D0121778

WITHDRAWN

SILENT COUNSEL

SILENT COUNSEL

A NOVEL

KEN ISAACSON

WINDERMERE PRESS, INC.

SILENT COUNSEL
© 2007 by Kenneth J. Isaacson

LCCN: 2006907610

For information:
Windermere Press, Inc.
1465 Rte 23 So., #190
Wayne, NJ 07470

Manufactured in the United States of America

Cover and interior design by www.kerndesign.net

ISBN: 0-9788622-4-4
ISBN: 13 978-0-9788622-4-4

For my sons, Brandon, Devon, and Jared
For my mother, Muriel Isaacson
And to the memory of my father, Frank Isaacson
With love

Acknowledgements

The idea for *Silent Counsel* came to me quite some time ago, upon reading a true account of a hit-and-run incident along a highway in Florida, in which a novel legal question was raised: Can the simple name of a client be "privileged information"? Although that case resolved itself before the issue was decided by the courts—the driver had an attack of conscience, and came forward on his own—the article got me thinking. What if the attorney-client privilege was interpreted to protect disclosure of information as basic as the identity of an attorney's client?

With this question in mind, I set out to write *Silent Counsel*. From the germ of an idea, to a finished product, is a long road, and it takes a lot of people to make it a reality. My thanks are due to the following:

Dr. Wesley Blank and Andy Kossowsky, who helped me with certain technical aspects of the story, as did numerous anonymous members of the online discussion groups of Yahoo!'s Sunfish Sailor and Google's alt.autos.bmw.

Carol Ingram and Linda Campesi, who read the very first draft, and whose enthusiastic response encouraged me to keep going.

My many friends at Mystery Writers of America. I can't say enough about MWA—just being among the extraordinary people there was inspiration enough to continue on when the going was rough.

Valerie Cornell, my editor, whose insightful comments and input helped make the final product so much stronger.

The wonderful people at Windermere Press, who took a chance.

Brad Meltzer, who always made sure he was available, and who gave me inspiration, moral support, and advice. Brad, you are a true *mensch*.

And my amazing wife, Sylvia, who always believed, and never gave up.

[A] lawyer shall not knowingly...
reveal a confidence or secret of a client.

Disciplinary Rule 4-101(B)(1)
American Bar Association
Code of Professional Responsibility

If the rule of law is this nation's secular faith, then the members of the Bar are its ministers. A lawyer is the mediator between his client's desires and the sovereign's commands. His aid is sought because of the relative ignorance of those to whom the law is but a collection of dim mysteries. When confronted with the awesome power of the criminal process, a client is never more in need of professional guidance and advocacy. In this setting, an instinct for survival compels a defendant to confide in an attorney. The necessity of full and open disclosure by a defendant... imbues that disclosure with an intimacy equal to that of the confessional, and approaching even that of the marital bedroom.

Any interference with the intimate relationship between attorney and client may do profound violence to the individual privacy of the client. Instead of receiving the protection that counsel can provide, the client unwittingly reveals his innermost thoughts to the unscrupulous. Such an invasion is unconscionable. The privacy between attorney and client is but an extension of the client's personal privacy... [T]he lawyer's duty to respect confidences is beyond dispute...Even in the courtroom, where the search for truth is of singular importance, an evidentiary privilege surrounds those confidences... The fundamental need for secrecy between attorney and client is clear.

Supreme Court of New Jersey
State v. Sugar
84 N.J. 1 (1980)

CHAPTER 1

The metallic blue BMW responded to the driver's slightest touch. He barely feathered the accelerator, and the Z4's powerful three-liter, 255-horsepower engine propelled the roadster through the curve. He depressed the clutch, nudged the gearshift into third, and applied just a little more pressure to the gas. The sports car reacted, and virtually hurled him into the straightaway. Because the temperature on this third Saturday in June had already been well into the nineties when he had started out in the morning, he had taken down the convertible top, and a hot wind whipped through the car. He inhaled deeply and breathed in the fresh sea air.

It was unusual for him to go in to work on a weekend, but the foreman at one of his sites had called him this morning with some nonsensical problem. Ordinarily he would have troubleshot it over the phone, but since he'd taken delivery of the Bimmer last week, he'd found himself looking for excuses to go for a spin. *Almost forty years old,* he thought, *and I'm acting like a kid with his first set of wheels.* He had put in a perfunctory appearance at the site, made his escape, and was now cruising along the waterfront before making his way back to the Garden State Parkway for the drive home.

He slowed and pulled alongside the curb, tipped his wraparound sunglasses back on his head, and looked out over the water. A brisk wind had developed, and the bay was alive with sailboats from the nearby Raritan Yacht Club. Some of the smaller craft that were tacking against the wind tipped precariously, and their crews, secured to the masts by harnesses and cables, stood atop the gunwales and leaned far out over the water to keep their boats aright. Masters, testing the limits of their craft.

His hand caressed the black leather of the passenger seat, and he once more considered whether he should have gone with the beige. The contrast would have been nice, and he knew the lighter color wouldn't absorb so much of the heat in the summer, but in the end he'd gone with the sleek elegance of classic black. The blue-black combination was striking, and the entire car exuded power.

He wondered what the limits of his piece of machinery were. He couldn't very well check the claimed top speed of 155 miles per hour, at least not here, but the boast of zero-to-sixty in 5.6 seconds was easily verifiable. He craned his neck around and saw that the long, straight expanse of Water Street was quiet and empty. His time trial would, by its very nature, take only a matter of seconds. It would be over before any trouble could ensue.

Dropping his Oakleys back over his eyes, he took the leather-wrapped steering wheel in his left hand, and rested his right on the shift knob. The clutch went down with just the right amount of resistance, and he pushed the gearshift forward into first. He looked at his wristwatch, and waited as the second hand crept forward.

A glance in the side-view mirror confirmed the continued stillness of his self-styled test track. The second hand swept past twelve, and he simultaneously popped the clutch and punched the accelerator. There was a squeal of rubber against asphalt, and the car lurched forward.

As he shifted quickly through the gears, his eyes flitted between speedometer and road. The acceleration was, as he'd expected, impressive. The needle leaped to fifty in what seemed no time at all, and it was still climbing. He glanced down at his watch to check his progress, and saw that he still had time to make his mark.

THWACK! He looked up.

What the fuck?

THUD!

Something bounced on his hood, smacked into the windshield, and rolled off onto the street. "What the fuck?" he repeated, this time aloud. He slammed on the brakes and skidded to a stop. He turned around, and looked out over the back of his open car.

That's not a kid, is it? Shit. Oh shit.

A small boy. Lying motionless in the middle of the street.

Where the hell did he come from?

He reached for the door handle, his hand shaking.

Not good. Not good. He's not moving. Just came out of nowhere, I hit him, now he's not moving.

His mind swirled, and he was dizzied by the cacophonous uproar pulsing in his head. Not only his hand, but now his entire body was shuddering, quaking uncontrollably.

Dead? Couldn't be. But what if? Could I have killed him?

He forced himself to breathe. Tried to force his racing mind to slow down.

I have to think.

He looked down the street, past the figure in the road. No one there. Quickly, side to side. No one. Forward, also clear.

Have to think…Can't…

He willed his foot to be still, but it continued to quiver as he pressed on the clutch. His right hand trembled, but he managed to move the gearshift into first.

I'll figure out what to do. But not here.

There was another screech of tires, and he sped away.

CHAPTER 2

Beethoven's Sixth Symphony played in the background on Scott Heller's compact disc player. The serenity of the first movement was counterpoint to the urgency with which the attorney punched the keypad on his telephone. "Stefanie," he pleaded into the intercom, "How much longer before it's out of here?"

His associate, Stefanie Handler, answered. "Relax, Scott. It's all set. Charles will be out of here in two minutes." She hung up and bolted from her office to find the paralegal assistant. He was just keying the client number into the photocopier so he could begin copying the complaint.

"For Chrissake, Charles! I thought that thing was ready to go. Scott's in there freaking out, and I told him you were halfway out the door already. What the hell happened?"

"Come on, Stef, you know nothing's short of DEFCON 1 around the law offices of Roth Stern. Did *le Grand Fromage* forget to mention that in addition to absolutely, positively needing me to file this thing as soon as possible, he also wanted me to make copies of all of the depositions in the *Billingsley* action? Right away?"

Charles dropped the forty-page complaint into the automatic

document feeder and punched the copy button.

"Oh, and do I remember a letter he thinks he got 'about eighteen months ago' from 'some guy' he met at a lecture he gave? No, I don't remember a letter from 'some guy,' and he doesn't remember what lecture. So I had to drop the two emergencies and look through his file on lectures and conferences, and see if I could figure out who this guy is he can't remember, who maybe wrote to him about a lecture he forgot, and try to find the letter that he only thinks the guy might have written to him, but when he's not sure. Because *if* the guy wrote to him, he *might* have mentioned something in his letter that'll be helpful in the *Hilton* suit."

Stefanie smiled. "He was right, though, wasn't he? You probably dug through the file, narrowed it down to two or three lectures, found four or five letters, and one of them was from someone who wrote to him about some arcane legal theory that'll probably end up being the key to *Hilton*. Right?"

Charles removed the photocopies from the sorter bin, and stapled the law firm's blue backers on them.

"Yeah, so big deal, the man's a walking Palm Pilot of information." He grinned. "But it's not like he's a genius or something—it was more like two years ago, not eighteen months."

He handed Stefanie the copies of the complaint, and dropped the original into the manila envelope that already held the summons, the civil cover sheet, and the $350 check to cover the fee for filing a complaint in the United States District Court for the Southern District of New York. As he headed for the elevator, she picked up the telephone and buzzed Scott. "It's gone," she said.

■   ■   ■

Scott Heller hung up, rose from his desk, and turned to face the window that stretched across the width of his office and wrapped around the corner to run half its length. Twenty stories below, he saw the buses and taxis of the Monday afternoon rush inching up Madison Avenue. The sidewalk was a sea of heads, bobbing chaotically in the seemingly Brownian movement of microscopic particles colliding at random with each other, though Scott knew that at street level there were two opposing hordes, one making its way north and the other heading south, with each individual instinctively negotiating his or her way through the mob, avoiding collision.

The copper roof of St. Patrick's Cathedral, one block south, gleamed in the late-day sun. A few years ago, it had been the green that copper turns when it oxidizes, and Scott had watched from this window as workmen went about refurbishing it. Visible just past St. Pat's was the digital clock atop the Newsweek Building. It was 4:27.

Scott turned from the window. Tall and fit, impeccably dressed and immaculately groomed, he appeared the quintessential corporate attorney. Newly-pressed dark gray suit, starched white shirt, with solid yellow suspenders and a yellow and gray printed tie. A professional and confident air about him that comforted clients while at the same time telegraphed to adversaries that he was a force to be reckoned with.

Only the diamond stud earring in his left ear clashed with the traditional image, and gave a glimpse into his slightly outrageous side. He'd gotten his ear pierced while in college at MIT, and for a while he'd worn a two-inch gold hoop—his way of ensuring that he stood apart from the tech nerds who had dominated the campus. When he'd started interviewing for a job as a summer associate after his second year of law school, he took it out, but when his girlfriend Jody—now his wife—had seen him *sans* earring, she'd taunted him and accused him of selling out. "Besides, if a damn law firm is going to pass up a graduate of MIT and an editor of the Columbia Law Review just because he wears an earring, then it's being run by idiots with no business sense, and you shouldn't be hitching your star to *that* wagon anyway." Jody had convinced him to keep the earring, but his compromise was to trade the flamboyant hoop for a modest stud. He had come to view his little symbol as a reminder never to take himself too seriously.

He crossed his office to the stereo, ejected Ludwig van and replaced him with Bon Jovi, and turned up the volume. At thirty-five years old—and male to boot—he knew that his enthusiasm for the long-haired pop idol put him in the minority, but he enjoyed the music nonetheless. Jon belted out "Have a Nice Day" while Scott found the last draft of the *Driscoll* complaint and plopped down onto his L-shaped black leather couch. He put his feet up on the steel and glass coffee table, and leafed through the complaint without really looking at it.

Driscoll v. Marcus, et al. was due to be commenced when Charles filed the complaint with the clerk of the federal court downtown at Foley Square. It was a stroke of luck that Scott had snagged this case as early as he had, and his was sure to be the first class action lawsuit filed against Eddie Marcus and Leonard Milstein, the officers of Marlen Industries, Inc.—news that they had manipulated the market for Marlen stock in order to sell their own holdings at fraudulently inflated prices had hit the street only ten days ago. In just one trading session, Marlen's stock had plummeted from $34 a share to $1, and a thirty-three point drop, multiplied by approximately fifty-seven million shares outstanding, meant a loss to shareholders of more than 1.6 billion dollars. It was Scott's job to make Marcus and Milstein pay for that loss.

Because so many shareholders would have identical claims against the officers, and it would be impossible for all of them to actively participate in a lawsuit, the law permitted the use of a "class action." One plaintiff petitioned the court to be appointed as a representative of all claimants similarly situated, and if the court was satisfied that the plaintiff would adequately represent the unnamed claimants' interests, the matter would be certified as a class action. The class members would then reap any benefit won by their representative. This was the type of case that Scott thrived on—his practice was limited almost exclusively to high-stakes federal class actions, and his reputation as a shrewd and effective force to be dealt with was growing among the closed community of hard-hitting lawyers specializing in this field.

A handful of other class action suits was sure to follow, but since they would all be based upon the same events, the court would undoubtedly direct that they be consolidated. Scott would be able to argue, probably successfully, that they should all be consolidated into *Driscoll*—his action—since *Driscoll* had been filed first. This assured Scott a lead role in prosecuting the case—not to mention a lion's share of what promised to be a substantial fee award.

The legal fees at stake were extremely high, and the competition among class action lawyers like Scott was fierce. So when Scott's college buddy Kevin Driscoll, who owned a block of Marlen stock, called him to ask whether he had a claim for damages, Scott hit the ground running. And today, less than a week after Marlen's collapse, *Driscoll v. Marcus, et al.* was about to be started.

The intercom chirped, and his secretary's voice announced: "It's Charles." Scott picked up the receiver and punched the blinking button.

"Yeah?"

"Hey sahib. I know how wired you are. I just wanted to let you know it's done. And I checked today's index. No other filings against the company or any of the officers. We're first."

"Time to rock and roll then," Scott said, grinning. "Now for the fun part. Why don't you take the rest of the day off?"

"You're too kind, massa." Charles answered. "If I got on the subway to head back there now, just so I could turn around and go home, you'd have to pay me overtime."

"Yeah, well, that too. Anyway, thanks."

Scott hung up. He glanced at the clock, and saw that it was almost five. Not quite his usual quitting time, but today's successful filing merited an early evening. He tossed a few things into his attaché case, and had just latched it shut when his intercom chirped again.

"Scott, there's someone on line one for you, but he won't give his name."

"Aw, come on, Karen. It's probably some salesman trying to sell me mutual funds. Tell him I've taken a big enough beating already, and I'm keeping everything under my mattress from here on in."

"I don't think so. He says he wants to hire you, and that it's urgent. He won't give me any details, but he says he was referred to you by a mutual friend."

"Okay, I'll take it." It was bad form to turn away business.

"Scott Heller," he said into the phone.

"Mr. Heller, I need a lawyer. Win Honnicutt suggested I call you."

Win Honnicutt was Scott's law school classmate and former colleague at Gersten Golub Levy & Schmidt, the Wall Street firm where they had begun their careers. He'd managed to make it through three years at Columbia to orientation at Gersten Golub before Scott learned the true name that he had inherited from his great grandfather: Thurston Winslow Barton Honnicutt IV. The imposing name only hinted at the legacy that came along with it. Win could actually trace his roots back to colonial Virginia, where the ancestral Honnicutts began as traders who through the generations established and built an import-export dynasty that his father—the venerable Thurston Winslow Barton Honnicutt III—ruled to this day. Win turned out to be the black sheep, renouncing his position as heir apparent to the Honnicutt industry throne in favor of such a disreputable profession as the law. And his decision to leave the corporate law department of a major Wall Street firm to open a small general practice catering to individuals who could barely afford his fee confirmed to his family that he was clearly insane.

"Is it any wonder I didn't advertise my name?" he'd once asked Scott, who couldn't understand his friend's aversion to his illustrious heritage. "Shit—you can't imagine the pretentious nitwits I was surrounded by growing up. Oliver Wendell Harding Brown, Jr., Rupert Reginald Winston Smythe III, Little Lord Fauntleroys all of them. You dream up the most pompous, obnoxious, spoiled brat of a rich kid, and he was my boarding school chum. No siree, just plain Win Honnicutt suited me fine."

When Win had made the split from Gersten Golub, he'd tried to lure Scott along. But although Scott eventually left the big firm for something less grand, he had stuck with the corporate practice that he'd grown to enjoy. Win regularly chastised him for staying in the ivory tower of the corporate elite, and routinely regaled him with war stories from the trenches of practicing law "among real people." The war was apparently in pitched battle needing fresh recruits, as Win had recently rented one of his vacant offices to an experienced criminal lawyer who had just moved from New England, to help with the overflow of cases.

Insisting that as a true friend he was obliged to round out Scott's professional experience, Win occasionally referred some matters Scott's way that were otherwise outside the scope of his usual practice. Every once in a while, someone called and said "Win sent me."

Scott shifted the telephone receiver. "All right, first tell me your name, and then let's see what I can do for you."

"I want you to consider this conversation a privileged communication. You're not to disclose what we talk about to anyone. Is that acceptable?"

Scott's curiosity was piqued. The caller, all business, had still not identified himself. "Okay. Consider this a privileged communication." He reached for a pad and pen. "First, tell me your name."

"Later. If a person committed a crime, and wanted to give himself up, could you try to work out a deal with the prosecutor?"

"That's really not my area. A few years ago I handled some white-collar criminal matters, but these days I mainly do corporate litigation. I'm sure I could refer you to a good criminal lawyer, though."

"No. I want you. Win said you're the best. At least hear me out."

Good old Win. "Okay, I'm listening. Go ahead."

"Did you hear about that hit-and-run in New Jersey? Where that kid got killed?"

"Yes, of course," Scott said. Six-year-old Benjamin Altman had been run down in front of his house in Perth Amboy over the weekend. He had been playing in his front yard Saturday morning, and his father, Marc, went inside for a minute to answer the telephone. Marc heard screeching tires, and rushed outside to find his son dead in the street. The car that had cut Ben down was nowhere in sight. According to the media, the PTA of Ben's school had already collected ten thousand dollars, which was being offered as a reward for information leading to the arrest and conviction of the driver.

"Do you know something about it?" Scott asked.

"Yeah, I guess you could say that. I did it."

Scott sat up. "And what do you want me to do?"

"I can't take it. When it happened, I panicked and ran. Now I've got to turn myself in. But I want you to see what kind of deal you can work out with the prosecutor before I do. Win said you could do it. He said you wouldn't let me down."

Scott reached up and fingered his earring, twisting it around and back between thumb and forefinger. This could be interesting. The matter was high-profile, so there would be a lot of press. The guy might not be a terribly sympathetic character, but hasn't it been said that there's no such thing as bad publicity?

"Well, if I were to help you, I'd need a lot more information. *If* I were to help you. We'll need to meet." He swiveled to face his computer, and clicked open his calendar. "I can see you on Thursday. Hold on for my secretary, and she'll schedule an appointment."

Good old Thurston Winslow Barton Honnicutt IV, Scott thought again after he hung up. *What did you send me this time?*

CHAPTER 3

"**W**here are you, Vince? Hello, Vince?"

Vincent Saldano sat staring at the sixty-inch, high-definition plasma TV recessed into the shallow cavity in the wall of his den. His wife's voice startled him, and he brought the screen into focus to see Katie Couric wrapping up the Thursday edition of the *Evening News*. Though the television had been squarely in his line of sight, he had been gazing not across the short space that stood between him and his high-tech, top-of-the-line entertainment center, but rather across the five days that separated his previously blissful existence from the hell into which he had descended when he had become a killer.

"Earth to Vince," his wife, Patty, said. She passed a hand in front of his face and wiggled her fingers.

"Huh? Oh…I guess I was zoning out." He did his best to put on a smile, but he was sure it came across more like a tortured grimace. "What did you say?"

"I didn't say anything. I just thought you were going to bore a hole in the TV with that laser beam of a stare you had going. I don't think you were on the moon—you were in another galaxy."

What do you expect? he wanted to scream. *I killed someone! An innocent little kid! What do you fucking expect?*

He was amazed that she couldn't read it. On his face. In his manner. Wasn't his terrible secret just oozing from his pores, like the stench of fetid sweat? Didn't guilt and shame coat every word he spoke, so that anyone listening couldn't help but hear the message he was powerless to cover up? *I am a monster! A killer of children!* He considered himself a good judge of people, and felt sure that if someone he knew—certainly someone he'd been married to for nearly fifteen years—was concealing such a horror, he would know.

But except for the lawyer he had contacted, no one knew.

"No, not another galaxy, hon. Just zoning," was the best he could muster.

Vince looked around the room. Since he and Patty had moved to Saddle River two years ago, they'd done a lot with the house. *Manor*, he reminded himself, *not house*. The listing had described a six-bed, five-bath manor on a two-acre gated estate with a pool and cabana, just twenty miles outside of New York City. Asking price, a mere $3.5 million. He'd been able to shave a little off the final figure, but he was now carrying a mortgage slightly in excess of $2.5 million. And he had poured a lot into the place since then.

It wouldn't have been possible without the inheritance from his father three years previously. Until then, his trust fund had been throwing off enough income to supplement his own and to allow Patty and him to live comfortably, but it wasn't until his father had passed away—and the trust corpus, along with a substantial amount more, had devolved upon him—that their financial situation really peaked.

The bright, window-filled den was a haven for his collection of electronic toys. Above a broad fireplace surrounded by a black granite hearth hung a vivid reproduction of Kandinsky's *Counter Gravitation* that, at the touch of a button, slid aside to reveal a five-inch-deep nook in which the wafer-thin big-screen TV was mounted. Inconspicuously embedded at strategic locations in the room's walls and ceiling were six surround-sound speakers that delivered high-fidelity, stereophonic, digital sound. A DVD player, a six-disc CD changer, and a stereo receiver were all tucked out of sight in a recessed cabinet beneath a picture window that looked out over one of two redwood decks. The components were hardwired to a single infrared sensor just beneath the TV, and controlled by a universal remote with the push of a few buttons.

The heart of Vince's home computer network—a wireless broadband router and four-port switch, and a high-speed cable modem—were in this room as well. Any one of his three desktop computers—in the den, his bedroom, or his upstairs study—as well as his notebook computer, could access the Web through a shared Internet connection that he controlled from here. With the technology evolving as quickly as it was, he found himself replacing his computer equipment every twelve months or so, but he loved the challenge of keeping his network at the cutting edge of all of the advances.

Vince had given Patty free rein throughout the rest of the house, but this room was his. When his wife had pleaded for permission to hire Enrique, the flamboyant interior decorator, the quid pro quo was this: the den was off-limits. Patty could commission Enrique, and together they could do what they wanted, but their authority stopped at the threshold of the den.

The compromise had worked well. Patty had proven to have quite an artistic eye, and Enrique showed himself adept at refining and then executing Patty's vision. And while Vince clung to the illusion of autonomy in his sacred den, truth be told he paid close attention to the progress of Patty and Enrique, and didn't stray too far afield of their example.

The result was a Saldano manor that rivaled anything gracing the pages of *Architectural Digest*. And now he stood to lose all of it. Because of an irresponsible, self-indulgent display of testosterone.

What a stupid, fucked-up stunt that had been.

The stand-up thing to do was to turn himself in. But shit, the lawyer said he could possibly get up to thirty years. Thirty years! Oh, but it's not likely. That's just if the charge is aggravated manslaughter.

It could be just reckless driving, with no jail time. Could be. Don't worry, the lawyer had said. The prosecutor will be reasonable.

Fuck that, hoping the prosecutor would be reasonable. Expose himself to the risk of being put away for thirty years, hoping for reason? *I don't think so.* He told himself it was Patty he was thinking about. How could she handle such a thing?

No, he could do the right thing, but at the same time minimize the risk to Patty and himself, and everything they'd built together. The lawyer negotiating on his behalf with the prosecutor had been forbidden to reveal his name unless and until a deal was in place—a deal that was acceptable to Vince.

If he just walked into the prosecutor's office, he'd have nothing to bargain with. It would be like laying his head down on the chopping block and pulling back his collar to give them a clear shot. But this way, the prosecutor ought to be more than willing to be reasonable. He was confident the authorities wouldn't find him on their own—he was sure no one had seen him. There was bound to be a lot of pressure to solve the case, so a lawyer calling up out of the blue would be a godsend. And Vince would have some leverage—he, through his lawyer, could threaten to vanish into the woodwork if the prosecutor wasn't quite as reasonable as he wanted.

What prosecutor wouldn't see the logic in taking that deal? Negotiate something reasonable, or risk never finding him.

Vince hoped it didn't come to that. He wanted to do the right thing, not run and hide like a coward. But for Patty's sake he had to do this carefully. *It's Patty I'm thinking about, isn't it?*

He had time to figure out what he would do if it didn't work out. Face the music, or disappear? He'd like to think he knew what course he would take, but there was no reason to ponder it too deeply now—it was a question he might never have to answer.

He was reassured in one regard, though. If he did decide to stay hidden, the authorities couldn't force the lawyer to talk. The lawyer would claim that his client's identity was privileged information. An attorney can't reveal privileged information to anyone.

From what he'd learned about the attorney-client privilege,

though, he knew there was some chance a court might disagree that his name fell within the scope of protection—the privilege was more usually applied to communications of substance. So there was *some* risk a judge might order the lawyer to talk. And there wasn't an attorney he knew of who would defy the court and risk his law license, just to protect a child-killer.

But Vince had that base covered, too. If it went that far, the lawyer could never betray him, even if he wanted to.

It won't come to that, though. One way or the other, he told himself, I'll do the right thing.

CHAPTER 4

"So what can you tell me?"

"Not much, Loo," Detective Roy Kluge answered. "I'm afraid we don't have a lot."

Roy Kluge sat across from his lieutenant, Rob Weber. Kluge, a sixteen-year veteran with the Perth Amboy Police Department, was a big man, with sandy hair close-cropped in a military style that featured a precisely-groomed flattop. His commanding officer, whose long face, jowls, and rheumy eyes resulted in a striking resemblance to a basset hound, wasn't due to return from his two-week vacation until Monday, but his compulsive nature had brought him into the station this Friday morning. He had been greeted with news of the Altman tragedy and the resultant investigation.

"Well, tell me what we do have. For Chrissake, the guy couldn't have vanished off the face of the earth. It was a Saturday morning, beautiful weather, and the boardwalk must've been crawling with people. You mean to tell me no one saw a car plow into a kid and burn rubber outta there?"

Kluge shared Weber's frustration. A hit-and-run death demanded a quick resolution, but when it was a young child playing in his own front yard, the heat really got turned up. For Kluge, there was even more at stake—he and the boy's father, Marc Altman, had gone to Perth Amboy High together. About twice a year, he and his wife met the Altmans for dinner. He could barely imagine what his former classmate was going through.

Nevertheless, all the detective could do was shrug.

"There was nobody in the immediate area at the time."

"Awright. Just tell me what we have."

Kluge flipped the pages of his notepad, but spoke without looking at it.

"I got the call at about ten thirty. When I got there, the uniforms had already been on the scene for almost an hour. The Altmans' neighbor,"—here he glanced down at his notes—"Victoria Lewis, had called it in. She'd just come home from the bagel shop and found the father in the street holding the kid. While I was talking to Mr. A. inside, the mother got home from running some errands. The body hadn't been moved into the ambulance yet, and she saw her kid laid out on the street and lost it. EMT sedated her, and since the ambulance wasn't doing the boy any good, they used it to transport her to Raritan Bay Medical."

"What about the incident? Tell me what you've found."

"Car was traveling north on Water. It's hard to say from the skid marks exactly how fast it was going when it hit, but right now we put it at about fifty. The kid was obviously thrown some distance from the point of impact, and judging from where Mr. A. found him, and where the skid marks start, it looks like he was hit at full speed. I don't think the bastard even tapped the brakes till after he'd hit him.

"There's a second set of marks that the vehicle made when it accelerated after stopping. Looks like it was a rear wheel drive, judging from the relation between where the skid on braking ends, and where the patch on acceleration starts. And, the acceleration patch shows some fishtailing, which would also indicate a rear wheel drive.

"We recovered some residue from the tires, but I don't know if we'll be able to make anything out of it. We also found a plastic disc, an inch or so across, in the road. Our guys think it might be a knockout plug that comes from a car's bumper. Covers the towing eye. If that's what it is, it might've popped outta this car, but I can't tell you that for sure. Might've been lying in the road from someone else."

"Any other physical evidence?" Weber asked.

"Nope."

"What about witnesses? Anybody see anything?"

"Haven't turned up anyone yet. We've gone door-to-door, starting south of the house and working north. Like I said, Mrs. Lewis, the next-door neighbor who found Mr. A. holding the kid, wasn't home when it happened. Neither was her husband. We haven't hit on anyone who was around yet.

"The car continued north up Water. We've hit all the houses on up to the 'T' at Smith, and on the first block or so of the streets intersecting Water between the Altmans' and Smith. So far, nothing. I'm figuring he sped up to Smith, turned left, and just headed out of town."

"Awright," said Weber. "Anything else?"

"Unfortunately not, Loo. Not at this point."

"Okay then. Keep me in the loop."

■   ■   ■

Kluge had put it off for most of the week, but felt he was ready for this afternoon's visit. The Altmans were observing *shivah*, the traditional seven-day period of mourning, and it was time for Kluge to pay his respects to his former schoolmate and his wife. There were a number of cars in front of the house, so he drove past, made a U-turn, and parked on the opposite side of the street along the boardwalk.

The Altmans' house looked out over Raritan Bay, where the

Arthur Kill and the Raritan River met. Like the other houses along that stretch of Water Street, the Altmans' two-story colonial was built atop a hill that rose about twenty feet above the level of the street. Thick ivy covered the nearly vertical rise, and concrete steps led from the sidewalk to a front yard that sloped gently further upward to the house. A walkway stretched across the grassy yard to the porch where Marc Altman had sat just minutes before a ringing telephone had summoned him from his son.

Kluge climbed the wooden porch steps, against which Ben had been rebounding a rubber ball moments before his death. The first cops on the scene last Saturday had found the ball in the street, and the theory was that it had rolled down the walkway and concrete steps, and that Ben had run after it.

The detective raised his hand to rap on the front door, but remembered he'd learned that the custom was to enter a Jewish house of mourning without knocking. He let himself into an open foyer with a ceramic-tiled floor and a cathedral ceiling. The brightness, furnished by sunlight streaming in through a circular window above the door, seemed almost inappropriate in a place of bereavement.

Muted voices filtered down a hallway from the den in which he had initially interviewed Marc. He followed the sounds and passed what he assumed to be a mirror hanging on the wall, but it was obscured by a black sheet. Once before he had observed covered mirrors in a house of *shivah* when he and his wife had visited a close family friend whose father had passed away. The friend had explained that Jews at one time believed that the soul of a person might be caught in the mirror and snatched away by the ghost of the deceased, so mourners who looked at their reflection thought they might be placing themselves in danger.

About a dozen people filled the den. To accommodate them, a number of folding chairs had been set up around the edge of the room, supplementing the floral print sofa and love seat. Most of the people, however, were standing in groups of two or three, speaking softly to one another. A few stood around a table that was filled with cakes and pastries. Marc saw him, and hurried over.

"Roy. Thanks for coming." Marc pumped Kluge's outstretched hand.

"Yeah, well," Kluge mumbled, searching for words. "How are you holding up?"

Marc shrugged. "I've just been in a daze the whole week. It's still all so unreal."

"How about Stacy?"

Marc looked uneasy. "She hasn't said a word to me all week. She blames me. Shit, Roy, *I* blame me..." His voice trailed off.

"Don't say that, Marc. It was an accident. A horrible, tragic accident."

Marc shrugged again. "Go say hi to Stacy. I'm sure she'll appreciate your being here. Come. She's talking to friends of ours from Pennsylvania. I'll introduce you to them."

Kluge followed Marc to where Stacy was sitting on a low wooden chair, almost the kind that a child would sit on. Another Jewish custom he had learned of—the mourners were to avoid comfort. Stacy's shoulder-length black hair was pulled back, and she wore no makeup or jewelry. The vacant look in her reddened eyes added to the tired look on her face.

A couple knelt in front of Stacy, talking with her. They rose when Marc and Kluge approached, and Marc made the introductions.

"Greg and I were just saying to Stacy that it's been too long since the two of you have been to see us," Amy Bartlett said to Marc. "You came out when we bought the farm, but that was two years ago. It's time for another visit. When things settle down, you should think of coming out for a while."

"Amy and Greg have this magnificent farm, tucked away in the heart of the Pennsylvania Dutch country," Marc explained. "You're right," he said to Amy. "We'll make a point of getting out there."

"Okay then," Greg said. "We'll expect it." He turned to Stacy, who sat in silence. "We've got to get going. You take care, Stacy." He leaned over and gave Stacy a peck on the cheek, and Amy did the same. Stacy continued staring straight ahead as the two well-wishers left.

"Sweetheart," Marc said. "Roy Kluge is here." He spoke to her as if she were unaware of her surroundings. "I'm going to leave the two of you to talk." To Kluge, he said "Thanks again for coming." The men shook hands, and Marc left them.

Kluge pulled a folding chair in front of Stacy's chair and sat down. He took her hand in both of his, and told her how sorry he was.

"I know everyone has probably been saying the same thing, but if there's anything I can do for you, please tell me. I mean it."

"Have you found him yet?" Stacy asked. Her voice croaked, as if she hadn't spoken in days. Kluge had to lean forward to hear her.

"No, Stacy, we haven't."

"Find him. That's what you can do for me."

"We'll do our best." He stood. "I don't want to intrude, but I wanted to let you know we're thinking about you. I'll leave you to your friends now."

Stacy reached out and took his arm. "No, wait. Please stay. Do you have any leads? Any clues at all?"

Kluge sat back down, ill at ease. This was not the time or place to be discussing police business.

"There's really not much to go on. We've canvassed the neighborhood, but we haven't been able to find anyone who saw anything. We've posted notices along the boardwalk, urging any witnesses to come forward, but so far, nothing. We just haven't uncovered anything yet that's likely to lead us to the driver."

"If you learn of anything, please let me know. I want to know."

Kluge assured Stacy that he would keep her informed, and rose once more to go. This time Stacy stood and walked with him to the door.

"The animal deserves to burn in hell, Roy. Please find him."

She turned and strode back to her little wooden chair, silent once more.

CHAPTER 5

"**I** can't believe you really want to represent scum like that," Jody Heller said to her husband. She climbed out of the swimming pool and reached for a towel. "He killed a child and then ran away."

The vicious heat wave that had kept virtually everyone in the tristate area in their air-conditioned homes and offices for the last six days had finally ended. For a week, the temperature had already been near eighty by sunup, and had soared past a hundred by early afternoon. Today the mercury had peaked at ninety, and it wasn't half as muggy as it had been, so people were able to venture outside to enjoy the last day of the weekend in the fresh air.

The evening was downright balmy, and Scott and Jody took advantage of the break in the weather for an after-dinner swim in the backyard. They had finished eating about an hour ago, and their daughter Alex, exhausted from her hard playing at day camp, had gone straight to bed. After clearing away the dinner plates, they had changed into their bathing suits and gone outside.

The western sky was a pastel blend of reds, pinks, and blues, gently illuminated by a sun that had moments ago tipped over the edge of the horizon and now hung out of sight just beneath the earth's rim. Jody had switched on the underwater light, and the pool shimmered and glowed.

Scott had met with his new client three days earlier, but had not had a chance to describe the conference to his wife until this evening's dinner. To his surprise, Jody had reacted strongly to his undertaking.

"Come on, Jo," Scott said from his lounge chair. "I met him, and he's not a monster. When it happened he panicked, but the important thing is that he wants to give himself up now."

"But the papers said he was doing more than fifty when he hit the kid. He had no business speeding like that. I mean, he wasn't on the Garden State Parkway—he was driving down someone's street. You know how you freak when any of the neighbors whip past our house." She stood at the foot of Scott's chair, and briskly massaged her scalp with the towel to dry her short brown hair.

"First, he says he wasn't going that fast, and second, from what I understand nobody sticks to twenty-five on that stretch of Water Street. Besides, he says the boy just bolted out from nowhere. Look, this guy definitely has to face the consequences, but I really don't think he's a piece of scum."

"Still," Jody pressed on. She put one foot up on the edge of Scott's chair, and toweled her leg. "Even if he wasn't going fifty, and even if the kid jumped out of nowhere, what kind of person can smack into someone, let alone a child, and just speed away? I'm telling you he's an animal. For God's sake, Scott, think of the poor kid's parents. I would die if something like that happened to Alex. And you'd defend the guy who did it?"

"But don't you see, Jo, you feel this guy is some bottom-feeder because you're reacting like a mother."

"Oh, I see. A typical woman's reaction. You know—"

"No, no." Scott held his hand up to stop her. "All I'm saying is you're not exactly impartial. Try and start with the idea that this guy is a regular person like you or me. Suddenly WHAM! Something like this happens. Don't you think his judgment might get clouded for just a second? Don't you think even you or I might panic and run? I'm willing to give him the benefit of the doubt. Like I said, as far as I'm concerned, the important thing is that he wants to come forward now."

Jody was not mollified. "I don't know, it just seems that only a real dirtbag would run away from the scene like that." She plopped down in the lounge chair next to Scott's.

"Anyway, Scott, you don't even do criminal law. You're a corporate litigator. Why do you even want to do this?"

"I told you, it's one of Win's deals. I know he jokes about sending stuff like this to me to 'round out' my professional development, but the truth is, he does it only if he needs my help. Usually, it's either a conflict of interest that prevents him from taking it on, or he's jammed up with other pressing business. If he's referred this guy to me, it's for a reason, and I can't let him down.

"Besides, I met the guy, and regardless of what you think, he is not Evil personified. And as far as the criminal law part goes, all I'm going to do is make some phone calls and probably have some meetings with the County Prosecutor to try to work out a plea bargain. If we make a deal, that'll be the end of it. If I can't, and the thing has to go any further, the guy understands that he has to find an experienced criminal lawyer. Either way, my involvement will be limited."

"Well, I just don't have a good feeling about this," Jody said. "If I were you, I'd think long and hard about getting into bed with this creep." She stood up, picked up her towel, and started toward the house. "And speaking of bed, come on in, it's getting late."

She climbed the stairs from the pool to the redwood deck, and when she reached the sliding glass door that led into the kitchen, she turned back to Scott. "You keep calling him 'the guy.' What's his name?"

"I can't tell you."

"What do you mean you can't tell me?"

"It's privileged information."

Jody looked confused. "How can it be privileged information?

I thought privileged information was private stuff that you and your client talk about. I just want to know his name."

"Well, his name *is* 'private stuff.' He told me his name in confidence. He's forbidden me to tell the prosecutor who he is. I'm supposed to try to work out a deal on what you'd call an anonymous basis."

"God, Scott, isn't that going to be impossible? Won't the prosecutor want to know who he is before agreeing to anything?"

"Yeah, probably. I don't think it'll work either, and I told the guy so. But he wants me to try. And like I said, if I can't do it, I'm out of it."

Scott moved toward the door to enter the house, but Jody blocked his way.

"Okay. So even if his name *is* privileged information, you won't even tell me? I'm not the prosecutor, I'm your wife. It's not like I'm going to run and tell anyone. Just tell me his name."

"I can't. I'm the guy's lawyer, it's privileged information, and it's as simple as that. The Code of Professional Responsibility forbids lawyers from disclosing client secrets. The courts take the Code very seriously, and so do I. I can get into serious trouble—I could even get disbarred—if I reveal privileged information. I can never tell his name to *anyone*, unless he says I can."

Scott stepped around Jody, and went inside.

CHAPTER 6

Scott awoke at his usual seven thirty. To make it to his midtown Manhattan office by nine, he generally left his home in Englewood Cliffs, New Jersey around eight fifteen. He had the option of taking the bus into the city, or of driving, and though most people thought he was crazy to want the hassle of a car in Manhattan, Scott preferred to drive. The house was just minutes away from the George Washington Bridge, and the trip across the Hudson and down the west side of Manhattan took anywhere from a half hour to an hour, depending on the traffic. The bus ride to the Port Authority Bus Terminal took just as long, and then he would have to contend with the New York City subways to get to his office. Driving was actually more relaxing.

Parking the car in midtown every day was expensive, but, hell, he could afford it, so why not? Besides, last year had been a good one, and he had leased himself a fire engine red Porsche Boxster. The two-seater was useless on the weekends for transporting Scott, Jody, and their nine-year-old daughter Alex, and it didn't really make much sense to let the sports car sit in the driveway all week. It was true that the difference between a boy and a man was the price of his toys—and Scott was a man who liked expensive toys.

Though Scott was the first one up this morning, by the time he'd shaved, showered, and dressed, Jody was already downstairs in the kitchen preparing Alex's lunch for camp. Alex's bus wasn't due for another forty-five minutes, so Jody would let her sleep just a little longer before waking her.

"What's on your busy schedule today?" Scott asked. He put his arms around Jody's waist from behind, and planted a kiss on the back of her neck.

"Oh, nothing special. Probably just do my lady of leisure impersonation. You know, go to the pool club and lie around until I have to get back here in time for Alex."

"Why the pool club? What's wrong with Club Heller?" Scott asked, motioning with his head toward the pool in the yard.

"The other ladies of leisure will be lounging at the pool club, not at Club Heller," Jody teased. "But tonight, if you're up for it, I'll meet you out back for a midnight swim. Bathing suits optional."

Scott leered at Jody. "It's a date. But bathing suits not an option."

▓   ▓   ▓

Thirty minutes later, Scott was crossing the upper deck of the George Washington Bridge into New York. For Scott, the trip between home and office each day was more than just getting physically from one place to another. It was, even on bumper-to-bumper traffic days, a significant factor that contributed to his overall mental health.

One thing that Scott had come to learn about the practice of law and about himself was the importance of being able to leave the pressures of the office at the office whenever possible, and to recognize that there was life after work. To call the daily drive from Manhattan to Englewood Cliffs—from office to home—a "cleansing process" would be taking it a bit too far, as that implied that Scott considered his work dirty in some way. Rather, the drive home gave him the chance to shift gears from the pressure-filled day, much in the way an athlete will cool down by walking a few laps around the track before heading for the shower after a hard run.

For Scott, the Hudson River was a dividing line. Each evening, as he crossed the GWB, he did his best to leave his office worries behind him in New York. Because of the nature of his work it was not always possible, but this is what he strove for. By the time Scott reached home, he was relaxed and at ease, even after the most tension-packed day.

If the evening ride home was Scott's "cool-down" period, the morning drive to work was the time for him to do some mental stretching before plunging into the rigors of the day. Crossing over into New York each morning, Scott would allow himself to begin planning his day, reviewing the goals he had set for himself the evening before, and ticking off in his mind the things he would have to do that day to achieve them.

He planned to spend this morning reviewing some research that his associate Stefanie had done on an arcane point of law that the adversary in one of his cases had raised. Then, he had a luncheon date with a prospective client, after which he was due in federal court for oral argument of an application to set the amount of attorneys' fees his firm would receive in a case they had just concluded. When he got back from court, he would call the Middlesex County Prosecutor's office in New Jersey and find out who he could speak to about Win's pet project.

He worked his way through traffic down the west side of Manhattan toward Fifty-seventh Street, where he would cut across town to the parking garage, and thought of his conversation with Jody the night before. After they'd gone inside, she'd once again asked him about "the guy." He'd again refused to tell her his name. Jody had first accused him of not trusting her, and then of being "too technical" about his obligation under the Code of Professional Responsibility. When he'd made it clear that he could not, and would not, reveal his client's identity even to her, they'd decided to assign him a fictitious name to make their conversations about the case less awkward.

At least Jody had lightened up at that point, as she tried out suitable names for "the guy." She'd thought of all the truly evil figures she could, and among the candidates she suggested were Adolf, Osama, Beelzebub, and even Satan. Scott had played along and made some suggestions of his own, including Voldemort—"you know who" of Harry Potter fame. In the end they'd decided that their name for "the guy" would be simply "Guy." At first, Jody had balked, complaining that there was nothing evil about the name, but Scott had reminded her that Guy Fawkes was an English villain who in 1605 had tried to blow up the Houses of Parliament, and that each November 5 the British burned Guy in effigy. Satisfied that Guy had achieved at least a minor place in the annals of malevolence, Jody had accepted the designation.

"You know I always wish you success in your cases, but this one gives me the creeps," she had said. "Here's to Guy's downfall."

The crosstown traffic on Fifty-seventh Street was light. Scott handed off his car to the garage attendant and walked the few blocks to his office. At the lobby newsstand, he picked up copies of the *Wall Street Journal*, the *New York Times* and the *Newark Star-Ledger*, all of which he would skim over coffee before settling down to work.

■   ■   ■

The offices of Roth Stern were located on Madison Avenue between Fifty-first and Fifty-second Streets. Madison Avenue did not carry with it the image of Park Avenue, but Scott and his partners considered the additional rent that the firm would have to pay for similar quarters just one block east to be a frivolous expense, even though they could afford it. Roth Stern depended on more than a prestigious address for its reputation.

The suite of offices on the twenty-first floor was tastefully decorated, but not overdone. When Scott and his colleagues formed the firm, Scott had convinced his partners to "keep it simple." Barry Stern—actually Barry's wife, who had assumed the role of interior decorator—had worked up a plan that included a lot of teak and marble, which would have been magnificent if executed. Barry had argued over dinner at Smith & Wollensky that as a start-up business without a track record, the firm had to present an image of success in order to attract business and engender confidence in its clients.

There was a lot of truth to Barry's argument—how secure could a client with a multi-million dollar problem feel entrusting his fortunes to a bunch of *shleppers*? But Scott had persuaded his partners that most clients would be put off by too grand a display of conspicuous consumption, which would make them wonder if the fees they were being charged were not just a little too high. The subliminal message Scott thought their firm ought to cast was that they were successful enough to be comfortable, but were not too greedy.

"I know we have to project an image that suggests financial success," Scott had conceded. "But why load up on expensive furniture and stuff that just sits there looking good? Let's spend our money on things that'll show our clients we're committed to delivering top-quality product. There's a lot of new technology out there in the way of computers, telephones, and other office equipment. If we create an environment that's obviously at the cutting edge of that technology, we'll show our financial success through our expensive surroundings, and those expensive surroundings will demonstrate our commitment to professional excellence."

Scott's partners could not argue with this logic, and since it was just as much of an ego trip to be able to play with the latest techno-gadgets as it was to be surrounded by marble, teak, and leather, Scott's approach was accepted. Barry Stern's wife graciously went back to the drawing board, but this time with Scott as consultant. When Roth Stern Conway Heller & Mulhearn, as the firm was first known, opened its doors a few months later, the furnishings themselves were modest, but there was hardly an office- or law-related technological toy on the market that could not be found within. The overall effect was extremely impressive, and Scott and his partners found that the gadgets actually did help them in the practice of law.

Roth Stern beat the odds—many new law firms in New York never made it past a year or two, but after four years Scott's firm had both a solid history and a bright future. And most importantly, Scott could honestly say that he enjoyed going to work each morning.

The route that Scott had followed to the formation of Roth Stern was a typical one. After graduating from Columbia Law School, he had begun his career at the large New York firm of Gersten Golub Levy & Schmidt. With more than five hundred lawyers in their New York office, and a like number spread out among branch offices in Newark, Boston, Washington, and Los Angeles, Gersten Golub specialized in high-powered corporate litigation.

Gersten Golub paid its lawyers a lot of money, but Scott soon learned that the horror stories he had heard in law school about big firm life were all too true. It did not take a genius to realize that spending no fewer than six days a week from 8:00 a.m. to 11:00 p.m. in the office might be a way to make a living, but was certainly no way to make a life. After a while, all Scott had to do was look around him to see the type of person his seniors had become, and his resolve to find an alternative hardened.

By the end of his second year, around the time that his friend Win had the balls to strike out on his own, Scott began interviewing with smaller firms in the city. He ultimately made the switch to Felsher & Hazen, a twenty-lawyer firm specializing in shareholder class actions and derivative suits. There, he became close with junior partner Barry Stern, and over the next few years Scott gained a wealth of experience and knowledge. Stern was a rising star at Felsher & Hazen, with excellent lawyering skills, a knack for dealing with people, and an ability to attract new clients. When, about four years after Scott had joined the firm, Barry Stern decided that his partners were not giving him a big enough piece of the pie and that he could do better in a firm of his own, he naturally turned to Scott and offered him a chance to join him.

Barry also reached out for his close friend, Sharon Roth, who was a partner in another firm in the city, and Scott introduced the two of them to his law school classmate Maureen Mulhearn, who was anxious to escape the fate that awaited her at Gersten Golub. To round out the team, Michael Conway, another Felsher & Hazen lawyer, was invited to join.

The concept of Roth Stern Conway Heller & Mulhearn was born, and six months later the partnership opened its doors. The firm developed an outstanding reputation among the bar specializing in federal securities litigation, and its lawyers were kept busy.

In keeping with the recent trend toward shortened names, just last year the firm dropped the "Conway Heller & Mulhearn," and became simply Roth Stern. The firm expanded, bringing on two associates to help push the work out the door. The partners decided that they needed a presence in New Jersey, so Scott and Maureen got themselves admitted to the Jersey bar, and they opened a branch office in Newark, where Maureen became resident partner.

In addition to being kept busy, Roth Stern's partners began accumulating significant personal wealth. Scott was happy. He had found his niche.

■   ■   ■

The office had begun to awaken. Lawyers and secretaries filtered in, computers were booted up, and copy machines were switched on. E-mail was checked, and faxes that had come in overnight were distributed to their recipients. Telephones began to ring.

Review research with Stefanie, have lunch with a new client, attend oral argument in court, and then call the prosecutor about Guy. Better get started—the day was pretty full. Scott put his newspaper aside.

He shuffled through the papers on his desk and found Stefanie's legal memorandum on the Hewett Technologies class action lawsuit.

"Good morning, Stef," he said into his speakerphone when she picked up the intercom. "Grab some coffee, and come explain to me why you conclude we can't question Mr. Lyons at his deposition on a matter that's expressly mentioned in Hewett's most recent 10-K filing, which Lyons himself signed."

CHAPTER 7

Michelle Dolan lunched at her desk. The egg roll dipped in hot mustard, which she had been working on bite by bite over the course of the past half hour, qualified as "lunch" because her usual noontime fare was just handfuls from the one-pound bag of Fritos (or Doritos, or Cheez Doodles) stashed in her bottom desk drawer, washed down by a can of Diet Coke. This afternoon, though, one of her colleagues had been in the mood for Chinese food, and had volunteered to make a run for anyone who was interested.

Between bites of egg roll, Michelle added items to the list of things for her investigator to do on the Perez case. One Saturday evening, not too long ago, Anthony Perez—drunk out of his mind—had fallen asleep behind the wheel of his friend's Chevy Blazer. When tested at the hospital emergency room, his blood alcohol level had been so high that even if he had been awake he probably would not have seen the red light that he hurtled past to broadside the Toyota Celica GT in which twenty-one-year-old Jim Collins and his eighteen-year-old girlfriend Ellen Mitchell were driving home from their date.

Jim had been killed instantly, and Ellen, who had been thrown from the car, had sustained critical head injuries and was now in a coma. Perez had been spared from serious harm, save for a concussion and a number of broken ribs. When the police arrived at the scene, he was rambling about trying to find an "all-night body shop" to fix his friend's car "or else he'll kill me."

Anthony Perez deserved to spend a good deal of time behind bars, and Assistant Prosecutor Michelle Dolan hoped to put him there. Michelle had joined the Middlesex County Prosecutor's office after graduating from Washington University Law School in St. Louis, Missouri two years ago, and had been with the Death by Auto Section for the past nine months. She had spoken on the telephone yesterday afternoon with Perez's lawyer, who had rejected her plea bargain offer. Michelle had offered Perez the opportunity to plead guilty to death by auto and serve seven years. If the offer wasn't accepted, Michelle had said, she would press for aggravated manslaughter and seek the maximum sentence of thirty years. Perez's attorney—an old-timer who knew the ropes—had laughed, and told Michelle that he was holding out for a plea of reckless driving, with no jail time. "Sweetheart," he'd said, "my man will walk if we go to trial, and you know it."

The sad thing was, Perez's lawyer was right, to a degree. Historically, incidents involving death by auto had been treated in the courts more like automobile accidents than crimes, and culpable drivers had usually gotten away with little or no significant consequences. Great strides had been made in recent years toward recognizing death by auto as the crime it was—a form of homicide—but still, with the elements of proof necessary, and all of the factors coming into play to determine first responsibility, and then penalty, bringing such a case to trial was always a crap shoot.

This sickened Michelle. Her fingers located the photographs of Jim Collins that had been taken at the crash site and later at the morgue. He was no less dead than had Perez shot him through the heart with an assault rifle. If that had been the case, Perez's lawyer would have been begging Michelle to do a deal at only seven years.

As it was, she would charge Perez with aggravated manslaughter, manslaughter, assault by auto, reckless driving, and whatever other lesser included offenses were warranted, and Michelle would just have to hope that something substantial stuck.

"Mint chocolate chip today. Want some?" Jeremy Milne stood in the doorway of her small, windowless office.

Michelle looked up from the picture of Collins and smiled at the interruption. Sweet Jeremy, about to begin his third year of law school at Rutgers Newark, and interning for the summer at the prosecutor's office. Two months ago, he had been assigned to help Michelle with legal research to oppose a motion to suppress evidence in another of her cases. A week after they'd met, they'd started sleeping together. Knowing her predilection for junk food, Jeremy had taken to surprising her with afternoon snacks.

"Absolutely."

"Thought so," Jeremy said, tossing the pint container to Michelle. "You look busy. Catch ya later."

"Thanks, Jer," she called after him. "Later."

She smiled again, anticipating the evening with the law student. Michelle didn't kid herself—she knew it was just for fun. At twenty-seven, she was four years older than Jeremy, and she suspected that the real draw for him was the idea of sleeping with an "older woman." He made no secret of the fact that he continued to date others, but Michelle didn't care. She knew she was no incredible beauty. Not unpleasant-looking, mind you, just on the unremarkable side. Not really overweight either, but not what you would call petite. All in all, in the looks department, neither grand prize nor booby prize. But Jeremy made her feel good, and she was keeping the whole thing in perspective. So they had dinner together a lot, spent some nights at her place when her roommate was away, some at his place when she wasn't, and never talked too seriously.

She pried the cover from the Häagen-Dazs, and was searching her desk drawer for a spoon, when the telephone rang.

"Attorney Scott Heller for you," announced the receptionist.

Michelle jabbed the blinking light. "Michelle Dolan."

"Ms. Dolan, my name is Scott Heller. I'm an attorney with the firm of Roth Stern. I've spoken already with Mr. Perone from your Intake section, who referred me to the chief of your Death by Auto section. Mr. Delinko isn't in today, and his secretary passed me on to you. I hope you can help me."

"I'll try. What can I do for you?"

"Are you familiar with Ben Altman? The accident in Perth Amboy?"

"Only what I've read in the papers."

"Well, I'm calling on behalf of the individual who was responsible. I've been retained to enter into negotiations with the prosecutor's office to try to work out a deal. Quite frankly, the man panicked and ran when it happened, but he's anxious now to resolve the matter."

"And what's your client's name, Mr. Heller?"

"I'm sorry, but I can't tell you that right now. What I'd like to do is come in and meet with you to discuss a way to reach an agreement."

"I can tell you, Mr. Heller, that our negotiations won't proceed very far unless you tell me who your client is."

"We'll see, Ms. Dolan. Please just hear me out."

◾   ◾   ◾

"So they danced around a little on the phone, him refusing to tell her who his client is, and her insisting that no deal could be made if she doesn't know who he represents."

"And what happened?" Kluge asked.

Weber replied. "He convinced her to at least meet with him and discuss the matter further. Dolan made it clear to me that there's no way her office will agree to a plea without knowing who's doing the pleading, but she didn't want to just blow the attorney off. She wants to keep the lines of communication open and work on him to convince his client to give himself up."

Kluge sat across from Weber, in the latter's office. He had just begun his Tuesday morning shift, and was about to head out, when the lieutenant had summoned him into his office with news of the call he'd gotten from the assistant prosecutor the previous evening.

"So what's next?"

"The lawyer meets with Dolan tomorrow. All we can do is wait and see."

"What about the lawyer? Who is he?"

"Guy by the name of Scott Heller. Out of some corporate law firm in New York, with a branch office in Newark."

"Want me to go talk to him?"

"Nah, not yet. Let's see what happens tomorrow with Dolan. If he still refuses to talk, we'll have you pay him a visit."

"Good enough. Lemme know."

■　　■　　■

"Doc, what kind of bullshit is this? Why are you wasting your time?"

Michelle sat in one of the two chairs opposite Rich Delinko's desk. Long ago, her colleagues at the prosecutor's office had dubbed her "Doc." On intra-office memos and distributions lists, the attorneys were referred to by their initials, and Michelle was "M.D." Hence, the Doc. To her, it was better than "Mish."

Delinko, the chief of the Death by Auto section, continued.

"How many files do you have on your desk? They all have defendants, right? The police, their job is to find the perps. The prosecutor—that's us." He waved his arm to show Michelle who the prosecutors were around here. "Our job is to prosecute the perps and put them in jail after the police do their job. You called the Amboy police and passed on this lawyer's name to them, didn't you?"

"I told you I did."

"Then let them do their job, and you go back to the files on your desk and try to put those bad guys away."

"Is that an order?"

"Oh, come on, Doc, what do you mean 'Is that an order?' You know I don't order you around. But we really do have enough of our own work around here to do without taking on the cops' work too. Let the boys in blue find this guy."

"Listen, Rich, I know better than to say I have extra time on my hands, but all of my files are under control. I just want to have this meeting with Heller and see what comes of it."

The section chief looked frustrated.

"What makes this hit-and-run any different from all of the others that've come through here the past six months?" His tone softened. "Look, Doc, it's a terrible thing when some asshole gets behind the wheel and snuffs someone, but that doesn't mean we make like we're Gannon or Friday on Dragnet and start playing detective."

"Rich, the kid was only six years old. You saw his picture in the paper. And the picture of his parents. This *isn't* like the other hit-and-runs. The rules are different when it's a kid like this."

Delinko shifted in his chair and leaned forward.

"Okay, okay. Meet with Heller tomorrow. See how far you get. But that's it. After tomorrow, I want you back on your cases. Now *please* go get some work done."

CHAPTER 8

"Scott Heller to see Michelle Dolan," Scott said to the receptionist. "I have a two o'clock appointment."

The young woman sitting at the desk smiled.

"I'll let her know you're here. You can have a seat," she said, and motioned to a row of uncomfortable-looking wooden chairs lined up against the wall. Scott sat down, and managed to find a current *New Jersey Law Journal* among several outdated issues of *People*, *Reader's Digest*, and *Newsweek*.

Scott had spoken with his client after his initial call with Dolan, and had repeated his feeling that the time would come when the client's name would have to be revealed in order to reach a deal. The client remained firm. Under no circumstances was Scott to disclose his identity unless and until an acceptable plea agreement was in place. Only after Scott assured him that his name would remain confidential did he allow Scott to go ahead with the meeting.

Scott expected this afternoon's meeting to be a short one.

"Ms. Dolan will be right with you," the receptionist said, smiling once more.

A moment later, Michelle Dolan appeared. Scott replaced the newspaper and rose, and the prosecutor extended her hand. "Mr.

Heller, Michelle Dolan."

"Nice to meet you," Scott responded, shaking her hand. "Thanks for agreeing to meet with me."

"My office is pretty cluttered, so I reserved a conference room where we can talk. Come on in, and we can get started."

Scott picked up his attaché case. "Lead the way."

Michelle turned and led Scott past the reception desk and down a corridor lined with offices. Those on the left were on the interior, and had no windows, and Scott assumed they belonged to the more junior staff attorneys. The windowed offices on the right, Scott assumed, were occupied by the more senior lawyers.

Michelle stopped outside an interior conference room, flicked on the light switch by the door, and stepped aside to allow Scott to enter. She followed him in and closed the door. Windowless, and large enough for only a conference table that accommodated at most six people, it was a cramped and airless room. Michelle chose a seat at the far side of the table, forcing Scott to sit with his back to the door, facing only the three unadorned walls of the small room. The image of the type of police interrogation room commonly portrayed in the movies came to his mind.

When Scott had taken his seat, Michelle began.

"Mr. Heller, I don't want to waste my time or yours. When we spoke on the telephone, I told you that this meeting would go nowhere if your client insisted on remaining anonymous. This office will not negotiate a plea bargain in the dark. But you were very persuasive about wanting to come in here to talk.

"I made it as clear as I could that this pre-condition—the disclosure of your client's identity—is non-negotiable. I suppose the only reason I agreed to meet with you was the hope that in the meantime you'd be able to convince your client that his interests would best be served by coming forward. Quite frankly, I've taken a lot of heat from my superiors for what they see as a waste of this afternoon."

Scott shifted uncomfortably in his seat.

"Are you prepared to tell me who your client is?" Michele continued.

"I'm sorry, Ms. Dolan, but it's not my call. I'm not authorized to tell you who he is."

"Oh, don't be sorry, Mr. Heller," Michelle said. "Unless you're apologizing for wasting my time." She stood. "It seems we have nothing further to discuss."

Scott gestured with his hand, waving her back into her seat.

"Wait, please. Let's talk this through."

Michelle did not move. "Mr. Heller, I'll say it again. No name, no deal. It's really pretty simple."

"Look, I can understand the prosecutor's reluctance to negotiate in the dark, as you put it. But we're talking about a death by auto case. That's an offense where the sentence range is five to ten years. It's not as if there's a tremendous amount at stake here."

Michelle sat back down. "If so little is at stake, why is your client so afraid?"

She did not wait for a response. "I'll tell you why, Mr. Heller. He won't come forward because this is not just a death by auto case."

The assistant prosecutor continued. "The police investigation is making pretty good progress. And either you're not being candid with me—which I don't fault you for given the hand you've been dealt—or your client is holding back on you. Not only did he cause that boy's death by driving recklessly, which is what we have to prove for death by auto, he did it under circumstances showing 'extreme indifference to human life.' That raises his offense to aggravated manslaughter.

"You see, he knows that the more serious charge is waiting for him, and he's afraid that if he comes forward without a plea bargain in place, I might not deal. Then he faces up to thirty years, and in his mind he walked right into it.

"But what you have to tell him is that he's fooling himself if he thinks we won't find him. And when we do, he's going to be facing that same manslaughter charge. The difference will be that I'll be less inclined to deal with him then.

"Go back and tell him. Come in before we come and get him. It's his only hope.

"And now, I have to get back to work. I'll show you out."

On his way down in the elevator, Scott looked at his watch. The meeting had lasted less than five minutes.

CHAPTER 9

"**M**ay I be excused?"

"Yes, but first put your plate in the dishwasher."

Alexandra Heller carried her dish to the sink, rinsed it off, and placed it in the dishwasher. She brushed her long brown hair off her shoulders with a one-two backhand flick—a mannerism she'd copied from her mother before Jody had cut hers short, and one that Scott found disconcertingly grown-up for a nine-year-old—and smiled.

"There," she proclaimed, and she scurried out of the kitchen.

"Hey, what about your glass?" Jody called after her. "And your knife and fork?"

"Oops!" Alex hurried back in to take care of the overlooked items.

"*Now*, you're excused. Where're you off to?"

"Just outside to play with Jacklyn."

"Okay, but in front of the house. I want you in by nine, because it'll be getting dark soon."

"No problem." Alex ran for the front door.

Alex had, as usual on summer evenings, rushed through her dinner—Jody and Scott had barely started eating. But at least in the summer, when Alex stayed up later, the three of them got to sit down at the table together.

"By the way, Jo, you'll be happy to know that Guy is about to become a *former* client of mine. My part in his case is just about finished."

"Thank God! What happened?"

"Not much. I met with the prosecutor this afternoon, and it was a waste of time. She started by asking me my client's name again, I told her I couldn't tell her, and it went downhill from there. It was a very short meeting."

He described his encounter with Michelle Dolan.

"So what happens now?"

"I don't know how much of what Dolan says to believe. I have no idea what 'evidence' she's talking about, and she could be bluffing. But Guy has to take all of this into consideration in deciding what to do."

"But you're out of it, right?"

"It's only a matter of time. There's nothing else to do unless he tells me I can reveal his name, and judging from my previous conversations with him, I'm sure he's going to opt for staying out of sight. That was the whole idea of this whole thing. And if he decides to just fade into the woodwork, I'm done."

"What did he say when you told him what happened at the meeting?"

"I haven't spoken to him yet. I tried paging him on his beeper, but he didn't call me back. I'll try him again in the morning."

Jody stood and carried her empty plate to the sink. "Well, Scott, you know how I feel. The sooner you're finished with Guy, the better. Get through to him tomorrow and end it."

■　　■　　■

The next morning, Scott paged his client and received a return phone call within minutes. After listening to Scott's report on his meeting with Michelle Dolan, and her insistence that he give himself up or face aggravated manslaughter charges, the client said he would think about it. It took him only half an hour to call back with his decision.

Scott telephoned Dolan to report.

"Ms. Dolan, it's Scott Heller. You've been up-front with me, so I wanted to give you the courtesy of this call. My client will not be coming forward at this time. I guess you and I have nothing further to discuss."

CHAPTER 10

Tomorrow, Saturday, would be twenty-one days since it had happened. To Vince, it had been an eternity. Each day since then had been a nightmare in which time crawled at a snail's pace to maximize the duration and extent of his suffering. Each day allowed him—no, forced him—to relive the events of three weeks ago over and over again.

THWACK! He knew now that the jarring sound he had heard had been his speeding roadster colliding with little Ben Altman. His two-and-a-half-ton masterpiece of German engineering smashing into a forty-five-pound child.

THUD! That was the sound a small body made when it landed on the hood of a rocketing BMW Z4, after being shattered and flung into the air like a rag doll.

THWACK...THUD.

THWACK...THUD.

How many times had he heard that sequence play in his head over the past three weeks? Enough, he feared, to drive him crazy.

How long had he looked away from the road? A second? Less? How long was too long? As it was, he'd had his eyes elsewhere for a lifetime. Ben Altman's lifetime.

He'd done a lot of foolish things in his life, in prep school at Choate, and later in college in Boston. Some stuff he'd gotten into trouble for, but nothing had ever been serious enough to have lasting consequences of any real significance. He'd never before given any real thought to how fine a line there was between action and responsibility.

Every day, again and again, he played out different alternatives. Marty, the man in charge of the construction site, called to tell him he'd encountered a problem. Instead of rushing to the site for no useful reason, he made a few calls from home. For God's sake, he was a property owner and developer, not a fucking foreman. His BMW stayed in the garage, and Ben Altman lived.

Or, after his token appearance at the site, he got into his car and instead of cruising the waterfront, he headed straight out Smith Street to the Parkway and home. Then, too, the boy lived.

It was the same with the other scenarios that ran constantly through Vince's mind. In all of them, he had done what he was supposed to—acted like a responsible grown man instead of a pubescent hothead with raging hormones—and Ben Altman was still alive. In all of them except the one that had really happened.

Is that what it comes down to? Picking up the phone instead of driving the car? Or taking one route home instead of another? Can so much depend on such impulsive decisions?

No matter how many times Vince went over it in his head, it came out the same.

I may as well have taken a gun and shot that poor boy between the eyes. I may as well have gotten up that morning and said, "Let's go kill me a kid."

The negotiations with the prosecutor had not gone as he had hoped. A week had passed since his lawyer had called to tell him of the abortive meeting with Michelle Dolan, and the threat of an aggravated manslaughter charge. Now he was plagued not only by the continual repetition in his mind of the horrific events of that Saturday morning, but by the dread of facing thirty years in prison as well.

The minutes, hours, and days crawled by.

CHAPTER 11

Scott Heller had expected Roy Kluge at three o'clock, and the detective was already ten minutes late. Over the last week, since Kluge began calling to arrange the meeting, Scott had done his best to avoid the whole thing, and now that he'd agreed to it he just wanted to get it done with.

When Kluge had first telephoned the previous Friday to talk with him, he had been out of the office and hadn't had to deal with it. It had been somewhat disconcerting to hear from the police—he had truly believed that his role in this whole matter had ended with his advice to the prosecutor that his client had chosen not to come forward at this time—and he wasn't quite sure how to handle an inquiry by the authorities.

Having thus been forewarned that the detective was reaching out for him, Scott had instructed Karen to put the detective on the "carousel." Communications from people on that merry-go-round got hopelessly lost in a cycle of missed messages and return calls. From then on, whenever Kluge called, Scott was "in a meeting," "on another line," or "in court." Carousel calls were never ignored outright—rather they were returned at inconvenient or unlikely times. Scott made sure that each morning at eight o'clock, when

Kluge arrived to begin his shift, the detective would find that he had missed at least two callbacks—one at about six the night before, and another at about seven thirty that morning. When Kluge telephoned again, he would be advised of another reason why Scott was unavailable, and would take another spin on the merry-go-round.

But nobody could accuse Scott of being non-responsive.

Yesterday, after nearly a week of getting the runaround, Kluge had tried a different approach. When Karen advised him that Scott was "with a client," the detective asked to be connected with Sharon Roth, the firm's senior partner. "Tell Ms. Roth I need to question her about Scott Heller's involvement in the Ben Altman homicide."

That message had been repeated to Roth's secretary, Abby, when she took the call. When Kluge was told that Ms. Roth was in a meeting, he instructed Abby to pass her a note stating that he was holding in order to speak with her about urgent police business.

Sharon quickly summoned Scott to her office to find out why a Perth Amboy detective was calling *her* about *his* involvement in the Altman investigation. To say that Sharon was displeased was to put it mildly. "We can't be perceived to be obstructing a police investigation. Deal with it."

Duly chastised by his partner, Scott had returned to his office and picked up Kluge's call. If Kluge had been surprised that Scott was suddenly available, he hadn't shown it. Scott explained that he would be of little help to the investigation—his client had forbidden him to speak about the matter.

"It would be a colossal waste of your time to travel all the way in to New York to have me repeat that face-to-face."

"But Mr. Heller, it's no longer a matter of what your client has or has not authorized you to do. You're in possession of material information relating to an ongoing homicide investigation, and I have to question you about it. Let's not make this any harder than it needs to be."

"I don't think you understand," Scott had replied. "Any information I might have is the result of privileged communications between my client and me, and it's not my place to decide whether or not to reveal those confidences. A client can seal the lips of his or her attorney. My client has asserted the attorney-client privilege, and I'm forbidden by law from violating it. So, I can't help you."

"Mr. Heller, I'm not prepared right now to debate with you the scope of your obligation to cooperate with a homicide investigation. You and I do have significant matters to discuss, and while I appreciate your desire to spare me a futile trip into the city, I don't think that a meeting with you would be wasted. I have to insist that you see me."

So it was, yesterday afternoon, that today's meeting with Roy Kluge had been arranged. But it would, as he had told the detective, be pointless. The attorney-client privilege prevented him from speaking about anything of substance. Scott just wanted to get the meeting out of the way and get back to work.

■　　■　　■

Detective Roy Kluge stuffed the receipt for the Lincoln Tunnel toll into his shirt pocket and inched his way forward. Christ, even at two forty-five in the afternoon the traffic into the city was murder. Bumper-to-bumper from the exit off the Turnpike and across Route 495. At a crawl down the helix to the toll plaza. And of course, a couple of tollbooths were unmanned. He closed his window so he wouldn't choke on the heavy exhaust fumes, wondering as he did so how the toll collectors stayed alive.

Of the three tubes, two were presently devoted to outbound traffic. Kluge inched his way, along with what seemed to him to be the entire population of northern New Jersey, toward the two lanes of the only city-bound tunnel. A strict adherent to the rules of "alternate merge," he allowed the minivan slightly ahead of him to the right to slip in front of him. He tried to ease in behind the van, but an attractive young woman no more than twenty-five, driving a red Audi TT, maintained her position just inches from the van's rear bumper and refused to yield. A toot from Kluge's horn brought a shout of "fuck you" through her open window, and just in case Kluge couldn't hear her, she flipped him the bird as well. He considered once more his theory that on-the-spot execution of asshole drivers would result in more civilized road conditions—the truly incorrigible ones would be removed from the scene permanently, and the educable ones would be deterred by the knowledge that anyone they offended would blow their brains out while society applauded. Not only would those behind the wheel be more courteous to one another, but judging by the present number of drivers who were clearly beyond reform, the roads would be far less crowded after the initial wave of executions. Lacking this desirable alternative, however, Kluge just smiled and waved to the young lady.

A week ago, Kluge had sat in Weber's office as the lieutenant described the telephone call he had received from Michelle Dolan, the assistant prosecutor who had met with Heller. She had reported that Heller remained firm in his insistence that his client's name stay confidential until a deal was struck. Dolan had repeated to Heller that there was no sense in talking any further, and that was that.

"We're gonna have to go talk to him," Weber had said.

"Well shit, getting the name from him should be easy. If he won't talk, the A.P. can just convene a grand jury and subpoena him. Then he has to tell us."

"Maybe. But it hasn't reached that stage yet. Right now, the prosecutor just wants us to go see him. I know his office is in New York, but I prefer you go there to question him. And when you get there, don't worry about being discreet. You know, flash your badge to the receptionist, and announce that you're there to question Heller in connection with the investigation into Benjamin Altman's death. If his colleagues don't know ahead of time you're coming, and why, I want you to do your best to make sure they know by the time you're leaving. I'm hoping his partners won't appreciate that their pal is in the center of a criminal investigation, and that there's a cop snooping around their offices."

After a week of missed calls and mixed messages, Kluge hadn't yet made up his mind about Heller. The lawyer claimed that he wanted to be helpful, but that his hands were tied because of his client's assertion of the attorney-client privilege. Yet Kluge had no doubt that Heller had been doing his best to avoid him. He hoped to have a better feel for the lawyer after this afternoon.

Sandwiched between two New Jersey Transit buses spewing dense black exhaust, the current of vehicles finally carried Kluge into the mouth of the tunnel, and once inside, the traffic picked up just a bit of speed. When he emerged in Manhattan, he proceeded east on Fortieth Street, hoping to make the light at Eighth Avenue lest his car fall prey to the host of street people at the corner hustling change in return for "cleaning" windshields. No such luck, and as he slowed to a stop at the intersection, he flicked on his windshield wipers to ward off an approaching entrepreneur armed with a filthy rag.

The city was crowded and busy as usual, and people overflowed from the sidewalks onto the traffic-clogged streets. Kluge worked his way slowly across town toward Madison Avenue, and he was forced to consider whether asshole pedestrians ought to be added to the list of those liable to be shot for discourtesy on the road. He realized that would be impractical. The city would become a ghost town.

When he finally pulled into an underground parking garage two blocks from Roth Stern's offices, he saw by his watch that he was twenty minutes late. He hurriedly exchanged his keys for a stamped ticket, and trotted up the ramp to the street.

He didn't expect that Heller would have had a change of heart, and would now tell him what he wanted to know. But, as Lieutenant Weber had suggested, he was ready to see what kind of trouble he could stir up at Roth Stern while he was there.

CHAPTER 12

The elevator opened onto the twenty-first floor of 473 Madison Avenue, where Roth Stern had its offices. The lobby was illuminated by reflected light emanating from concealed halogen fixtures. A sleek black leather couch stretched across the mirrored wall opposite the bank of three elevators, and in front of the couch sat a smoked glass coffee table on which was arranged an assortment of newspapers and business and law journals. To the right stood a chest-high, steel-gray laminated receptionist's counter. At both ends of the lobby, open doorways led to suites of offices.

Kluge approached the counter, where a young woman wearing a telephone headset sat talking to a remote caller. Without stopping her conversation, she smiled and held a finger up to Kluge indicating that she would be with him in a minute.

"Yes, of course, Mr. Craig. I'll leave another message for him, but he's been in a meeting all day and he hasn't even seen your other two messages."

She paused and nodded.

"Yes, Mr. Craig. I'll see to it that he gets all three messages the minute the meeting ends."

She pressed a button on the console in front of her and looked up at Kluge, smiling once more.

"Now, sir, may I help you?"

Kluge retrieved his badge from his pocket and held it up for the receptionist to see.

"Roy Kluge from the Perth Amboy Police Department. I'm here to question Scott Heller in connection with the hit-and-run death of Ben Altman. Mr. Heller's expecting me."

"Yes, I overheard you were coming. That poor boy," she sighed. "And his parents...I can't imagine what they're going through. Have you caught the animal who did it?" She paused. "And what could Mr. Heller possibly know about all this?"

Kluge thought it significant that the woman did not seem to know Heller's connection. A case like this would be gossiped about around the coffee machine or watercooler, so if she didn't know, probably the others on the staff were ignorant as well. Well then, time to make waves.

"No, we haven't caught him yet. But that's why I'm here. Mr. Heller's his lawyer."

The young woman looked startled. "Omigod. Really? I didn't know we were involved in any way." Her surprised expression turned into one of concern as the import of what Kluge had just said sank in. "You know, then, I shouldn't be talking to you about your investigation. And I probably shouldn't have said what I just did. About the guy being an animal, I mean. Him being a client and all." The look on her face told what she really felt, though.

"That's okay, ma'am, but it may well be that we'll end up talking further anyway," Kluge said. "Depending on how cooperative Mr. Heller is, I may just have to question everyone here at Roth Stern."

The receptionist appeared disconcerted at this news.

"But I don't know anything," she protested. "And the fact that Mr. Heller is representing the driver will be news to most everyone here...But really, I don't think I ought to be talking to you about it."

Her reluctance to talk notwithstanding, there was something about her—maybe her expression of disgust when she had said the word "animal"—that made Kluge think she might be an ally at some later time. He decided to plant the seed.

"Ma'am, what's your name?"

She hesitated.

"Look." Kluge smiled and held his empty hands up as if to show he was unarmed. "I'm not writing it down or anything. I just feel dumb calling you 'ma'am' all the time."

"Julie," she said.

"Julie, you were right before. The person who ran Ben Altman down, and then sped away without so much as a 'howdy-do,' is an animal. And about what his parents must be going through? You were right about that too. You can't imagine it.

"My job is to find the creep who ran Ben down, and to take him off the road, because five'll get ya ten the guy was juiced up or stoned, and this wasn't the first time he got behind the wheel all fu—uh, all messed up. And unless we find him, he'll drive like that again, and someone else'll be crossing the street at the wrong time and the wrong place. And then we'll be trying to imagine what *that* poor slob's family is going through."

Kluge knew he was being melodramatic—Christ, he sounded like Joe Friday on Dragnet—and he wondered if he had gone too far. But judging by the consternation on Julie's face, his speech was having the desired effect.

The detective leaned in a little closer and lowered his voice. "Your boss knows who that animal is. And he refuses to tell the prosecutor what he knows. Julie, if you're trying to imagine what Ben's parents are going through, try to imagine their anger and frustration in knowing that that guy is still out there, that Mr. Heller knows who he is, and that he refuses to do anything about it."

Julie lowered her eyes. "I didn't know."

Kluge reached inside his pocket, pulled out a business card, and placed it on the counter. "If you think of anything you ought to be telling me, call me."

Julie looked at the card, but made no move to pick it up.

"Now," Kluge said with a smile, "I think you'd better let Mr.

Heller know I'm here. I'm already almost a half hour late, and God knows it was hard enough getting this appointment in the first place."

Julie regained her composure, picked up the telephone receiver, and punched a key on the intercom. "Karen, Detective Roy Kluge is here to see Mr. Heller." Pause. "Okay, I'll tell him."

"Mr. Heller's secretary will be out in a minute. Make yourself comfortable."

■   ■   ■

"Okay—showtime." Scott was standing outside Sharon Roth's door. "Karen's bringing him into the conference room in a minute."

Scott's partner rose from behind her desk. The first thing one noticed about Sharon Roth was her flaming red hair—curly and thick. She was about five and a half feet tall, slender, and very pretty, and she wasn't afraid to use her looks to her advantage in a profession still dominated by members of the old-boy network. Many were the ogling male attorneys whom she had left at the courtroom door or conference room table wondering what had hit them, after miscalculating the acumen of such an attractive adversary.

"Showtime it is," she replied, and she followed Scott into the conference room.

The black-gray-steel-glass motif evident throughout the office carried through into the conference room. The wall behind Scott and Sharon, as they entered, was translucent glass through which silhouettes and shadows could be seen. Opposite them, a window overlooking Madison Avenue ran the width of the room. Lengthwise, the walls were covered with a light gray, ribbed cloth, and along one of these walls lay a dark gray credenza atop which sat a brushed stainless steel coffee carafe and eight black mugs. In the center of the room was an ebony conference table surrounded by eight chairs covered in black fabric. Hanging on the walls, lithographs colored in deep greens and blues, bright yellows, and sharp reds added life to the room.

They remained standing until Kluge was ushered in. When first meeting someone he had only before spoken with on the telephone, Scott was always interested to see how well his mental impression of that person matched his or her actual appearance. Scott had expected an archetypical cop, and that was what stood before him. The hulking frame, thick neck, and buzzed haircut fit the profile, as did the meaty hand that the detective extended in greeting. There was no mistaking Roy Kluge for what he was, and his very presence was discomfiting to Scott.

"Detective Kluge, I'm Scott Heller." He shook the policeman's hand. "And this is my partner, Sharon Roth, who you've spoken with."

After Sharon and Kluge exchanged greetings, the two attorneys took their seats on the side of the table along the wall with the credenza, and Scott motioned to the chair closest to the door, facing the window. "Please, Detective, make yourself comfortable."

Kluge sat, and Scott continued. "I hope you don't mind if Ms. Roth sits in on our meeting. She and I discussed the matter, and we both decided that in view of the sensitive nature of the case, we would all be better off if both of us were present."

"No problem," Kluge said. "I know both of you are busy, so I'll try to be brief. As you know, I'm investigating the hit-and-run death of Benjamin Altman. You have attempted to negotiate a plea bargain on behalf of the driver. You've spoken and met with Assistant Prosecutor Michelle Dolan. You've refused to reveal who your client is, claiming protection by the attorney-client privilege.

"Now, Mr. Heller, my understanding of the attorney-client privilege is that it protects communications between you and your client. I don't want to know what this person told you, and I don't want to know what you told him. I just want his name. It's as easy as that."

Scott shook his head slowly from side to side. "I'm sorry, Detective. I already told you on the phone that I can't help you. The fact that you don't want to know the substance of my conversations with my client doesn't change anything." The lawyer paused. "Can I explain?"

Kluge nodded.

"The attorney-client privilege goes back a long way, and the reason for it is to ensure that clients will receive adequate legal counsel and representation. In order for an attorney to properly advise a client, there must be free and frank communication between them. The attorney must have all the facts, or else his advice is likely to be flawed. He must know the harmful information as well as the helpful. If the attorney could be forced to reveal what his client tells him, then the client would likely hold back information that the attorney must know in order to do his job.

"Now, you're right when you say the privilege protects *communications* between attorney and client. And you probably know that not *all* communications between attorney and client are privileged—the law protects only those communications that the client intends as confidential. But in this case, when my client communicated his name to me, he intended that it remain confidential.

"If I, or any attorney, can be forced to disclose the identity of a client who has come to me in confidence, then under certain circumstances—such as those present in this case—the entire purpose of the attorney-client privilege would be defeated.

"Assume for a minute that a client comes to me and says 'I've been arrested for bank robbery. I'm guilty and I need you to represent me at trial.' The client's statement to me that he's guilty is a classic example of privileged information. You couldn't force me to reveal whether he had admitted his guilt to me, and I'd be committing a serious ethical breach if I told you of his admission."

Scott paused as he poured himself some water and sipped at it. Then he continued.

"Now assume a client comes to me *before* he's arrested and says 'I just robbed a bank. What can you do for me?' And assume that I make some inquiries on his behalf, and the police ask me 'So who is this person you're trying to plea-bargain for in this bank robbery?' My simple disclosure of my client's name would in effect reveal the very subject matter of what he and I discussed—his guilt in the bank robbery. Under those circumstances the privilege protects his name from disclosure."

Kluge considered this. "But with your real client, we already know the subject matter of your discussions. You've already told Ms. Dolan that he was the driver of the car that ran Ben down."

Scott nodded. "That's precisely my point. In both of my examples, the privileged information is 'I, Joe Blow, robbed the bank.' In my first example, where you've already arrested Joe Blow and placed him on trial, although you know who the 'I' is, you don't know what Joe Blow told me—'I'm guilty.' If you asked me to provide that missing piece of information, I couldn't, because it's privileged.

"In my second example, though, while you may know *what* the client told me—'I robbed the bank'—you don't know *who* the client is. In neither case do you know the full communication that the client imparted to me: 'I, Joe Blow, robbed the bank.'

"Just as in the first example my disclosure of Joe Blow's statement would reveal the confidential admission of Joe Blow's guilt, so too in my second example would the disclosure of Joe Blow's name."

Throughout this analysis, Kluge had been sitting back in his chair, listening. He now leaned forward, forearms on the table.

"Mr. Heller, Ms. Roth, I'm not a lawyer. I don't know all the technicalities about the attorney-client privilege. What I do know is that a little boy is dead and that you know who killed him."

Kluge had brought with him a brown 8½-by-11-inch envelope, which he had laid on the table in front of him when he sat down. He opened the flap, pulled out some photographs, and placed the first one faceup in front of Heller.

"This is Ben. It was taken in the beginning of last month, before he crossed paths with your client."

Scott looked down at the picture. It showed a smiling young boy wearing a "Happy Days Camp" T-shirt, a baseball bat slung over his shoulder.

"This is Ben after he had the pleasure of meeting your client." Kluge laid another photo on the table next to the first. Not wanting to see it, Scott nevertheless shifted his gaze to the second picture. It had been taken at the scene of the accident, before the ambulance had taken Ben's body to the morgue. Ben was not visible in the photograph—his body was covered by a white sheet. Scott was relieved that the picture was not more graphic, but seeing the lifeless, shrouded mound lying in the road was powerful stuff. He tugged at his earring absently, and his shoulders drooped.

"Please, Detective, don't," Scott said. "Can't you see my hands are tied?"

Kluge went on—he still had one more picture. "Here's Ben's parents," he said, and he dropped it on top of the other two. "They don't have a son anymore."

Now Sharon spoke up. "One minute, Detective. You have no right to do this." She spoke calmly and forcefully. "I myself don't know the client's identity. But as for Scott, you have no right to lay a guilt trip on him. The matter is not in his control. He has no choice. He cannot help you."

She reached in front of Scott and slid the three photographs back across to Kluge.

"No, those are duplicates. They're for you to keep." Neither Scott nor Sharon made a move to pick them up. "Look, Mr. Heller, you seem like a nice guy. You have your job to do, I have mine. Maybe there is something to this attorney-client privilege, but if there is, it stinks. From what I've learned, it's not so cut-and-dried—Ms. Dolan over at the prosecutor's office tells me she can make you talk. So it's not over."

He stood to leave. "Thank you both for your time."

◼   ◼   ◼

When Kluge passed through the lobby, where Julie was talking on the telephone, he saw that the business card he had left on the counter was no longer there. He stepped onto the elevator, and turned to wave a good-bye to the receptionist. She waved back, but quickly looked away.

Heller wasn't going to talk. Weber had thought just a visit from the cops would do it, and that it wouldn't be necessary to go the grand jury route. The attorney did seem troubled by the whole thing—he didn't appear eager to shield the driver—but he evidently took his ethical obligation of confidentiality very seriously. They'd have to consult with Dolan, and see what the next step would be.

Kluge exited the elevator on the ground floor and looked at his watch. *Shit. It's after four. Fuckin' rush hour. The streets are gonna be jammed, and the tunnel'll be a bitch. Shit.*

CHAPTER 13

Kluge's escape from the city was all that he had feared. In the sprawling buildings and towering skyscrapers of Manhattan there are more than four hundred million square feet of office space, which if laid out at street level rather than piled up story upon story would cover an area of nearly two-thirds of the whole island. About two and a half million people work in that space, and every day they have to travel to and from their homes, apartments, co-ops and condos. Shortly after four every afternoon, the mass evacuation of midtown begins. Those who dwell in Manhattan make their way south to neighborhoods like Chelsea, Greenwich Village and SoHo, or north to the Upper West Side or the Upper East Side. More than one and a half million of the workers live someplace other than the island, and every morning and evening they have to find their way across or through one of the eleven bridges or tunnels connecting the borough to the surrounding communities.

By the time Kluge had retrieved his car from the parking garage, the exodus was in full swing. As if released by floodgates, rivers of workers flowed from office buildings to form a sea of people on the sidewalks of the broad avenues and the narrow side streets. The streets quickly became clogged with buses and taxicabs, and with automobiles of those fool enough to have driven themselves into the city earlier in the day.

Kluge had parked in the garage beneath 437 Madison Avenue, at Forty-ninth Street, and though he was only about a mile from the entrance to the Lincoln Tunnel, the drive across Forty-ninth Street and down Ninth Avenue took almost an hour. By then, the backup at the tunnel had reached severe, but routine, proportions, so traffic was being redirected to an alternate approach about six blocks further south. A half hour more found Kluge, nerves frayed, fighting for position at the mouth of the tunnel—the hell with alternate merge.

The detective eventually made his way through the tunnel, across Route 495, and onto the New Jersey Turnpike, where the traffic was more bearable, though not by much. The hour being what it was, there was little for him to do except head for home.

First thing Monday morning, Kluge met with Weber. He described the law firm's physical appearance so Weber could visualize the setting. He detailed his conversation with Julie, the receptionist, and described his gut feeling that she might be of some use at a later time. Then he recounted his meeting with Heller and Roth.

"Up until yesterday," he said, "I really did have a negative impression of him. When we spent that week or so playing telephone tag, I was sure he was avoiding me, and I figured it was your typical lawyer protecting his client by making himself unavailable.

"But now, I don't think that was it. I'm still sure he was playing hard-to-get, but I think it was because he really doesn't know what to do, and by avoiding me he wouldn't have to figure it out. We're forcing him to realize that this attorney-client privilege stuff might prevent him from doing what he thinks is probably the right thing."

"So, whaddya make of it all?" Weber asked.

"I think the bottom line is if he had his druthers, he'd nail the guy. But his view of the law and his code of ethics tells him he can't."

"Look, Roy," the lieutenant said. "I would guess that most lawyers faced with this situation just need the protection of a subpoena or a court order, and then they'll talk. These lawyers worry about paper—what the record shows—so later when someone questions what they did, they could point back to something in the file and say 'See, I did it the right way.'

"What I understand from Dolan is a situation like this can play out in a few ways. Heller could be subpoenaed before a grand jury. If he is, he could either obey the subpoena and testify, or he could refuse, claiming the privilege. If he refuses, the A.P. could seek a court order to compel him to comply with the subpoena. If the court finds that the privilege doesn't apply, it would order Heller to testify. If he still refuses, he's in contempt of court and he goes to jail."

"Well if that happens, Loo, he can't stay in there forever," Kluge interjected. "Eventually he'll get tired of sittin' there and speak up."

"It's not that easy, Roy," Weber responded. "Dolan says that even if the lower court holds him in contempt and orders him to jail, he would probably appeal, and his imprisonment would probably be stayed in the meantime. Then, either the Appellate Division or the Supreme Court could disagree with the lower court, and hold that Heller's right. Then he doesn't go to jail, and he doesn't have to talk.

"On the other hand, his appeals could be turned down. Then it depends on just how principled he is—he obeys the final court determination and talks, or he continues his silence and goes into the slammer."

"Well hell, Loo, I don't care how principled this guy is, he's not gonna sit and rot forever. Sooner or later he'll have enough, and he'll give the perp up to get out."

"Maybe," said Weber, "Maybe. But Dolan says with civil contempt, since the object of imprisonment is not to punish, but to coerce compliance with a court order, if the court finally decides that the prisoner is *never* gonna talk, and that further jail time is futile, he walks. Dolan told me of cases where mob guys have been thrown in jail for refusing to testify, and after a year or so the court realizes they're not gonna turn. The judge has to cut them loose because otherwise the imprisonment becomes punitive instead of coercive.

"Now, I'm not suggesting that I expect Heller to willingly rot in a jail cell for a year or two. I'm just telling you the different ways this could play out. What I want to know from you is: Does Heller just have his eye on the record? Will a piece of paper—a subpoena or a court order—in his file be enough? If we just go through the steps and build his record for him, will he come across? Or will he go to jail 'on principle'?"

"Jeez, Lieutenant, I'm good, but Dr. Joyce Brothers I'm not. I only met with the guy for a half hour. But I'd have to say there's more going on here than him just worrying about covering his ass. How far he'll take it, and whether he'd actually walk into a jail cell because of what he believes, I can't say. My bet is that it's not as simple as being able to point to a piece of paper in his file and saying 'See, I did it by the book.'"

Weber sighed. "I'm afraid you're right, Roy. This isn't gonna be easy…How's the investigation going otherwise?"

Kluge had a small spiral-bound notebook in his hands, but he spoke without referring to it. "Well, we still haven't come up with any witnesses, but we've been able to identify the make, model, and color of the vehicle. Remember that plastic disc we found in the middle of the street? Looks like it *was* a knockout plug, and the good news is that the lab guys were able to trace it by its specs and color." He glanced down at his notes. "It's from a 2006 BMW Z4, Montego blue metallic."

"So we know what kind of car we're looking for," said Weber. "Well, it's more than we had yesterday. What can we get from Motor Vehicles in Trenton on this?"

"I already started the paperwork with them. I'm getting a list of all of the registered owners of Montego blue '06 Z4's in town. That shouldn't take too long. I figured I'd start with Amboy, because even though we don't know if the perp is from town, we gotta start somewhere. We'll know soon enough how many people we have to question, and I could always expand the search later, depending on what turns up."

"What about the Altmans' neighbors? Nobody saw anything useful?"

"Nah, we've come up dry there. We really blanketed the area, and no one remembers a speeding car." Kluge paused. "No, let me say that another way. No one remembers a *particular* speeding car. We got people telling us what we already know. That part of Water Street is heavily traveled, and we've always had a problem with speeders there. It's a long stretch from Lewis to Gordon, and since there are no intersections, cars really travel. A speeding car is nothing out of the ordinary, so even if someone saw one, they wouldn't take much notice."

"But now we know what kind of car it was," Weber interjected. "Maybe we ought to go back. Now, instead of asking everyone 'Do you remember a speeding car,' we can ask 'Do you remember a speeding blue BMW.' Look, even if we know what kind of car we're looking for, it'd still be nice if someone remembered seeing it, or even who was driving. Z4's a sporty-looking car. Maybe someone'll remember."

Kluge shifted in his seat. "Uh, Loo, we really don't have the manpower to go talk to everyone again."

Weber thought for a moment. "We don't have to go back to everyone. Eliminate the ones who've already told us they weren't home at the time. Eliminate the ones who said 'No way, I didn't see anything, I was in the backyard all day, I was inside all day and didn't look out the window, blah, blah, blah.' Go back to the ones who said 'Yeah, I was around, but who the hell remembers one fast car to the next?' Maybe with those people, a description of the car will jog their memory.

"And let's post some more flyers along the boardwalk, with a description of the vehicle. Also, poke around more south of the Altman house. Till now, we've been concentrating to the north, to see if anyone remembers seeing a car speeding from the scene. Now that we know what kind of car it was, let's see if anyone below the scene remembers seeing it before the accident."

"Will do, Loo. Anything else?"

"Nah, that's it for now. Just keep me advised."

Both men agreed that Scott Heller was the key. The meeting concluded with Weber undertaking to reach out for Michelle Dolan to discuss what she could do from her end to force the attorney to talk.

■　■　■

"Unfortunately, Lieutenant, the decision to bring the matter before the grand jury isn't mine to make."

Michelle Dolan shifted the receiver from one ear to the other and took a gulp from her can of Diet Coke. In front of her, her desk was cluttered with police reports, lab reports, interview notes, and other material from the Perez file. Michelle's efforts to negotiate a plea bargain had failed, and Anthony Perez was due to go on trial for aggravated manslaughter in just two days.

Photographs of Jim Collins and Ellen Mitchell, Perez's victims, were tacked to the bulletin board opposite Michelle's desk. Some of her colleagues thought the posting of the pictures gruesome, but some time ago Michelle had found it to be a useful device when getting ready for a trial. In the final days before beginning a trial, when she had to concentrate all her efforts and mental energy on preparing, she would select from the file a photograph of the victim—not a grisly picture taken in death, but one that portrayed the victim as he or she was before the tragedy—and would pin it on the wall where she could see it from her desk. Whenever she felt she had done all she could on a particular aspect of the matter, or simply grew tired from an exhausting day of poring over the minutia that must be put together to build a case, a glance at the photo would remind her of exactly why she was there, and would inspire her to go over things just once more to be sure she hadn't missed anything.

Lieutenant Weber had telephoned her moments ago about Scott Heller, and Collins and Mitchell beckoned her from across the room to return to the autopsy report, which she was reading for the third time that day. *One more minute, guys. Just let me finish this call.*

"Lieutenant, you don't have a suspect, and we don't have a case to present to the grand jury. Granted, the law allows the grand jury to inquire into matters where it's apparent that a crime has been committed, even though no complaint has been filed against a particular individual, but the decision to pursue such a matter with the grand jury is beyond my authority."

"Then who can make that decision?" Weber asked. "Right now, I'm sorry to say that this lawyer is all we've got. We really need to learn what he knows."

"I'd have to take it up with our section chief, Rich Delinko. But between you and me, he wasn't too thrilled about me taking the time even to just meet with Heller the first time around, and I can guess how he'll feel about devoting more energy to this. He thinks I'm spinning my wheels because the court would uphold the privilege. I know I told you Heller could be subpoenaed. But it just doesn't look like that's going to happen."

"Well at least talk to your boss and see what you can do. I don't want this guy to walk."

Michelle promised to do so before the end of the day, and hung up. She glanced at the photos on her corkboard, and plunged back into the medical examiner's report.

■   ■   ■

Some hours later, Michelle glanced at the clock on her desk. The clock was a big clunky thing, gold-plated and crystal, more suited for a fireplace mantel than a desk, but it was a gift from her parents so there it sat. When Michelle had passed the bar exam, her mother and father had been bursting with pride and had wanted to buy her something for her office, though at the time she had neither an office nor even a job. One morning, UPS delivered this clock to Michelle's apartment, and though Michelle thought it hideous, she placed it on her desk on her very first day of work, and had kept it there ever since. The clock showed that it was nearly five.

She had promised Weber that she would broach the subject of Scott Heller with Rich Delinko, so she put aside the outline of facts she hoped to prove through the testimony of the police officer who was the first on the scene of Perez's crash, and headed into Delinko's office. She waited while Delinko finished a telephone call, and then brought him up-to-date on the Altman matter, ending with Weber's plea for intervention by the prosecutor's office.

"Doc," Delinko sighed, sounding a bit exasperated, "I just don't see it. Like you said to the cop, they have no suspect, and we have no case.

"Cases, I got plenty. All with suspects. All just barely making their deadlines because I don't have enough A.P.s to work them. I thought our deal was that you'd meet with this Heller guy and see what you could do. If nothing came of it, you were going to leave it alone and do your real work."

"Yeah, but—"

"Now Doc, don't be working those sad eyes on me, or getting goofy about 'poor little Ben.' It's not going to work this time. You talked me into letting you meet with Heller because of that, and it didn't lead anywhere. How can I justify putting any more time into this? I mean, from what you tell me, I think the court will ultimately agree that the privilege applies. If Heller's all the cops have, then they're going to have to look harder for something else, or consider closing their file on it too.

"Now I know you don't like it if I give you orders, so I'm giving you a very strong suggestion. Unless and until the police come up with a suspect, leave the Altman matter alone."

The next morning, Michelle telephoned Lieutenant Weber and apologetically told him that the prosecutor's office would not be pursuing the investigation.

CHAPTER 14

Stacy was alone on a Sunfish, a small, light, single-sailed boat scarcely big enough to carry two people. Choppy water buffeted the craft. Thick, nimbostratus clouds had gathered to crowd out the sun in an ominous display of force, and the temperature had plummeted. The wind had risen from a gentle breeze to nearly twenty knots, and Stacy leaned backwards over the port gunwale, tiller in her right hand, mainsheet in her left, trying to keep the vessel from going over. The starboard gunwale threatened to dip below the lapping waves to flood the tiny dinghy, but Stacy hiked herself out even further and succeeded in avoiding disaster.

Even as it started, Stacy knew, or at least sensed, that it was a dream. It was *the* dream, and although Stacy knew how it would turn out, there was nothing she could do about it. Previous times, she had tried to will herself awake, but the dream's grip was always too strong. She had resigned herself to the fact that when it came, there was nothing she could do but ride it out to its conclusion.

The Sunfish was about fifty yards from the shore, where the Arthur Kill and the Raritan River flowed together opposite Stacy's house on Water Street. She was trying to guide the boat in, but it would be tricky even under ideal sailing conditions because there was no dock or pier to which to moor, or even a sandy beach on which to run aground. Instead, a six-foot-high wall of rocks, which Stacy would have to climb in order to reach the boardwalk, awaited her. There would be nowhere to tie the boat, but she already knew that the fate of the vessel was simply not an issue in the events soon to unfold. Nevertheless, Stacy made a mental note to remember to raise the centerboard when she came within ten yards of the wall, lest it be dashed along the shallow bottom closer in.

One reason she knew this was a dream—aside from having experienced it a number of times before—was that had this been reality, the rock wall and boardwalk would have hidden the road from her view, leaving only the houses atop the hill visible. But in her dream, she could see the stretch of Water Street in front of her house, and she was petrified to find Ben—strangely two years old again—sitting on a blanket, in the middle of the street, playing with a toy truck.

What is he doing out there? This is crazy! Sitting in the middle of the street, playing. And where the hell is Marc? He's supposed to be keeping his eye on Ben. I have to get there fast, before a car comes along. Damn this storm, and damn Marc too!

Stacy pushed the tiller away from her, pulled in on the mainsheet, and ducked under the boom as the small boat came about. With only fifteen or so yards to the rock wall left, she hustled to pull up the centerboard. This made the craft less steady, but she was fast approaching the shore.

At the last moment, she turned the bow directly into the wind, stopping all forward motion and causing the craft to sidle up to the wall. The sea was still pretty rough, though, and the vessel was pounded sideways into the rocks, and bounced up and down on them for good measure. From this close in, Ben was hidden from Stacy's view and she rushed to scale the wall and climb onto the boardwalk. The violent motion of the sailboat made it hard for Stacy to get a firm hold on the slippery rocks, but somehow she hoisted herself out of the boat, leaving it to be battered against the craggy shore.

It had begun raining a few moments before, and Stacy was now soaked to the skin. Shivering, she scaled the rocks, grabbed the tubular railing at the edge of the boardwalk, and swung first one leg, and then the other, over onto the concrete walkway. She glanced back and saw the Sunfish being pulled downstream by the current, still being pounded on the rocks by the rough sea.

She turned back toward Ben. A grassy strip, approximately fifty feet wide, separated the boardwalk from the street. Her two-year-old son still sat on his blanket, in the middle of Water Street, playing. And now she could see Marc, sitting on their front porch. Reclined on a lounge chair, he held a drink in one hand, and raised it to her as if in a toast.

Asshole! You're supposed to be watching Ben. What the hell is he doing out in the middle of the road?

Then she heard it. The car horn. Not the blaring horn of someone trying to warn of impending disaster. But rather the erratic honking of a drunken reveler toot-toot-tooting some syncopated rhythm to an unheard song. In her dream, though she could not yet see the car, she could hear the driver. He was laughing and humming.

Then she saw it. The car. She couldn't tell what kind it was, just that it was big, and dark, and fast. It hadn't been there a second ago, but now there it was, a few houses up the street, hurtling straight for Ben. Its windows were tinted black, and Stacy could not see the driver.

She looked up at the porch, and Marc still sat there. He smiled and waved, incognizant of any danger.

"Mom," Ben called. "Will you play ball with me? I asked Dad, but he didn't want to." Another telltale that this was only a dream: though Ben appeared to be only two years old, he spoke with the mature voice of a six-year-old.

Things started happening fast now. Ben, who until now had been oblivious to the approaching car, heard the horn and turned toward the sound. The horn had ceased its staccato bursts, and was now sounding a loud continuous wail. Whether it was because the driver was reacting to the sight of Ben in the road, or was just ending his musical accompaniment with a flourish, Stacy could not say.

Stacy had already broken into a full-out run, and was racing toward Ben. Conscious as she was that she was dreaming, she always expected herself to be trapped in slow motion, the way dream sequences are often depicted in the movies. But no. With the car bearing down on Ben at an unrelenting pace, Stacy, in sheer panic, ran in her dream far faster than she could in actuality. But even had it been the first time Stacy had lived this dream, she knew she would never make it in time. The car was too close, she was too far, and Ben was now frozen in terror—his mouth wide open in a silent scream.

Though she and the vehicle raced at full speed, Stacy's thoughts raced even faster. Knowing that she was in the process of seeing her precious baby being taken from her, in these last short seconds she saw in her mind's eye, and remembered, the joy of his birth, and the wonder of his early years. His first words, his first steps, and so much more. And she saw with deep sadness the future never to be. His proud performance at his bar mitzvah in his thirteenth year, his first girlfriend in high school, and his departure for college. She saw the wedding she would never attend, the daughter-in-law she would never know, and even the grandchildren she would never get to spoil. In these last seconds, she saw it all.

"Mommy!" cried Ben, finally finding his voice. "MOMMY!" The car slammed into him with horrific force. He was thrown into the air, and came down with a sickening sound. The car sped away.

■　　■　　■

Stacy woke up shaking. The morning light filtered in through the blinds, and she wrapped herself in her comforter, as if to form a cocoon in which she could stay, protected and undisturbed. She shuddered as she remembered her all-too-recurring dream. How often had she been haunted by the surreal depiction of the look in Ben's eyes, and the sound of his terrified cry, in that last instant before he was killed? In reality, had he seen what was about to happen to him? Had he cried out for her before being hit? She hoped not, and prayed that his end had been mercifully instantaneous.

Why did she pray? To whom? To a cruel god that took babies from mothers? If there was a God, he must be punishing her. But wasn't she a good mother? *Yes, I was. And a good person. I'm a good person, too.* Why, then? Why would God do such a thing? She could think of no reason.

Then there is no God. It's all a bunch of crap. The synagogue and the Rabbi. The Shabbat services. The Passover seder. All of that tradition. For what? So I could lie here grieving for my baby, wanting to die?

Stacy lay there, once again considering taking her life. But that would require commitment, planning, execution. Stacy hadn't the will to commit herself to brewing a pot of coffee, much less to killing herself. If she could lie there in bed and just *allow* herself to die, she would. Indeed, she came as close to that as she could, staying in bed, curled up under the covers until forced to get up. But she hadn't the strength to *make* anything happen.

She stirred, and was thankful to find that Marc was no longer in bed—hopefully he had already left for work. Except for a blowup when they were getting ready for the funeral, she hadn't said a word to him since the accident, and he was keeping his distance. Thank God—or whatever—for her mother, who had taken charge of Stacy's well-being. Without her, Stacy might have had to actually rely on Marc, and with the hatred she felt for him now that would have been impossible.

This morning was Tuesday, and more than three weeks had passed since Ben's death. Stacy's parents had rushed from their home in eastern Pennsylvania the afternoon of the accident, and following the seven-day *shivah* period her father had gone back, leaving her mother to stay "until Stacy's back on her feet." Her mother had proven to be a godsend.

There was a quiet knock on the bedroom door, and her mother entered.

"Stacy, hon, it's ten thirty already. I think you should get up."

Stacy turned to face her mother.

"Besides," her mother added, "Detective Kluge called first thing this morning, and you need to call him back. There's been some kind of development in the case."

■   ■   ■

The telephone call from Detective Kluge left Stacy stunned. Two weeks previously, she had learned from him that there was a lawyer out there who knew who had run down her son. She had been heartened, then, to know that the prosecutor was to meet with the lawyer to try to negotiate the killer's surrender, but what Kluge had just told her rendered her speechless. The lawyer refused to talk, there was a legal procedure that possibly could force him to, but the County Prosecutor had "other priorities," and was not going to go after the lawyer. She had screamed through the phone at Kluge. "You're kidding, aren't you? Other priorities? What could possibly be more important?"

Stacy had come directly downstairs when her mother had awakened her, and had called Kluge at the station house. He was not there, and she left word to have him return her call. Then she set about waiting.

Kluge's call had finally come shortly after noon, and had found Stacy in the kitchen, lining her cabinets with paper, the contents emptied onto the counters. Shortly after she had placed the call to Kluge, her mother had left to do some food shopping and other errands. Stacy, full of nervous energy and restless anticipation, sought something to distract her while waiting.

Since Ben's death, her existence was a void. Having given up her profession when he was born, Stacy's life had revolved around her son. Every stage of Ben's growth had given her such joy. How often had she wished she could freeze time? An infant in her arms, sucking at her breast. Hadn't she wanted that to last forever? Until he'd started crawling around the house, learning to explore. That. That was fascinating to watch. If he could only stay like *that* forever. But then he'd begun to speak...

And so it had gone, with every phase of Ben's development. Whenever Stacy had thought Ben couldn't possibly become more awesome or enjoyable, he had quickly grown to be so. Soon she had realized that the only way to hold on to the pleasures that Ben continually, and inevitably, outgrew was simply to have more children. Another infant to hold in her arms. Another baby to crawl through the house. Another toddler learning to talk, first just parroting words to convey simple concepts, and later building phrases and sentences that offered a glimpse into the wondrous little personality being so delicately formed. Stacy had come to imagine an almost endless supply of children, a house full of baby Altmans.

Her dream of a large family had been shattered about three years ago. At first, she began having irregular periods, sometimes experiencing bleeding as often as every two weeks. Thinking that her cycle was just "a little screwed up," Stacy ignored the anomaly for a few months, but finally grew concerned when it continued. She mentioned the problem to her gynecologist, Dr. Weinstein, who recommended an endometrial biopsy, an in-office procedure which would allow him to extract and test tissue from the inner lining of the uterus. The biopsy revealed what he called "endometrial carcinoma." In other words, Stacy had cancer—a tumor on her endometrium. If left untreated, the cancer would eventually spread throughout her body.

To a terrified Stacy and Marc, Dr. Weinstein had explained that luckily the disease was in its early stages, and the prospect for recovery was therefore excellent. The treatment he recommended, however, was to remove the uterus, the fallopian tubes, and the ovaries. Stacy would no longer be able to bear children.

A second and third opinion later, Stacy and Marc had concluded that this course of treatment, drastic as it seemed, was the wisest choice. The operation was a success, and the physical recovery was, indeed, complete. Dr. Weinstein explained that the surgery had revealed that her cancer was "stage 1A grade 1," restricted to the endometrial lining. This meant that Stacy needed no chemotherapy. No radiation treatment. She could go on as before.

But Ben Altman was forever to remain an only child. Over the last three and a half years, Stacy had been forced to continually remind herself that she'd done the right thing.

After the operation, her devotion to Ben had deepened. Stacy was reluctant to consider that her experience could have caused her to love Ben any more than she already had, but she could not deny that her relationship with her son had become closer. With him, Stacy had seen to it that there were no ordinary moments. No mundane times. She had done her best to enrich his existence, and what she had gotten back from him in return had been priceless.

Now he was gone. What was she now to do with the long empty hours of the day? She had only just learned how to occupy the six hours of daily free time that Ben's school or day camp had given her, and now there was an infinite amount more to fill.

Except for her mother, she had no one. Although strict Jewish custom would have had Marc remain home to mourn a full thirty days, the tension between them was so great that he had chosen to go back to work early. It wouldn't have mattered if Marc had stayed home instead—it was all because of him that Stacy's world was turned upside down, and she despised him for that. As for her friends, they all had children Ben's age, and though every one of them was making an effort to comfort her and spend time with her, she found it painful to be with or talk to them. Stacy found herself resenting her friends for still having their children.

And so, to fill the vacant hours, Stacy became obsessed with the house. Upon waking every morning, she would clean from top to bottom, vacuuming, dusting, polishing, and scrubbing. Over the last three days, Stacy had cleaned out all the closets, and donated all the old, unwanted items to a local charity. Today she was attacking the kitchen pantry and cabinets. She had already emptied the cabinets onto the counters and dusted the interiors, and was at work fitting the shelves with flowered contact paper, when Kluge finally returned her call.

Kluge listened to Stacy's unbelieving protestations. "Look, Stacy, I know how you feel. You know how important it is to me, personally, to find the person responsible. As far as the prosecutor's concerned, it's important too. But they have limited resources, and they have to make judgments on how to allocate them. They've apparently decided that they would have to spend a lot of time and energy trying to get this lawyer to talk, and that in the end the court would agree with him that the attorney-client privilege applies. They just have too many other cases where the return on the investment of their resources is more likely to be better, so those are the cases that they have to go with. Prosecutors don't like to pick fights they don't think they're going to win."

"But there must be a way to convince them to do something!" Stacy cried. "For God's sake, unless you have leads you're not telling me about, this lawyer is the only way you're ever going to find the guy. You yourself told me that the more time that goes by, the less chance you'll ever find him."

"Stacy, you know I can't tell you any details about the investigation, but I'm not revealing secrets by telling you we haven't gotten very far. Lieutenant Weber tried to convince the prosecutor to pursue it, but the assistant he's been dealing with tells him that the decision has been made and there's nothing she can do about it. We just have to hope for a break in our investigation."

"Roy, I know the police are doing all they can, and I'm thankful for that. But I'm really afraid that you'll never find that driver without this attorney's help. Forget the prosecutor. Tell me who the lawyer is and I'll call him. Or go see him. I want him to look me in the eye and tell me he won't help me find who killed my son."

"Jeez, Stacy," Kluge said. "I can't do something like that. Give you the name of a witness and have you go talking to him? I can't."

Stacy pushed on. "Then the prosecutor. Tell me who the assistant prosecutor is and I'll go talk to her. Maybe I can convince her to do something. This attorney-client privilege stuff is ridiculous. Everybody seems so worried about the driver's rights. I thought these days the prosecutor was supposed to worry about the victim's rights too. Ben has a right to rest in peace. His killer should be found."

Kluge sighed. "You're right. Judging from Lieutenant Weber's conversation with the prosecutor I don't think it'll do any good, but you're entitled to talk to her and let her know how you feel. Besides, even if I didn't tell you who she was, you'd be able to find it out from the prosecutor's office. The assistant's name is Michelle Dolan. She's in the prosecutor's Death by Auto section. Give her a call and let me know what happens...and good luck."

　　　　　■　　　■　　　■

After her initial exclamation of disbelief, Stacy had somewhat calmed herself during her telephone conversation with Kluge. But after hanging up the phone, a sense of outrage developed as she considered exactly what was transpiring. The "system" that was supposed to protect and help her was going to ensure that her son's killer would escape justice.

She had never been one to mourn for the criminal defendants she read about in the newspapers who complained that their rights had been violated by supposedly illegal searches and seizures, or by the police's failure to advise them of their right to remain silent, or whatever other technical excuse their lawyers could come up with. Though she knew why the law protected the rights of the accused, and was familiar with that old saw—"Better that one hundred guilty men should go free than one innocent man be imprisoned"—as far as she was concerned, the reality was that if you were arrested and put on trial for something, it was a pretty good bet you were guilty.

This attorney-client privilege nonsense was just another one of those technicalities that lawyers used to protect their guilty clients. Predisposed as Stacy was to view such a tactic with disdain, the fact that it was being used to shield her son's killer made it personal, and all the more offensive. She had to do something about it. No one else seemed inclined to.

Stacy sat down at the kitchen table and dialed the number Detective Kluge had given her. Ms. Dolan was in a meeting, she was advised, and was expected to be free in about an hour. Stacy gave her name, but instead of leaving her telephone number, she volunteered to call back later. She did not want to spend the afternoon sitting by the phone waiting for the prosecutor to get around to returning her call.

The kitchen was in chaos. Cabinet doors wide open, their contents piled on the counters below. Stacy looked at the clock and saw that it was almost one thirty. A half hour ago it had seemed very important to her that her dishes, pots, and pans be stored only in the cleanest of cupboards. Now, she hadn't the patience to straighten out the mess she'd created. She'd wait for her mom to help her.

Her mother was still out, so Stacy was home alone. Since she had not yet showered, and had an hour to kill before trying the prosecutor again, she headed upstairs to her bathroom, where she undressed. She filled the Jacuzzi tub with hot water, turned on the jets, and stepped into the steaming swirl. She lay back and closed her eyes, purposefully concentrating on one knotted-up muscle after another, willing each one to relax.

She pondered her upcoming call with the assistant prosecutor. *I have to convince her to see me. I can't let her refuse me over the phone. It'll be harder for her to tell me to my face that she has more important things to do than try to find my son's killer. Maybe she has kids of her own. Maybe she'll understand.*

Having lingered in the bath long enough, she washed herself and shampooed her hair, and reached for the nearby spray nozzle to rinse the suds from her head. She stepped out of the tub, wrapped herself in a large terry towel, and padded over to the vanity. Little puddles of water trailed behind her on the white ceramic tile floor.

Blow-drying her hair did not take long, and she pulled it back in a ponytail. She slid into a pair of blue denim jeans that had been left in a heap next to the bed, and found a loose-fitting white man-tailored shirt in the closet, which she pulled on, leaving the shirttails hanging out.

By the time she made her way back downstairs, forty-five minutes had passed since her call to the prosecutor's office. Though it was still fifteen minutes early, she decided to try Dolan again now. She dialed the number, and upon her request was connected.

Moments later, Stacy had an appointment to meet with Michelle Dolan on the following Monday. It could not have been easier, and Stacy could not have been more surprised. Rather than giving her the brush-off she had expected, Dolan had seemed sincere, sympathetic, and even apologetic. Though Dolan had initially faltered when Stacy came right out and asked to come see her, the hesitation was only momentary. Dolan cautioned that she didn't think she would be able to help her—the decision not to proceed had not been Dolan's—but she, Dolan, welcomed the chance to sit down with Stacy and discuss the matter. Today was Wednesday, and she was due to start a trial tomorrow which was expected to last until Monday. They agreed to meet at Dolan's office at two o'clock on Monday afternoon.

■   ■   ▓

The next six days passed slowly for Stacy. She didn't even think of saying anything to Marc of her telephone call with the prosecutor, or of her upcoming appointment, but she had talked animatedly about it with her mother. Her mother cautioned against expecting too much to come of the meeting, reminding her that Ms. Dolan had already told her that there was nothing further she could do. "I know, Mom," Stacy had said. "But I can't just sit. There's got to be a way to convince someone to do something." "Just be careful," her mother had warned. "The more you expect, the more you'll be disappointed if nothing comes of it."

Stacy thought about what she actually did expect to come of the meeting. Intellectually, she knew that what Ms. Dolan had explained to her made sense from the state's point of view. It wasn't that they didn't think Ben's case was important. It was because other important cases, where the chance of success was more certain, would suffer if they chose to pick this fight with this particular lawyer. Stacy knew she had no logical argument to counter this reasoning. So what was it that she expected?

Damn it. She expected to make them see that this was her son they were talking about. They deal with this stuff every day. It's easy for them. For God's sake, Stacy had learned that there were so many of these cases that the prosecutor had a whole "death by auto" section to handle them. What's one more file to these lawyers? Is it like just another leaky faucet is to a plumber? All in a day's work? Do they realize that the decisions they make and the actions they take affect real live people? And this attorney-client privilege stuff. Maybe Ms. Dolan could explain to her how the law could possibly make it okay to keep this murderer's identity secret. To Stacy it was a simple matter. Someone ran down her son. This lawyer knows who did it. Make the lawyer tell who it is. Period.

If nothing else, she would make sure Michelle Dolan understood how tormented she was by the thought that that animal was still out there.

Stacy just drifted through the week, waiting.

CHAPTER 15

Oh, shit, Michelle Dolan thought as she hung up the phone. The receptionist had just buzzed her to announce that Stacy Altman had arrived for her two o'clock appointment. Michelle had carefully avoided mentioning the upcoming meeting to her boss, hoping that he'd perhaps be in court when the time came, and she would be able to get Stacy in and out without his seeing her. No such luck today—Michelle had seen Richard Delinko moments before, heading into his office. *He'll have my head if he finds out about this.*

When Stacy had called her the previous week and asked to see her, Michelle was at first inclined to refuse, mindful of Delinko's "suggestion" that she leave the matter alone. But she decided that there was no harm in sitting down and talking with the distraught mother. So as not to mislead her, Michelle made sure Stacy understood that the prosecutor was not actively pursuing the matter at present, and that their meeting was unlikely to change that. Stacy said that she understood, but wanted to meet anyway.

In view of what she had advised Stacy, Michelle wasn't quite sure why she'd agreed to the meeting herself. *I guess Delinko was right—it's because of "poor little Ben."* As a member of the County

Prosecutor's staff, Michelle felt a responsibility to the boy and his family to see that justice was done, and she did not agree with the decision to drop the investigation. She felt frustrated, and even a little guilty, at the thought that the prosecutor—and she herself, by association—might be seen as letting the Altmans down. Maybe she saw the meeting with Ben's mother as a way of dealing with these feelings.

Well, I'll see her, do my penance, and move on.

■　■　■

The woman waiting for Michelle in the reception area was dressed in white cotton slacks and a sleeveless red and white checked blouse. She looked up as Michelle approached, and extended her hand in greeting.

"Ms. Dolan? I'm Stacy Altman. Thanks so much for seeing me. I do appreciate it." She shook Michelle's hand firmly.

"Nice to meet you," Michelle responded. "Why don't we get started? I've managed to dig myself out of the clutter in my office, so we can talk in there. Right down this way." Michelle led the way, and Stacy followed.

Michelle sat down at her desk, and Stacy took one of the two seats across from her. The attorney glanced from the files on the floor to the papers on her desk, and groaned inwardly as she thought about the amount of work they all represented—and about the fact that her meeting with Stacy Altman was an "unauthorized" diversion. Her eyes flitted to the door, and she wondered if Delinko would stick his head in, as he did every once in a while.

Although Michelle had indeed begun to dig out of the aftermath of the Perez trial, the excavation had not yet hit pay dirt. What had until recently been apparently disorganized heaps of papers, notes, briefs, and pleadings were now neatly squared-off piles covering most of Michelle's desktop. But the papers still needed to be sorted, and eventually attended to. Her floor had been a repository for a jumble of redweld files, each representing a case that required action. Now they were at least lined up in orderly fashion beneath the corkboard opposite her desk. But all of those files had been ignored during the previous week, and she now needed to turn her attention to them. She had done little more than take inventory of what was there, and already had an idea of what a busy week lay ahead of her.

As for Mr. Perez, the jury had rejected Michelle's plea to find him guilty of aggravated manslaughter, and had returned a verdict of assault by auto. Michelle knew that she had established each and every element of aggravated manslaughter beyond a reasonable doubt. Michelle also knew that often, though the evidence clearly supports, or even demands, one finding, the jury disregards it and reaches a different conclusion for reasons wholly unrelated to the proof. And this jury had, for its own reasons, decided that they were not going to throw the book at this defendant. In the end, they must have been swayed by the picture Perez's attorney had painted—a young man, from a disadvantaged background, who despite a lack of schooling had "pulled himself up by his bootstraps" and become a "productive member of society" holding down a responsible job. This "momentary lapse of judgment" ought not ruin this man forever, the lawyer had argued. The jury obviously agreed, and had opted to convict Perez of the lesser offense of assault by auto.

The judge was to sentence Perez four weeks from now, and Michelle would not know until then how much time, if any, the man would spend behind bars. This particular judge had a reputation for being fair and conscientious, and she knew that whatever sentence was imposed would be the product of an intelligent, thorough analysis of the situation. But the maximum term for assault by auto was a whopping eighteen months.

She turned back to Stacy. "Mrs. Altman, I'm happy to meet with you, but I already explained that there's nothing more we can do now. So I'm not really sure what we can accomplish here this afternoon."

"Please, call me Stacy." She played with the strap of the small handbag that sat in her lap. "I know what you've told me already," she said. "But I just can't believe this matter is simply going to die like this. Don't you understand how important it is to me that the driver who ran down Ben be found? You can't imagine what this is doing to me."

"Stacy, 'imagine' is all that I really can do, because I won't insult you by telling you I *know* what you're going through." Michelle glanced at the door again, and lowered her voice a bit. "Whatever you might think about the prosecutor's decision not to pursue this any further, I want you to know that it's not a decision that I agree with. But my hands are tied. I can't do anything about it."

"Ms. Dolan. Can I call you Michelle?" Michelle nodded. "I just don't know where to turn. The police won't tell me exactly what's going on, because it's a 'pending investigation.' But from the vague reports they give me it's obvious they're not getting anywhere. You tell me that there's a lawyer out there who knows who did it—one word from him and the guy's in custody—but you also say he can't be forced to tell what he knows. A *privilege* to keep silent! How sick is that?

"And to make matters worse, you say this 'privilege' isn't even a sure thing—if put to the test, maybe a judge would force this lawyer to talk. How do you think I feel knowing your boss has decided that finding my son's killer just isn't worth the effort of even trying?"

Stacy reached into her handbag, took out a photograph, and passed it to Michelle. It was a copy of Ben's camp picture that she had given the police. She glanced over at the row of files on the floor, and then back at Michelle.

"Michelle, this is not some nameless, faceless victim in one of the many cases that comes through this office. This is Benjamin David Altman, my six-year-old son. Tell me it isn't 'worth the effort' to find his killer."

Michelle sighed. "Stacy. You don't know me very well. You don't know me at all. I do not work files with faceless victims. I prosecute men and women who are responsible for taking the lives of mothers, fathers, children, and loved ones. That folder over there?" She pointed toward one of the files on the floor. "Steven Birch. Nineteen years old. Sophomore at the University of Michigan, home for a week for spring break. The Friday night before heading back he and a few pals from high school went out to dinner, and afterward, as he was getting into his car, Russell Hardaway, twenty-three years old, slammed into him with his red Dodge Stealth. Russ's girlfriend, in the front seat with him, had, uh, let's say 'distracted' him.

"The folder next to it? Dan Hughes. Forty-five years old. Father of four children—Ian, 16, Melanie, 14, Jaime, 12, and Seth, 8. Dan commuted to New York, where he worked as a security guard in an office high-rise. Caught the 5:30 bus into the city every day. One morning in March, he was crossing Route 18 to get to the bus stop. It was still dark, and Kevin Sprague, a forty-nine-year-old investment banker driving a black Mercedes without its lights on, ran him down. Witnesses say Sprague had to be going at least seventy. He was talking on his cell phone, and had stretched over to the back seat to get his laptop."

Michelle moved some papers on her desk, and found the photos of Anthony Perez's victims.

"And here's Jim Collins and Ellen Mitchell. Two real nice kids out enjoying being with each other one night. In a few weeks, I'll find out what will become of Mr. Perez, who broadsided their car as they came home from the movies."

Stacy's eyes had followed Michelle's from file to file, and she now gazed at the photographs that the attorney had produced.

"I don't mean to lecture," Michelle said. And her tone was soft and sincere. "I just want you to understand that I take my work and my responsibility very seriously. My friends tell me I take it too seriously. But the decision about Ben's case has been made, and for the time being, unless the police catch a break, there's nothing more that I can do."

Stacy's shoulders slumped. "Michelle," she said, desperation evident in her voice. "What should I do? What *can* I do? He's out there. He killed my son, and he's out there. I have to do something."

The two women sat in silence for a moment, and Stacy spoke again. "Let *me* talk to the lawyer. Tell me his name, and let me go see him."

Michelle opened her mouth to speak, but Stacy cut her off.

"I know, I know. You can't. Pending investigation, and all. But you're giving up. You're not investigating. If you won't follow it up, why can't I?"

More silence, as Michelle considered the question.

"Stacy, you're asking the impossible. I just can't do that. But I do think there's something that you can do. Do you have a lawyer?"

"Well, not exactly." She thought a moment. "There's a guy who helped us with a problem we had with a contractor who did some work in the house. But that was years ago. Why?"

Michelle looked at the clock on her desk. It was 2:20, and she was sure that Delinko was going to pop in any second. She'd better hurry this up.

"If our office were to pursue this, we'd subpoena the lawyer to appear before the grand jury for questioning. When he refused to answer, we'd ask a judge to hold him in contempt of court, and that's when we'd argue about whether the attorney–client privilege applies or not. That's where the test would be.

"Now, since we're not going to do that, it's up to you. Of course, you can't convene a grand jury, but you can start a civil suit."

Stacy thought for a moment. "Wait a minute. I'm confused. Who would I sue? The whole problem is that I don't know who the driver is. And you won't tell me the lawyer's name, so how can my lawyer subpoena him to even try to find out?"

"Even though you don't know who the driver is," Michelle explained, "you can still start a lawsuit against him in a fictitious name. It's called a 'John Doe action.'"

Stacy looked puzzled.

"Oh, you come across it mostly in product liability cases, where someone is injured, but isn't quite sure of the proper party to sue. Like when the asbestos cases were first brought. People knew they had been harmed, they knew it was asbestos-related, but they had no way of knowing which particular asbestos manufacturer had made the product that had injured them. If you were one of those people, the law would actually let you start an action called '*Stacy Altman versus John Doe.*' When in the course of the litigation the name of the actual manufacturer became known, its real name would be substituted."

"So how does this help me?"

"Well, your attorney could start a wrongful death action against 'John Doe,' the driver of the car. And in the framework of that action, your attorney could use the legal process to try to find out the driver's identity."

"But the link to the driver is the attorney, and you won't tell me who that is," Stacy said. "If you were pursuing the matter, you said you would subpoena the attorney before a grand jury. How could my lawyer subpoena the attorney without knowing who it is?"

"Stacy, it just isn't up to me to give you the attorney's name. As much as I'd like to help you, I could lose my job if I breached confidentiality on an open investigation like that. But once you get a lawyer involved to help you, who knows what will be? Maybe your attorney could put pressure on my superiors. Maybe he could force them to give up the lawyer's name under the Freedom of Information Act. One thing I've learned since I started practicing law—once you put a matter into the hands of the court, you never know what'll happen. I mean, you know what the law is. You know what ought to happen. But the judge might have his own ideas. And even if he's wrong, and ultimately overturned on appeal, sometimes the damage has already been done, and can't be undone."

Stacy listened and nodded.

"But Michelle, there's no guarantee that I'll be able to find out the lawyer's name, much less get him to reveal who the driver is?"

Michelle sighed. "That's right. I wish I could be more encouraging."

Stacy thought for a moment.

"This is ridiculous! There's a guy out there who ran Ben down, but his identity's being protected by some lawyer. And that lawyer's identity is being protected by the County Prosecutor. I feel like I've followed Alice down the rabbit's hole. Something's wrong here." She shook her head.

"Please believe me," Michelle said. "I'd like to help you, but I just can't. Take my advice and get a lawyer. In the meantime, if anything changes from this end, I'll be sure to let you know."

The two women exchanged closing pleasantries—Stacy just slightly less cordial, and quite a bit less optimistic, than when she'd arrived—and Michelle showed Stacy back to the reception area.

■   ■   ■

Michelle watched the elevator doors close. She couldn't blame Stacy for being upset. The attorney-client privilege clearly pitted important competing interests against each other—the individual's right to fully informed counsel against nothing less than society's quest for truth and justice. As a lawyer who was fully aware of the logic of, and necessity for, the privilege, Michelle often had a hard time accepting some of the circumstances under which it was applied. She could imagine how difficult it was for a layperson, to whom the law was often just a jumble of arcane rules, to understand.

She headed back to her office, and passed Rich Delinko in the corridor. *Well, I'm finished meddling with the Altman case, so I won't have to dodge him anymore. I can tackle that mountain of work that's waiting.*

Back at her desk, she was haunted by Stacy's helplessness. I don't know where to turn, she'd said. And what had Michelle offered her? The idea of a John Doe action was a good one. It would allow Stacy to test the privilege just as well as the prosecutor could before a grand jury. But without the attorney's name, Stacy was going nowhere. Get yourself a lawyer. That was Michelle's big contribution to the solution. Great. Probably a big comfort to Stacy.

Damn it, the woman was entitled to the information, the attorney's name. She was right. The state had decided to do nothing.

Why not let the boy's mother pick up the ball? She couldn't interfere with an investigation that wasn't taking place, could she?

Michelle saw that Stacy had left the photograph of Ben behind. Little Ben, in his camp T-shirt, baseball bat slung over his shoulder. She made up her mind. She knew that her professional responsibility was to keep silent—it would be a breach of policy to give out any information to Stacy. But she knew what was right, too. Michelle tried to put herself in Stacy's position, and knew that she, too, would be compelled to take action. In light of the prosecutor's decision to do nothing, it wasn't right to stand in Stacy's way.

Determined, she reached for her yellow legal pad.

■   ■   ■

Two days after her meeting with Michelle Dolan, Stacy received an envelope in the mail. There was no return address on the plain white wrapper, but it was postmarked "New Brunswick, NJ." Inside was a single sheet of yellow, lined paper, on which was printed in neat block letters:

Scott Heller, Esq.
Roth Stern
473 Madison Avenue
New York, NY 10022

Beneath it was a simple message: "Good luck." There was no signature.

CHAPTER 16

Alex Heller was not having a good day at all. The camp bus, which was driving her home from a long day at Ivy League Day Camp, was steaming hot. The bus counselor had made them shut all the windows because Billy Holmes had thrown a paper airplane out of his window, and when the counselor had hollered at him he'd made an obnoxious face and even spit his gum out the window. Boy, was he in for it tomorrow, when Coach Nelson, the camp director, found out! But she still didn't see why they all had to burn up with all the windows closed, just because of stupid Billy Holmes. So what if everybody else on the bus had started hooting and hollering when the counselor yelled at Billy? Alex had to admit that Eric Granger's imitation of the counselor when he ran up the aisle and stood over Billy wagging his finger, mimicking the counselor's yelling, was kind of funny. But the counselor got all kinds of pissed off, and ordered them all to sit in their seats quietly and to close their windows. Didn't they know her dad was a lawyer? She'd have to ask him at dinner if he could start a class action against the counselor. She knew he was good at that.

And the bus ride wasn't the worst part of her day. She was really mad at Jacklyn, who until this afternoon had been her best

best friend. Earlier in the afternoon, just after snack time, Alex was standing outside the Canteen, and Kyle Brenner started talking to her. Kyle was ten, a year older than she was, and she thought he was cute. Jacklyn saw them talking, and started giggling, and even came right up to them and started teasing them. Jacklyn was SO IMMATURE! She thought all boys were gross. And for the rest of the day she teased Alex, and whispered stuff to the rest of the girls in the bunk. And then ALL OF THEM started teasing her about Kyle being her boyfriend and stuff. Boy, she couldn't wait till next summer. Her parents said next year she'd be old enough to go to sleepaway camp. She was sure the girls there would be more mature.

At least things weren't as babyish at Ivy League as they were last year. Last year she was in the "Smurfettes." The counselors had picked that name for her group because they said she and her friends were too young to choose their own name. Smurfettes! How EMBARRASSING! This year, she and her bunk-mates were allowed to vote on a name, and they picked the "Ladies of Ivy." A little more grown-up, she thought.

And last year, a counselor had to be with them every second of the day. Even when they went to the BATHROOM! They had to go in a group, according to a schedule. If one of them had an emergency, a junior counselor had to go along. At least this year, she could go to the bathroom without a counselor tagging along.

Jacklyn's teasing had made the day pretty rotten. Later, when it came time to find seats on the bus for the ride home, Jacklyn tried to apologize to her. But even though Jacklyn was her best best friend, and Alex kind of felt that she could at least be just her *best* friend for a while, the teasing really made her mad, so she just didn't feel like making up with Jacklyn right now. Instead Alex teased her back about the time she admitted that Josh Katz had kissed her on the cheek on the playground after school one day, and that she'd liked it, and Jacklyn got all kinds of mad, and started calling her names, and then they both swore they would never talk to each other again, and now Jacklyn wasn't even her friend, let alone her best friend, or her best best friend. What a lousy day.

The bus turned onto Mountain View Drive, and pulled to a stop. Jacklyn's stop. Jacklyn stared at her as she walked down the aisle to get to the door, and Alex thought she looked a little sad. But they had sworn that they would never talk to each other again, so Alex didn't say anything. But she felt a little sad too.

Alex lived just around the corner from Jacklyn. The bus turned onto Apple Ridge Crescent. Alex was lucky. The bus route went right past where she lived, so she was picked up and dropped off in front of her house. She gathered up her duffle bag, which held her wet bathing suit and towel, and half a Snickers bar left over from afternoon snack, and walked toward the door. As she passed Billy Holmes, he stuck one of his feet out into the aisle on purpose, and Alex tripped over it. Boy, what a dork. She stepped on his foot, on purpose, and he started yelling, calling her names. Without thinking, he threw the "B" curse in there, and the last thing she heard as she climbed down the three steps of the bus was the counselor yelling at Billy again. Well, he was having a worse day than she was.

■　　■　　■

"Hello, may I please speak to Scott Heller?"

"May I tell him who's calling?"

"Yes, this is Alexandra Heller."

Of course, everyone at her father's office knew who she was, and they even recognized her voice. Alex could have just said "Hi, can I please speak with my father?" and Julie, the receptionist, would know who it was. But Alex preferred to be businesslike when she called her father's office, and her formal manner had become a little game between her and Julie.

"I'll see if he's free, Miss Heller. Please hold on."

Alex knew her father was very busy when he was at work, and she was allowed to call him only once each day. That was usually right when she got off the school bus or camp bus. This afternoon, though, she had delayed her call long enough to describe her miserable day to her mother over a big helping of vanilla ice cream. After rinsing her bowl and placing it in the dishwasher, she had found the phone.

"Hi, honey. What's up?" No matter what was going on at work, her dad was always cheerful when she called him.

"Nothin' much. Except that I've just had the worst day of my whole entire life. Not counting when Peeps died." Peeps had been her parakeet.

Alex recounted the events of the afternoon once more, and her father gave her the same advice that her mother had. Try to make up with Jacklyn. Alex figured it must be the grown-up thing to do.

"Maybe tomorrow, Dad."

They chatted another minute, and Alex heard her father's intercom in the background.

"Oops, gotta run, sweetie. Phone call. I love you."

"I love you too, Daddy. See you tonight."

■ ■ ■

"There's a Veronica Howell on line one for you, Scott," Karen announced over the intercom. "She says she may have a new matter for you to handle."

Scott said his good-bye to his daughter, and reached for his pen and a yellow legal pad. He was happy for the added interruption. A minor turf war had erupted among plaintiffs' counsel in the *Driscoll* case, and as lead counsel it fell to Scott to referee the skirmish. From among the numerous lawsuits that had been filed across the country in connection with the demise of Marlen Industries, and ultimately consolidated into Scott's action, no less than eight different law firms still had roles in prosecuting the efforts. The deposition of Kevin Driscoll had been completed, and defendants had deposed a number of the other representative plaintiffs as well. The committee of plaintiffs' counsel had compiled a list of individuals on the defendants' side who must be deposed, and Scott now had to deal with a number of inflated egos and decide who was going to be responsible for each deposition. At the root of the problem, of course, was money. Whatever fee was ultimately awarded by the court had to be split among all of plaintiffs' counsel, and each firm's share depended, in large part, on the amount of time it put in. Everybody wanted a piece of the pie, and most could be heard to complain that someone else's slice was bigger than his. Scott was reviewing an exchange of correspondence among some of the law firms, in which each was pitching to be assigned responsibility for the next pretrial examination. He had just finished reading a self-serving letter from an attorney in Atlanta who was convinced that he was the obvious choice to conduct an upcoming deposition more than two thousand miles away in Oakland, when Alex had called.

He would talk with this potential new client, and then get back to deciding who got to go on a road trip to California.

■   ■   ■

So far, Veronica Howell sounded good. Whenever Scott spoke with a potential new client, he immediately began assessing four different things. With respect to the legal case that the client was calling about, he made a preliminary judgment first about liability and then about damages. When one party sued another, both of these elements were critical. In the liability phase of a lawsuit, the plaintiff must prove that the defendant did something that was legally wrong. But establishing liability was not enough. In the damages phase, the plaintiff must prove that the defendant's wrongful act actually damaged him. He must also demonstrate the extent and amount of that damage. Proving liability without damage, or damage without liability, gets the plaintiff nothing. Therefore, from the outset, Scott began to form a judgment on both of these issues.

The third element that Scott looked at early on was the plaintiff. Was she reasonably articulate? Would she be easy to work with? Would she follow advice? What kind of picture would she present to the jury? Sympathetic, or antagonistic? Amiable, or not? It was far easier for a jury to make an award to someone they liked.

The potential for a large fee award. That was the fourth thing that Scott appraised up front. Because, face it—he was in business. To make money. The best plaintiff, with the strongest liability case, and good damages, wasn't worth much to Scott if there was little promise for a meaningful fee to be made. To a large extent the greater the damage, the more likely it was that there would be a high fee, but this was not guaranteed. And, a half-million dollar fee earned in a case that took three or four years to litigate was worth far less than the same fee earned in a year or two.

Scott's initial impression of Ms. Howell as a potential client was positive. She spoke clearly and intelligibly. She did not ramble on about irrelevancies, and answered his questions concisely and in a to-the-point manner. Of course, he had not yet seen her, and would have to reserve further judgment on her promise as a client until then, but his first impression was a good one.

The case she was describing sounded strong, as well. Two years ago, Galway's, a nationwide restaurant chain, had instituted a program in which diners received points for every dollar they spent in any of their restaurants across the country. When the promotion was inaugurated, the parent company, Galway Eateries, Inc., had published a schedule of prizes for which points could be redeemed. The prizes ranged from a free dinner entree, to free promotional clothing, all the way to wide-screen televisions, sophisticated entertainment systems, and even ocean cruises, all depending on the amount of money spent dining at Galway's. Last month, Galway's had published a new schedule of prizes, and the number of points required for each category had been substantially increased. The restaurant was taking the position that the new schedule applied to all points redeemed, and all prizes claimed, from the date the schedule was published, regardless of when the points had been earned. Therefore, diners who spent the last few years accumulating points with the intention of redeeming them for the more valuable prizes suddenly found that those prizes were no longer available at the previously-advertised level. They either had to accept prizes of lesser value, or spend more money eating at Galway's in order to earn the needed extra points.

"That doesn't seem fair to me," Scott heard his caller complain.

Scott agreed, and pointed out the similarities between the Galway program and airlines' "frequent flier" promotions where points were earned for every mile flown. "In fact, two years ago I successfully litigated a class action against Universal Airways when they tried to do the very same thing."

"Actually, that's how I got your name. I had mentioned this to my sister, and she remembered that a few years ago she got some kind of notice from the court that she was a member of a class in a lawsuit against Universal. The papers said that she didn't have to do anything, but that if there was any kind of recovery in the action, she would share in it. A few months later, she got some vouchers in the mail that she was able to use for free airline tickets. She dug out some old papers and found your name on them. So here I am."

To Scott, Galway's liability appeared clear from what he had learned so far. Damages, it seemed, could be considerable although not earthshaking. No single diner would have suffered in any significant way, but the number of class members nationwide would be rather high, and when their damages were aggregated, the numbers would take on more substance.

Attorney's fees? Well, the potential was there. The case did not sound like a gold mine, but he wouldn't lose money on it either. With such clear liability, Galway's was likely to seek an early settlement, but not without putting up some kind of token resistance at first. That would suit Scott just fine, because if Galway's were to cave in too quickly, the court would not be likely to approve a meaningful legal fee. On the other hand, the court would not be apt to approve too large a fee, even if the litigation were long and protracted, because the type and amount of damages that Scott could foresee would not justify it. The bottom line for Scott was that he thought he could turn a profit.

"Well, Ms. Howell, what we need to do is schedule a meeting here in my office so we can go over this material in more detail... How does Thursday sound? Hold on, and my secretary will set up a time that we can get together."

"Great." Scott's new client sounded enthusiastic. "Looking forward to meeting you."

■   ■   ■

Jody Heller drifted on the lounge that floated in the shallow end of the pool, her feet dangling in the water. Alex had changed into her bathing suit after her phone call with her father, and she was now practicing her cannonballs off the diving board. Jody rocked peacefully as the waves from her dives petered out into gentle ripples by the time they traversed the length of the pool. The early evening sun was well on its way from its perch in the afternoon sky, but it still had enough strength to warm mother and daughter as they enjoyed ushering in the day's end together in their backyard.

When Alex had gotten home from camp, she had found her mother sunning herself out back on the deck. Jody usually waited in the front for the bus to arrive, on some pretext of yard work or something, but this afternoon she'd dozed off next to the pool. Jody knew that her daughter would be annoyed to know that she contrived to be outside when her camp bus was expected—Alex was going through an "independent" stage, and any sign that her parents were babying her was met with objection. But although Alex was nine years old already, Jody continued to keep close tabs on her comings and goings. Scott sometimes accused her of being overprotective, and encouraged her to give Alex a bit more leeway, but Jody was ever so reluctant to cut the apron strings that bound her baby to her.

Alex had gotten off the bus, let herself in through the garage, and spied her mother through the plate glass window sleeping in her lounge chair. Still smarting from her traumatic day at camp, she had convinced Jody to come inside to fix her a snack. After Alex's phone call to Scott, the two Heller women had retired to the pool for a lazy late afternoon by the pool.

"Oh, I forgot to tell you. Daddy's got to work late tonight, sweetheart," Jody said.

Alex stepped out onto the diving board. "Ooooh. Can we bring in Chinese food?"

"I think we can arrange that. Let me know when you're hungry."

"Mom. I'm always hungry," Alex called. She bounced off the board and curled herself into another cannonball.

CHAPTER 17

"**M**s. Howell is here," Julie announced over the intercom. "I've shown her to the conference room."

"Be right in. Thanks."

Scott reached for his jacket, checked himself in the mirror behind his office door, and straightened his tie. He had dressed this morning in his gray pinstriped suit, which he usually saved for court appearances, but this morning, instead of a courtroom advocate, he was a salesman. His visitor, with whom he had spoken on the telephone three days earlier, was thinking of buying his services, and Scott was ready to make his pitch and close the deal. He was good at it.

"Ms. Howell," Scott greeted her warmly upon entering the conference room. "I hope you found us without any trouble."

His guest was seated at the ebony conference table. As she rose to greet him, he thought there was something vaguely familiar about her, but he couldn't place it. He was pleased, though, to see that his initial impression of his potential client, formed earlier in the week on the telephone, was proving to be accurate. Veronica Howell was attractive and likable. Someone a jury could relate to.

"Yes," she said, shaking his hand. "I mean, no...no trouble."

"Well then, why don't we get started? Before business though, I'd like to show you around the office."

Scott had not yet sat down, and he held his hand out toward the door to begin the tour.

"No, thank you, Mr. Heller. I'd prefer to get to the point."

Scott dropped his arm to the side, and moved to take a seat. "Of course," he said, instantly all business. He motioned for his guest to sit, and he did the same.

"Those are the documents I asked you to bring?" He nodded at the manila envelope on the table in front of the woman.

"No, Mr. Heller." She opened the envelope flap, removed its contents and slid the single sheet across the table to the attorney. "And my name is not Veronica Howell."

Scott was confused as he reached down and turned over what this woman who was not Veronica Howell had placed in front of him. He grew even more perplexed when he recognized the face of Ben Altman looking up at him. It was the same photograph Detective Kluge had shown him when they sat in this same room three weeks earlier. He would not soon forget that face.

And that's when he remembered *her* face—from the other picture that Kluge had virtually forced upon him at the end of their meeting. His stomach sank as he realized who was sitting before him.

"Mrs. Altman?" he asked tentatively, though knowing full well that that was the true identity of his mystery guest.

"Yes, Mr. Heller, Stacy Altman. Ben's mother." She hesitated, a bit uneasy. "I-I'm sorry about getting in to see you this way, but I didn't think you'd meet with me if I'd told you who I was up front."

She was right about that—he would not have agreed to see her. What was the point? But how did she find him? Surely not the police.

"How did you get my name?" He didn't know what else to say.

"That's not important," Stacy said, deflecting the question. She shifted in her seat. "Look, I don't know where to turn anymore. My son is dead. The police can't find who did it. You know who it is, you won't tell, and the prosecutor says they won't even try to make you. I just don't understand..."

So, the prosecutor *was* accepting his exercise of the privilege. They won't force the issue, and that was a relief. But now this. This was uncomfortable, to put it mildly.

"Mrs. Altman, I know it's hard to understand. I feel for you. I really, really do. But the law is clear. The information you want is privileged, and I just can't reveal it. If I did, I could lose my license."

"Your license." Stacy was speaking softly. Sadly, not agitated or bitter. "Do you have any children, Mr. Heller?"

"Yes, I do. A little girl."

"Then think about what you just said. God forbid something terrible should happen to your daughter, and someone talked to you about the importance of his license." Her voice was weak, and quavering.

Damn it, thought Scott. This was *not* his problem. He'd taken a call from a client, done his job, and now he was through. How that job affected this woman was not his responsibility. Make this woman go away.

"Mrs. Altman. I know what you must be feeling. But what you're asking is just not possible. I cannot help you. I can't."

Stacy appeared close to tears.

"Now, I have to ask you to leave. I'm very sorry, but there's nothing I can do for you. Maybe the police will find him."

He was on his feet, holding his hand out toward the door again, this time to escort her out. Stacy rose silently and walked out ahead of Scott.

They reached the lobby, and Scott pressed the button to summon the elevator. Julie looked up from the reception desk. "Oh, Mr. Heller, Alex just called. She's home from camp, and wants you to call."

The elevator arrived, and Scott extended his hand to say good-bye. Stacy made no move to accept it, and she stepped into the open car. She looked at him. "Go. Alex must be your little girl. Call her. Talk to her. Enjoy her."

The elevator doors closed.

■   ■   ■

Scott finished his telephone call with Alex. It had been a typical day at camp. Alex and Jacklyn had made up the day after their falling-out, and Alex reported today that they were best best friends once more. Alex had called as soon as she had gotten home, and finding that her father was busy in a meeting, she had headed out to the pool with her mother to wait for Scott's return call.

Scott promised to be home in time for a family dinner, instructed his daughter to give her mother a great big kiss for him, and said good-bye.

He swiveled his chair to face out over Madison Avenue, leaned back, and rested his feet on the credenza beneath the window. His fingertips were steepled in contemplation, his forefingers tapping nervously against one another.

Stacy Altman. The boy's mother. That was uncomfortable, wasn't it? Scott didn't for an instant question where his responsibility lay. It was just that the issue was so rarely put before him in such stark terms. In fact, the issue had never been put before him in this way. He did not practice criminal law, and didn't usually encounter crime victims. In his civil law practice, he was always keenly aware that real people, with real problems, were involved, and that helping a client achieve a benefit usually meant that his adversary's client was going to suffer in some way. But that was his job—to help his clients with their legal problems. He represented them zealously, within the bounds of the law. He always treated his adversaries and their clients with respect, and acted in accordance with the Code of Professional Responsibility, which set forth the rules of ethics governing the legal profession. As long as Scott conducted himself honorably, the fact that successfully representing someone resulted in some detriment to another was something he could live with. If he refused cases on the basis of the amount of harm that might befall the other side if he did his job properly, he would be a very hungry lawyer.

He asked himself why this should be any different. Criminal defense lawyers must face this question every day. What Stacy Altman was going through must be unbearable, but Scott couldn't be expected to take on her burden, could he? He had been hired by his client to perform a legitimate service. He had tried, and in fact failed. He had deceived no one, and had dealt with the authorities in a straightforward manner. And they even apparently agreed with him that his hands were tied. His involvement in the matter was over. No, he had done nothing wrong, could not be held to blame for Stacy Altman's terrible misfortune, and could, with a clean conscience, tell her there was nothing he could do for her. His client's identity was privileged information which he could not divulge. It wasn't fair for her to come to his office and try to make him feel guilty. It was not his problem.

Scott turned back around to face his desk. Somewhere among the papers was another letter from Howard Gilman, the lawyer from Atlanta who had wanted to be assigned the upcoming deposition in Oakland in the *Driscoll* matter. Scott had assigned the task to Gerald Blackwell, whose law firm was conveniently located in San Francisco. Gilman, who had apparently been looking forward to an all-expense-paid visit to the West Coast, was griping that he was better suited to conducting this particular examination. Scott located Gilman's letter, found the microphone for his voice-recognition software, and watched as the response he dictated appeared on his computer screen. He tried to put Stacy Altman out of his mind.

CHAPTER 18

The Royal Hunan Restaurant on Pell Street, in Manhattan's Chinatown, bustled with lunchtime activity. Scott would not have known that it was the Royal Hunan unless Win had told him, as there was no sign outside, and no menus anywhere to be found. Almost all the tables were occupied, mostly by Chinese, and waiters dressed in black pants and white shirts hurried about with trays of steaming, aromatic delicacies.

"One of the perks of working just off of Foley Square," Win said, as he picked up another steamed dumpling with his chopsticks and dipped it into the sweet sauce in front of him. "Client of mine—a prostitute who works not far from here—introduced me to the place."

He popped the dumpling into his mouth.

"See," he said, with a grin. "I represent whores, just like you. Mine walk the streets, and yours prowl the corporate boardrooms."

"Hey, wait a minute," Scott protested. "Get your players straight. I represent the oppressed shareholders who get screwed by the crooked corporate elite. I'm one of the good guys, remember? I bring lawsuits to vindicate the rights of the downtrodden." He grabbed the last dumpling.

"Oh, gimme a break, Heller. You don't believe that bullshit, do you? Suing or being sued—it's all the same in what you do. Your clients'll sue anybody, anytime, just to make a quick buck. You're all whores. Your plaintiffs, your defendants, and all of you lawyers who represent 'em. You guys have no social redeeming value whatsoever."

"Yeah," said Scott. "And putting the likes of Pussy Galore back on the street is a major contribution to the quality of life in New York?"

Win shrugged. "I do what I can to preserve the diverse nature of our fair city. From diversity comes strength, variety is the spice of life, melting pot—all of that. And by the way, Pussy Galore was a Bond girl, not one of my clients."

"Whatever. You get my point. Anyway, from what you've been telling of your practice lately, the citizens of New York have you to thank for quite a lot of spice. You're turning into a real jailhouse lawyer. Why the sudden preoccupation with criminal law?"

"Just one of those things. I started handling a couple of cases, did okay with them, and boom! Word of mouth passed from some satisfied customers. There's only so many real estate closings and wills you can do without going batty. This criminal stuff is a nice change. I've told you about Jack Doherty, haven't I? Had a practice just outside of Boston, and moved to New York about six months ago. He was working out of his apartment in Brooklyn till I rented him one of my vacant offices. He helps with my overflow in a lot of areas, and vice versa. Turning out to be a pretty synergistic fit."

The dishes from the appetizer were taken away, and the main course laid out—a chicken and shrimp concoction that Win had negotiated with the waiter when they had arrived. Scott's host smiled, and pointed to the dish. "What'd I tell you? Magnificent, right?"

Win waited as Scott helped himself, and then filled his own plate.

"Carolyn keeps asking me when we're going to get together again with you and Jody. She accurately points out that when you and I were at Gersten, the four of us spent a lot more time with each other. Ever since you've become a snobbish advocate of the corporate elite, you don't seem to have the time for us common folk."

Scott laughed. "For some reason, Win, when I think of you, the term 'common folk' doesn't leap to mind."

"Well, anyway, tell Jody that Carolyn is asking about her." He scooped some rice with his chopsticks. "So, you seemed pretty upset when you called last week. What's going on?"

It was Tuesday afternoon, and the previous Friday, the morning after Stacy Altman had surprised him at his office, Scott had telephoned his friend. The two had arranged to have lunch, so Scott had met Win about a half hour ago at his office on Worth Street, and the two of them walked the few blocks to Win's Chinatown find.

"It's that friggin' case you referred to me."

Win cocked his head to the side, and narrowed his eyes.

"Say what?"

"The hit-and-run driver."

"Heller, what the fuck are you talking about?"

"The Altman hit-and-run driver. The guy who ran over the kid in Perth Amboy."

Win put down his chopsticks and placed both of his hands palms down on the table in front of him.

"I have absolutely no idea what you're talking about, my friend."

Now Scott stopped eating.

"What do you mean you have no idea what I'm talking about? The guy called me and said you told him to."

"Nope. Not me. Must have been another Thurston Honnicutt. There's quite a few of us, you know. But remember, I'm Thurston *Winslow Barton* Honnicutt. The *Fourth*." He went back to his meal.

"Wait a second. You're telling me you didn't send some guy over to me in June? That he just called me out of the blue and decided to tell me 'Win sent me'?"

"Yeah, that's just what I'm telling you. The last case I sent over to you was back in January. You remember—the domestic violence thing. Guy accused of making terroristic threats against his ex-wife. Threatened to run her over. Bitch deserved it, as I recall. I'd much rather've seen you defending him for actually doing it, not just saying he would. Whatever happened with that, anyway?"

"Not now, Win. This is serious."

Scott explained to Win what had happened, beginning with the mysterious client's initial telephone call, and ending with Stacy Altman's appearance at his office the previous week.

"This is not good," Scott concluded. "Why would someone call me and lie about something like a referral?"

"Oh, come on, Heller, stop being so melodramatic. Maybe you misunderstood him. Maybe he was telling you he wanted *you* to *win*, not that Win sent him. I dunno, but if it'll make you feel better, call the guy and ask him."

"You bet I will. I don't like this. I got a client who lied to me, and a grieving mother masquerading as a new client to get in to see me. And you're telling me I can't even blame you for it? I need to know what's going on."

"Now there's something new," Win said, as he poured himself some green tea. "Clients who lie. Don't think I've come across any of them before."

■   ■   ■

When Scott had finished his lunch with Win, he walked to the corner of Mott and Pell and hailed a taxi. The cab made its way uptown on streets clogged with midday traffic.

Was he making too much out of it? Maybe Win was right. Maybe he'd misunderstood what his client had said on the phone. But no, he was sure the guy had said that Win told him to call. How would someone know to use Win's name with him?

The cab dropped him off in front of his building. He paid, left the driver his customary generous tip, and hurried upstairs to his office. It was about two o'clock, and his afternoon was light. He would call his client and ask for an explanation.

At his desk, he opened the address book he maintained on his computer, located the entry he was looking for, and double-clicked it. The client had left him only a pager number, and Scott punched it into his phone.

"I'm sorry. The number you have reached is not in service. Please check the number and dial it again."

The recorded voice took Scott by surprise. Thinking that he might have dialed incorrectly, he hung up and tried again.

"I'm sorry. The number you have—"

Scott hung up.

He knew he was calling the right number. He had used it previously to contact his client. When he had asked for a more direct way of communicating, he'd been told that this was the surest method. The pager was always on, always nearby. Instead of a voice mail message at home or on a cell phone, which might not be retrieved for a number of hours, a page was certain to reach its mark without delay.

Except now. The pager number led to nowhere. And Scott had no way of contacting his client.

CHAPTER 19

The weekend. Scott Heller and his daughter Alex were engaged in their Saturday morning ritual—preparing breakfast. Within wide boundaries set by Scott, Alex had full discretion over the menu. The possible choices included eggs, any style, French toast, pancakes, bacon, sausage, fresh fruit, and a variety of fruit juices. Today, Alex had chosen pancakes, sausage, and orange juice. Scott was now dutifully searching the pantry for the semi-sweet chocolate chips that Alex had announced would be mixed generously into the pancake batter.

"And then I think we'll slice a banana on our plates too," Alex told her father. She fetched one from the basket hanging over the kitchen counter. "It'll make the dish look nice."

It had been about two weeks since Scott had found that his client's pager had been disconnected. Upon making that discovery, Scott had tried to find another way to contact him, but that proved to be impossible. When he had received the first telephone call, almost two months ago, he had turned the client over to Karen to set up the initial consultation, and as was customary she had collected the necessary information to open up a new matter. Never having had the need to look at those records before, it was only after his lunch with Win that Scott learned that his client had given Karen no address. The only contact information that the firm had was a pager number and an e-mail address—the client asked that any written correspondence and any bills be sent to him by e-mail. Given the firm's penchant for high-tech productivity, Karen had not thought the request unreasonable. A call to directory assistance, as well as an Internet search, showed no listing.

An e-mail to the address on file bounced, returning a "no such user" error. The address proved to be a "throwaway" address that many services provide free of charge. Go to a website, create a username, and establish a mailbox. Check your e-mail from any computer by logging on to the service's website. This particular user had closed his account, and the provider, citing privacy considerations, refused to disclose any information about its customer.

Frustrated rather than concerned, Scott put the matter out of his mind. There was no real reason to contact the client—Scott's role in the matter had been completed, and Stacy Altman's appearance in his office seemed to have been just an isolated uncomfortable incident.

Scott had decided to chalk it up to experience and move on.

Alex was mixing the chocolate chips into the bowlful of pancake batter, and Scott was frying the sausage at the stove, when the door chime sounded.

"Jody," he called. "Could you get that? I got my hands full."

Scott heard his wife open the door. "Wait here," she said, and the door closed shut. Jody appeared in the kitchen.

"Uh, Scott, someone's here with 'important papers' for you."

Scott pursed his lips in puzzlement. He handed Jody the fork he was holding, and pointed to the frying pan where the sausage sizzled. "I'll be right back."

Scott opened the door to find a man in his late fifties, with a thick neck and a weathered face. Cop, or ex-cop, is what came to Scott's mind.

"You Scott Heller?" the man asked.

"Yes. Who are you?"

"Mitchell Halk, Mercury Subpoena Service," the man responded politely. He handed Scott the papers he held in his hand. "You've been ordered to appear for a deposition in the case of 'Stacy Altman against John Doe' in ten days, at the law offices of Frank O'Connor in Woodbridge. Here's a copy of the Order, signed by Judge Lawrence Adams, and a copy of the Complaint that's been filed by Stacy Altman. Sorry for the intrusion."

Mitchell Halk turned, and walked to his car.

■   ■   ■

"I thought it was over." Jody was obviously upset. "A judge is *ordering* you to appear? What does this mean?"

Few lawyers relish being called upon to give a deposition. They're used to asking the questions, not sitting there answering them under oath. Testifying is an annoyance. It's time-consuming, and nobody pays you for doing it. For Scott, this latest development was supremely irritating—this was more than he had signed on for.

Irritating, and a waste of time, but of no real significance. He would appear for the deposition, and would assert the attorney-client privilege in response to any questions about the identity of his client. It would be a short deposition. This Frank O'Connor must realize how the deposition would go, so he was no doubt prepared to test the applicability of the privilege in court on a motion to compel Scott to answer. That would require even more of Scott's time, but he was confident of the result. After all, the prosecutor agreed that Scott's position was a strong one.

A short deposition, and a quick court proceeding. That would be that.

A picture of Stacy Altman sitting across his desk, pleading with him, came into his mind. He forced it out. Damn her.

"Oh, honey, it's just routine. Part of the job—you know. It's nothing to worry about."

"Let's eat!" piped in Alex, who had been sitting quietly at the kitchen table. "The pancakes are getting cold!"

CHAPTER 20

The Middlesex County Superior Court was among the places and institutions that Mike Harrison covered for the *Middlesex Herald*. At least twice a week he visited the court clerk's office to check the newly filed actions for anything of interest. He looked forward to the day that the New Jersey courts went completely online, as other jurisdictions had, so he would be able to punch up the information from his office. At least the court was computerized within the clerk's office so he no longer had to rifle through index cards.

Tri-State Environmental Corp. versus Midstate Recycling, Inc., et al. He made a note of that one. One of his colleagues, Lou Rice, had been following allegations of corruption in the waste-hauling business—what a surprise—and he might be interested in this. According to the computer summary, Tri-State's claim was based on the state's RICO statute—Racketeering Influenced and Corrupt Organizations. Among the co-defendants were a few county officials, and the claim was that Tri-State was being precluded from certain geographical areas in favor of Midstate, and that "official pressure" was in part responsible.

Another one caught his eye. *Stacy Altman versus John Doe.* Altman. Wasn't she the one whose kid was run down a couple of months ago? Barbara Lewis had done a few pieces on that, right after the accident. The computer showed that it was a wrongful death action. Against John Doe? That was something Harrison hadn't seen before. Maybe he'd take a look at this one and see if something was there. Suing John Doe was an interesting angle. He wondered what was going on.

■   ■   ■

"Come on, Scott, you're not doing it alone. I'll go with you as your lawyer."

Sharon Roth stood with Scott Heller in Roth Stern's small kitchen, stirring her first cup of coffee of the morning. Scott had finally mentioned the weekend visit he had had from the process server five days earlier, and had also made the offhand comment that he intended to go to the deposition himself.

"I guess you're right, Sharon."

"You know I'm right. However simple it's going to be, you should have a lawyer representing you. I'll do the objecting, and I'll do the arguing with O'Connor. You'll sit there and keep your mouth shut. You're right about one thing, though. It should be a short deposition."

■   ■   ■

It wasn't a major story, but there was enough there to justify Mike Harrison's probing just a little bit, and keeping his eye on things. The computer showed that the only documents in the court file were the complaint, a certification from Altman's lawyer, Frank O'Connor, and an order compelling the deposition of a Scott Heller. Harrison had pulled those documents and read them through. In his certification, O'Connor described how Altman didn't know who the driver of the car that had run her son down was, that Heller was an attorney who represented the driver, and how he was apparently the only person who could identify "John Doe." After a few calls to the Middlesex County Prosecutor's office, Harrison learned that the authorities were not pressing Heller because he claimed that the identity of his client was protected by the attorney-client privilege.

Back at his desk in the newsroom, Harrison considered his next move. A call to Stacy Altman for a statement. Chances were that she would refer him to O'Connor, her lawyer, but it was worth a shot. Then, a call to Heller for his reaction to the lawsuit and to the order requiring him to appear. According to a notation in the court file, Heller had been served with a copy of the order last weekend.

The court case probably merited mention in the *Herald*—a short follow-up to a tragic accident.

■　　■　　■

"Damn it, Karen," Scott snarled into the intercom. "Who did that guy on the phone say he was when he called? Someone with new business?"

"Yeah, why?" came the response.

"A reporter. He was a damn reporter."

He had no reason to be upset with his secretary—he knew she had asked the caller his name and business before putting him through. This Mike Harrison had no doubt neglected to mention that he was a reporter.

Annoyed as he was at having had to fence with a newspaper reporter—had he actually said "no comment" a number of times?—he was even more upset at what the call represented. The press was interested in this lawsuit that the boy's mother had started, and in his own role in it.

He remembered what he had originally thought when he had considered the pros and cons of taking on such a potentially controversial client as this hit-and-run driver: *There's no such thing as bad publicity.* Well, he pondered now, that was when he was going to represent someone being brought to justice. The adversarial system working at its best. The prosecution striving to demonstrate the guilt of the accused, him defending the rights of the alleged wrongdoer, and the system working as designed to mete out justice. Even a plea bargain before trial—which is what Scott had sought to achieve—represented the system at work.

But now, he would be seen as standing in the way of the system. Protecting someone from having to submit to judgment of any kind, all in the name of some abstract technicality. Cheating the people of their right to call upon someone to account for his actions.

No, thought Scott. Maybe there was such a thing as bad publicity.

CHAPTER 21

"They never did find that guy who ran over the kid in Perth Amboy," Patty Saldano said.

It was Saturday morning. Vince Saldano and his wife had finished breakfast, and as was their custom they lingered at the kitchen table with their coffee, she with one of the local newspapers and he with the *New York Times*.

Vince looked up from an article about the recent spate of suicide bombings in Israel. It had been a while since he had consciously thought about the accident.

"What brought that to mind?"

"This piece here," Patty said. "It says the boy's mother has started a lawsuit, and she's trying to find out the name of the driver."

Vince tried to appear calm. As nonchalantly as he could manage, he asked, "What's it say there?"

"It's complicated. The guy apparently has a lawyer, but the lawyer won't say who his client is. Claims it's 'privileged information.' So the mother's started a lawsuit against the driver, except since she doesn't know who it is, the action is against 'John Doe.' Now, she's subpoenaing the lawyer and trying to make him talk. It says here that if he continues to refuse, the whole thing can turn into a court battle about what's privileged information and what's not."

"Really?" Vince was sure his discomfort must be apparent, but Patty didn't seem to notice.

"Yeah, can you imagine? How horrible. The lawyer is actually protecting the guy who did it. What a coward the driver is. To hide behind a lawyer like that… And the lawyer. Imagine protecting such a creep. What that poor mother must be going through."

Patty continued to tell Vince what she thought about the vile attorney and his despicable client, but he was no longer listening.

He was trying to figure out how he could possibly wait until Monday morning before calling his lawyer to find out just what was going on.

■   ■   ■

Scott Heller hurried into his office and picked up the phone. He had been in a meeting in the conference room—the firm's regular Monday afternoon get-together to discuss routine administrative matters—when Karen had buzzed him to say that Glenn Ericson was on the line.

"Well, I'm glad you called," he said, before he'd even sat down at his desk. "I've had a hell of a time trying to find you. To begin with, I've spoken with Win Honnicutt. He doesn't know who you are, and he certainly didn't refer you to me. Let's start by you explaining to me what's going on here."

"Do I have anything to worry about when you testify at your deposition tomorrow?" The client spoke as if Scott had said nothing.

"Now wait a second," Scott said. "You can't expect me to continue representing you if you're not honest with me. You lied to me about how you came to me. You gave me a pager number that's been disconnected, an e-mail address that's not in service, and no other way of getting in touch with you. This is *not* how I conduct business. You'll either have to answer some questions for me, or I'll have to withdraw as your attorney."

"Withdraw from what, Mr. Heller? As a matter of fact, you don't really represent me in anything now, do you? I hired you to work out a deal with the prosecutor, and you couldn't. When the prosecutor refused to bargain, your services were no longer needed."

"But you can't leave me with no way of getting in touch with you."

"Why's that? I no longer need your services, and you have no reason to contact me. In case you haven't noticed, the whole idea has been to avoid leaving a trail that leads to my door."

"Yes, but—"

"But what?"

"We've gone over that before. There won't *be* a trail to your door. The attorney-client privilege prevents that."

"The attorney-client privilege? Come on, Mr. Heller. You've been subpoenaed for a deposition by the attorney for Ben Altman's mother for the express purpose of discovering who I am. We both know it's a coin toss whether a court will agree that my name is privileged. Do you really think I'm going to stake my entire future on some technical legal rule?"

"But suppose the court orders me to talk? Do you think you're safe just because *I* don't have your address or telephone number? If the court orders me to, I'll give them your name. They'll find you eventually."

"You think so? Did *you* try finding 'Glenn Ericson'? How'd you make out?"

Scott paused, realization coming over him.

"That's not your name," he said weakly.

"I had to build in some protection. Just in case."

This was not how Scott had expected this conversation to go. He calmed himself, and thought a moment before answering.

"Then what difference does it make if I invoke the privilege tomorrow or not? I can just tell the truth—you gave me a bogus name, and I don't know who you really are. It won't do you any harm."

"An added layer of insulation, Mr. Heller. Call it misdirection. I figure the longer everyone thinks that *you're* the key to this whole thing, the less energy they'll be putting into other ways of finding me. And I've done a little looking into how this privilege works—even though you don't represent me anymore, whatever you and I discussed while you *were* my lawyer stays privileged. So whether you like it or not, you're obligated to keep my secret."

"Now wait a minute. You can't force me to be part of some scheme of yours."

"Oh, spare me the tantrum, Mr. Heller. The rule only allows you to reveal information to prevent me from committing an illegal or fraudulent act. I've already *done* all my 'committing,' so there's nothing to prevent me from doing. You *can't* say anything. And please don't give me any of that high-and-mighty stuff. I'm sure this won't be the first time you advocate a position you find distasteful. That's what makes you such a good lawyer, isn't it? The ability to argue a position you don't agree with?

"Besides, what are you going to say? That you were stupid enough to take on a client without even getting his name and address? Who's going to believe that? They'd probably think you were lying to protect me. No, you're better off invoking the privilege. That, people will believe."

He *was* stupid. For getting mixed up in this in the first place. Jody had been right. What had she asked him, first thing? *Why do you want to represent scum like that?* Good question…no answer.

"Your silence tells me you know I'm right. So, I can assume you'll do the right thing at your deposition tomorrow? Invoke the privilege?"

Scott tightened his grip on the telephone receiver. In what was perhaps a juvenile effort to avoid giving Ericson—or whoever he was—any satisfaction, he answered noncommittally.

"I'll think about it," he spat. "Now, I have legitimate work to do."

He hung up before the man who wasn't Glenn Ericson

could answer.

■   ■   ■

Jesus fucking Christ! That's another fine mess you've gotten us into, Ollie.

Scott sat at his desk, chair swiveled around so he could stare out over Madison Avenue, the meeting in the conference room forgotten.

The guy was right. *The "guy." Now* I *don't even know what to call him. What a fucking mess.* How could he go to a deposition and admit he didn't even know who his client was? If they believed him, he'd look like a buffoon. If they didn't, he was a liar.

He had to think it through logically. It was probably true that there was no longer any attorney-client relationship between him and...Guy. Even if that were so, the attorney-client privilege *did* still apply to the communications they'd had during the relationship. But would he be breaching a confidence if he simply revealed that he didn't know the client's name, and told the bogus name he'd been given? He couldn't see how.

So what would happen if he came clean? Besides looking like an ass? O'Connor would probably subpoena the firm's records, to find any information that could possibly lead to the client's identity. So the battle about privilege would continue. And, maybe more importantly, the firm would become more deeply entangled in an unsavory legal battle. That was not something Scott looked forward to dragging his partners through.

Could he justify continuing to assert the privilege? Knowing what he did now—which is that he didn't know anything worthy of protection? He remained convinced that under the circumstances of this case, if he *did* know his client's identity it would be privileged information. So technically speaking, if he were asked to name his client, answering that question by saying that that information was protected by the attorney-client privilege would be accurate. The information *was* privileged—never mind that he didn't know it.

The more he thought about it, the more he convinced himself that that was the way to go. He wouldn't have to admit on the record that he'd been duped by his client. He wouldn't expose his firm to unnecessary legal hassles fighting subpoenas for internal records. And there was the chance that this thing would go away once and for all—maybe the court would accept his position that the privilege applied, and everyone would just leave him alone.

Scott turned back to face his desk. Now that he'd decided what course to take with O'Connor at the deposition, he still faced some questions. What should he tell Sharon—his own attorney? How many times had he excoriated his own clients for keeping secrets from him? *Nope. Doesn't apply here.* He'd keep quiet. This whole thing would blow over. No need to complicate things by fessing up to his partner.

Jody? That was an easy one. He couldn't bear the inevitable "I told you so." Jody didn't need to know about this twist either.

Go to the deposition, plead the privilege, and move on.

Scott headed for the conference room to see if his meeting was still in session.

CHAPTER 22

Frank O'Connor did not project the image of a keen legal adversary. He had a slightly rumpled appearance, and his hair always looked about a week overdue for a trim. He wore suits that hung on him loosely, to some extent concealing the few extra pounds that he carried, and there was invariably a spot on his tie or his shirt that bore silent testimony to his most recent meal. Those who had never faced him in court before usually watched with some amusement as he made his way up the aisle to the counsel table, sometimes fumbling with his briefcase, often apologizing to the judge as he shuffled papers into some kind of order that would allow him to begin his presentation.

But when he addressed the court, all doubts about his legal acumen were removed. He wasted no words, focused quickly and sharply on the problem, and drew a clear and persuasive road map that led convincingly to the result he was advocating. The second time you opposed Frank O'Connor, you did not underestimate him.

This morning's stain—on his bright yellow tie—was ketchup, from the plate of eggs, bacon, home fries, and toast that the waitress had placed before him moments ago.

"Breakfast's a very important meal," he said to his client, Stacy Altman, who sat across from him in a booth at the Woodbridge Diner. "Usually, things get so busy during the day that it's nearly four o'clock by the time I can even think of grabbing lunch. And, when it comes to depositions, you never want to be hungrier than the witness or his attorney. I like to push right through lunch whenever I can. Witnesses who start focusing on their hunger let their guard down. They just want to finish."

He took a sip of coffee.

"Anyway, that's why I asked you to meet me for breakfast—this way we can get ready for this morning while I get my sustenance." He smiled.

"No problem, Mr. O'Connor." The lawyer glanced up from his plate, a forkful of eggs poised at the ready, and he moved to speak. Stacy cut him off. "I know. You told me already. 'Frank.'"

He shrugged. "Hey, I'm almost forty, but whenever someone says 'Mr. O'Connor' I still always turn around to see where my father is. What can I say?"

"Well, okay…Frank." She fingered the bran muffin that lay uneaten on her plate. "Do you really think Heller will talk?"

"Ah, that's the sixty-four thousand dollar question, isn't it?" O'Connor put his fork down, and dabbed at his mouth with his napkin. "Will he talk today? Probably not. Will the court order to him talk when we file our motion to compel? I think so. There's no governing precedent going our way, but luckily there's none going against us either. Since the law's unsettled, we try, and if we end up in court, we make our best pitch to the judge and hope he sees things our way. And then, depending on how things go, we go up the ladder of appeals and see who gets tired first and gives in. There's no simple answer, and the road from here to there isn't easy."

"But if we know that he's going to refuse to answer your questions, why do we have to go through this charade? Why can't we go right to court and ask a judge to make him answer? This seems like a waste of time."

"We have to do this to build a record. Last Friday afternoon, his partner Sharon Roth and I spoke on the phone, and we discussed whether Heller should simply claim the privilege and refuse to appear at all. If he did that, I would have the grounds to make a motion to hold him in contempt, and we'd get the issue of the privilege before the court then. But we both agreed that there are some questions that there's no argument I'm allowed to ask. Appearing today and answering those questions will help narrow the issues that the judge will ultimately have to rule on."

"What type of questions?" Stacy asked.

"Questions that'll help establish whether or not the privilege applies. Assume for the minute that the communication of a client's name *can* be privileged just like any other communication between client and lawyer can be. The privilege attaches only when certain conditions are met. The client must mean for the communication to be confidential, and he must communicate the information to the lawyer privately. No one other than the client and the lawyer may participate in the communication. For instance, if you confide something to me as your attorney, but your friend is here listening, there's no privilege. The friend's presence destroys the confidentiality. Also, if you discuss our confidential communication afterwards with someone else, the privilege is destroyed—you've shown you no longer care for it to be confidential. With Heller, if we can discover that the conditions that give rise to the privilege weren't met or preserved, we don't even have to get to the tougher question of whether a client's name can be privileged information.

"So, there will be a little bit more to today's deposition than just 'Good morning, Mr. Heller, tell me the name of your client.'"

He leaned forward toward Stacy, forearms resting on the table. "By the way, you never did answer my question—how *did* you come up with Heller's name?"

Stacy hesitated. "I don't know if I really want to say. Someone went out on a limb, and I don't want her to get in trouble."

"You know that anything you tell me from here on in is privileged information, don't you?"

Stacy winced. "That 'privilege'! That's the whole damn reason

I'm here!"

"Well, it does serve its purpose. And for the moment, rather than focus on how the privilege is working against you, accept the fact that in your dealings with me, the privilege benefits you. If I'm to help you, you have to know that what you tell me in confidence goes no further.

"Anything short of 'Hey Frank, I'm on my way to the bank to knock it over' is absolutely privileged."

Stacy looked at him quizzically.

"Even the attorney-client privilege has its limits," O'Connor explained. "About the only thing that's not privileged is a statement to an attorney of your intention to commit a serious crime, or your statement that you're in the process of committing one."

He paused for a forkful of home fries. "And," he said, after swallowing, "in my opinion, the simple name of one's client. I don't think that's privileged either, under the circumstances of this case. When all is said and done, I do think we'll end up learning what we want from attorney Heller."

■   ■   ■

They finished at the diner and walked the short distance to O'Connor's office, just one short block off Main Street. The Law Offices of Frank T. O'Connor were located in a small suite on the second floor of a converted firehouse—rather a quaint environment. There were offices for O'Connor and his two associates, a small law library that doubled as a conference room, and a small kitchen that also housed a photocopier, a fax machine, and the office supplies. All modestly furnished.

"When the court reporter gets here, show her in to the conference room," O'Connor said to his secretary. "Have Mr. Heller and Ms. Roth wait in reception when they get here, and let me know." He ushered Stacy into his office. "We have a few minutes, so why don't you have a seat?" He sat down at his desk, and pointed to a chair opposite him.

"I don't really have to explain too much of what's going to happen, do I? When I represented you in that construction case of yours, both you and your husband were deposed, and if I remember right, you sat in on the defendant's deposition. Same drill this morning. Heller will be here, along with Roth, who'll be representing him. Then there will be you, me, and a certified shorthand reporter. The reporter will swear Heller in, I'll ask questions, and Heller will answer. Or, Roth will object and advise him not to answer. And the reporter will take everything down and have it typed up."

Stacy nodded.

"Well then, try to relax. And by the way, did you see Saturday's *Herald*?"

"It's probably sitting at home somewhere. Why?"

"Page ten. Us. Just a small item recapping the accident. And the revelation that a lawyer named Scott Heller knows who did it, but refuses to say. It tells of our lawsuit, and of Heller's upcoming deposition."

"Good. I want people to know what's going on."

"I agree. Publicity is good."

O'Connor's secretary appeared at the door. "Excuse me. Mr. Heller and Ms. Roth are here."

"Okay. Tell them I'll be out in a minute. Have them wait in reception, though. I'll bring them into the conference room."

Then, to Stacy he said, "Come. You'll wait in the conference room while I get them."

He led Stacy to the library, which was a windowless room, three walls of which were lined floor-to-ceiling with bookshelves. Along the remaining wall ran a credenza, atop which was a telephone. The room was brightly lit, to combat the lack of natural lighting.

A large rectangular oak conference table stood in the middle of the room. At the head of the table sat the reporter, who had set up her stenographic machine on a tripod. Yellow legal pads lay in front of four of the chairs, two on each side of the table, facing each other.

"I'll sit here," O'Connor said, pointing to one of the two chairs nearest the reporter, on the side facing the door. "You'll sit on my right. Heller will sit opposite me, with his back to the door, and Roth next to him."

■   ■   ■

Scott had driven this morning directly to Frank O'Connor's office. Sharon, who lived in Manhattan, had taken the New Jersey Transit train to Woodbridge and had met Scott downstairs, in front of O'Connor's building. When they presented themselves to O'Connor's secretary, who apparently doubled as his receptionist, they were asked to wait while O'Connor was summoned. A moment later, O'Connor escorted them to a conference room. Although Scott had known that Stacy was entitled to be at the deposition, he had hoped she would pass on the opportunity. To his dismay, she was seated at the table.

"Mr. Heller, I think you and Mrs. Altman have already met. Ms. Roth, Mrs. Altman," O'Connor said, introducing the two women.

Scott Heller extended his hand. "Good morning, Mrs. Altman."

Stacy neither rose from her seat, nor offered her hand in return. But her gaze was fixed on Scott. When he realized that Stacy was not going to respond, Scott lowered his hand and sat down. Sharon simply nodded to Stacy as she took her seat, but Stacy did not acknowledge her, either.

"Okay," O'Connor said. "Let's get started." He turned to the court reporter. "Please swear in the witness."

The young woman addressed Heller. "Please raise your right hand. Do you swear that the testimony you are about to give in this matter will be the truth, the whole truth, and nothing but the truth, so help you God?"

"Yes, I do."

The reporter continued. "State your full name for the record."

"Scott Heller."

As Scott had expected, O'Connor briefly laid some groundwork. He quickly established that Scott was indeed an attorney, having gotten his law degree ten years ago. After spending two years as an associate attorney in a large New York City firm, he'd joined a smaller firm, where he stayed for another four years. Then he, along with four other lawyers, had formed the firm now known as Roth Stern.

"Mr. Heller, are you aware of an incident that occurred on June 17 of this year, which resulted in the death of a six-year-old child named Ben Altman?"

"Yes."

"How did you first learn of it?"

"I read about it in the newspaper."

"Then you are aware that Ben's death was the result of being struck by a car?"

"That's what I read."

"Did there come a time when you were contacted by someone claiming to have driven the car that was involved in the incident?"

"Objection," Sharon interjected. "By asking whether the person contacting Mr. Heller 'claimed to have driven the car,' you are asking him to divulge the contents of a communication between lawyer and client. That matter is privileged, so I advise Mr. Heller not to answer."

Scott saw Stacy stiffen in her seat. She had not taken her eyes off him since they had begun.

"I'll rephrase it," O'Connor continued. "Did there come a time when you were contacted by someone wishing to retain your services in connection with the incident?"

Scott glanced at Sharon, who nodded.

"Yes. I received a telephone call on June 19."

"You were in your office at the time?"

"I was."

"Was anyone else in your office with you?"

"I was alone."

"To your knowledge, was anyone else on the line with him?"

"I didn't say that the person who called me was a 'him.'"

"Well, was it a man or a woman?"

Another objection came from Sharon. "Disclosure of the person's gender helps to establish his or her identity, which as you know we claim is privileged information. Therefore, I advise Mr. Heller not to answer."

"Ms. Roth, to avoid awkwardness in phrasing the questions and answers, can we agree to refer to the client as 'he' or 'him'? We can stipulate that such references are for convenience only, and do not establish the gender of the client."

"Yes, that's acceptable."

"Then, Mr. Heller, to your knowledge was anyone else on the line with him when he called?"

"No. Not to my knowledge."

"And did the caller ask you to contact the County Prosecutor on his behalf regarding Ben Altman's death?"

"Objection."

"I'll rephrase that. Following your telephone conversation with the caller, did you contact the County Prosecutor on his behalf?"

"No, not immediately. I first met with the caller."

"Where was this meeting?"

"In my office. And no, Mr. O'Connor, no one else was present. The client asked to meet me early in the morning, and we met in my office at seven o'clock, Thursday, June 22. My partners, associates, and office staff were not yet in, and my client and I were alone. In fact, the client insisted on that."

"And was it following that meeting that you contacted the prosecutor on his behalf?"

"That's correct."

"Did the client specifically instruct you to keep his name confidential?"

"That he did. Those were his exact instructions. I was not to reveal his identity unless and until the prosecutor reached a plea bargain agreement with me."

"Did you have any further telephone conversations or meetings with him?"

"No other meetings. I spoke with him perhaps two or three more times. And no, no one else was present or on the line."

"And since then, have you revealed his name to anyone?"

"No sir, I haven't."

"Finally, for the record, I ask you, Mr. Heller, what is your client's name?"

As Scott considered the irony of the question that he knew all along had been coming, and his inability to answer it even if he wanted to, Sharon jumped in with her protest.

"Objection. I advise Mr. Heller not to answer."

Scott felt like a fraud—even his friend, partner, and lawyer didn't know what he knew.

"With all due respect, Mr. O'Connor," Scott said, and he now turned to Stacy before continuing. "And I do apologize to you, Mrs. Altman, for your loss and your pain. But I must refuse to answer that question because it is privileged information."

Stacy did not move. The hatred with which she regarded him was palpable.

"I have no further questions," Frank O'Connor said. "Thank you for coming."

■　　■　　■

After the conclusion of the deposition, Scott and Sharon retrieved Scott's car from the nearby municipal parking lot. Scott pondered the morning's events as he passed through the toll plaza at Interchange 11 of the New Jersey Turnpike, and proceeded north toward the Lincoln Tunnel.

He'd turned a corner at the deposition, and he wasn't entirely comfortable with the direction in which he was headed. Though he had known from the start that he'd be called upon to guard his client's identity, even in the face of a police investigation, the appearance of Stacy Altman in the flesh had been troubling. But he'd nevertheless been able to justify his position. He was a lawyer. His client had imparted information to him confidentially. That information was privileged and he could not disclose it. He'd felt bad that Mrs. Altman was so deeply affected, but that did not justify his breaching his duty to his client.

Now, though, his silence was no longer dictated by pure ethical considerations. Instead, he was allowing himself to be governed by self-interest. The simple desire not to look foolish.

He tried to step back and examine the situation objectively. When he had debated the issue with himself the day before, he'd decided that his original analysis had been accurate—if the client *had* told him his name, it would be privileged information, and he could not be required to reveal it.

Today, he had been asked the name, and it was perfectly accurate to respond that the question sought the disclosure of privileged information. Why should it matter that the reply had the added benefit of preventing him from looking like an ass?

Was it because the honest answer was "I don't know," and how could that answer possibly convey confidential information protected by the attorney-client privilege? Was it because even though he could justify what he was doing by resorting to an exercise in tortured semantics, the bottom line was that his answer was dishonest?

No, that couldn't possibly be it. It was his responsibility as a lawyer to uphold the sanctity of the attorney-client privilege, however severe the consequences might be. That was the driving force behind his actions.

"Hey, Scott. Where are you? Seems like someplace far away."

His so-called client had chided him with the observation that one of the things that made him such a good lawyer was his capacity to argue a position he didn't agree with. Another virtue that the client hadn't mentioned was his ability to take virtually any set of facts and construct a legal theory to get things to come out his way.

"Huh? Oh—nowhere. Just thinking about what a busy afternoon I have ahead of me. And hoping the tunnel traffic isn't too horrendous."

Content for now with the decision he had made, he glanced in his side-view mirror, spotted an opening, and punched the accelerator of his Porsche.

CHAPTER 23

"Yes, good morning, Detective Kluge, it's Frank O'Connor. I represent Stacy Altman. Thanks for taking my call. How are you today?"

"Not too bad, Mr. O'Connor. What can I do for you? It's a terrible thing, what happened to the Altmans."

"Mrs. Altman is with me in my office now. As you may know, I've started a lawsuit that we hope will force attorney Heller to tell us who's responsible. But I'm also interested in learning how the police investigation is going. What can you tell me?"

Roy Kluge was naturally wary of lawyers. And discussing ongoing investigations—with anyone—wasn't something he did. But there wasn't much to tell.

"I wish I could give you good news. I'm afraid we're not coming up with much. Interviews of neighborhood residents have not uncovered any useful information. No witnesses have come forward. Physical evidence we recovered at the scene has allowed us to determine the kind of car involved, and we're following that up. But so far, nothing really helpful in terms of identifying the perpetrator."

"Can you try to keep me informed, Detective?"

"Mr. O'Connor, to the extent I can, I will. I take this case kind of personal because it was a kid, and because Mrs. Altman is such a nice lady. But however slowly it's going, it is an ongoing investigation, and—"

"Yes, I know. There are limits on what you can tell me. All I'm asking is that you tell me what you can, when you can. Nothing more."

"That, I'll do. And please give my regards to Mrs. Altman."

Kluge hung up the phone. He hadn't told O'Connor the details. Not that there was much to withhold. They knew they were looking for a 2006 Montego blue Z4—but they had known this a month ago. They had finished interviewing the twelve Perth Amboy residents who owned such cars, with no success. Most could demonstrate beyond doubt that they were somewhere else at the time of the accident, and with respect to the others, there was simply nothing to tie them to the incident. He now had to expand the inquiry to Z4 owners from areas surrounding Perth Amboy. Notwithstanding Kluge's devotion to making progress in this case, he had other responsibilities, too, and the Altman matter was just one of many that he could attend to.

So, he was little further along now than he had been two months ago when they'd first determined the make, model, color, and year of the car. But he was not about to give up.

■   ■   ■

O'Connor replaced the receiver in the cradle, and thought about what the detective had just told him.

"They know what kind of car it was," he said to Stacy, who was sitting across from him in his office. "I don't really think Kluge has told me everything he knows, but my bet is they don't have much more than that to go on."

"They'll never find him, Frank."

"Scott Heller is clearly the key," O'Connor responded. "Which brings us to business."

O'Connor passed a document across his desk to Stacy.

"I've prepared a motion seeking to compel Heller to answer the questions about his client. Technically, he's not in contempt of court right now. We make the motion, and hopefully Judge Adams orders him to answer. If he still refuses, then he's violated a court order and can be held in contempt."

"What's this?" Stacy asked, referring to the document O'Connor had just handed her.

"That's an affidavit for you to sign in support of the motion. My affidavit will describe the deposition and Heller's refusal to answer questions. Yours will describe the factual background of the incident itself, and what's happened to you since then. I know it's not pleasant to go over that stuff and see it in print, but I want the judge to have something from you personally when he's considering this."

O'Connor showed her a plastic-covered booklet he had on his desk.

"This is a copy of last week's deposition. I had the stenographer rush it, and it arrived by messenger yesterday afternoon. I'll submit a copy of the deposition with the motion, so Judge Adams will have everything.

"Take a few minutes to read through your affidavit, and if it's all right you can sign it, and I'll notarize it. I have a courier coming by in an hour to pick the motion up, serve a copy on Sharon Roth as Heller's attorney, and file it with the court.

"And, oh yeah. I'm sending a copy of it to Mike Harrison, that reporter at the *Herald*. I want to keep him interested. I mean, what the heck?"

■   ■   ■

Sharon stepped into Scott's office, took a seat on the couch, and waited for him to finish his telephone call.

"What's up?" he asked Sharon, when he had hung up.

"Messenger just dropped this off," she said, holding up some papers. "O'Connor's motion to compel."

I guess she's not going away. Not that I really expected her to.

"Well, no surprise there. Have you read it through yet?"

"I skimmed it. It's what we expected. The simple identity of a client is not privileged information. And he includes a rather soppy affidavit from Mrs. Altman about Ben, the incident, and how much the loss has affected her. Totally irrelevant to the issues on the motion. An obvious attempt to tug at Judge Adams's heartstrings."

"Oh, Adams is smarter than that. I've made a few inquiries about him. Before taking the bench, he practiced criminal law. He's used to protecting the rights of unsavory types, and he's not likely to be offended by the workings of the attorney-client privilege. He'll figure out what the law requires, and decide accordingly. Do they cite any legal precedent for their position?"

"Nothing directly on point. But we didn't expect there to be any. Mostly a general discussion about the privilege, what it's meant to protect, and an argument that a client's own name is not a 'communication' within the scope of the privilege."

"I guess we ought to submit a brief in opposition. When's the hearing date?"

"Sixteen days. Friday, September 15. Opposition papers are due Thursday, September 7. Then they get a final crack at a reply by Monday, the 18th."

Scott glanced at the calendar on his desk.

"Okay. Eight days to put together a brief. More than enough time. I'll take care of it. Just ask Karen to make a copy of the motion papers for me."

Sharon rose to leave.

"And Sharon," Scott said. "I appreciate this."

"Yeah, Scott. Not exactly the kind of law practice I want the reputation for.'"

■   ■   ■

The small courtroom was crowded. Long rows of wooden benches were filled with lawyers and their clients, and those who could not find seats stood against the dark paneled wall along the back of room. Moments before, O'Connor had shepherded Stacy down the side aisle and had squeezed both of them into place not far from the front of the room.

He glanced at his watch, which said 8:55.

"When our case is called, you'll come up to counsel table and sit with me," he said, pointing toward the front of the packed courtroom. "Unfortunately, it's a crowded calendar today, and we're a good two-thirds down the list. The judge might not even reach us until after the lunch break."

"Then why did we have to be here at nine?"

"The motion calendar is called at nine," O'Connor explained. "Sometimes it's crowded, sometimes not. The court doesn't schedule these things—every second Friday is a motion day, and anyone can bring on a motion on that day, provided he files his papers by the deadline. You can have fifty to a hundred motions scheduled before one judge on a motion day. But not all of them will have oral argument like everyone here. Some will waive argument, and ask the judge to make his decision based on the papers they've submitted. Others, the judge will have reviewed beforehand, and he'll notify the parties that he doesn't want to hear oral argument, and that he'll decide on the papers. Other motions, the parties will adjourn to another day for some reason or another. And still others, the parties will come to some agreement, and the motion will be withdrawn.

"The rest of us," O'Connor waved his arm, indicating the crowded courtroom, "We all sit and wait our turn."

"Seems pretty inefficient, if you ask me. Look at all these lawyers just sitting around. And charging their clients for their time, no doubt. Wouldn't it make more sense for each case to have a scheduled time, instead of having this circus?"

O'Connor laughed. "Every once in a while, a client will ask me 'What time is our appointment with the judge?' Of course it would be better from the point of view of the lawyer and the client. But it doesn't work that way. Like I said, cases settle. Cases get adjourned. And then the judge would say 'Okay, send in the 9:30 case,' and be told 'Oh, that just settled.' 'Okay, then send in the 9:45 case,' and be told 'They're not here yet, it's only 9:30.' Then it would be the judge who was sitting around waiting. Nope, that system wouldn't last very long. So, we sit around and wait, to make sure the judges are kept busy."

Stacy shook her head. "But look at this zoo. With so many cases coming at him all at once, how can a judge give any single case the attention it deserves? It seems like it would be impossible."

"Unfortunately, to some extent you're right. Most judges do their best, and many are very good at what they do. They listen, they analyze, and they rule. But yes, sometimes the sheer volume affects the depth of the consideration they can give to a particular case.

"Of course," O'Connor smiled, "that's why you pay me the big bucks. To package and present your case in a way that gets the important message across in the most succinct and compelling way, so we can make the most of the limited attention we can get from the judge."

Package and present is what O'Connor had done. A week after he had served the motion papers on Roth, she had filed an opposition brief. O'Connor had analyzed it, and a few days later filed a reply brief, rebutting the opposition. He was confident that his legal analysis was correct—the name of Scott Heller's client was not privileged information, and Heller should be required to disclose it—but he knew all too well that Stacy's assessment of the system was sadly accurate. Too often, what should happen and what did happen in court simply did not connect.

They sat in silence for a moment, and then Stacy spoke.

"This judge. What's his name? What do you know about him?"

"Lawrence Adams. Early fifties. Been on the bench about ten years. Before that, he practiced criminal law. He's intelligent, thorough, and fair. Smart is good for us, because although there's no easy answer, I think on a thorough legal analysis we're right. We need a judge who's capable of seeing that."

A door at the front of the courtroom opened, and through it stepped a tall, gray-haired man wearing a black judicial robe. A young woman seated at a desk just inside the doorway sprang to her feet and called out "All rise!"

In one motion, everyone in the courtroom stood. More slowly, conversation died. Judge Adams waited until there was complete silence, and then proclaimed "Be seated" as he himself sat.

"Good morning, everyone," the judge began. "We have a crowded docket this morning, so let's get started. When you're called for oral argument, keep in mind that I've read all the papers you've submitted, so don't start from scratch with me. There are a lot of people here today, so please don't waste their time or mine just reading your brief to me. Speak only if you have something useful to add."

Judge Adams reached inside his robe, produced a pair of half-glasses which he perched upon his nose, and referred to the list of cases in front of him.

"Byrnes against Regal Motors," the judge called.

Two lawyers, one a man, and the other a woman, rushed forward and passed through the swinging wooden gate in the railing that separated the public seating area from the front of the courtroom. After both took a moment to arrange their papers on the two counsel tables facing the judge's bench, the woman launched her presentation to the judge.

"Thank you, ladies and gentlemen, we'll break for lunch now and reconvene here at one thirty."

O'Connor looked at the clock on the wall behind Judge Adams. It was a few minutes past noon, and the fifth case of the day had just concluded. He turned to Stacy.

"Okay. Time enough for a sandwich downstairs at the snack bar. There's really not enough time to go outside the building for lunch."

"A can of soda will do me fine," Stacy said, offering him a weak smile. "My stomach is doing flip-flops."

"Well, it won't be too much longer today. It looks like we're second on the list when we get back from lunch. A few hours from now, and we'll know which way this thing is headed."

CHAPTER 24

"*Altman versus John Doe*," the court clerk called.

Court had reconvened following the lunch break, and when the clerk had called the one case that had been ahead of them on the remaining list, an attorney had stood and advised the judge that she and her adversary had come to an agreement during lunch, and she was withdrawing her motion. The judge had made a notation on the pad in front of him and instructed the clerk to call the next case.

O'Connor stood in response.

"Ready for the movant, Your Honor."

Across the room, Sharon Roth stood.

"Ready in opposition," she said.

O'Connor walked through the gate to the front of the courtroom, and on to the two wooden tables that faced the judge's bench. As previously instructed, Stacy followed close behind. On each table stood a stainless steel carafe of water, with a stack of paper cups. O'Connor placed his papers in front of him on the table marked "Plaintiff" and remained standing, as Stacy did next to him. Roth did the same at the table marked "Defendant."

"Good afternoon, counsel," said the judge. "Please give your appearances for the record, and be seated."

"Good afternoon, Your Honor. Frank O'Connor for Stacy Altman, the moving party. With me at counsel table is Mrs. Altman."

"May it please the Court. Sharon Roth, from Roth Stern, for Scott Heller, a non-party witness."

Judge Adams motioned for them to sit down.

"This is a troublesome case. I've read all the papers, and done a lot of thinking, and this is a troublesome case."

The judge adjusted the glasses on his nose. "Well, Mr. O'Connor, it's your motion. Why don't you begin?"

"Thank you, Your Honor," O'Connor began, rising once more. "I'll be brief, because our position is set forth fully in the papers you have before you." He took a sip of water from the cup he had filled when they sat down.

"This case is about truth and justice. Now I know that sounds a bit theatrical, Judge, but it happens to be true. Of course, every case that comes before this Court is a search for truth and justice, but in this case, Your Honor must take an active role in directing that search.

"A serious wrong has been committed. Three months ago, someone killed Mrs. Altman's son. In this lawsuit, she seeks to hold the killer responsible for what he did. But she must find him first. For Mrs. Altman, this case is a search for truth—to discover what happened to Ben, and to find who is responsible. And it's a search for justice, to lay responsibility where it belongs.

"But the case has implications that go beyond one mother's quest. It's often remarked that trials result not in discovery of the truth, but instead in a determination of whose version of the 'truth' will prevail. Your Honor is faced with a rare instance in which we know precisely where to look for the truth. Not my version. Not some defense counsel's version. But God's honest truth."

He was pointing to Sharon Roth.

"Ms. Roth's client, Scott Heller, *knows* who ran down Ben Altman. When the Court orders Mr. Heller to disclose that God's honest truth, justice will be served.

"What stands in the way is the long-standing custom of protecting the confidentiality of communications between clients and attorneys. I do not belittle this privilege—I seek only to make sure it is not applied improperly. And here is where I will rely on the legal brief I have submitted, and spare the Court further comment. In that brief we've shown that the information we seek—the name of Mr. Heller's client—is not a communication that falls within the attorney-client privilege. What is more, we show that even if a client's name were within the privilege, that privilege against compelled disclosure is not absolute, and the circumstances of this case warrant an exception.

"In short, Your Honor, Mrs. Altman comes before you today with her goal nearly achieved. She has already found the truth that she is looking for." O'Connor was pointing at Roth again. "She needs your help simply to be able to hear it.

"Please don't shield the holder of that truth and turn Mrs. Altman away with instructions to 'keep searching.'"

O'Connor took his seat.

"One question, Mr. O'Connor," said the judge.

The lawyer stood again.

"Yes, Your Honor."

"I take it there is a police investigation? Do you know the status of that investigation?"

"To my knowledge, the investigation is ongoing. The detective in charge has advised me that physical evidence discovered at the scene has allowed the police to identify the kind of car that struck Ben, but that no further progress has been made." O'Connor took this opportunity to advance his argument. "Attorney Heller is the only available link to the driver."

"All right then," said the judge. "If you have nothing further to add, we'll hear from Ms. Roth."

Sharon Roth took a sip of water and rose.

"Thank you, Your Honor," Roth began. "I too shall be brief. I agree with Mr. O'Connor. A terrible wrong has been committed. I feel for Mrs. Altman. She should seek out the perpetrator and bring him to justice. And, I agree with the Court. This is a troublesome case. The Court must balance the time-honored and hallowed right of a client to confer in confidence with his attorney against the right of an individual to have complete access to all relevant evidence needed to pursue a legitimate civil claim.

"While it may be a troublesome conflict, I think that upon analysis the Court will agree that the scale tips the balance in favor of protecting the privilege.

"First, the name of Mr. Heller's client *is* within the privilege. Our own Supreme Court addressed this question in *In re Kozlov*, a case in which an attorney was held in contempt of court when he refused to comply with an order directing him to disclose his client's identity. There, Chief Justice Hughes expressed 'the most serious doubt...of the validity of any inflexible thesis that the identity of the client, as distinguished from the substance of his professional confidence, is outside the ancient privilege deemed to exist between attorney and client.' Quoting from a case decided by New York's highest court, he observed that 'usually, it is not the client's name but the client's communication to his lawyer which is held to be sacred, and so, ordinarily, there is no need to conceal the name to preserve the confidence. But here the client's communication had already been divulged...and it was the client's name that deserved and needed protection.'

"That is precisely the case here—the substance of the communication from Mr. Heller's client to Mr. Heller is already known. He apparently has indicated his responsibility for the terrible tragedy in which Mrs. Altman's son was killed. It is the client's name that deserves and needs protection.

"The Chief Justice went on to hold that under these circumstances the court must engage in a balancing test between the public interest in the search for truth and the attorney-client privilege itself. He held that there must be a legitimate need of a party such as Mrs. Altman to reach the evidence sought to be shielded. There must also be a showing of relevance and materiality of that evidence to the issue before the court.

"We do not deny that these elements are present here.

"But Chief Justice Hughes also held that it must be shown that the information being sought cannot be secured from any less intrusive source. To justify breaching the sacred privilege, there can be no other way to obtain the information.

"In the present case, the police continue to investigate the matter. While that avenue of discovery remains open, which does not intrude on the attorney-client privilege, we respectfully submit that this Court is not justified in invading the client's confidentiality.

"We do not mean to suggest that if the police are not successful in their investigation that a breach of privilege would automatically be justified, however. There may yet be less intrusive ways of obtaining the information. But the pendency of the police investigation relieves us of the need to consider the existence of those other alternatives now.

"In short, Mrs. Altman has not demonstrated any entitlement to breach the attorney-client privilege, and her motion must be denied."

Roth thanked the judge and took her seat.

Judge Adams, who had been listening intently, adjusted the eyeglasses on his nose once more, and shuffled some papers in front of him. He appeared to be in thought. A moment later he looked up and addressed O'Connor and Roth.

"Counsel, I want to thank you for your professional presentation. The papers that both of you submitted were informative and helpful, and your oral argument was clearly focused. I am prepared to issue my ruling. While I am no less troubled now by the circumstances of this case than when we began, I believe that my duty is clear. Both of you, and your clients, can be assured that I have given this matter my careful consideration."

O'Connor, who was watching the judge intently, felt Stacy stiffen in her chair next to him.

"Our judicial system strives to mete out justice. The system is premised on the notion that truth must be pursued wherever it leads. Now, the attorney-client privilege is an integral part of our system. Indeed, by fostering open and frank discussions between client and lawyer, the privilege is an important tool in the search for the truth. The lawyer can learn all of the facts, and the client need not worry that what he tells his lawyer will go any further.

"On the other hand, that privilege can operate to frustrate the search for truth as well. An attorney with relevant evidence can be forbidden by the client from disclosing it.

"Such circumstances are not unknown to our system of justice. Indeed, the federal Constitution has within it certain rules that, when properly applied, result in the exclusion of concededly relevant evidence when it is deemed to be for the greater good. An example of this is the exclusion of evidence that is obtained by authorities in violation of a defendant's Fourth Amendment right to be free from unreasonable searches and seizures. Another is the exclusion of a defendant's own confession if that confession was obtained in violation of his Fifth Amendment right against self-incrimination.

"In each of these examples, the Court purposely closes its eyes to evidence it knows to be there, and knows to be relevant. Why? Because we have made the judgment that on the whole our system of justice, and by extension society, will be better off promoting certain values and freedoms, even at the expense of some harsh individual results. For instance, we feel that we are better off enforcing our right to be free from unwarranted invasions of our privacy by the state, even if it means that occasionally a guilty party will go free. That is why we will exclude evidence that is seized from a defendant in violation of his Fourth Amendment right even though we know that that evidence will help convict him.

"In today's case I am called upon to make a similar judgment—under the circumstances of this case, does the public interest in protecting the attorney-client privilege outweigh an individual's right to access to relevant evidence? Notice that I did not say that this is a balance between the rights of Mr. Heller's client against the rights of Mrs. Altman. I believe we must view this question as one in which the public interest is involved.

"Mr. Heller possesses knowledge that is necessary for, and relevant to, the cause of action that Mrs. Altman seeks to assert against the individual responsible for the death of her son. That person, Mr. Heller's client, confided in him as his attorney, undoubtedly expecting that anything he said to Mr. Heller would be held by him in the strictest confidence. He was relying upon the well-established attorney-client privilege. Mrs. Altman asks me to breach that privilege and direct Mr. Heller to divulge his client's identity.

"As a preliminary matter, I find that under the circumstances of this case, the name of Mr. Heller's client *does* fall within the protection of the attorney-client privilege. In this case, where the content of the communication between attorney and client is for all intents and purposes already known, it is the client's very name that needs the protection of the privilege.

"Therefore, I turn now to consideration of whether or not the privilege is to be put aside under the facts present in this case. I have concluded that Mrs. Altman has not demonstrated sufficient cause for me to invade the sanctity of the privilege. If the privilege is to have any meaning, the circumstances under which it will be thrown aside must be strictly limited. If a client must always worry whether a judge is going to one day deem his conference with his attorney to be fair game, the privilege becomes worthless. Therefore, such confidential communications will be ordered disclosed only in the most extreme circumstances.

"That Mrs. Altman has a legitimate need for the information she seeks, and that such information is relevant and material to the issues in this case, is beyond dispute. In my opinion, however, she fails to establish the final requirement that would justify abrogating the privilege—that the information cannot be secured from any less intrusive source. There is an ongoing police investigation into the incident, which if successful will reveal the identity of the perpetrator. It therefore appears that the information Mrs. Altman seeks may well be available from a less intrusive source.

"I caution both sides against drawing any conclusions from today's ruling about what I may decide should the police investigation fail. I do not mean to imply that in those circumstances I would necessarily rule that the privilege is to be set aside. Nor do I suggest the opposite. Such a determination must await another day, if at all. All that my holding today means is that the pendency of the police investigation leads me to conclude *today* that ordering Mr. Heller to disclose his client's identity is unwarranted.

"Accordingly, plaintiff's motion to compel Mr. Heller to disclose the identity of his client is denied."

CHAPTER 25

"So it really isn't over yet, is it?" Jody asked.

They sat at the dinner table, sipping wine. It was Friday night, and Alex was spending the night at Jacklyn's. Together, Jody and Scott had cooked dinner, opened a bottle of Merlot, and enjoyed a quiet meal. Eventually, the conversation had turned to the events of the day.

Scott had been exuberant when he told her of the judge's decision, but when she pressed him for details, he had to admit that there was the potential for more legal wrangling.

"I just want that Guy out of our lives," Jody said. "And Stacy Altman too. I mean, I feel for her and all, but she's just too...pushy."

"Well," Scott replied, "I think it's over. Like I said, Mrs. Altman might decide to appeal, but if she does, for the most part it won't involve me. It'll just be legal briefs for the Appellate Division, and Sharon already said she'd handle it if it comes to that. But I just don't see the App Div reversing Judge Adams—his decision was well-reasoned, and supported by precedent. I think the appeals court would affirm. And we don't even know she'll appeal."

"Oh, she'll appeal all right. Look at how she set you up, with that phony appointment. She's determined. And besides, you said that the judge left open the possibility that if the police investigation doesn't come up with anything, he might change his mind. You think she won't go back to court in a few months if the police don't find him? I know she will. I don't like it."

Scott sipped his Merlot. "You worry too much, Jo. The court has said I don't have to testify. If a higher court says I do, I will. And in the meantime, Sharon'll handle whatever legal stuff comes up. So what if Mrs. Altman appeals? As long as I do what the court says I have to, I have nothing to worry about. I'm not going to think about it anymore, and you don't have to either."

"I hope you're right, Scott," Jody said. She poured the last of the wine for both of them. "I just get this feeling about her."

■   ■   ■

Monday afternoon, four fifteen. Alex was into her fourth week of school—fourth grade already—and had arrived home about an hour ago. Responding to the door chime, she ran into the foyer and poked her fingers through the slats of the mini-blinds that covered the full-length oval glass window in the front door, so she could see the front stoop.

"Mom, there's a lady at the door."

"Okay, Ali, here I come."

Jody opened the door to find a tall, thirtyish woman, her black hair hanging freely to her shoulders. She was dressed in denim jeans and a brown leather jacket.

"Mrs. Heller, I'm Stacy Altman, Ben's mother."

Jody stiffened. "Ali, honey, go inside," she said, still looking at Stacy. "I'll be in in a minute."

"Who's Ben?" Alex asked.

"Inside, Alex. Now."

The girl looked quizzically at her mother, then at the intruder, and then back at her mother. She turned, and headed up the stairs.

Jody made no move to invite Stacy in. Keeping the screen door between them, she glared at Stacy.

"What do you want?" she asked. The iciness in her voice was undisguised.

"I want to know who killed my son."

"You have no right to come here. This is a legal matter between you and my husband, and it's being handled through his office. I know how painful this must be for you, but you have no right to come here like this."

Stacy bristled. "No, Mrs. Heller, you don't have any idea how I must feel. When I leave, your daughter—Alex, is it?—will come downstairs, and your life with her will go on. Three months ago, I couldn't begin to imagine life without Ben. So don't tell me you know how I must feel."

"This is a legal matter between you and my husband," Jody repeated. "The judge has said that what you are asking for is privileged information. Scott can't help you."

"That's bullshit, and you know it. You know the difference between right and wrong, and so does your husband. Do you think a rule made up by lawyers and judges can change that? The rule is wrong, plain and simple. Your husband ought to have the balls to recognize that and do the right thing."

Jody took a step back from the screen door. "Please leave. I don't want to be rude, but you can't stay here. I have nothing to say to you, other than to tell you I'm sorry for your loss. Really, I am."

"Spare me your sympathy, Mrs. Heller. Everyone is so sorry for me. But no one has the guts to take a stand." Stacy drew herself up straight. "Be sure to tell your husband I was here. If he thinks the judge's decision ended this, he's mistaken. And if he thinks I'm just going to rely on the legal system to help me, he's wrong there too. This isn't over. Not by a long shot."

Without another word, Stacy turned and headed for her car.

■   ■   ■

"She what?" Scott asked, at once both angry and incredulous.

"Just what I said, Scott," Jody said. "She came here to the house. She just left."

At Jody's insistence, Karen had interrupted Scott in a meeting. His wife rarely disturbed him at work, and he was initially worried that something had happened to Alex. Scott had rushed into his office to take the call, and though relieved that Alex was all right, he was troubled by what his wife was telling him.

"You told me it was over, Scott. That except for some nice little legal maneuvers, both Guy and Stacy Altman would be out of our lives. But she came to our house. What did she mean she's not going to rely on the legal system? That sounds like a threat to me. And besides, how did she even know where we live? I'm scared."

"Well, I don't like the fact that she came out to the house—she probably tracked us down online. But I really don't know what she could do. She suffered a setback in court, and she's frustrated and emotional. I don't think there's anything to worry about."

"Scott. You've been saying that ever since you took this case on. You were supposed to make a few phone calls for that creep and be done with it. But you've been subpoenaed, deposed, and hauled into court. And now some crazy woman is stalking us at home."

"Jo, she's not 'stalking' us. She came there once."

"You know what I mean. This doesn't have *you* worried?"

"I don't like it, but I'm not really worried. I think she's just venting," Scott said. "But I'll mention it to Sharon, and see what she thinks about the whole thing."

■   ■   ■

Scott replaced the receiver. He couldn't deal with Stacy Altman right now. Three other lawyers, adversaries in one of his class action lawsuits, were waiting for him in the conference room to resume the settlement negotiations he had interrupted in order to take Jody's call. He walked out of his office on his way back to the meeting, but Karen motioned to him from her desk.

"Another call," she told him. "Brian Hardwicke."

Scott groaned. Brian Hardwicke was a senior partner at Sechrest Hardwicke & Toombs, a large accounting firm, and a particularly good Roth Stern client. Scott had represented the firm in a number of lawsuits over the past few years, and one thing he'd learned through that was that Brian Hardwicke did not like being put off. When he wanted to talk to his lawyer, he wanted to talk to him *now*. Scott wasn't aware of any pending matters with Hardwicke's firm, so the call might be about new business. Better to take the call now than to have Karen tell Hardwicke that he was in a meeting. He returned to his desk.

"Brian, how are you?" Scott said, hoping he sounded cordial enough. "It's been a while, hasn't it? Staying out of trouble?"

"I should be asking you that question," Hardwicke said with a hint of an edge in his voice. "I just got off the phone with some reporter. Wanted to know how I felt about Sechrest Hardwicke & Toombs's lawyer protecting the identity of some child-killer. What's that all about? You representing damn child-killers now?"

Reporter, thought Scott. He remembered a call coming in that morning from the fellow who had done a story or two on the case. The message had said that he was working on a follow-up, now that the judge had made his ruling. Scott had not returned the call. What the hell was he doing calling Brian Hardwicke?

"Oh that," Scott said evenly, though he began twirling his earring furiously. Hardwicke lived on Long Island, where the Altman matter was not big news, so there was no reason for him to be familiar with it. "I wouldn't quite say I'm protecting a child-killer." Scott briefly explained the background, and described his role. "It's actually an interesting legal question. If Mrs. Altman appeals, we may end up making new law."

"Don't give me that crap," Hardwicke said. "Don't get me wrong, that's why I come to you—you're a damn good lawyer. Count on you to put a positive spin on the mess you're in. But what the hell is that reporter doing calling me? And he even let slip that he'd be talking with more of your clients. It seems that the story he's doing is about how lawyers use technicalities to accomplish unjust or immoral results, and one angle of the article is how your own clients view this. I refused to give him my opinion, but he intends to mention my firm and me—and the fact that I refused to comment. I have to tell you, I'm not happy about this.

"And besides, what *are* you doing protecting that creep? From what this guy told me on the phone, he ought to be turned over to the cops to face the music, attorney-client privilege or not."

What a hypocrite, Scott thought. Hardwicke has no problems when those "legal technicalities" work in his favor. "Creative arguments" is what they are then.

"Relax, Brian," Scott said. "The whole thing will blow over. And as far as mentioning you in the story goes, the day after it's printed, no one will even remember. But hey, thanks for the heads-up on this. I guess I should call this reporter and talk with him, so I could maybe head off any further disturbance to you and my other clients." Scott rifled through the message slips on his desk. "Was it Mike Harrison from the *Middlesex Herald*?"

"That's the one. Call him, and call him off. I don't want to be bothered again."

"Will do, Brian. Good talking to you, in any case. Let's get together for lunch soon. I could make this up to you."

Scott said his good-bye to Hardwicke. *Shit. This thing is out of control.* He sighed, gave a final spin to his diamond stud, and headed back into his meeting.

CHAPTER 26

Scott and Win sat at a table in the Royal Hunan Restaurant, and watched as the waiter set down a large serving dish, bearing what Win had enigmatically described as "a wonderful secret."

"Trust me—you'll love it."

When the waiter had left, Win convinced Scott to try it. He was glad he did. But Win still refused to reveal its contents.

After the two ate in silence for a while, Win spoke.

"So, counselor, it seems this case of yours is giving you nothing but *tzooris*, huh? What's the latest?"

"Like I told you. This Altman woman has really shaken Jody up, coming to the house yesterday, and all. And I've got to tell you, I'm not too thrilled about it either. You may be used to dealing with the unbalanced, but not me, Win. I'm in uncharted territory."

"You're not considering talking, are you?"

"I don't see how I can. I'm between a rock and a hard place. It would have been easier if the judge had ruled against me. If he'd just ordered me to answer the damn question, this would be over."

"Yeah, Heller, but you wrote such a brilliant brief, Adams didn't have a choice but to go your way. What a curse, to be so clever. So if you're not gonna rat out your client, what are you gonna do?"

"I don't think I have any choice. Keep quiet. Maybe I'll get lucky. Maybe she'll appeal, and I'll lose."

"That's the spirit. Strive for victory, pray for defeat."

"But there *is* something else. I want to try to find Guy."

Win looked up from his plate.

"The client, you mean?"

"Yeah. I don't like the idea of being cut off like this. So out of control."

"And if you find him?"

Scott shrugged. "I dunno. Talk some sense into him maybe?"

"Yeah, right. When you find his address, you can send him a pair of handcuffs, with directions to the nearest police station. That what you have in mind?"

"I don't know what I have in mind. But I'll feel better if I know where to find him. When I spoke with him, he was so adamant about staying hidden. And arrogant. Right now he has the upper hand. If I can find him, then at least maybe he won't be so cocky."

"I get it. It's a macho thing."

"No...Yes...No. Not exactly. I just don't like being played like this. And I'll be more comfortable if I know how to contact him."

"Well, what do you know about him?"

Scott thought for a minute.

"I have a fake name, a pager number that's been disconnected, and an e-mail address that's no longer in use. I've made calls to the pager and e-mail providers, but couldn't get anything from them. Internet searches for the name came up empty in New York and New Jersey."

"The name he gave you, even if it is a fake, might be useful in tracking him down anyway. It might be a variation on his own name." Win paused in contemplation. "Did he at least give a bogus address? Maybe we could figure out something from where he *said* he lived."

Scott shook his head. "Karen took the contact info, and the pager and e-mail was all he gave her. Didn't seem like a big deal to her at the time—we encourage electronic communication. Who'd've thought it would be a problem?"

"Oh, I forgot. You deal only with the finest, most upstanding constituency. Client of mine would never give me his pager number. Only his supplier and his best customers get that. What else? What about his retainer payment? Trace him through the bank? These days, it's hard to fake an ID for a bank account—you might be fronting money for Al Qaeda. What's the deal there?"

A sheepish look from Scott.

"Jesus, Heller. You *did* take a retainer payment, didn't you?"

Scott ducked his head, almost apologetically. "Well, yes…But he, uh, paid with money orders."

Win shook his head in disbelief.

"Money orders? That didn't seem a bit strange to you?"

"I didn't know. Until I found out his pager number and e-mail address were no good, and checked the accounting file for more contact information."

"Is that standard procedure for Roth Stern? Taking money orders for retainers? Sometimes *I* have to, but let's just say the individuals comprising my clientele don't usually have banking references of the same caliber that yours do."

Scott sighed.

"I don't handle that stuff. I mean, I decide what size retainer to take, but accounting takes it from there. I quizzed the staff—seems our Guy apologized for not having a proper bank check. Said he'd just switched banks, and there'd been a mix-up with his new check order. Hence the money orders. It seemed reasonable to accounting."

"And you tried tracing them?"

"Yeah. They were Postal Service money orders. Maximum amount is a thousand dollars each, and the retainer was five, so there were five money orders. You can pay for those things in cash, with no ID required unless you buy more than three thousand dollars in a day. Then you're supposed to fill out a form and present ID. I've filled out the paperwork to get whatever information I can, but who knows how long that will take? Besides, I'm sure he covered his tracks. You know, bought them at different times, in different places."

"Security video? At the post office?"

Scott waved off the question. "Win, we're not talking national security here. We're talking dumb attorney. Can you imagine the red tape I'd have to cut through to get someone even to listen to a request for a review of video?"

Win thought for a moment. "You met with him once, didn't you? What's he look like?"

"Uh, let's see…Fortyish. About six feet tall, average build. Black hair, not too short, not too long."

"You are one sorry excuse for a lawyer, Heller. My clients would have wet dreams for an eyewitness as brain-dead as you."

Win moved the rice around in his bowl with his chopsticks, deep in thought.

"Seems to me that the pager number and the e-mail address are the only things we have to go on, then."

"Yeah, I'm ahead of you on that. Buddy of mine, from MIT, has a computer security consulting firm. He tells me that from one of the e-mails I got from the guy, there's a good chance he can trace the message back to the computer that sent it. Says there's all sorts of information in e-mail headers about the different servers the mail goes through on its way to its recipient. He told me about how the authorities have been able to track down hackers who introduce some of the more virulent computer viruses into the Net—they were once able to trace a virus all the way back to a particular computer in Russia. I'm forwarding the two e-mails that my secretary got from the guy to him tomorrow so he can see what he can come up with."

Win looked thoughtful.

"Well, okay then. How about letting me see what I can do with the pager number? I know a guy who might be able to run it down. Got him off some identity theft charge last year. What a racket he was running. You can't believe how vulnerable all your so-called 'confidential information' is. I'll bet that if there's a way to find out who was at the other end of that pager number, this guy can do it."

"You got this guy off? Some more of that spice you're providing to our city?"

"Yup. He's an expert hacker, or cracker, or whatever the hell they call themselves. I'll find out if there's any way he can worm his way into the pager provider's computer network, and access the subscriber's information. When you get back to your office, shoot me over the provider's name, and I'll see what my guy can dig up."

"Will do, Win. Thanks."

"*De nada.* In the meantime, let me know what your computer geek finds out about the e-mail. You got me curious now."

CHAPTER 27

"O'Connor wasted no time. His appeal arrived by messenger while you were out."

Sharon was waiting for Scott when he returned from lunch. He followed her into her office, where she handed him a packet of papers.

"Along with it is a motion to have the matter heard on an expedited basis. He argues that with every day that goes by, the trail to the driver grows colder, and the risk of him vanishing increases. Since you're the only link to him, your testimony is needed as soon as possible."

Scott looked up from the papers. "My recollection from the court rules is that we have ten days to respond to the motion. Anything in here that changes that?"

"Not that I saw. I assume that you're going to handle the opposition papers?"

"I suppose so. I don't really have a choice, do I? I can't very well ask you to do it."

"Well, Scott, that brings us to the next thing. What's our plan here? Where are we going with this thing? Wouldn't you say it's getting out of hand? What with reporters calling clients, and clients calling us, and all?"

"I know, I know," said Scott. "That's not the half of it." He told her of Stacy's visit to his house the previous afternoon.

"This is more serious than I thought," Sharon said when Scott finished.

"No argument here," Scott agreed. "I just don't know what to do."

With that, Karen stuck her head in the door of Sharon's office.

"Scott, sorry to interrupt, but Stacy Altman is on the phone for you. I told her you were in a meeting, but she insisted I let you know. She said you were expecting her call."

Scott and Sharon exchanged glances.

"Tell her I can't be interrupted," Scott said. Karen turned to go.

"No, wait." He turned to Sharon. "I think I ought to talk to her. But I want you on the line with me to listen. Just in case."

Karen had returned to the door. "What line is she on?" Scott asked her.

"Three."

Scott reached across Sharon's desk, jabbed at line three, and activated the speakerphone.

"Hello, Mrs. Altman," he began, his fingers fiddling with his earring. "I have you on the speakerphone because Sharon Roth is listening." Ordinarily he would ask his caller if she minded having someone else listen in. He did not extend that courtesy to Stacy.

"I suppose you think that Judge Adams's ruling is the end of this," Stacy began. Out of habit, Scott began taking notes of the conversation.

"Well, actually no, I realize that it's not, because we got a copy of your appeal this morning," Scott replied. "But more to the point, let's talk about your visit to my house yesterday." Scott hoped she would be rational.

"I keep my business and my personal life separate," he continued, "and I would appreciate it if you would keep all your contact with me on this matter here at my office. In fact, since you're represented by counsel, it would be more appropriate if you and I didn't have any direct contact. The communications should really be between

Mr. O'Connor and Ms. Roth."

"I'm very sure you'd like to insulate yourself from responsibility," Stacy responded. "Tell yourself it's strictly business, turn it over to your lawyer, and forget about it. But it's not that easy. I won't let it be that easy."

"Mrs. Altman, I'm trying to be reasonable with you. But yesterday, coming to my house, you crossed the line. You can't do that."

Stacy all but exploded. "I can't do that? Who the hell are you to tell me what I can and can't do? And what line did I cross? The line that you've conveniently drawn to protect you from the consequences of your actions? You keep on spouting this crap about professional responsibility. But what about personal responsibility? Your problem is that you think as if you *are* a lawyer. But you're not. You're a *person* who happens to practice law. You can't practice law at the expense of your personal morals. And I can't believe that personally you believe in protecting that scum."

Scott stole a glance at Sharon. "I'm sorry, Mrs. Altman," he said, "but I can't help you. And I beg you not to take it personally. I have a daughter of my own, and can imagine what you're going through. But you're asking me to do something I can't do.

"Your lawyer has filed an appeal. I have no personal allegiance to this client, and I'll do whatever the court finally decides I have to. If the court orders me to disclose who my client is, I'll be on the telephone to Mr. O'Connor within minutes. But unless and until that happens, I can't help you.

"Which brings us back to yesterday. My wife was very upset by your visit. From here on in, I'm asking you to see to it that all contact about this matter be only between Mr. O'Connor and Ms. Roth. Stay away from my home and my family."

There was a momentary silence on the other end of the line. Then, Stacy spoke.

"Now you listen to me, you arrogant bastard. I don't give a damn how upset your wife is. As far as the appeal goes, I have very little faith in the system, so I'm not about to rely on it to get what I need. As between you and me, I do take this personally, and I'm not dropping it. One way or another, I'll make you understand that you can't run away from this. Expect to hear from me again." And she hung up.

■   ■   ■

A somewhat shaken Scott Heller looked across the desk at Sharon Roth. For herself, Sharon appeared a bit bewildered.

"What the hell do you make of that?" Sharon asked.

"You got me," Scott replied. "But I sure don't like the sound of it. I don't need an adversary with a personal grudge. 'You can expect to hear from me again.' What do you think she means by that? She's going to start harassing me?"

"I don't know, Scott. But like I started saying before, you have to give some thought as to where this thing is going. Is this really a battle you want to be fighting? And I have to be looking at it from the firm's viewpoint, too. We have a reporter calling our clients. In addition to affecting our relationship with them, if he publishes a not-so-flattering story, we'll have to deal with the negative publicity as well. For your sake and the firm's, I think you ought to be looking for a way out."

"You're not telling me anything I haven't already thought about," Scott said. "But I've done the research. I have no choice. If I reveal the client's name, I risk disbarment in a disciplinary proceeding, as well as civil liability in a claim that can be brought by the client." Scott paused. "And I suppose you realize that since I'm a partner in the firm, the firm has exposure in any civil action that the client might bring."

Sharon sighed. "Jesus, Scott. What a mess. We'll be better off if we lose the appeal and the Appellate Division orders you to talk."

"Yeah, I thought of that too. But it's not as if we can just throw the appeal. We have an obligation to oppose it competently and vigorously, and we have to do it as if someone might review our performance one day. Otherwise, if we lose, we expose ourselves to the possibility that the client might sue us for malpractice on the appeal.

"We have to do our best to win for this guy, regardless."

Sharon sighed again. "And hope that our best isn't good enough. Jeez, what a mess," she repeated.

CHAPTER 28

The school bus rounded the corner of Mountain View Drive and neared the T-intersection with Apple Ridge Crescent.

"Gotta go, Jacklyn," Alex Heller said. She stood in the aisle, and slung her book bag over her shoulder. "Call you later!"

"Bye, Alex," came a singsong refrain from Billy Holmes. Jacklyn's hand shot up to stifle a giggle, and Alex glared at her. On her way down the aisle past Billy she murmured a "G'bye" to him, and then rushed off the bus.

Since school had started, Billy didn't seem quite as stupid as he had in camp, and Alex had noticed that he was kind of cute. Jacklyn, though, in her usual immature way, teased her as often as she could. About Billy, or about *any* boy that so much as said "hello" to her.

For a best best friend, Jacklyn sure could be a pain.

Alex skipped down the steps, just behind Melissa Porter, who lived around the corner from her on Mountain View. "Bye, Lissy! See you tomorrow."

To her relief, her mother was not standing at the bus stop waiting. She was in fourth grade, could walk the half-block home by herself, and didn't want everyone on the bus to see her mother treating her like a baby. The first few days of school, her mother had come to the bus with her in the morning, and met her there in the afternoon, but Alex finally had had a grown-up talk with her about it. Melissa, who was also in fourth grade, walked by herself. Granted, she didn't have to cross any streets to get home, but the bus always stayed put, with its red lights flashing, until Alex made it safely across Mountain View. Once across that street, all Alex had to do was walk three houses down, and she was home. "I can do that, no problem, Mom. You let me play outside in front of the house. Walking home from the corner isn't any different."

Her mother had finally agreed, after extracting a promise from her that she would come *directly* home from the bus.

She ran across Mountain View, and turned to watch the bus pull away. It was still pretty warm out, being only September, so she meandered along at a leisurely pace. *Mom said "directly." She didn't say "fast."*

As she neared her house, she saw there was a car parked right in front. The woman in the car looked vaguely familiar. It was that lady that rang the doorbell yesterday. The one that upset her mother.

The woman leaned over from the driver's seat and let down the window on the passenger side.

"Alex," she called.

Alex stopped and turned toward her.

"When you go inside, tell you mother that Mrs. Altman said hello."

Alex was puzzled, but she nodded and waved.

When she got to the door, she looked back over her shoulder and saw the car pulling away.

■   ■   ■

"Mommy, who's Mrs. Altman?"

Alex was seated at the kitchen table, enjoying her customary after-school milk and cookies. Jody was brewing herself a cup of tea, about to join her.

"Why do you ask?" Jody asked. "Where did you hear that name?"

"She told me to tell you hello, that's all."

"She what?"

"She said to say hello to you," Alex repeated, a little annoyed that her mother didn't understand this simple greeting.

"Alex, where on earth did you talk to Mrs. Altman?"

Alex was a bit concerned about her mother's tone. Had she done something wrong? She didn't think so.

"Just now, outside," she told her mother. "A lady was sitting in her car out in front, and when I came in she said to tell you that Mrs. Altman said hello." Alex dunked one of her chocolate chip cookies into her milk and took a bite. "That's the same lady that was here yesterday, isn't it?"

"Outside? Now?" Jody rushed to the living room window, and Alex joined her. There was no one there.

"She left when I came in," Alex told her mother.

"Did she stay in the car? She didn't touch you, did she?" Jody asked her daughter, agitated.

"Mommy, you're scaring me. Who's Mrs. Altman?" Alex asked again. "Did I do something wrong?"

Jody put her arms around Alex. "Oh no, honey," she said. "Mrs. Altman is just someone who's involved in one of the cases Daddy's working on at the office. That's all."

"Then why does she keep coming here to talk to you?" Alex asked. "Are you helping Daddy with his case?"

"No, Ali, I'm not. And I don't know why she's coming here to me. I wish she would stop."

"Then ask her to," came the innocent response.

"Oh honey, I wish it was that easy."

■　　■　　■

"Okay, okay. Slow down. First of all, is Alex all right?"

"I told you, she said Stacy didn't touch her. She stayed in the car and just talked to her."

God damn that woman. He was furious. And though he was trying not to show Jody, he was getting worried. This invasion of privacy was getting out of hand.

"Scott, can't you do something about this? Bothering us at our house is one thing. But talking to our nine-year-old daughter…" She let that thought hang. "I'll bet she was purposely waiting out there for Alex to get home from school."

"Let's not jump to conclusions," Scott said. "She feels she's getting a raw deal from the system, and she's frustrated. Let's not read too much into this."

"Honey, please. Sometimes you can be so naive. Can't you see that there's more to it than that? This woman is trouble. The whole case is trouble, and I told you that from the start. Now we have some crazy woman stalking us. You have to do something."

"All right, all right. Just calm down." Scott thought a moment. "I'll have Sharon call Frank O'Connor. Maybe he'll talk to Mrs. Altman. In the meantime, let's try not to overreact."

"Okay. See if Sharon can call him right away. I'm telling you, this woman is trouble."

■   ■   ■

Frank O'Connor hung up the telephone and shook his head in disbelief. It was just after five, and Sharon Roth had caught him on his way out the door for the evening. He hoped there was a reasonable explanation for what she had just told him, but he couldn't think of one. He'd better find out what this was all about.

He located Stacy Altman's telephone number, and keyed it in. No one answered, so he left a voice mail message, saying that it was very important that he speak with her as soon as possible. He left his cell phone number.

About an hour later, as he sat at home over a Lean Cuisine entree, he got the return call. After exchanging pleasantries, he got to the point.

"Stacy, I got a disturbing phone call from Sharon Roth this evening. She said you've been harassing Scott Heller's wife and daughter. What's that all about?"

There was a momentary pause before Stacy answered.

"Oh, come on, Frank," she said. "I haven't been harassing anyone. I wanted to talk to Scott Heller in person, so I went to his house yesterday. He wasn't there, but his wife was. I spoke with her for a minute at the front door. This afternoon I decided to try again to see if I could find him at home, but he wasn't there. I just happened to get there at the same time their daughter got home from school, and I said hello to her. I didn't harass anyone."

"Well, Sharon said you threatened Heller this afternoon, while she was listening on the speakerphone. She said you told him you're going to make it personal, and that he was going to hear from you again."

"For God's sake," Stacy said. "Whose side are you on anyway? It *is* personal. That's the whole point. Since when can't I try to appeal to his conscience? While you're off doing whatever you do in court with his lawyer, why can't I try to talk to him on a personal level? I can't help it if confronting the issue head-on makes him uncomfortable. That just shows me that he knows I'm right."

O'Connor sighed. "Well, from what you've described, I don't think you've done anything wrong. But I'm advising you to be careful. I don't think it's a good idea to be showing up at his house again. You and I both know you can't expect to find Heller there in the middle of the day during the week, so there's no legitimate reason for you to be going there. And for God's sake, stay away from their daughter. Don't do *anything* that might even *look* like you're harassing her. That'll get you into hot water faster than you can imagine, whether it's innocent or not."

"Oh, Frank, you sound as paranoid as they do. Relax. I won't do anything out of line. I'm just trying in my own way to get through to Heller."

Stacy paused, and then continued.

"Just think of it as my effort to reach an out-of-court settlement with him."

CHAPTER 29

Stacy sat up in bed, shivering. She had had that dream again. The one in which an infant Ben sat in the middle of the street in front of their house, transfixed by the sight of the speeding car bearing down on him. As every other time the dream had forced itself upon her, she ran as fast as she possibly could, to try to scoop him from the car's path. As always, she was too late, and was forced to hear her son's terrifying scream—MOMMY!—and the sickening thud of the car impacting on flesh and bone.

She squinted at the green LED readout on her clock radio—it was 5:20. Just as well, as the alarm was set to go off in ten minutes. She swung her legs over the side of the bed and sat up. It was still dark out, so she felt for the lamp on her night table and turned it on.

The other side of her bed was, of course, empty. In the three months since the tragedy, she and Marc had had nothing to do with each other. She'd become obsessed, he'd said. You're insensitive, she'd responded. We have to move on, he'd countered. Our son is dead, she'd reminded him. And the monster who's responsible is still out there.

Marc had moved into the spare bedroom a while back. Stacy didn't miss him.

It was Wednesday morning, and she wanted to make it to the Hellers' house by seven thirty, in time for Alex's school bus.

Frank O'Connor's telephone call yesterday had all but convinced her that she was on the right track. Scott Heller was sitting up and taking notice. She had invaded his private realm, and that was making him uncomfortable. His reaction had been predictable. Smugly thinking he could direct the action, he'd had his lawyer call her lawyer with instructions for her to back off. It was important for her to send the message that it was she, not he, who was in control. Therefore, she wanted to be right back there in his face immediately on the heels of Sharon Roth's call.

She showered quickly, and while still in her robe went downstairs to the kitchen. A freshly brewed pot of coffee was waiting for her, courtesy of her Krups coffeemaker, which she had programmed the previous night before going to bed. She poured herself a mug, and prepared a bowl of instant oatmeal, which she heated in the microwave.

By six thirty she was on the road. She was not accustomed to traveling at this hour, and was surprised at the volume of traffic already clogging the New Jersey Turnpike. Nevertheless, she felt she had left herself enough time to be in place at the corner of Apple Ridge and Mountain View before seven thirty. She did not know when Alex's school bus picked her up, but she was pretty sure she would make it in time.

She rounded the corner onto Mountain View, and up ahead saw a young girl she recognized as the one who had gotten off the bus with Alex the day before. She did not, however, see Alex. Good. She had made it in time.

Stacy slowed and pulled alongside the curb just feet from where the girl waited. Being at the T-intersection with Apple Ridge, she was afforded a view of the Hellers' house not far down the block. She wondered whether Jody would accompany Alex to the bus, or whether Alex would come alone. That the other girl was there without her mother suggested that the neighborhood practice was to send the children on their own. Just as well, Stacy thought. All she was going to do was say hello as she had done the day before. She knew she had struck a raw nerve by talking to Alex then, and Alex would no doubt report this morning's encounter as well. A horrified Jody would complain to Scott, who would now be feeling control slipping away. Stacy wondered how long it would be before Scott realized that she was not going to just go away.

There came Alex now. Book bag once more slung over her shoulder, she was sauntering up the street by herself. As she neared the corner and noticed Stacy sitting in her car, Stacy could see a glimmer of recognition in the girl's eyes. Her mouth tightened, apparently when she realized who Stacy was, and she quickly looked away. *That means her mother told her to be careful of me. Good.*

"Good morning, Alex," Stacy called through her open window.

Alex glanced toward her, but turned quickly away.

"How are you this morning?" Stacy asked.

The girl stood motionless, this time not even looking toward Stacy.

"Did you tell your mother hello, like I asked?"

This time, Alex turned to her and nodded slightly. But then she moved closer to the other girl waiting for the bus, and turned away again.

"Good girl. Have a good day at school. Maybe I'll see you tomorrow."

Stacy saw the girl stiffen. She put the car in gear and drove off.

■   ■   ■

"Well it didn't work, did it?" It was more a statement of fact than a question.

"No, obviously not," Scott replied to his wife. Neither of them was in a very good mood.

Scott and Jody sat in their den. He on their black leather couch, and she on the matching love seat. It was eight fifteen, and just minutes ago they had put Alex to bed for the night. Ordinarily, they would now turn on the TV, and catch a mindless prime time network show. However, at dinner tonight, Alex had given them some disturbing information that they needed to discuss.

"Mommy, I saw that lady again this morning," she'd announced.

Jody had tightened her grip on her fork and glared at Scott.

With a little prompting, Alex had recounted the morning's events for her parents, ending with Stacy's suggestion that she might be back tomorrow.

"I don't like her," Alex said. "She gives me the creeps."

Scott jumped in before Jody could say anything. "Oh, sweetheart, you don't have to worry about her. I'm making sure she doesn't bother you or Mommy anymore." Scott knew he was in for an earful from Jody, but he didn't see any reason why Alex should hear it and become even more upset.

Jody took his cue, and said, "Ali, you're right to be careful when strangers talk to you. But don't you worry about tomorrow. I'll walk you to the bus and wait with you till it comes." She turned to Scott. "And in the meantime, Daddy will talk to Mrs. Altman again, and make sure that she leaves us alone."

In her trusting way, Alex seemed to accept this. They finished dinner, and afterward Jody and Alex read to each other for a bit. But after Alex was in bed, Jody made it clear to Scott that she wanted to talk to him about Stacy.

So, with Alex tucked safely away, Scott and Jody had retired to the den. "Well then, what are you going to do?" Jody asked, after Scott acknowledged that Sharon's call to Stacy's lawyer had clearly not warned her off.

"I'm not sure, I'm not sure," Scott said, frustration evident in his voice.

"For God's sake, Scott, this whole thing is ridiculous. The hell with this stupid principle you're so busy upholding. This has gotten out of hand. Just tell her what she wants to know. Your goddamn client deserves whatever she's going to dish out for him."

"Jody, not this again. We've gone through it how many times? I'm not fighting for principle, and I'm not fighting for my 'goddamn' client. I'm fighting for my license to practice law." He had raised his voice, and he paused for a moment to calm down. "I'm sorry. But don't you understand that it's not my decision to make? If it were a crime, and they could send me to jail, would you insist that I tell her?" He paused again, though he did not expect a response. "If it would help, think of it as a crime. They can't send me to jail, but they could disbar me. How would you suggest I earn a living then?"

Jody sat silently.

"Until a court tells me that I have to talk, I just can't. It's that simple."

"Damn it, Scott," Jody said. "That woman is harassing us, and frightening our daughter. That can't continue. You got us into this, and you better get us out. Fast."

Jody stood and went upstairs.

■   ■   ■

"You're walking me to the bus, aren't you?"

Jody stood at the kitchen counter, pouring herself a second cup of coffee. She turned to her daughter, who had looked up from her bowl of Corn Pops to pose the question.

"Honey, I told you not to worry. I'm going to go to the corner with you, and wait there with you until the bus comes." She took a sip from her mug. "And you know, there are some things that moms can do even better than lawyers. If Mrs. Altman is there, I'll tell her myself that she better leave you alone." She smiled at Alex.

"Thanks, Mom. She better listen."

"You're right, if she knows what's good for her." Jody tousled Alex's hair. "Now finish up and get ready, or else we'll be running for the bus instead of walking."

By the time Alex had finished her breakfast and loaded her book bag, it was 7:20. "See, I told you," Jody chided her daughter.

"Now we have to hurry." Just as well, though, Jody thought. If that woman was going to be at the corner, the less time she and Alex had to stand there, the better.

As Jody and Alex approached the corner, Jody's pulse quickened. There Stacy was, as promised. Her car was parked at the curb, just feet from where Alex's friend Melissa stood waiting for the bus. As they drew closer, Jody could make out Stacy sitting calmly at the wheel.

"There she is, Mom," Alex said, alarmed.

"Relax, Ali. Nothing's going to happen." Nevertheless, Jody took Alex's hand in hers.

Stacy was watching them as they approached. Since she was parked directly at the bus stop, the only way for Jody to avoid her would be to wait with Alex on the other side of the street. Jody was not about to let Stacy determine their movements like that. This was going to stop.

She grasped her daughter's hand firmly, and strode past Stacy's car. When they came abreast of the open window, Stacy smiled and greeted Alex. "Good morning, Alex," she said, ignoring Jody.

Alex stiffened, and tightened her grip on her mother's hand.

"Go over there and wait with Melissa," Jody told Alex. Alex hurried to her friend. Jody bent down to the open window.

"I don't know what your game is, or what you're trying to prove," she said through her teeth, "but stay away from my daughter."

Stacy returned Jody's gaze with a neutral expression on her face, but said nothing.

"Do you understand what I'm saying?" Jody asked. "Leave us alone. I will not allow you to terrorize my daughter."

Still, Stacy said nothing. She smiled and rolled up her window, both symbolically and physically blocking out Jody's demand. She fixed her gaze now on Alex, totally ignoring Jody.

Jody could do nothing but turn and walk to where her daughter stood, where they both waited until the bus came five minutes later.

■   ■   ■

"You don't understand," Jody shouted at her husband through the telephone. "The woman is dangerous!"

She had returned to the house just moments before, and now stood in the kitchen with the cordless telephone. Scott had left early for work that morning, and she had reached him on his cell phone.

"Okay, Jody, relax, and tell me again exactly what happened."

"Stop telling me to relax! You weren't there, and didn't see the look on her face. She totally ignored me, and just kept staring at Alex. I don't blame Alex for being scared. I am."

"I understand," Scott said. "I know it's upsetting, but I really don't think there's anything to worry about. Do you really think I'd allow you or Alex to be put in danger? She's just trying to psyche me out, that's all."

"Psyche you out?" Jody said. "Psyche *you* out? I can tell you she's psyching *me* out. And she's scaring our daughter."

"I'll talk to Sharon when I get to the office. Maybe she'll have an idea."

■ ■ ■

That afternoon, Jody made sure she was at the bus stop fifteen minutes before the bus was scheduled to arrive with Alex. Five minutes after Jody got there, Stacy appeared and parked at the same place she had earlier in the day. Jody felt herself trembling, but did her best to ignore the woman. The bus arrived, and Jody rushed to the curb to take Alex's hand when she stepped off.

"Let's go, Alex. Quickly."

It was Thursday afternoon, and the week had been a tense one. Stacy had confronted them every day so far, and Jody was becoming increasingly alarmed. That night, after Alex was in bed, Scott and Jody readdressed the issue. "All right," Scott said. "Here's what we're doing. We're going to ask Judge Adams for a protective order forbidding Stacy from coming within a hundred feet of you,

Alex, or me.

"The application for the order to show cause will be ready to file in court tomorrow. It will require Stacy to appear in court for a hearing to demonstrate why the judge shouldn't enter a protective order."

"Yeah," Jody said. "But how long before a hearing? And what about in the meantime? I don't want to go through another week like this."

"I know. Hopefully, the judge will schedule the hearing for Monday morning. But regardless of when the hearing is, when we present the order to show cause, we'll ask Judge Adams for an immediate temporary restraining order. If the judge grants us a TRO, Stacy will have to stay away from us until he decides what to do at the court hearing."

"I just wonder if she'll listen to a court order," Jody mused. "She's nuts."

CHAPTER 30

"Stacy, what in God's name have you been doing?"

"What are you talking about, Frank? What's wrong?"

It was just after two o'clock, and Stacy was getting ready to make the drive back up to Englewood Cliffs to be there in time for Alex's return from school. It was Friday afternoon, and Stacy had greeted Alex at least once every day that week. The round-trips each day were time-consuming and wearing, and she was beginning to wonder if she was wasting her time. She could tell that Jody was affected by her presence, but since Sharon had called O'Connor, and he in turn had called her, there had been no communication from the other side. She was starting to get discouraged. Why was Scott Heller so stubborn?

"I'm looking at a temporary restraining order forbidding you from coming within one hundred feet of the Hellers," O'Connor told her. "And we have to be in court first thing Monday morning to convince Judge Adams why he shouldn't make this temporary order permanent. According to Scott's and Jody's affidavits, you've been harassing them and terrorizing little Alex." Frank paused. "Stacy, this is serious. What's going on?"

Stacy's cheeks flushed. A restraining order! He thought he was going to use the system to beat her? She'd already decided that wasn't going to happen. When was he going to realize that?

"In simple terms, Frank, what does all this mean?"

"It means just what I said. The judge has ordered you to appear in court on Monday morning to demonstrate why he should not permanently order you to stay away from the Hellers. And until then, when he makes that decision, you are forbidden to go anywhere near them."

Stacy's mind was working. Two can play at the same game. How could she use the system?

"I want you to be very specific," she said to her lawyer. "Exactly what does this temporary order forbid me from doing?"

"I'll read it to you," O'Connor said. "It says 'Until further order of this court, it is hereby ordered that said Stacy Altman is enjoined and restrained from coming within one hundred feet of the Heller residence at 8 Apple Ridge Crescent, Englewood Cliffs, New Jersey; from coming within one hundred feet of Scott Heller, Jody Heller, and/or Alexandra Heller; and from telephoning the Heller residence.'"

"And what will happen on Monday morning in court?" Stacy asked.

"I told you. The judge will decide if he should make this prohibition permanent."

"No, I mean exactly what will happen? Will Scott be there? Will Jody and Alex? Do I have to be there?"

"Well, I don't know who besides Sharon Roth will be there on the Hellers' behalf. They're entitled to be there, but not required. They've already said what they want to in their affidavits. Now, you get to tell your side. It looks like we'll be working over the weekend, putting our submission together. The question is, what do we tell the judge? What's your defense?"

"Wait a minute," Stacy interrupted. "Slow down. What happens if we don't do anything?"

"You mean if we don't submit any opposition papers, and we don't show up?"

"Yeah. What then?"

O'Connor paused as he considered the question.

"Judge Adams would give the Hellers what they're asking for. He'd change the temporary restraining order into a permanent injunction."

"So, unless and until the judge changed that order, I just wouldn't be allowed to come within a hundred feet of them, or telephone their house, right?"

"That's right."

"If we don't show up, could the judge add any surprises? You know, order something in addition to that?"

"No," O'Connor answered. "He wouldn't be able to do anything else, without first giving you notice and an opportunity to be heard. Why? What are you thinking?"

"I don't want you to do anything."

"No opposition papers? No appearance Monday morning?"

"That's right. Ignore it."

O'Connor exhaled audibly.

"Stacy, I don't think that's wise. I never feel comfortable defaulting in any situation. First of all, you'd pretty much be admitting all the things they said you did. And it just doesn't look good in the eyes of the court. I'd rather see you submit a simple affidavit denying that you meant to harass them, but agreeing to keep your distance. Then at least you come across to the court as being reasonable."

"No," Stacy said. "I'm through playing the game. I mean, I'll let you do that appeal thing, because you've already started. But the system sucks, and I've discovered I'm being naive if I think I can influence the outcome by playing along. I'm telling you to ignore it."

"Now Stacy, you're not going to do anything foolish, are you?" O'Connor said. "The judge has entered an order, and if you disobey it there can be serious consequences."

"Oh, don't worry, Frank. I'm going to listen *exactly* to what the judge says. Now, I have to run. I have business to take care of."

Stacy glanced at the clock after she hung up the telephone. She had no intention of missing Alex's afternoon bus, but in light of what O'Connor had just told her, it was important to get to the bus stop early. She took care of one little thing first, and then she grabbed her car keys and headed out.

■   ■   ■

Stacy turned the corner onto Mountain View at three o'clock, twenty minutes before the bus was scheduled to arrive. Good, Jody had not yet gotten there, she observed. She parked her car in what had become her usual spot—just feet from where the bus would let Alex off. From the intersection, she glanced up Apple Ridge Crescent to make sure Jody was not on her way. There was no sign of her. She stepped over to where the bus would pull up to the curb, and turned to face up Mountain View Drive, from where she had just come. Taking measured steps, she counted as she walked along the sidewalk. Before leaving the house, she had seen that the tiles on her kitchen floor were each twelve inches on a side, and she had measured her gait. She was now pacing off what she estimated would be one hundred and fifteen feet from where the bus would stop.

Her car, she would leave. She was under a restraint, but not her automobile. When Jody and Alex arrived at the corner, Stacy would be in strict compliance with Judge Adams's order.

■   ■   ■

Jody had been relieved by Scott's telephone call, though she remained skeptical. Scott had told her that Judge Adams would hold a hearing on Monday morning, but that in the meantime, he had signed a temporary restraining order directing Stacy to stay away from them. "If she disobeys, she'll be in contempt of court, and the judge could put her in jail," Scott had said.

Relieved but skeptical. She had been there again this morning, before the order was entered, smug as ever. Jody really did think the woman had lost it. Would she ignore the judge's order? Jody almost found herself hoping she would. Let her go sit in jail for contempt of court. She couldn't bother them from there.

Jody looked at the kitchen clock, and saw that it was 3:10. Restraining order or not, she was not allowing Alex to walk to or from the bus alone. Time to go pick her up.

She neared the intersection, and her mouth dropped open. Stacy's car. *I knew it. She is nuts. She's defying the judge.*

Jody drew closer, and saw that Stacy was not, as usual, seated in the car. Nor was she standing at the bus stop. Now Jody was confused as well as concerned.

Then she saw her. About two houses up the block, standing there watching her. Startled, Jody drew in her breath, and quickly looked away. But her eyes were drawn back to look at this woman so obviously pained by her loss that she was driven to lurk about as she did. *No! I will not start to pity her. I just want her out of our lives.*

Jody's thoughts were interrupted by the sight of the approaching school bus, which had just turned onto Mountain View. On its way to the stop it would pass by Stacy, who had been staring at Jody, and who now turned to fix her gaze on the school bus. Stacy waved in the direction of the bus as it passed her. She then turned back to Jody, and even at this distance Jody could see the slight smile on her face.

More convinced than ever that the woman was dangerous, any fleeting sense of pity for her left Jody. The bus reached the curb, and Jody heard the doors opening. She rushed to retrieve Alex, and as she hurriedly started toward home, she glanced back over her shoulder.

Stacy was watching. And she was still smiling.

CHAPTER 31

Sharon stuck her head into Scott's office.

"Protective order's signed," she reported. "Come on into my office and I'll tell you about it."

Moments later, Scott was seated across from Sharon, who sat at her desk. She had handed him the two-page order that Judge Adams had signed earlier that morning, and when Scott finished reading it, he looked up.

"Great, but Jody called this morning to tell me that Stacy was there again today, hovering just outside the legal limit, like on Friday afternoon after the TRO was entered. So I guess having this order gives us some degree of protection, but it looks like she'll just continue to harass us from a distance."

"Well, we'll have to keep our eye on things, and maybe consider asking the judge to modify the order," Sharon suggested.

"We may well have to," Scott agreed. "But now, tell me what happened in court."

"For one thing, our application was unopposed. No opposition papers, and no appearance in court."

"Really?" Scott asked, eyebrows raised.

"Yeah. I was surprised, as was the judge," Sharon said. "But I did have a heads-up on it. O'Connor left a voice mail message for me early this morning, as a courtesy, just to let me know that no one would be appearing. I guess in retrospect, it's not that surprising. I mean, what could they have said in defense?"

"Then oral argument must have been pretty short and to the point," Scott observed.

"It was. The judge didn't have any other matters on for this morning, so he wasn't on the bench when I got there. When I checked in with the court clerk, he already knew that O'Connor would be a no-show. So he let the judge know I was there.

"Adams took the bench, and when we went on the record he asked if I had anything to add to our papers, which I didn't. He remarked for the record that Altman hadn't filed any opposition, and hadn't appeared, and indicated that he was granting the application. I handed up the proposed order, and he signed it. That was that."

"Good job," Scott said. "I'll fax a copy of this over to O'Connor right away. And then I want to call Jody and let her know. Now we'll see what good it does."

■   ■   ■

The clicking of computer keyboards filled the *Middlesex Herald* newsroom as reporters hurried to file their stories. Two televisions at one end of the room were turned on, volume muted. One was tuned in to CNN, and the other to News 12 New Jersey, a local cable news network. Mike Harrison sat at his desk, having just finished the feature he was working on. A few more taps of the keys and his work was electronically transmitted to his editor one floor above.

Earlier, he had made a note to himself to check in with Stacy Altman before the end of the day. He knew from the court records that Scott Heller had obtained a temporary restraining order on Friday, and that his application for a permanent one had been scheduled for today. A call to the docket clerk revealed that the application had been granted, unopposed. He clicked the mouse and brought Stacy's telephone number up on the screen.

"Mrs. Altman? Mike Harrison here. From the *Herald*. Remember?"

"Oh yes," Stacy replied. "You've written a few articles on what's happened."

"That's why I'm calling. I wanted to find out how you're doing," Harrison began. "I see that Judge Adams just entered a restraint against you, and want your comment on it. According to the court papers, you've been harassing the Hellers, but I didn't see any submission from you. I'd like to get your side of the story."

There was a momentary silence, as if Stacy was considering whether to respond to him, or just brush him off. Then Harrison heard her sigh.

"Oh, I guess there's no harm in talking to you," she said. "In fact, it'll probably help. I mean, the more people that know about what's going on, the better, as far as I'm concerned."

"Then why don't you tell me. Heller's court papers said you're stalking his family. What's that all about?"

"I wouldn't quite put it that way. But I won't deny I've been in his face as much as possible." She told him of her visits to the Hellers' house, and her vigil at Alex's bus stop. "I don't know how else to get to him. It infuriates me that he won't step back and see how wrong it is, what he's doing. I guess I sound pretty crazy, don't I?" she asked.

Harrison paused only slightly. "No, Mrs. Altman," he replied. "Not crazy. Frustrated. And rightfully so, as far as I'm concerned. So, if you can't talk to Heller directly now, what are you going to do?" Harrison asked.

"I haven't thrown in the towel yet," Stacy responded. She told the reporter how, since the restraining order provided that she could not come within one hundred feet of the Hellers, she had paced off the forbidden distance, and taken to coming as close to Alex Heller's bus stop as was legally permissible. "I'm going to continue to do that. They have to know that I'm here to stay. But I hate the fact that I have to modify my behavior because some judge says I do...I have half a mind to just thumb my nose at the whole lot of them and march right up to Heller's front door, restraining order or not."

Mike Harrison considered what Stacy Altman was telling him. He hadn't really given much thought to where he was going with the story—stories like this usually determined their own course, and he just followed. But as a journalist—he preferred that designation to "reporter"—he could occasionally guide the story along a desired path, and could even jump-start a story that might have stalled along the way. Not that he ever went overboard to the extent of creating news where it didn't already exist. He did try hard not to cross that line. Rather, as a champion of the public's "right to know," he sometimes simply had to take a more proactive role to make sure that the story's participants realized the importance of bringing their tale, with all its details, to press.

So far, Harrison had been satisfied with how this particular drama was unfolding. Little Ben's death had the local residents pretty stirred up. News that someone knew who was responsible, but refused to talk, ensured that interest in the story continued. The revelation that it was a lawyer who knew, and that he was relying on some legal technicality—that was a bonus. What better scoundrel than an attorney hiding behind a technicality? Even better, with a judge taking the lawyer's side and upholding the attorney-client privilege, the system could be blamed as well.

And now the mother was being told that not only did the system refuse to do anything to help her, but she herself was forbidden from taking action.

All in all, he would have preferred the judge to have gone the other way—he felt for the Altmans, and would have been happy to see Scott Heller forced to give up his client. And the news story would have progressed from there with no problem. On the other hand, though, another example of society's protecting the criminal instead of the victim was something the people always loved to hate, and loved to read about.

But what was going to happen next? Judge Adams had ruled that Heller did not have to talk, and Mrs. Altman was prohibited from helping herself. If Mrs. Altman simply accepted that determination, the story would peter out. He could write a wrap-up berating the system, and the boy's mother would no doubt agree to an interview, but that would be the end of it. On the other hand, if Mrs. Altman took on the system, and pressed ahead, then there was much more.

He hoped things wouldn't stall here. Maybe Mrs. Altman needed some encouragement.

"Would you really consider doing something like that? Violate the restraint" he asked.

"Oh, I don't know. My lawyer told me that if I do, I'd be in contempt of court and could be thrown in jail. But I'm starting to think that that would be a small price to pay if it'll help me get what I'm after."

Harrison paused. "Well, you know, it's not that likely that the judge would actually throw you in jail. He'd probably just give you a warning. At least, in my experience that's what I've seen in cases like this." Harrison didn't really have experience in "cases like this," and didn't know if what he was saying was accurate, but if he was going to have anything to write about, Stacy was going to have to take some action.

"One thing is for sure," Stacy declared. "I'm not giving up. I don't know exactly how, but I am going to find out who killed my son."

Stacy promised to keep in touch, and hung up.

■   ■   ■

Shortly after her telephone call with Harrison, Stacy was on the road to meet Alex's afternoon bus. She mulled over in her mind the conversation she had just had with the reporter. She hadn't really been serious when she'd said she would consider violating the court order, but Harrison's comments had made her stop and think. She didn't have much confidence that her appeal would be successful, and she wasn't getting very far on her own with Heller.

In fact, he'd won the first round by getting Judge Adams to sign the restraint. Harrison seemed interested in helping her—he'd told her that as soon as there was something to write about he would do a follow-up story.

She was frightened about the prospect of being sent to jail if she defied the court order, but she thought her lawyer was exaggerating that possibility. He was probably using that as a scare tactic for what he thought was her own good. For her part, she tended to agree with Harrison's assessment—the judge would probably make a big show of things, and warn her that he meant business. But in the meantime, she might be able to get some publicity. Mother seeking justice for her slain son, taking on the system.

The more she thought about it, the more sense it made.

By the time she finished her musing, she was rounding the corner onto Mountain View Drive. Up ahead at the bus stop, she saw Jody already waiting. In that instant, she made up her mind.

Instead of keeping the distance required by the retraining order, she continued right on until she was abreast of Jody. She pulled up to the curb, turned off the motor, and took a deep breath. She was about to willfully violate a court order, and she knew that the Hellers would seek whatever remedies were available under the law. She wondered what she was setting in motion. The image of Ben, in the driveway that last morning as she pulled away in her car, crept into her mind. She held up her head and got out of the car. She strode over to Jody, who appeared both startled and frightened.

"You're not supposed to be here," was all Jody could manage.

"Not supposed to be here?" Stacy repeated. "There are a lot of things that are not supposed to be. My son is not supposed to be in a wooden box. Your husband is not supposed to be protecting a child-killer. The court is not supposed to be more concerned about the rights of some piece of garbage than it is with justice. So don't lecture me on what's not supposed to be."

Jody's expression hardened. She reached into the back pocket of her jeans and retrieved a piece of paper which she unfolded and held out to Stacy.

"Mrs. Altman, this is a copy of an order signed by Judge Adams this morning."

Stacy made no move to accept the document. "I know about the order."

"Then you know that Judge Adams has forbidden you to be here. So I suggest you leave immediately, or I'll call the police."

"Yes, why don't you do that?"

Jody faltered.

"What's the matter?" Stacy asked. "Oh…cell phone must be sitting on the kitchen counter. Why not run home and call from there? Alex's bus will be here any minute, but I'll be glad to walk her home so she's not alone. Children shouldn't be left alone."

Jody's fists clenched at her side. "Don't you dare threaten my daughter," she said with a stony stare. "I don't care what you've been through—it doesn't give you the right to take it out on my family."

"It seems that you and your family are good at pointing out what's 'supposed to be' and what's 'right,' but until your husband starts *doing* what he's supposed to and *doing* what's right, I'm not interested in listening. So save it."

Stacy gestured to the court order that was still in Jody's hand. "No piece of paper any judge signs is going to stop me. But all your husband has to do is tell me who ran down my son, and you'll never hear from me again."

Jody folded the order and put it back in her pocket. "I'm sorry it will come to this, Mrs. Altman," she said. "But you're not leaving me any choice. I know a bit about how the system works, and I'll make sure you're punished for contempt of court."

Jody turned from Stacy and did her best to ignore her in the remaining minutes until Alex's bus arrived.

■   ■   ■

"I can't believe you did this. It's true what she says in here?"

Stacy sat in one of the armchairs in Frank O'Connor's office, across the desk from her attorney.

The Hellers had wasted no time in seeking the court's intervention. Stacy had confronted Jody at the bus stop only yesterday, and at two o'clock this afternoon she had received a telephone call from O'Connor, who insisted that she come see him at once. Sharon Roth had faxed him an Order to Show Cause which scheduled a hearing for the following morning to determine whether Stacy should be held in criminal contempt of court.

"This is very serious," O'Connor had told her over the telephone. "Do you have any idea what Judge Adams's reaction is going to be when he sees this?" He had sounded extremely upset, and even a bit angry, as if it were he, not Stacy, who had been accused of wrongdoing.

On her drive back from Alex's bus stop the previous afternoon, Stacy had contemplated what she had done. She had broken the law. But she didn't consider her transgression to be in the same class as what she viewed as "real" illegalities—like robbing a bank. One reason for that was that bank robbery, as were most other crimes, was morally wrong. What she had done was, in the truest sense, justified. In fact, she had thought, civil disobedience—the purposeful disregard of a rule of law in order to protest—played an important role in society. Besides, she wasn't hurting anyone.

Oh, she realized that she was, in some way, invading the Hellers' privacy. But it was warranted by the circumstances. You could even say they deserved it because of Scott's stubborn refusal to do the right thing.

Contempt of court. Jody had threatened her with that at the bus stop. Stacy had turned the phrase over in her mind, and realized that she couldn't have said it better herself. If that was what she was to be charged with, then maybe the charge was appropriate.

These reflections during her car ride home yesterday had led her to an important decision—she was discharging Frank. She no longer wanted a lawyer. If she intended by her actions to protest the hypocrisy of the legal system in preferring some killer's rights over Ben's and hers, then she herself would be hypocritical hiding behind some lawyer as an advocate.

"Oh, Frank," Stacy said. "Do you really think that I care about a judge's reaction at this point?"

"Stacy, this is serious," Frank repeated. "It's contempt of court."

"This all reminds me of something Mae West supposedly said once," Stacy said. "I forget what she did, but a judge said to her, 'Madam, are you trying to show contempt for this court?' and she replied in that voice we all know so well, 'No, Your Honor, I was doing my best to hide it.' You're damn right I have contempt for that court. But I don't see any reason to hide it."

"But Stacy," Frank said. "You're not giving me much to work with here. I'm not sure what I'll be able to do for you at tomorrow's hearing."

"Well, that brings me to the next point. I'm going to do this on my own. I appreciate all you've done for me till now, but from here on in, I'm going to represent myself."

Frank shifted in his seat. "I don't think that's a very good idea," he said. "You're obviously emotional about this, and that doesn't make for clear thinking. You can find yourself in a lot of hot water. Maybe you want to think about this."

"I've already given it a lot of thought," Stacy told him, "and I've made up my mind. No matter what you do for me, no matter how brilliant your appeal to the Appellate Division is, the courts are going to side with Heller. I've accepted the fact that I'm not going to win playing by the rules. So I'll just have to do it my way."

Frank grimaced. "I don't know about this, Stacy," he said. "I don't think you're making a very wise decision."

"Look, Frank, if you have to cover yourself for the all- important 'record,' write me a letter telling me that I'm acting against your advice. Hell, I'll even countersign the damn thing. But you're not going to change my mind," she insisted. "And, tomorrow, I want you to withdraw my appeal. There's no sense clogging up the court system with that loser. Anyway, the judges have more important things to do. Like coddling some rapist, or making sure some death row inmate isn't being deprived of his right to watch television."

Frank looked uneasy. "Well, I can't force you to keep me on. Just be careful. And if you change your mind, I'm here."

The lawyer spent the next twenty minutes reviewing the Hellers' contempt application with Stacy, and explaining to her the procedures for the motion the following morning. Stacy stayed and listened, but only at Frank's insistence. Her frame of mind was such that she was willing to just let the chips fall where they might. But she remained and allowed her now-former lawyer to discharge this one last duty to her.

"Good luck tomorrow," Frank said as he walked her to the door. "And remember, if you change your mind, or if you need me, call."

CHAPTER 32

tacy woke the next morning more than just a little nervous. Court was not until ten, and it was only seven thirty, so after showering she forced herself to have a light breakfast. Then, back upstairs in her room, she stood in front of her open closet pondering what to wear.

At first, she considered dressing casually, but then had second thoughts. Maybe Mae West hadn't been totally off the mark in at least trying to hide her contempt for the court. For all her brave talk about not caring, Stacy was growing fearful about what she had set in motion. She decided that offending the judge by dressing inappropriately would be pushing it.

She had been out of the workforce for so long that she had no business suits. And most of her more formal wear was more appropriate for dinner or the theater than for a court appearance. Finally, she settled on a navy blue skirt that came just below the knee, and found a white silk blouse to go with it. As close to business attire as she could find.

When she had dressed, she went to the kitchen and poured herself a second cup of coffee. Despite her determination not to take this morning's proceedings too seriously, she sat down at the table and reviewed the Hellers' motion papers once more. She had decided that she was not going to say anything in her defense, but was simply going to respond to whatever Judge Adams asked of her.

At nine o'clock it was time to go. Stacy shut off the coffeemaker, gathered the motion papers, her purse, and her keys, and left for the half-hour drive to New Brunswick.

Frank had explained to her that today would not be a regular motion day, so the courtroom was not likely to be crowded like the last time they'd been there seeking to compel Heller to testify. Instead of waiting through a calendar call of fifty or so motions, Frank had told her to expect that her case would be the only one scheduled for ten o'clock, and that the matter would be heard promptly at that time.

At 9:35, Stacy joined the line of people waiting to pass through the metal detector at the security checkpoint just inside the entrance to the courthouse. Once through, she proceeded directly to the elevator, remembering from her last visit that Judge Adams was on the fourth floor. Upon exiting the elevator, she made her way to the courtroom. Another twinge of uneasiness came over her as she opened the door and walked in.

To her relief, the courtroom was empty, save for a young man seated at a desk in the front corner of the room. The prospect of facing the judge in front of a courtroom filled with people had not been appealing to her. The clerk looked up as Stacy entered.

"Are you here on the Heller Order to Show Cause?" he asked pleasantly.

"Yes, I am," Stacy replied. "I'm Stacy Altman."

The man made a notation on the sheet in front of him. "Ms. Roth, who represents the Hellers, hasn't checked in yet. Is your attorney here?"

"I don't have an attorney anymore," Stacy said. "I'll be representing myself."

The clerk raised his eyebrows. "I don't see any opposition papers in the file," he added. "Do you have anything to submit now?"

"No sir."

"All right," said the clerk. "You can have a seat until Ms. Roth arrives. In the meantime, I'll let the judge know that you're appearing *pro se*."

Stacy looked at him quizzically.

"Without an attorney," explained the man. He rose and exited through a door that apparently led to the judge's chambers.

Moments later, the courtroom door opened and Sharon Roth walked in. She regarded Stacy only in passing, as her eyes surveyed the empty courtroom.

"Good morning, Mrs. Altman," she finally said in a formal tone. "Is Mr. O'Connor here yet?"

"Mr. O'Connor doesn't represent me anymore. I'm appearing *pro se*. Without an attorney," Stacy explained.

"Yes, I know what *pro se* means," Sharon said. "And I have to say I'm surprised," she continued. "This is a pretty serious matter to be handling yourself. But, it's your choice." She shrugged indifferently and turned away.

A moment later, the clerk reappeared from Judge Adams's chambers. "Oh, Ms. Roth," he said upon seeing Sharon. "Everybody's ready?" The man looked from Sharon to Stacy, and back to Sharon.

"I am," Sharon said, and then looked at Stacy, who simply nodded.

"Very well. Why don't you set up at counsel table, and I'll let the judge know you're ready."

Not exactly sure what to do, Stacy watched Sharon proceed through the swinging gate on the railing that separated the public seating area from the front of the courtroom, where the two counsel tables were arranged before the judge's bench. Sharon sat at one of the tables and took what appeared to be a copy of her motion papers from her briefcase, and Stacy passed through the gate and seated herself at the other table. Just as she did so, the door to the judge's chambers opened, and the clerk rapped sharply on the doorjamb three times.

"All rise," he said in a strong voice. "Court is now in session. The Honorable Lawrence Adams presiding."

The judge entered, climbed the two stairs leading up to his

bench, and addressed Sharon and Stacy. "Good morning. Please be seated." He reached into his pocket and retrieved his reading glasses. Then he nodded to his clerk, who pressed a button on the tape recorder on her desk.

"The matter before the Court is *Altman vs. John Doe*. Nonparties Scott Heller and Jody Heller have brought on an Order to Show Cause to adjudicate Stacy Altman in contempt of court for failing to abide by a restraining order previously entered in the case forbidding her from coming within one hundred feet of any member of the Heller family."

The judge looked up at Stacy and Sharon. "I note for the record that Sharon Roth is appearing for the Heller family, and that Stacy Altman is appearing *pro se*. I note also that the Court has received no opposition papers from Mrs. Altman. Am I correct, Mrs. Altman, that you are submitting no opposition?"

Stacy hesitated. "No, Your Honor," she said. "I mean, yes, Your Honor, you're correct."

Judge Adams looked surprised. "Very well then, we'll proceed," he continued. "I've read your papers, Ms. Roth," he said, turning to Sharon. "They're quite clear, and they make out a *prima facie* showing of the entry of a valid order, and the willful disobedience by Mrs. Altman of that order. Do you have anything to add to those papers?"

Sharon rose. "Only to reiterate, Your Honor, that Alex Heller is absolutely terrified of Mrs. Altman, as is Mrs. Heller. Mrs. Altman has no legitimate reason to have any contact with any member of the Heller household, and she certainly has no legitimate reason to violate this Court's clear and unambiguous order."

Sharon took her seat, and Judge Adams turned to Stacy.

"Mrs. Altman, on Monday, September 25, I entered an order restraining you from, among other things, coming within one hundred feet of any member of the Heller household. You've seen that order?"

"Yes, Your Honor."

"Mrs. Altman. Please stand when you address the court," the

judge interjected, not all too pleasantly.

Stacy rose, flustered. "I'm sorry, Your Honor."

"You've seen a copy of the order?" Judge Adams repeated.

"Yes sir."

"When did you first learn of it?"

"On Monday afternoon, Your Honor."

"How?"

"My attorney told me about it on the phone."

"And yesterday, did you go to Alex Heller's school bus stop, as described in the motion papers?"

"Uh, yes sir."

"And did you come within one hundred feet of Mrs. Heller and her daughter?"

"Yes."

"In fact, you walked right up to Mrs. Heller?"

"Yes."

The judge looked down at the papers in front of him. "And did you say to her, 'No piece of paper any judge signs is going to stop me'?"

Stacy shifted uneasily and remained silent.

"Did you?"

"Yes sir," she responded softly.

"And you knew at the time you approached Mrs. Heller that your actions were in violation of my order, did you not?"

"Uh, yes sir," came the quiet response.

"Well, Mrs. Altman, do you have any explanation? Can you give me a reason why I should not hold you in contempt of court?"

Suddenly, this whole thing did not seem to Stacy to be the good idea it had the day before. Her defiance of the judge, or her decision to face him without Frank. She looked down at the table and rifled through her copy of Sharon's motion papers, the only thing she had brought with her, as if the answer to Judge Adams's question might be there.

"Well, Mrs. Altman?" the judge insisted.

"Your Honor," Stacy began, finally finding her voice. "I lost my son. Mr. Heller knows who killed him. I'm only trying to find out who's responsible."

Judge Adams's demeanor grew even sterner. "Mrs. Altman, I'm well aware of the circumstances that bring you here. And I have the utmost sympathy for you with regard to your loss. But if you think for one minute that that entitles you to ignore a direct order of this court, and as a result terrorize a young child and her family, you are mistaken. You have brought your efforts to find the responsible person to this court, in the lawsuit you began. I made a ruling that the attorney-client privilege prevents Mr. Heller from speaking, and I understand that you have appealed that ruling to the Appellate Division. You must await the Appellate Division's decision. You cannot take matters into your own hands. You must follow the rule of law.

"Ordinarily in a case like this, I would simply warn you, and assume that you would recognize that I mean business, and give you a chance to abide by my order. But I believe that there are extenuating circumstances in this case. First, the well-being of a nine-year-old girl is at issue. Alex Heller is afraid to leave her mother's side because of you.

"Second, you have given me no reason to believe that you would heed my warning. You said as much directly to Mrs. Heller. If 'no piece of paper any judge signs' is going to stop you, then I'm afraid I must find another way. I can impose a fine upon you, but I'm not confident that that would get the message across to you. And I don't think it would do much to ease Alex's or her mother's fears.

"I'm afraid you've left me no choice but to order your arrest. I sentence you to three days in the county facility. That should give you ample time to consider how to conduct yourself in the future."

Stacy had taken her seat. She now grew faint as she heard the judge's pronouncement. Jail? Three days? This is not what was supposed to happen.

The judge continued. "It is now 10:20. I will allow you until three this afternoon to make whatever arrangements you need before surrendering to the sheriff's office. There will be serious consequences if you fail to report to the sheriff at that time. Do I have your word that you will surrender at three o'clock?"

"But, Your Honor," Stacy said.

"No buts, Mrs. Altman. I can easily have you taken into custody right now. Do I have your word you will report to the sheriff at three o'clock this afternoon?"

Tears welled up in Stacy's eyes. "Yes."

"Good," the judge said. He beckoned to the court officer, who had been silently observing the proceedings from his post at the front of the courtroom. "Please tell Mrs. Altman where, and to whom, she should report this afternoon." Judge Adams returned his attention to Stacy and Sharon.

"That's all." He stood.

"All rise," said the clerk, as he too jumped to his feet.

The judge descended from the bench and left the courtroom.

Stacy was too stunned to respond to the clerk's call to rise, and Judge Adams was through the door to his chambers before she was able to jump to her feet. She avoided Sharon, and shuffled over to the court officer, head lowered and eyes looking down at the floor.

"I'm sorry, ma'am," he said to her. "I've read about what happened to your son. I have a little boy at home, too."

Stacy looked up at him, eyes brimming with tears, but she said nothing.

"Anyway, I've written out the instructions. We have an office on the first floor of this building. The deputy in charge during that shift is Bobby Luberto. By three o'clock, all the paperwork will be down there, but I'll make sure I talk with Bobby before then."

He handed the sheet of instructions to Stacy. "You take care now," he added.

Stacy took the paper from him and cast a glance over at the counsel table. Sharon had left, and was probably somewhere on her cell phone already, gloating to Scott about their victory.

Outside the courtroom door, Stacy succumbed fully to the tears, as frustration and fear overcame her. She wondered how she had lost control of the situation, but quickly realized she had never had any. It was not within her power to do anything. The driver of that car could hide, his lawyer could protect him, and the court could punish her for doing what any mother would do for her son. What a nightmare, to be so out of control. And now she was afraid of what was ahead of her. Jail! What would that be like? What kind of people would she encounter? How would she pass the time? Three whole days.

Lawyers huddling with their clients in the hallway all but ignored the sobbing woman, acknowledging her only to the extent of glancing in her direction and shuffling a few feet away. Stacy found the elevator, jabbed the down button, and hoped that the next car would be an empty one. The door slid open and Stacy stepped into a cab with one other woman who, like the others that Stacy had passed in the hallway, looked at her curiously and then ignored her.

A few moments later, Stacy sat at the wheel of her car, key in the ignition but engine idle. Her frustration and fear gave way to anger and outrage. She would not let them stop her. But what could she do? In a little less than five hours, she was going to jail, and would spend the next three days there.

She started the car, shifted into gear, and pulled out of the parking lot. She made her way onto Route 18, and then onto the New Jersey Turnpike north toward her home. She had stopped crying. A few minutes later she neared her exit, but with hardly a thought she sped past it, continuing north. She found herself drawn toward Englewood Cliffs.

Toward the Hellers' house.

CHAPTER 33

"So, cowboy, what has your cyber-sleuth come up with on the e-mail address?"

"Well, he's made *some* progress, but nothing definitive yet."

Win had caught Scott on his way out to lunch. He had planned to catch a quick bite with his associate, Stefanie, but when he'd heard that Win was on the phone, he'd sent her off without him.

"How so? I'm confounded by all this techno-magic. Me, I still can't understand how my phone knows how to connect to your phone when I punch in your number, never mind how one computer in one part of the world can actually hook up with a specific one continents away. I think it's witchcraft, and anyone who can actually make it happen should be burned at the stake."

"Yeah, Win, that attitude's easy to understand coming from a barbarian like you with a twelfth-century mentality. Have you broken down yet and gotten a photocopier for your office, or do you still have a scribe reproducing all of your stuff by hand?"

"Mimeograph. That's as far as I've gotten. Little letters, cut out in a stencil, and I can see how the ink goes through the little holes onto the paper. That I can comprehend...But tell me—what's your wizard come up with?"

"It's really pretty fascinating. Try to follow. When you send an e-mail, it actually goes through a number of different computers before it reaches you. Those computers are called 'servers.' Now, every e-mail contains a header, which is basically a road map leading from the sender's computer to yours. Every server that the message passes through adds an entry to the header. What you have to do is look at the header, and follow the map in reverse direction back to the source."

"Well, that sounds easy, even to a simpleton like me. I used a map once."

"Ah, but it's not always as simple as that. It's easy enough to find the e-mail header—it's usually not visible when you download your message, but depending on what program you use, it just takes a couple of mouse clicks to bring it up. The entries will look something like 'Received from blah-blah at such-and-such time.' It's not too hard to find the header entry that identifies the source computer—each server that adds information to the header adds it to the top line, so you just look down the list till you find the last 'Received from' line, which is actually the first.

"Every computer that's connected to the Internet has something called an 'IP address.' Stands for 'Internet Protocol.' Think of it as the computer's telephone number. The computer that the message was first received from will be identified by its IP address. Find out who the IP address belongs to, and you have your sender."

"So, you've made progress, but 'nothing definitive.' What's the problem?"

"To begin with, my guy tells me that there are ways to alter what the headers will show. It's called 'spoofing.' But it takes someone who's pretty sophisticated to do that, and I'm hoping that this client wasn't thinking like that when he sent the e-mail.

"The other thing is the IP address. Assuming the header shows the right IP address, the trick is to find the computer that has that address. There are two kinds of IP addresses—static and dynamic. When you have a permanent Internet hookup, you can get a static IP address. It's yours, and yours alone, all of the time. But most people connect to the Net only periodically, and each time they connect, they get a different IP address. Their Internet service provider has a block of addresses assigned to it, and when individual customers connect, the provider's server assigns the computer an address. You keep that address for as long as you're connected, but when you disconnect, that address goes back into the pool. Someone else connecting after that might get that address. And the next time you connect, you'll probably get a different address."

"Kind of like getting a new phone number each time you pick up the phone to make a call?"

"Exactly. Now, the headers on every e-mail you send out during a particular session will show the same IP address, but e-mails sent during different sessions may show different IP addresses."

"Well, static *or* dynamic, how do you find out whose address it is? I know there are reverse directories for telephones—look up a phone number, and find out whose it is. Anything like that for IP addresses?"

"Yes and no. It's pretty easy to trace an IP address online, but usually it'll just lead to the Internet service provider. You then need to find out from the provider which of its customers that address was assigned to.

"The problem there is twofold. First, the provider usually won't talk to you. You usually have to subpoena the information. Second, if the address was dynamically assigned, you've got to hope the provider still has a record of who had what address when. In my case, the e-mail I got from the client is nearly three months old, and it's likely that the IP address was dynamic. I have to hope that the provider still has records."

"So you've gotten as far as finding out who the provider is?"

"That's where we are. Luckily, I don't think I'll have to go the subpoena route. My guy is a real geek, and knows a lot of people in this area. He seems to think he'll be able to find someone who'll get him access to the records. The big question is whether the records will have the information we need."

"Well, bunky, it sounds like you have things under control."

"As much as I can hope for right now. My guy is digging around for more info."

"Okay then," Win said. "Now you got me curious. Let me know if you turn up anything else. I want to see you find this guy. I don't know why, but I feel kind of responsible, him using my name with you and all. Call me when you hear."

"Will do, Win. And stop pretending you're so clueless about computers. You somehow manage to e-mail me all the dirty jokes you get. My joke folder runneth over."

CHAPTER 34

Stacy drove north, toward the Hellers' house. She'd already been forbidden by the court to go anywhere near there, and held in contempt for ignoring the order. But it was important that they see she was not giving up. She was already going to jail for three days. What could the judge do? Add another day? She had come to realize that she had made a commitment that was bigger than a few days in jail.

She pulled into the Hellers' driveway without hesitating. She would catch Jody completely off guard—by now the Heller woman was sure to have heard of the penalty Judge Adams had imposed, and she would never expect Stacy under these circumstances.

The street was quiet, and Stacy saw no one around. There was no car in the driveway, and peering in through the garage door window, she saw that that was empty. Stacy went to the front door and rang the bell, though she now realized that there was probably no one home. A moment later she rang again, but no one answered.

She decided to look around. A stone walkway alongside the garage led to a gate in a six-foot-high wooden fence surrounding the backyard. Luckily, though the gate was latched, it was not locked. Stacy reached up and let herself in, and quickly glanced around the yard to assure herself that no one was there. She confirmed that she was alone, and closed the gate behind her.

Before venturing further into the yard, Stacy surveyed the scene. From the gate, the stone walkway curved to the right, along the back of the house, to a redwood deck that was reached by three wooden steps. A wooden railing surrounded the deck, and the railing was adorned with boxes brimming with colorful flowers. In the center of the deck stood a combination wet bar, grill, and food preparation area, and in one corner was a round, glass-topped table ringed by four wrought iron chairs and topped by a white umbrella. A bench was built into the entire length of the railing around the deck.

Another set of wooden stairs led from the back of the deck down to a walkway connecting to a small concrete patio at one corner of a swimming pool. A table stood on the patio, surrounded by four more chairs, all of white resin. A concrete walkway, about five feet wide, led around the perimeter of the pool. The area behind the pool was beautifully landscaped, and Stacy presumed that the shrubbery hid the pool's filter and heater from view. The rest of the yard was covered by a lush, green lawn.

Stacy climbed the stairs to the deck, and walked past the food preparation area to a sliding glass door. The vertical blinds were drawn open, and cupping her hands to shield the sun's glare, she put her nose to the glass to peek in. The door led to a breakfast nook adjoining a bright, open kitchen. Without even thinking, Stacy tried sliding the door, and she was shocked when it glided smoothly open.

She hesitated for a moment, and glanced over her shoulder around the yard. It did not appear that any of the neighboring houses had a view of the Hellers' deck. Stacy drew a deep breath and stepped over the threshold. As she slid the door closed, she became aware of how calm she was under the circumstances. She had just broken into someone's house, yet except for her quickened pulse she felt rather composed. Almost as if she had a right to be here. In a way, she thought, I do have a right. Scott Heller has invaded my life. Maybe not physically, as I'm now entering his, she thought.

But no less really. His actions have created consequences for me. Foreseeable consequences that he could control if he wished. Yet he's chosen to act as if he's an island unto himself, unconcerned with the effect he has on others. Doesn't that justify dealing with him in a special way?

She moved quickly out of the kitchen, through an adjoining formal dining room, and into a foyer by the front door. On the other side of the foyer was a living room. Behind her, directly across from the front door, was the staircase. She didn't expect to find anything—indeed she wasn't looking for anything. It's not as if she thought Scott would have any papers pertaining to his client here at the house. She simply wanted to see where he lived. Violate his privacy. Even though she intended to leave no trace of her visit, so he'd never even know she had been there.

Once at the top of the stairs, she was drawn to Alex's room.

■　　■　　■

Pete Baxter sat with his feet propped on his desk, leaning back in his chair. There was never much to keep him busy, so he got a lot of reading done. He was on a Douglas Adams kick now, and had recently finished *The Hitchhiker's Guide to the Galaxy* and *The Restaurant at the End of the Universe*. Now, he was halfway through *Dirk Gently's Holistic Detective Agency*. He was the only one at Slocum Security this morning. Greg Burnham, their salesman, was on the road, and Lou Tarantino, their technician, was on a service call.

The telephone rang, and Pete picked it up on the first ring. There was a momentary pause before a computerized voice began.

"There has been an unauthorized entry at the Heller residence at 8 Apple Ridge Crescent, Englewood Cliffs. The time was eleven forty-five a.m. on September 27. Please notify the authorities."

Pete sighed. Probably another false alarm. Clients were always forgetting to disarm their systems. They'd come in with an armload of groceries, go out to the car for more, and forget to punch in their security code in the meantime. Or they'd give a house key to a friend, and forget to instruct him in how to shut off the alarm. If the system wasn't disarmed within sixty seconds of a breach, the automatic dialer called Slocum and reported the event. Pete then had to first notify the appropriate police department, and next telephone the client at whatever contact number he had in his database. Nine times out of ten, though, it was a false alarm. In fact, within seconds of receiving the initial call, an embarrassed homeowner usually telephoned, reporting that he or she had simply forgotten to shut off the system. The client then had to repeat a security password to ensure that everything was copacetic so Pete could close the incident.

But the rule was that immediately upon receiving first notification, the police were to be called. If the police responded and it turned out to be a false alarm, the homeowner was subject to a municipal fine. But that was the homeowner's problem. Slocum Security would have done its job.

Baxter tapped a few keys on his computer, and brought up the telephone number of the Englewood Cliffs police department. He identified himself, and reported an alarm at 8 Apple Ridge Crescent. The desk sergeant on the other end of the line repeated the information back to him, thanked him, and hung up.

A few more taps on the keyboard, and he found the client's contact number in New York City. He placed his call, recorded the entire incident in the computer log, and went back to Douglas Adams.

■   ■   ■

Stacy sat on Alex's bed. On entering the room, she had briefly surveyed it, noting the pale yellow walls with the border of colorful stars near the ceiling. The walls were adorned with framed pictures of various Disney heroines—classics like Cinderella, Snow White, and Sleeping Beauty, and contemporaries like Belle from *Beauty and the Beast*, and Ariel from *The Little Mermaid*. Even Nala, the lioness from *The Lion King*.

The girl's bed was of brass, with a white bedspread and white dust ruffle. Next to it stood a dresser atop which were some framed photographs. Alex, apparently at a dance recital. Alex in a ski suit on a bunny slope. And family pictures. One of Scott, Jody, and Alex on Main Street in Disney World, one of the three on the deck of a cruise ship, and a more formal shot of the family from a studio sitting.

Stacy rose from the bed and moved toward the dresser. She absently picked up the Disney World photo. Ben had never been to Disney World. She sat back down on the bed as her eyes brimmed with tears.

She was jolted to attention by the sound of footsteps coming from downstairs. She leaped to her feet and peeked out of Alex's window, which looked out over the street. She gasped in horror at what she saw. A police car!

Stacy dropped the picture on the floor and ran toward the door leading to the hallway, where she collided with a policeman, gun drawn.

■   ■   ■

"Jesus, Stacy," Frank O'Connor said to her across the table. "What the hell were you thinking?"

The two sat in a bare consultation room adjoining a courtroom in the Bergen County Courthouse in Hackensack. Stacy had been taken from the Hellers' house, handcuffed, and transported to the Englewood Cliffs police station in the patrol car. Once there, she had given in to her great embarrassment and telephoned Frank to tell him what had happened. "I guess you're rehired," she had said to him. She was thankful that he had not lectured her, at least not then, and had simply told her to keep quiet and sit tight. She had been taken to a holding cell, and about a half hour later one of the officers told her that she was being brought before a judge at the county courthouse, and that her lawyer would meet her there.

Stacy found it difficult to meet Frank's eyes, and she sat staring down at the table that separated them.

"Frank," she said glumly. "I appreciated that you didn't lecture me over the phone, and I hope you won't now."

"Right," Frank said, suddenly all business.

"Your situation is not good. It's two thirty now, and you're due to report to the Middlesex County Sheriff to start your three-day contempt sentence in a half hour. You're obviously not going to make it. At least not on time. I've spoken with the sheriff, and I had no choice but to call Judge Adams to explain what happened. To say that he's angry would be putting it mildly. Instead of taking you into custody on the spot this morning, he trusted you. You've—well, you've made him look foolish. What you did today, in addition to being an illegal breaking and entering which you'll have to answer for to the judge here, was another violation of Judge Adams's restraining order, which you'll have to answer to him for. He intends to add another two days to your sentence, but technically you're entitled to a hearing before he does that.

"I've spoken with the prosecutor here, and reached an agreement. We'll appear briefly before Judge Doyle here, and you'll be released without bail into the custody of the Middlesex County Sheriff. His deputy will transport you to Judge Adams's courtroom. I tried to arrange it so I could drive you to New Brunswick myself, but neither the prosecutor, Judge Doyle, nor Judge Adams, was too enamored of that idea. I'll meet you at Judge Adams's courtroom. He'll hear us, and then formally increase your sentence. Then you'll be transported to the county jail, where you'll stay for the next five days. In the meantime, I'll try to work something out with the prosecutor here, so that when you're through with your contempt sentence you won't have to stay locked up until your trial for breaking into the Hellers' house."

"Then that's it," Stacy said simply. "Let's get it over with."

Frank rose, opened the door leading to the courtroom, and told the uniformed court officer that they were ready to see Judge Doyle.

■   ■   ■

"That madwoman was in our house! In our daughter's bedroom!"

Jody sat at her kitchen table, trembling as she spoke into the telephone.

"Okay, Jo, try and relax," Scott replied. "They have her in custody now. Everything's under control."

It had been about an hour since Jody had gotten Scott's call on her cell phone, and the police had just left the house. She had been out running a few errands, and in fact had been only a few blocks from the house when Scott had reached her. He'd explained that he had just gotten a call from Slocum Security, and cautioned her not to go into the house until the police had arrived and made sure that it was safe. "And call me when you know what's going on," he had instructed.

Jody had recognized Stacy's car in front of her house as she rounded the corner onto her street. She had remained outside, parked across the street, while she watched a police officer lead Stacy from the house into the patrol car. Meanwhile, a second officer emerged from the house, and Jody approached him and identified herself. The two policemen conferred briefly, and the second one then accompanied her into the house, explaining that the first would wait in the car with the intruder while he went through the house with her to determine whether anything was missing. "She doesn't seem to have anything on her, but there's a lot of paperwork to complete before we can search her car," the cop had explained. "We'd appreciate it if you'd look around and see if anything is out of order."

Jody had followed him into the house.

"By the way," the policeman added. "Do you recognize her?"

"I sure do." She told the officer just who Stacy was, and how she had been harassing her family in violation of a restraining order. "In fact," Jody said, "she's due to begin a three-day sentence for contempt of court in a few hours."

The officer shook his head. "I think she'll be a little late."

Jody had finished walking through the house with the officer, spoke briefly with him on the front lawn, and watched as he got into the patrol car with his partner and pulled away. She felt a chill as she saw Stacy staring intently at her from the back seat.

Once back inside, Jody telephoned her husband.

"She apparently came in through the back door. I must have left the door unlocked when I watered the plants on the deck this morning."

"Did she take anything?" he asked.

"I don't think so. But Scott, she was in Alex's room. The policeman said she collided with him running out of there. And the picture of us at Disney was on the floor by the bed." She shuddered.

"What are we going to do, Scott? I'm afraid to let Alex out of my sight now."

"I don't know what the answer is," Scott admitted. He promised her that he would finish up early at the office, and get home as soon as possible. They would talk more that evening.

Later that afternoon, Jody stood at the bus stop, waiting for her daughter. *At least this afternoon that woman won't be here to frighten Alex. But they can't keep her locked up forever.*

Anger and frustration churned her stomach. It had taken a drastic incident like this—one in which her family had been exposed to the actuality of significant personal danger—to get the court to do something. But what use was a legal system like that against a mentally disturbed woman who just didn't seem to care about the consequences of her actions?

What will I have to do to protect my family?

CHAPTER 35

When Judge Doyle finished with Stacy in Bergen County, a Sheriff's deputy from Middlesex took her from the courthouse and drove her, caged in the back seat of a police car, to New Brunswick. Upon Stacy's arrival at the Middlesex County Courthouse, she was taken to the basement, where she was turned over to another deputy, Bobby Luberto.

"Oh yeah," Luberto said. "Charlie, up in Judge Adams's courtroom, came down to see me about you this morning. Said I should go easy on you 'cause you seemed like a nice lady caught up in a bad situation. Told me to expect you around three o'clock." He glanced at the clock on the wall, which showed that it was nearly four thirty. "Been tied up somewhere else, huh?"

Stacy remained silent as she was fingerprinted for the second time that day. Luberto then escorted her to a small holding cell, and after Stacy stepped in, he shut the barred door. "Gotta keep it locked," he said almost apologetically. "Regulations."

Jail doors really do clang when they shut, Stacy thought, just like on TV. Not a pleasant sound, she was coming to realize. At least not from this side of the bars.

"What happens now?" she asked meekly.

"Oh, when Judge Adams is ready for you, his clerk will call down, and I'll bring you up to his courtroom. Word is, he's pretty upset with you. Charlie came down about an hour ago to see if you'd made it here okay. He's a nice guy, and was worried about you from this morning. Well, when you didn't show up, he had to let the judge know. Charlie called me and said the judge was pretty P.O.'d that you'd made him look like a fool. Said the judge wanted to know the minute you got here."

Luberto took a seat at a desk opposite the cell door, and took a sip from a paper coffee cup that had been sitting there.

"Look, I know what happened to your boy. It's a damn shame, and I don't know what I'd do if it had been my son. Now, Judge Adams is a good judge, a fair man. But crossing him…" Luberto trailed off. "Wouldn't want to be in your shoes this afternoon."

An electronic chime sounded, signaling that someone had entered the basement office. "'Scuse me," Luberto said as he stood. "Gotta see who that is."

Wouldn't want to be in my shoes. What did I expect? She recalled O'Connor's question to her earlier in the day: *What was I thinking?* She took a deep breath. No answer there. *I think I'm on autopilot.*

Five minutes later, Luberto came back. "Okay. They just called for you. Your lawyer's upstairs, and Judge Adams is ready for you. Time to go."

■   ■   ■

Luberto brought her into the courtroom through a door near the front of the room. To her right, at the long counsel table where earlier today she had sat by herself, she saw O'Connor, who nodded to her. To her left, she saw Judge Adams, robed and seated at the bench, looking stern. Luberto led her to a seat next to Frank and stepped back, staying close by.

"Are we ready?" Judge Adams inquired.

"Yes, Your Honor, we are," O'Connor responded.

"Very well then. Let's proceed." Judge Adams peered over his eyeglasses. "Mr. O'Connor, I believe you know why we're here." The judge addressed O'Connor, but his piercing glare was aimed directly at Stacy.

"Yes, Your Honor."

"Yes," the judge agreed. "We're here, Mr. O'Connor, because Mrs. Altman did not live up to her word. In fact, after promising me to stay out of trouble and to report back here promptly at three, and after I went out on a limb because I felt sorry for her, she did not stay out of trouble. Indeed, she went searching for it. She took advantage of me. She made me look foolish. What we're here to do now is to decide the consequences of her reckless behavior."

His gaze finally left her, and he looked over to O'Connor.

"I'll hear you now," said the Judge.

"Your Honor," the lawyer began. "I've spoken with Mrs. Altman about her actions. She realizes the seriousness of what she has done, and makes no excuse for it, as there is none. She knows that she must pay the consequence, and asks only that the Court take into consideration her contrition." O'Connor sat down. He and Stacy had agreed that the less said, the better.

Judge Adams seemed inclined to keep the proceedings short as well.

"Please stand, Mrs. Altman," the judge said, returning his attention to her. "My previous sentence of three days did not appear to have made the impression upon you that I'd hoped it would. I find that I must increase that sentence in light of your conduct. Therefore, I sentence you to five days. Sentence to begin immediately."

Judge Adams rose, and left the courtroom.

■   ■   ■

When Judge Adams left the courtroom, Deputy Luberto stepped

forward. "Mrs. Altman, you'll have to come with me."

"Can you give us a minute?" asked O'Connor.

"Sure," the deputy replied, taking a step backwards again. "But I have to stay right here."

O'Connor turned to Stacy, who was sitting silently at the table.

"Is there anything you need me to do?" he asked.

"Will they let me use the phone there?" She stared at her hands in her lap, not able to meet O'Connor's eyes. "I never even told my mother what happened this morning. What will I wear? I don't even have a toothbrush. Will they let me call her? Can she bring my things?"

O'Connor put his hand on Stacy's shoulder and squeezed gently. "Yes, they'll let you call her. And they'll explain to you what you can and can't bring. A few books might not be a bad idea."

Stacy finally looked up at O'Connor, fear in her eyes. "Don't worry, Stacy," he said. "You're going to the county facility to serve a five-day sentence for contempt of court. You're not a criminal, and they're not going to treat you like one. You won't be put in with murderers, bank robbers, or drug addicts, and you'll do fine. Take the time to catch up on your reading. Look at it as a little vacation."

Stacy managed a weak smile.

"Thanks, Frank," she said. "When I get out, we'll have to talk about the Bergen County thing. Will you help me with that?"

"Of course. But don't worry about that now. Take one thing at a time."

Luberto cleared his throat. "I'm sorry. We have to get going."

He stepped forward and led Stacy out of the courtroom.

■　　■　　■

Shortly after her arrival at the county facility, which was about fifteen minutes away in North Brunswick, she was permitted to telephone her mother. Her mother was shocked, and trying to calm her down had a soothing effect on Stacy. Stacy had checked with the deputy sheriff about what she could bring. Food, yes. Earphones and iPod, yes. Books, yes. Her prescription anti-depressant medication, no—drugs from the outside were not permitted, but arrangements to fill prescriptions through the jail's pharmacy could be made. She asked her mother to pack her a small bag with the permitted items.

The time did not go quickly, as O'Connor said it would. She was kept in a cell that measured about ten feet by thirteen. Adequate size for a business office, depressingly small for a bedroom, living room, and kitchen combined. Thankfully her quarters did not double as a bathroom as well, as those facilities were separate and at least available as needed. She was grateful that she did not have to share the small cell with anyone else, but after the first day she grew lonely. O'Connor had been right in his advice that she would not be kept with the criminal population, but it seemed that this week there was a shortage of people sent to jail for thumbing their noses at the court. So Stacy was the sole occupant of this particular block.

Though she had plenty of time on her hands, she could not concentrate on any of the books her mother had packed for her. She spent a lot of time dwelling on what had brought her here. She was a victim. She replayed in her mind the events of the past three and a half months, and tried to see where she had crossed over from being the victim of some nameless, faceless monster behind the wheel of a speeding car to a victim of the system of justice that now placed that monster's interests ahead of her own.

It didn't matter. Victim she was, and out of control. She had taken a step toward regaining it when she'd first hired O'Connor and had sought the court's help. But that control had been illusory, as she had come to recognize when Judge Adams had issued his first ruling, upholding the attorney-client privilege. Even as she had tried to keep it from slipping further through her fingers by reaching out directly to Scott Heller, it was like grasping at a rope of sand.

Though she had taken initiative herself, it seemed that for every step forward she took, she was forced two or three back.

There was a lesson to be learned. She spent the next few days thinking, and by the time she'd completed her five-day sentence she had figured out what that lesson was.

Take bigger steps.

CHAPTER 36

Stacy's mother picked her up at the courthouse in Hackensack. She was out on bail. Upon completing her contempt sentence in Middlesex County earlier that afternoon, she had been transported directly to the Bergen County courthouse to appear before Judge Doyle in connection with the breaking and entering at the Heller residence. O'Connor had met her there, and had opposed the prosecutor's application to hold her without bail. He really was good at what he did—it was the system that sucked, no fault of his—and he'd convinced the judge that she had been chastened by her stay in the Middlesex County facility, and that she would behave herself pending trial on the break-in. Since she had not yet succeeded in pissing off this particular judge and making him look like a fool, the judge was inclined to cut Stacy some slack. Bail was set at $25,000, and between the money Stacy had set aside for the lawyer's bill, and her savings, she was able to secure her release almost immediately. By five o'clock, her mother was driving her home.

"Stacy—"

"Mom," Stacy interrupted, "I told you I don't want to talk."

Stacy's mother shrugged, and the two women rode for some

time in silence.

Her mother tried again.

"But I'm worried about you," she ventured. "You can't just make believe that nothing happened. You went to jail. And now you're going to have a trial because you broke into that lawyer's house. You've got to get a grip."

"I don't want to talk about it," Stacy repeated slowly and deliberately.

Her mother did not try a third time.

■   ■   ■

Stacy soaked in the tub. She and her mother had not spoken the rest of the way home, and Stacy had gone immediately up to her room when they'd arrived home. Though she had showered every day when she was in jail, she had been looking forward to a nice hot bath. The aroma from the eucalyptus bath oil was relaxing.

Stacy lay back and mulled over the plan that she had formulated during the past few days. She had decided that the way to succeed— the way to move forward despite being forced two steps back for each step forward that she managed—was to take bigger steps. Bolder steps. In fact, she thought as she relaxed in the bathtub, one giant step that was sure to leave Scott Heller no realistic choice but to give her what she wanted.

When the idea had first come to her, she had dismissed it out of hand. It had been a fanciful notion, born of frustration and rage. But as she'd struggled with the realization that she could depend on no one but herself, this germ of an idea kept on surfacing. How could she make him see? How could she make him realize that this was about so much more than some abstract legal principle? *It's about flesh and blood. It's about my child.* And she had realized that the only way was to make it about his child, too. About his daughter, Alex.

Make it about Alex, and he'll understand.

Stacy stood, and reached for her terry robe. Dripping, she stepped from the tub, wrapped her hair in a towel, and continued her thoughts. Having made the decision to act, she was anxious to get under way. She was afraid of losing her nerve if she delayed.

It was six thirty on Monday evening. Too late in the day to do anything now. The school bus dropped Alex off at about 3:20, so tomorrow afternoon at that time, Stacy would make her move.

She dressed and went downstairs to find her mother. She now felt guilty about how she'd spoken to her earlier, and wanted to smooth things over. Stacy found her mother in the kitchen, fixing dinner for them both. Across the dinner table, Stacy extended the olive branch to her mother, beginning with a description of her five days in jail. Having first wanted to hear about it, her mother quickly grew uncomfortable learning about the small cell and the public showers.

After dinner, the two women cleaned the kitchen together, and the conversation became lighter. When the work was done, they browsed the TV listings, settled upon a movie on HBO, and moved into the living room. Within minutes of the opening credits, Stacy was asleep on the couch, her head on her mother's lap.

The next morning, Stacy woke with a sense of purpose. Her mother had awakened her briefly the night before to move her upstairs, and Stacy had slept the rest of the night peacefully. Now, she was ready to move.

Her first order of business after coffee and a shower was to pack an overnight bag. She did not imagine that she would be gone for more than one night, if that, so it did not take long to gather a few things together.

Next, she needed to rent a car. Her own Camry was an all too familiar sight on Apple Ridge Crescent, and its re-appearance on the Hellers' block was sure to raise an alarm. She wanted a car that would not stand out in the upscale neighborhood, and decided that an SUV would both fit in and be practical. She retrieved the Yellow Pages from the kitchen, returned to her bedroom so she could conduct her business without her mother hearing, and found a local Jeep dealer. The dealer indeed had rental cars available, and Stacy arranged to pick up a Grand Cherokee before noon.

Downstairs, on the kitchen table, she opened a road atlas, and over a fresh cup of coffee and a toasted English muffin, she traced a route from Englewood Cliffs to Interstate 80 west, ultimately finding her way south to Interstate 276 into Pennsylvania. The most direct way would have been simply to get back on the New Jersey Turnpike and head south, but Stacy wanted to avoid toll roads—and toll booths—to the extent possible. When her mother came into the kitchen to freshen up her own cup of coffee, and saw Stacy studying the map, Stacy told her that she had decided to get away for a few days to Pennsylvania, and spend some time at her friend Amy's farm.

"Oh, that's nice. It was so thoughtful of Amy to invite you out when she was here for *shivah*. It's about time you took her up on her offer."

"Yeah, it's a good opportunity to chill out," Stacy told her mother. "I want to make sure I remember how to get there," she said, pointing to the map. "I've only been there once before, and that was two years ago, with Marc doing the driving."

Stacy returned upstairs to finish dressing, and when she was done she sought out her mother to say good-bye.

"I'll see you in a day or two, Mom," she said, and kissed her on the cheek.

"You go relax," her mother replied. "It's a good idea to take some time. I hope this is a turning point for you."

"Yes, Mom." Stacy said. "I think it will be."

CHAPTER 37

Stacy judged that she was less than ten minutes from the Hellers' house when she pulled her rented Grand Cherokee into the parking lot of the Mayfair Diner. It was nearly two forty-five—about a half hour until Alex would be let off at her bus stop.

The problem that Stacy had been wrestling with when she had formulated her plan for today was how to ensure that Alex was alone at the bus stop without Jody there to meet her. In the days before Stacy had started her sentence, Jody was always there to greet her daughter at the end of the school day. Stacy had no reason to believe that things would be any different now. In fact, she expected that Jody would be even more protective of her daughter following the break-in at their house. Contemplating this problem the night before, Stacy had come up with what she hoped was a workable solution.

It was time to call Jody Heller. Stacy didn't think Jody would recognize her voice on the telephone—they'd exchanged only a few words in their various encounters—but she would do her best to disguise it slightly without sounding phony. She considered whether to stay in the car and call from her cell phone, or to go into the diner to find a pay phone. Although there was a chance that a call from the car might be recognized as originating from a cellular phone, and therefore make Jody suspicious once Stacy identified herself as calling from Alex's school, she decided that that was less risky than placing the call from the diner and having some waitress in the background shouting out an order for a corned beef on rye. She turned off the motor to eliminate any background noise, pressed "*67" to block Caller ID, and keyed in the Hellers' telephone number. After a deep breath, she pressed the send button.

"Hello," came a woman's voice.

Stacy hesitated for a split second, and plunged in.

"Is this Mrs. Heller?" she asked.

"Yes."

"Mrs. Heller, this is Annette Troy, the nurse at Quail Brook School. Your daughter Alexandra was in to see me this afternoon. She tripped in the hallway and bruised her knee. You know that it's our policy to just let you know of any incidents, however minor."

"Ms. Troy? I don't think I know you. Isn't Ms. Boyer there?"

Stacy had anticipated that Jody might know the nurse. "Ms. Boyer is out today. I cover the school district as needed, when the regular nurse is unavailable. You're right, we've never spoken before."

Jody seemed to accept this.

"Alex is okay, isn't she?" Jody asked anxiously.

"Yes, she's fine. A little antibiotic ointment and a Band–Aid were all that she needed. But she is a bit upset. It seems that someone pushed her, and she's more shaken by that than by her bruised knee. Alex is back in her classroom now, but I think that instead of sending her home on the bus, perhaps you should come pick her up. She could do with some pampering this afternoon."

Stacy held her breath, waiting for Jody's response.

"Of course. Yes, of course. I can be there in fifteen minutes."

"Good. I'll have her wait in the administration office for you."

"Okay. Thank you, Ms. Troy. I'm on my way."

Stacy pressed the end button on her cell phone. Jody had taken the bait, and would now be headed for Alex's school. The timing would be close. Alex's bus was due to drop her off in about twenty-five minutes, and Jody could be expected to return in about forty minutes.

Rather than take up her usual spot on Mountain View Drive, Stacy intended to wait for Alex nearer her house on Apple Ridge Crescent. She would park the Jeep past the Heller house, so she would have a view of both the house and the route that Alex would walk from the intersection of Mountain View and Apple Ridge. Stacy recalled that the girl who got off the bus along with Alex walked down Mountain View, so Alex would be out of the girl's sight as she walked toward her house. This gave Stacy a stretch of Apple Ridge Crescent along which to approach Alex unseen by anyone else.

To coordinate her arrival at the Hellers' house with that of the school bus as closely as possible, she drove slowly the rest of the way. She turned onto Mountain View Drive at twelve minutes after three, and continued one block past Apple Ridge Crescent in order to loop around to be facing the right way on the Hellers' street. Stacy was relieved to find very little activity in the neighborhood, and her hopes that she would encounter Alex alone were buoyed. Left on Mystic Drive, and left again on the far end of Apple Ridge, which was as its name implied crescent-shaped, and Stacy came to a stop one house away from number eight. It was exactly 3:15.

Her heart began to race, and she felt a bit light-headed. The idea that she was about to commit a crime of major proportions hovered just outside the envelope of her consciousness, and each time the thought succeeded in breaking through, she shook it off as she would an annoying mosquito buzzing around her head. The regular rules don't apply, she kept telling herself. If they did, things wouldn't have gotten this far in the first place.

Stacy's was the only car on the street, and this added to her uneasiness. She watched the digital clock on her dashboard register the passage of another minute, and she hoped that the bus arrived before too many more went by.

CHAPTER 38

The last of the buses were still being loaded when Jody arrived at the Quail Brook Elementary School. Jody slid into a parking space being vacated by a departing teacher and headed for the front door of the school.

The interior of the administration office was visible from the hallway through its floor-to-ceiling glass wall. The office served as an anteroom to the principal's own private office, and a counter that ran the length of the office separated four administrators' desks from a small waiting area. Frightened children summoned to see the principal sat from time to time on the two chairs that stood in the waiting area. So did children waiting for early release, or to be picked up by their parents for any other reason, and it was there that Jody expected to find Alex. As she reached for the doorknob to enter the office she saw through the glass that the chairs were empty.

From her activities with the PTA, Jody knew the woman seated at one of the desks behind the counter.

"Hi, Janice," Jody greeted her. "I'm here to pick up Alex."

"Oh, Mrs. Altman, is anything wrong?"

"Nothing really. The nurse called and said that Alex fell and scraped her knee. She suggested I come pick her up. More for pampering than anything else. But I wonder where she is. The nurse said she'd be waiting here in the office."

"That's strange. Ms. Boyer didn't say anything to me about it."

"Ms. Boyer?" Jody repeated. "I thought Ms. Boyer wasn't in today. It was Ms. Troy who called me."

"Ms. Troy?" Janice echoed. "Who's that?"

"I don't know. She said she was some kind of substitute or something. Are you sure Ms. Boyer was here today?"

"Well yeah. I just talked to her a few minutes ago. I think she's still in her office. Let me get her on the phone."

Jody waited.

"That's what I thought," Janice said when she hung up the phone. "Ms. Boyer was here all day. And she sure doesn't recognize the name Troy."

"But what about Alex? Where's Alex?" Jody asked.

"Not with Ms. Boyer. She hasn't seen Alex all day. And she didn't hear anything about Alex hurting herself."

"Well someone called me and told me to come pick her up. Where's her teacher? Is she still here?"

Janice walked to an intercom on the wall and spoke into it. She came back to the counter and shook her head. "Ms. Fine says that Alex went home on the bus as usual. She said she didn't know anything about Alex falling either. She put Alex on the bus herself, along with the others."

A feeling of dread came over Jody. *Oh my God. That woman was released from jail yesterday.* Could it be? Would she dare come back? She must have purposely orchestrated this so Alex would arrive at the bus stop alone.

Jody looked at the clock on the wall. The bus would be letting her off any minute. She ran for her car.

CHAPTER 39

Stacy had a clear view of the T-intersection ahead of her. The yellow school bus slid into view. A moment later it exited left, and Jody saw Alex and her schoolmate on the curb. Alex said something to the girl, and then looked around, apparently seeking her mother. She hoisted her book bag over her shoulder, looked both ways before crossing Mountain View, and started home.

Stacy's heart was pounding now. She started the car and shifted into gear, still keeping her foot on the brake. She made one last check and satisfied herself that no one else was on the street. She had no way of knowing whether anyone could see what was happening from inside their homes, but she would have to chance it.

Alex reached the curb and began to walk along the sidewalk to her house three doors away. It now occurred to Stacy that she had not given any thought as to how she would get Alex into the car, or how she would drive away with a kicking and screaming child. Nevertheless, Stacy eased her foot off the brake, and the car started rolling up the street slowly along the curb, closing the distance between it and the approaching girl.

The two came abreast of each other when Alex was still one

door away from her house. She glanced at the Jeep but did not appear to give it a second thought. At that instant, Stacy stopped the car and threw it into park. Because Alex had continued walking, she was now at the rear end of the Jeep, and did not see Stacy as she slid quickly to the passenger side door, opened it, and leaped out. In one fluid movement, Stacy threw her right arm around Alex's waist, lifted the child off her feet, and backed herself into the car again.

Stacy had moved so fast that Alex was inside the car before she even reacted. Stacy pinioned the girl against the car seat with her right arm as she reached across her and pulled the door shut with her left. Alex let out a yell and pulled at Stacy's arm, kicking her feet and trying to reach for the door handle at the same time. Stacy somehow managed to keep enough leverage on the girl while she shifted into gear with her left hand. Although she realized that speeding from the scene was not the wisest move, neither was remaining too long with a frantic child thrashing about in the front seat. She mashed on the accelerator.

Somehow, Stacy managed to keep control of both Alex and the car. When they had exited the Hellers' development and turned onto the adjoining state road, Stacy increased her speed to match the fifty-five mile an hour limit. Alex was still struggling against Stacy's arm to reach the door.

"Alex, if you open the door, you're going to get hurt. I need both hands to drive safely. I'm not going to hurt you, so relax."

The girl, who had been crying the entire time, stopped struggling, and Stacy took the wheel with both hands. Immediately upon being released, Alex started wailing even louder and began pummeling Stacy with her small fists. Stacy fought to keep control of the car with her left hand, as she warded off the blows with her right.

"For God's sake, Alex, you'll get us both killed!" Stacy shouted. "Stop it!"

Stacy's tone apparently frightened Alex, and she stopped her barrage. She continued crying hysterically, though.

"Where are we going?" Alex shouted. "Take me home!"

The gravity of what she was doing was beginning to sink in,

as were the difficulties she would encounter in carrying it off. Too late to turn back now, Stacy would have to get Alex under control. She considered stopping the car by the side of the road so she could talk calmly with the girl, but decided that keeping the car moving reduced the chances of Alex's making a run for it.

"Alex, I know this will be hard for you to understand, but I'll do my best to explain," Stacy began. "I want your father to tell me something, and he won't. I need a way to convince him to tell me, and when he knows you're with me, he'll tell me. Once he does, I'll bring you back home. We're going someplace where I can call him now."

Alex did not say anything.

"I'm not going to hurt you. I'm going to find out what I need from your father, and then you'll be on your way home."

Still there was no response from Alex, and Stacy glanced at her. The girl was sitting stock still, hands in her lap, eyes staring unfocused straight ahead.

Stacy felt a twinge of guilt, mixed with compassion. She realized how frightened the girl must be, but forced herself to shrug it off. Thankful for now that the girl was quiet, Stacy drove toward Pennsylvania in silence.

■　　■　　■

Still two doors away from her house, Jody reached to the visor above the windshield, depressed the button on the garage door opener, and held it down until she came into range. She stopped the car in the driveway and ran in through the garage, ducking her head to clear the still-rising door.

"Alex!" she called as she threw open the door leading from the garage into the mud room. "Alex!"

Alex knew the code for the keypad and could have let herself into the house by herself, but Jody had called the house from her cell phone and gotten no answer, so she did not expect to find her daughter inside. Jody had also telephoned Adrienne Lang, her next-door neighbor, to see if Alex was there. Alex knew that if for any reason Jody was not there when she got home from school, she was to go to Adrienne's. Adrienne had not heard from Alex.

She knew she would not find Alex, but Jody nevertheless ran from room to room calling her name. Melissa. Alex rode home on the bus with Melissa Porter. Maybe she knew where Alex was. Jody found the Porters' telephone number.

A few minutes later, Jody knew no more. Melissa's mother had questioned her daughter. Alex had ridden home on the bus, and had gotten off at the stop as usual. No, Melissa had not seen anyone waiting at the bus stop. She had come directly home, but had seen Alex start off in the direction of her own house.

Don't panic, Jody told herself. It's probably something innocent. She's probably just at another friend's house and neglected to leave Jody a note. That would not explain the telephone call from "Ms. Troy," Jody knew, but to acknowledge otherwise right now would drive her over the edge.

Jody ticked off a list of Alex's friends in her mind, and began calling their homes one by one. When she'd hung up from her fifth unsuccessful call, fear had firmly taken hold.

Alex was missing, and Jody knew that Stacy Altman had her.

■　　■　　■

Finally, Alex slept. Stacy continued west, watching for the signs to U.S. 202. They had been driving for nearly two and a half hours, and she estimated that she had another thirty minutes to go before reaching Amy and Greg's farmhouse. It was beginning to darken, and the building gloom imposed a sense of surreality upon Stacy.

As it was the tail end of rush hour, the highway was heavily traveled, and Stacy contemplated how inside each car was someone with his or her own life story—a complex past, a unique present, and a singular destiny. Alongside her now was a red Volkswagen Passat, driven by a middle-aged man dressed in a business suit. Stacy sometimes played a game with herself, observing strangers and concocting what she thought might be interesting, even exotic, personae for those people. But more often, instead of creating fictions for these strangers, Stacy tried to imagine their separate realities. She knew how complex a person she was, how much a product of her past experiences she must be, and she would marvel that every person who crossed her path, however casually, was also such an exceptional individual. When she was in a public place among strangers, the temptation was to think of those people simply as "walk-ons" in the drama of her own life. Out of her sight, they were insignificant, and indeed did not even exist. Sometimes, though, she would consider the fact that each of them was so much more than just a bit player in her own story. When they left her presence, their own personal dramas continued. The reality that her chance encounters with multitudes of strangers were just pinpoint intersections of complicated lives, each unique in its own right, was sobering.

The driver of the Passat next to her. What brought him here, to this very place, right now? What in his life's history dictated that at this moment he should be driving along Interstate 76 next to Stacy Altman? Was he simply driving home from work after a routine day at the office? Or was there more than met Stacy's eye? And when that man glanced innocently in her direction, to see what car was overtaking him in the passing lane, what did he see? No doubt he saw a mother driving with her sleeping daughter next to her, perhaps bringing the girl home from a ballet lesson. Certainly, he did not see an anguished, grieving mother turned kidnapper, fleeing the scene of her crime to hole herself up in a hideaway and arrange her hostage's ransom.

Stacy watched as the Passat exited the highway at the next ramp and vanished from her view, the driver's walk-on appearance in The Stacy Altman Story finished. The next act of the story, perhaps the climax, was to begin.

CHAPTER 40

Alex woke up shortly before they arrived at Amy and Greg's farm. Though she glanced periodically at Stacy, she otherwise sat silently and still, apparently resigned to the fact that there was nothing she could do.

"I have to go the bathroom," she said finally.

"We'll be there in a few minutes," Stacy replied. "Can you hold it?"

Alex squirmed, but nodded.

Night had fallen, and since Stacy had been this way only once before, she stayed alert for landmarks. Moments later she spotted a small white church, which was her signal to turn left off Route 34. Five more minutes and she would come upon the Bartletts' mailbox standing at the beginning of a dirt road that led through a cornfield to the farmhouse. Spying the mailbox, on which was stenciled its owners' name, Stacy slowed and turned onto the dirt road.

Shortly after Amy had paid her respects in Perth Amboy, she had called Stacy to see how she was holding up. Amy had mentioned that she and Greg would be gone the entire month of October, and had urged Stacy to treat the place as her own in their absence. The perfect getaway, she had called it. More like the perfect hideout,

Stacy now thought.

The Jeep bumped along the dirt road. Although it was dark, and there were no lights except for the car's headlamps, Stacy knew that a few hundred feet ahead stood a picturesque house made of stone. About fifty feet from the house, the cornfield ended and Stacy passed through an open gate into a grass meadow.

The road turned into gravel, and Stacy followed it around the house to the back where, across a small yard, there stood a two-car garage. She considered whether to see if there was room there for her car, where it would be out of sight, but decided against it. The house was well set back from the road, and the car was in any event around back, shielded from view. If she needed to leave quickly, time would be lost retrieving the car from the garage.

"Okay, Alex, we're here."

Stacy grabbed her overnight bag from the back seat, opened the driver-side door, and motioned for Alex to slide out behind her. Stacy took the girl's arm as she got out, and ascended the stairs to the door. Amy had told her that the key would be above the door frame, and it was.

Once inside, Alex went straight to the bathroom, as Stacy went quickly through the house reminding herself of the layout. When Alex reappeared, Stacy directed her to a chair in the living room.

"You wait here," she instructed. "I'm going to call your father now."

Stacy reached for the telephone, but hesitated. No, she would use her cell phone, in order to make it more difficult to track her location. She retrieved it from her bag, and punched in the Hellers' number, which she had committed to memory. As she pressed the send button to complete the call, her pulse quickened. Although she was nervous, and even scared, Stacy felt a sense of power. She had taken control.

"Hello," a woman's breathless voice answered before even the first ring had finished.

"Yes, Mrs. Heller," Stacy said. "I think you know who this is."

"My daughter! Where's Alex? What have you done with her?"

"She's right here with me. Put your husband on."

Jody hesitated. "He's not here right now."

"Very unfortunate, Mrs. Heller. Where is he?"

Jody paused. She had telephoned Scott after she had finished calling around to Alex's friends and determined that she was indeed missing. He had set out for home at once, and had telephoned her from the car a short time later. Of all the evenings for a traffic accident to tie up the George Washington Bridge! Outbound traffic was at a standstill, and there was nothing Scott could do but sit and wait.

"Uh, he's on his way home now," Jody answered. "But Alex. Is she all right? You haven't done anything to her, have you?"

Stacy ignored her questions. "You know what I want, don't you, Mrs. Heller? Why I need to talk to your husband?"

"Yes, yes. But Alex. Let me talk to Alex," Jody pleaded.

Stacy glanced at the girl, sitting quietly on the chair.

"For a minute. So you'll know she's okay. Make it quick."

Stacy strode across the room and handed the phone to Alex.

"Mommy?"

"Alex! Are you okay? She hasn't done anything to you, has she?"

"Mommy, I'm scared. Come take me home."

"Alex, sweetheart, everything's going to be fine. You just do what the lady says, and try to be brave, and you'll be home before you know it."

"But Mom, I want to come home now." Alex's voice quivered. "Please come get me now. I'm afraid."

Stacy took the phone back from Alex.

"Listen, Mrs. Heller. I've tried reasoning, and I've tried pleading. But your fucking attorney husband just doesn't want to understand how serious I am. He knows who killed my son, and one way or another, he's going to tell me who it is. You read the papers—that animal was going fifty miles an hour when he smacked into Ben. Do you know that he was going so fast that the police think my poor Ben's head cracked his windshield? After being thrown into the air like a doll? He was only six and a half years old, Mrs. Heller."

Stacy paused for a moment before continuing.

"You tell your husband I want to know who killed my son. I'll call back later…And don't even think about calling the police."

"Please don't hurt Alex," Stacy heard Jody plead. "Let me talk to her again. Please."

But Stacy cut the connection.

■   ■   ■

Jody heard the line go dead. She felt sick to her stomach, but did not make it to the bathroom. She doubled over in the hallway leading from the kitchen to the powder room, fell to her knees, and vomited. Her daughter. In the hands of that crazy woman. This has gone too far. To hell with the attorney-client privilege, to hell with the client, and to hell with her husband.

Jody stayed there on the floor for a moment, catching her breath. When she had sufficiently recovered, she got to her feet and cleaned up the mess she had made. She poured herself a glass of cold water from the refrigerator, and sat at the table to drink it. She was willing herself to be calm and not to panic. Though she had hoped against hope that Alex would turn up at a friend's house, having just absent-mindedly forgotten to leave word for her, she had known how unlikely that was. And she had known in her gut that Stacy Altman was responsible for Alex's disappearance. But hearing that woman's voice on the telephone—filled with anger and rage—scared her immeasurably.

Notwithstanding the panic she felt, she did not want to be hysterical when Scott finally arrived home. Her call to him earlier, when her search for Alex had failed, had been frantic. "Alex is missing!" she had cried. "She's taken Alex!" In what was becoming an all too common manner, Scott had patronized her. "Calm down," he had insisted. "Just tell me what happened."

Jody had convinced him that this was an emergency, and he'd started out for home. A half hour later he had called from the car, stuck on the approach to the George Washington Bridge. Jody had rushed that call because she knew she would be hearing from Stacy, and did not want to tie up the line.

When Scott finally did get home, Jody wanted to be in control of herself. For weeks, she had been telling her husband what a threat that woman was. Each time Stacy did something to validate Jody's concerns, Scott just took it in stride and told her he would handle it. He'd gotten a restraining order, a contempt citation, and an arrest warrant. Look where that had gotten them. Their daughter was in the hands of a lunatic. It was time for Jody to lay down her own law to her husband, and being hysterical would not help.

She had to believe that Scott would no longer resist. No legal principle could require him to place his own flesh and blood at risk. He would come home, Stacy would call back, and he would tell her what she wanted to know. Alex would be returned home, and their nightmare would be over.

■　■　■

Stacy hung up the telephone. Alex was back in her chair across the living room, crying.

Stacy went to the bathroom and splashed water on her face. She saw her reflection in the mirror. Only three months ago she had been just a mother, with a son and a husband. Now look at her. Her son was dead, she didn't want anything to do with her husband, and she was holed up in a farmhouse with someone else's daughter, the police probably looking for both of them by now.

She walked out of the bathroom, and saw that across the room, Alex had cried herself to sleep on the chair. There was really no danger that they'd be found—at least not yet. Even if the Hellers had been monitoring their incoming calls, Stacy had called from her cell phone. For some time, she had been meaning to upgrade her phone, but she was now glad she hadn't gotten around to it. The newer models had some kind of GPS chip in them, that made it simple to zero in on the phone's location. She was sure there was a way to deactivate that feature, but she didn't have to worry about it—hers was a relic from the dark ages that just made and received calls. Even so, she knew that somehow the telephone company could determine the cell antenna from which the call had been transmitted, and by that her general location, but it was unlikely that anyone would think to seek that information for a while. She had some time yet.

I can rest awhile. Then I'll call back to see if Jody has contacted her husband.

The farmhouse was remote, so there was nowhere for Alex to go if she woke while Stacy grabbed a nap. She lay down on the sofa, and within moments she was asleep.

■ ■ ■

Scott sat across from Jody at the kitchen table, the telephone between them. He had finally arrived home about fifteen minutes ago, almost two hours after he'd received Jody's panicked call that Alex was missing. Like his wife, he had hoped for an innocent explanation while at the same time knowing exactly what had happened. Then he got the call on his cell phone from Jody after Stacy Altman had telephoned. *That crazy bitch.*

The drive home had been agonizingly slow, with two lanes on the GWB shut down as a result of a multi-car crash. Stacy hadn't told Jody when she'd be calling back, and Scott wanted to be sure he was home in time for her call. But he'd been forced to sit, watching as emergency vehicles maneuvered to clear the way.

He had never dreamed Stacy would go this far. He was used to handling this type of thing through the courts. People have disputes and disagreements, and they settle such things in a civilized manner—as civilized as a court proceeding could be, that is. But to go to these lengths?

She's going to call back, and you're going to tell her what she wants to know, his wife had said to him.

The long ride home gave him a lot of time to contemplate the very real problem that confronted him. *I don't know what she wants to know. She wants my client, and I don't know who he is.*

How was he going to explain that to Stacy? Would she believe him? What would she do to Alex when she found out?

What was Jody going to do when *she* found out?

Now, sitting across the kitchen table from Jody, he at least knew the answer to *that* question.

"Let me get this straight," she said to him. Her initial urgent manner had given way to an icy, disdainful demeanor. She appeared calmed by the chance to shift her focus from Stacy, over whom she had absolutely no control, to her own husband, whom she could hold to task for having—at least in her eyes—mishandled the situation.

"Let me get this absolutely straight," she repeated. "You're telling me that after all this time, after three months of doing this guy's bidding, you don't even know who he is? That you've been protecting some goddamn coward who didn't even have the balls to tell his own lawyer his real name?"

Scott sat there in silence, nervously thumbing his earring. He'd told Jody everything he knew just moments ago.

"And you've known this for two months and haven't told me?"

"I've been trying to find him," Scott said meekly.

"Tell it to the madwoman who has our daughter," she said, and stormed out of the room.

◼   ◼   ◼

Shivering, Stacy sat up on the sofa. She had dreamed once more that she had watched helplessly as Ben was run down—and it always left her unnerved. She looked at her watch, and saw that she had slept just under an hour. Thankfully, Alex was still fast asleep on the chair.

She swung her legs over the side of the couch and stood up, considering what to do next. Jody had had enough time to let her husband know what was going on. She had also had enough time, Stacy knew, to alert the police. Stacy had instructed Jody not to contact the authorities, and she wondered whether, if anything like this had happened to Ben, she would have heeded the warning. Foremost in her mind would have been to get Ben back safely, and if that meant only complying with a simple demand, she probably would have done so without worrying whether the police ever caught the kidnapper.

She winced as that word entered her mind. *Kidnapper. I guess that's what I am. A kidnapper.*

Surely Scott Heller would simply tell her the name of his client now. God knows she didn't intend to harm Alex in any way, but she had to keep that possibility as a thought in the Hellers' minds if her plan was to work. Faced with even the remotest chance of anything happening to Alex, how could Heller fail to give in to her right away? It was absurd to think that his conviction about the sanctity of the attorney–client privilege could be stronger than his need to protect his own daughter. This ordeal ought to be over before the end of the night.

Alex stirred. Stacy looked down at the peaceful figure. The poor child must be so frightened, she thought. *Well, there's no reason why* she *has to think I might hurt her. At least I can do all that I can to make her feel at ease.*

The young girl opened her eyes, blinking. Upon seeing Stacy standing over her, she quickly looked around the room, apparently remembering where she was and how she got there. She drew in her breath in a gasp and hugged her knees, burying her head in her arms and curling up like a ball. She started to whimper again.

"Now Alex," Stacy said. "I'm not going to hurt you. I just have to talk with your father on the phone, and pretty soon after that, I'm sure I'll be taking you home."

Alex continued to cry, and did not look up.

"Alex…sweetheart…I'm sorry I'm frightening you. I really don't mean to. Try to understand that."

Alex lifted her head. "I'm hungry," she said.

"Okay, hon. In a minute. First I need to call your dad on the phone again, and after I'm done we'll go to the kitchen and find something to eat. How's that?"

Alex just nodded her head silently, and resumed her curled-up position. Stacy stroked the girl's hair gently, and then reached into her bag for the cell phone.

To be safe, Stacy had to assume that the Hellers had contacted the police in spite of her warning not to. She had to assume that they would try to track her location when she placed her call. She did not know how quickly they could learn from which cell the call originated, or once that was accomplished how fast they could actually pinpoint her location within that cell. That, she understood, was trickier, and involved triangulating her position from two different points while she was actually on the line. Best to keep the call short to minimize the risk. She truly believed that Heller would finally give her what she needed, and that she would be driving Alex home shortly.

She sat down on the edge of the sofa, punched in the Hellers' number, and glanced at her watch. She would allow herself no more than sixty seconds once the ringing began, and then she would have to hang up.

Someone answered on the first ring.

"Scott Heller here."

"I want his name."

"Alex. Let me talk to Alex. Is she all right?" Scott asked frantically.

"She's fine. Now tell me the name."

"Mrs. Altman, please," Scott pleaded. "Just let me talk to her for a minute. She must be petrified. She's just a little girl."

"And my Ben was even littler," Stacy retorted. "I am not fooling around here, Mr. Heller. How can you protect that coward? If you won't help bring him to justice, and the so-called 'justice system' insists on protecting *his* rights, then *I* have to do something. Now tell me who he is."

Only ten seconds left.

"I'll call you back soon, Mr. Heller." She hung up.

■   ■   ■

"Wait! Mrs. Altman!"

But the line was dead.

Scott looked across the table at Jody, who had returned to the kitchen when the phone rang.

"Now what?" Jody said, after Scott filled her in on what little Stacy had said to him before abruptly cutting the call short.

"I'm sure she'll call back. She said she would. She must be afraid of having the call traced. I guess we just have to wait."

Scott took a long swallow of Scotch, which he had poured for himself moments ago.

"Maybe we should call the police," he offered.

"No!" Jody exclaimed. "I have absolutely zero confidence that the 'authorities' can help us. Look at the mess we've gotten into thinking that the court can protect us from her. When she calls back, you'll just have to explain to her that you don't have the information the wants. You can't tell her what you don't know. She'll have to understand that. Then she'll just let Alex go, and that'll be the end of it."

Time dragged. They had no idea when Stacy might be calling back, though they both assumed it would be that night. It was nearly eight o'clock, but neither of them could think of eating. Scott resisted the temptation to pour himself another drink. He moved to the living room, where he tuned the TV in to CNN and stared unseeing at the screen.

Jody brewed some coffee and sat silently at the kitchen table waiting.

Stacy cut the connection as she heard Scott plead with her to wait. Though Heller had not yet told her what she wanted to know, she could not risk allowing the authorities enough time to triangulate the location of her cell phone.

As she rummaged through the kitchen of the farmhouse to find Alex something to eat, she thought about her next move. Another call was necessary, and she saw now that she would have to stay on the line for more than the one-minute limit she had imposed on herself. To minimize the chances of disclosing her exact location, she would have to make the next call from somewhere else.

She found some ice cream in the freezer. Not exactly an ideal meal, but there was no time now for anything more substantial. It would have to satisfy Alex for the time being. Stacy filled a bowl for Alex, and one for herself, and returned to the bedroom, where Alex waited quietly.

"Ice cream for dinner!" Stacy said, trying to sound cheerful. "Eat up, and as soon as we're done, we're going for a ride."

"Home?" the girl asked, sitting up straight. "You're taking me home?"

"Not just yet, sweetheart," Stacy told her. "One more call to your dad first, and then we should be on our way, though."

"Then where are we going?" Alex asked. "You said you'd take me home after you talked with my father, and you already did. I want to go home." Tears welled up in her eyes.

The girl had become somewhat docile, and easier to deal with, and Stacy did not want to lose that small advantage. She did her best to sound upbeat. "Yes, I know. But your dad didn't know the answer to my question and had to find it out. So I have to call him back."

"Then where are we going now?" the girl pressed.

"Alex, it's hard for me to explain. Just trust me. Everything will be fine. We just have to go for a short ride."

Alex was losing interest in her bowl of ice cream. Stacy sat down on the bed next to her and put a hand on her shoulder. "I know this is frightening for you. I'm sure that as soon as I talk to your father again, we'll be on our way home."

"You're not going to hurt me, are you?" Alex asked quietly.

"No, Alex, I'm not."

"You're the lady whose son got run over by a car, aren't you?"

"Yes. How do you know about that?"

"I heard my parents talking about it." Alex paused. "You must be very sad."

Stacy nodded.

"And my father knows who did it, but he won't tell you, right?"

"Yes, that's right."

Alex thought for a minute. "I think he should. Is that what you're calling him about?"

"Yes. And I think he's going to tell me when I call him back. So then we'll be able to go home."

"You must miss your son an awful lot," Alex said.

"I sure do. I miss him every day. Would you like to see a picture of him?"

"Sure," Alex said, her half-eaten bowl of ice cream now forgotten.

Stacy removed her purse from her overnight bag and found the wallet-sized photo of Ben that had been taken in school the previous year. She handed it to Alex.

"Gosh, he's cute."

Alex sat in silence for a minute.

"So if we're not going home now, where do we have to go?"

"Nowhere special," Stacy told her. "I just don't want to call your father from here again."

Alex shrugged. "I guess it's okay then. Let's go."

◼   ◼   ◼

Five minutes later they were in Stacy's car heading east toward the

Interstate. When they reached the highway, and were about thirty miles from the farmhouse, Stacy rang the Heller residence.

Again, Scott answered on the first ring.

"Tell me, Mr. Heller. Now."

There was silence on the line for a moment before Scott spoke.

"Mrs. Altman, please try to understand—"

"Are you insane, Mr. Heller?" Stacy interrupted. "Are you still going to protect him? Even now?"

"No, no…" Scott stammered. "What I mean is…"

■　　■　　■

Scott faltered, and stole a glance at Jody across the kitchen table.

"I don't know who he is."

Stacy exploded. "What kind of fool do you take me for?" she shouted. "What do you mean you don't know who he is? This is not a good time to be playing games, Mr. Heller."

"I'm not playing games, Mrs. Altman. I don't know his name. We met only once, and we've spoken on the phone a few times. He was very guarded about his personal information. Even though I'd explained to him that it would remain confidential because of the attorney-client privilege."

"His telephone number, then. Give me his phone number," Stacy said harshly.

Scott cleared his throat. "Uh," he stuttered. "I only have his pager number and an e-mail address. Neither of them works anymore. I'm telling you, this guy was private."

"Jesus Christ," Stacy said. "Putting everything on the line to protect some coward."

There was a moment of silence before Stacy continued.

"This changes things, Mr. Heller. I'm not bringing Alex back until I know who your client is, and I've made contact with him. What the hell good is an inactive beeper number or e-mail address to me? You've got to do better than this."

Blood drained from Scott's face. As out of hand as this had been, it was becoming even more so.

"But you don't understand. I'm telling you everything I know. You *have* to bring Alex back now. You have to."

"Mr. Heller. If you think I've come this far to walk away empty-handed, you're crazy. No, Mr. Heller, you're going to have to deliver him."

Scott was silent.

"You've just become a detective. Find him. I'll be in touch."

The line went dead.

■　■　■

Stacy's car was still traveling east on the Interstate. At the next exit, she looped around to head west, back to the farmhouse.

"Sorry, Alex. Change of plans. You'll be staying with me for a while."

CHAPTER 41

Throughout the evening, Jody had alternated between anger and an almost timid stillness. After Scott related to her Stacy's side of the conversation, there was panic.

"Scott…What are we going to do? We've got to do something. *You've* got to do something. You've got to find him!"

Scott tried to remain calm.

"I've been trying to. I have someone trying to trace an e-mail that he sent to me in the beginning. There might be a way to track it back to the computer it was sent from."

"Well, how long will it take? When did he start? Has he found out anything yet?"

Scott looked at his watch—eight forty-five. He retrieved his PDA and found his friend's telephone number.

"Al," he said, when his college buddy answered. "It's Scott. Listen, have you had any success tracing that e-mail yet? It's turned out to be a priority now. Kind of urgent, you know?"

"Hey, Scott," Al Prescott replied. "I was going to call you tomorrow. I'm afraid we've hit a dead end."

Scott's eyes involuntarily flicked up toward Jody.

"Shit, Al, that's not what I wanted to hear."

"Yeah, I know, pal. But it's a fact."

"What's the problem?"

"Well, you know the e-mail header showed the IP address of the computer that the message came from, right? And you know from there I found the ISP—the Internet service provider—that the IP number was registered to."

"Yeah…"

"I was able to hook up with someone at the ISP who has access to the logs of IP addresses. The one we want is in the pool of dynamic addresses. It's not assigned to any one particular account. Like I explained before, dynamic addresses are assigned to users every time they log on. Log off, and the address goes back into the pool."

"Right, you told me that last time."

"Here's the problem. Their log only goes back fourteen days. They'd be able to tell me who had that IP address on any day within the last two weeks, but that's it. The e-mail we're looking at was sent almost three months ago."

"Shit," Scott repeated, and he remained silent for a moment.

"Al, there must be a way. There's got to be. I can't begin to tell you how important it is."

Scott waited as his friend thought.

"I dunno, buddy," he responded. "I don't see any way around it. If you'd given it to me sooner, my guy would've been able to trace it. But the e-mail's too old now."

"This is not good. Shit, this is not good."

"Sorry I couldn't be more help, my man. Hi to the family, okay?"

"Yeah, Al," Scott said. "Thanks for trying."

Jody listened quietly as Scott explained what he had just heard. She seemed too exhausted and emotionally drained to react.

"Scott, I'm scared," she said softly. "What if you can't find him?"

Scott looked at her and took her hand in his. "Honey, I'll find him. And I really don't think that Stacy is going to do anything to hurt Alex. She wanted to force the issue, and she's done that. As long as she knows that I'm working on finding this guy, I really think Alex'll be all right."

"But Alex. She must be terrified."

"Yes, I know. But what counts the most is whether she'll be all right. And I think she will be."

"Oh God, Scott. I hope you're right."

◼   ◼   ◼

They had spent the rest of the evening quietly, as there was nothing that either of them could do. Though Scott reiterated his desire to notify the police—at least it would be doing *something*—Jody remained adamant about keeping them out of it. Finally, they went to bed, though neither was in the least bit tired.

Scott dozed from time to time, but awakened long before his usual seven thirty. He had a problem, and he needed a plan. He told himself that this was what he did for a living—problem-solving—and he willed himself to address it like any other problem. Until now, the e-mail had represented the best hope of tracking down Guy. Now that that had been eliminated, he had to find another way. Win had said he'd try to trace the pager number Guy had used. He'd check in with Win later, and he'd try to figure out another way of finding the guy.

He showered and shaved, and got ready for the office. Whatever resources he could muster to find Guy would be there. He would enlist Sharon Roth's help. He did not want word of Alex's kidnapping to get out, but he and Sharon had always been a good problem-solving team, and he could rely on Sharon's discretion.

Jody was awake also. She made him promise to let her know everything that happened during the day.

"She'll call again, and since it's daytime, she'll probably call your office. Call me as soon as you hear from her."

Scott assured her as best he could, and set off for the office.

There was no traffic, and forty-five minutes later he was at his desk in his office. He sipped a freshly brewed cup of coffee, and considered the problem before him. His client, identity unknown, had given him two names. For himself, he had taken the name Glenn Ericson, and he said he had been referred to Scott by Win Honnicutt. But Win said he hadn't referred anyone to Scott since the Altman incident. So how had Guy/Ericson come to hire him?

Scott discounted the notion that it was simply a cold call. Though rarely, he sometimes did get clients from out of the blue, whether by way of the firm's Web page, or even through the Yellow Pages. But Guy had known to use Win's name, so there must be some link to Win. If Win hadn't sent him, then Guy must have come to Scott through someone who knew Win. Someone Win had mentioned Scott's name to?

Then Scott had an idea. Win had referred clients to him before. Maybe one of those clients, happy with the result Scott had obtained, had passed his name on to Guy. Since Guy wanted to conceal his trail, he wouldn't have told Scott the name of his real source. But wanting a name to use as a referral source, he had seized upon one that he knew Scott would recognize—Win Honnicutt.

Scott turned to his computer, and logged on to the firm's local area network. Roth Stern was making progress toward becoming a completely paperless office. All documents in newly opened files were scanned, converted into digital form, and maintained on the server, and the slow process of converting the firm's existing files had begun. The time would come shortly when Scott would be able to access any piece of information from any file in the office from his computer. To date, the conversion had progressed at least to the point where all client information, whether on open or closed files, was in the database. One of the information fields was "referral source," and Scott initiated a search for all clients who had been referred to him by Win. Scott was surprised to see from the list that appeared on his screen a moment later that in the four years since Roth Stern had been in existence, Win had referred ten clients to him. To ensure that he was not leaving anything out, Scott took a moment to search for any clients that those ten had in turn referred to him. That search turned up an additional seven names. With a few more clicks of the mouse, Scott generated a report that listed the name, address, and telephone number of each client, which he instructed the computer to print.

He heard the front door to the suite open, and knew that it was Sharon. She, like he, was an early starter.

Scott went out to greet her and fill her in.

■   ■   ■

"Okay, Scott," Sharon said. "I agree. Tracking the e-mail would be great, and your source might still be able to figure out how to do it, but we can't sit back and just hope for that. This guy who said he was Glenn Ericson probably got your name from one of the clients on this list, and while we wait for some word on the e-mail, we have to work that list."

They were sitting in Sharon's office, she at her desk, and Scott in one of the chairs opposite her.

"Now, what we need to do is talk to each person on this list as soon as possible, and see which of them has referred someone to you recently."

Sharon was taking charge, and Scott was only too happy to let her do so. He was tired and emotionally drained, and not sure he could think objectively.

"We need to think what we'll tell these people," Scott said. "We can't just say that some guy retained us and gave us a bogus name, did you send him to us."

Sharon thought for a moment.

"Well, when someone refers a new client to us, we usually send them a thank-you note. How about if we call the clients on this list, and tell them that we discovered that by mistake no one ever wrote them to thank them for their recent referral? If they say 'I don't know what you're talking about,' we can make like we're just embarrassed about yet another bit of messed up paperwork."

"Yeah," said Scott. "But what if they say 'Oh, you're quite welcome,' what do we do? Say 'By the way, what was that client's name again?'"

"Let's deal with that when it comes up," said Sharon. "At least we'll be a step closer to finding the guy at that point."

"Okay, then. At least it's a start."

Sharon looked at the clock on her desk. "It's only eight fifteen. We really shouldn't start the calls until about nine. How do you feel about letting Karen know what's going on? That way she can help with the calls, and we'll get through them quicker."

"Fine by me. The faster the better."

CHAPTER 42

Stacy opened her eyes and sat up with a start. She glanced over to the bed and saw that Alex was, thankfully, still asleep. The girl had wailed the entire ride back to the farmhouse last night, and Stacy had had her hands full getting her back into the house. "Take me home! You promised we would go home after you talked to my father!" she kept on shrieking.

"I'm sorry, Alex. Change of plans," was all that Stacy could say.

They had arrived back at the farmhouse at about nine o'clock, and Stacy somehow managed to get the girl upstairs to the guest room, where Stacy and Marc had stayed during their visit two years ago. Once there, Stacy had sat herself on the floor, her back propped against the bedroom door, as she watched Alex throw things around the room, screaming hysterically.

"Everything will be okay, Alex. Everything will be okay," Stacy kept repeating, though she was beginning to wonder herself.

Except for the bowls of ice cream they'd only picked at when they had arrived earlier that evening, they had not eaten. Eventually, hunger and exhaustion overcame the girl and she fell asleep on the bed. Stacy covered her with a blanket, and found another blanket and a pillow for herself. She spread the blanket on the floor in front of the door and lay down. If Alex woke during the night, she would not be able to open the door, as Stacy's body blocked the way. Stacy finally drifted off, and she awakened as she had fallen asleep, contemplating the mess she had gotten herself into.

She had not slept comfortably, and was surprised to see that it was already after eight. After checking to see that Alex was still asleep, Stacy made her way downstairs. She was famished, and she expected Alex to be likewise when she woke up. Stacy was thankful to find a fully-stocked pantry, and the refrigerator had some essential staples as well. There were fresh coffee beans in a canister on the counter, and a quick search of the overhead cabinets turned up an electric coffee grinder. After starting the coffee brewing, she found a large cast-iron skillet, retrieved the pound of bacon she had seen in the refrigerator, and started it frying. While the bacon was cooking, she found a bowl, whipped some eggs, and added in a splash of milk, a touch of vanilla extract, and a sprinkling of cinnamon. She added six slices of bread to the mixture, and while they were soaking she melted some butter on the griddle she had begun heating. About ten minutes later, breakfast was ready.

She placed the French toast and bacon in the oven to keep it warm until Alex was up, and set the table. She wanted to do her best to put Alex at ease.

With breakfast ready and waiting, Stacy quietly made her way upstairs to peek in on Alex. The poor girl must be exhausted, she thought as she looked in on the still-sleeping figure. She turned and went back downstairs.

What next? What she had hoped would be a simple transaction had become immeasurably complex. She had been right about one thing. Immediately upon her taking Alex, Heller had ceased hiding behind his principles and had given in to her. But she had never dreamed that he would not have the information she wanted. It briefly occurred to her that he might be playing with her—that he might be giving her a story—but she dismissed it. He couldn't be that cavalier about his daughter's safety. *But I'm absolutely no further along than I was yesterday.*

What had she gotten herself into? She believed that Heller would try, was trying even now, to find out who and where his client was. But what if he was unable to? What if the client had covered his tracks too well? What was she going to do?

She had to talk to someone. Someone who would understand, and could advise her. She sighed. Ashamed as she was, she knew she had to call Frank O'Connor. She looked at the clock on the wall and saw that it was nearly nine o'clock. He would be in his office now.

Frank answered the phone himself.

"Frank. It's me. Stacy. I've done something really stupid. I'm in a mess, and I don't know what to do."

There was silence on the other end of the line for a moment. Then came the question.

"What now?"

"I have the Hellers' daughter with me. I met her at her bus stop yesterday, and forced her into my car." She told him of her telephone call to Scott, and of the client's deception of him.

"My God, Stacy! This is serious! You've got to bring her back! Where are you?" he shouted. "No, wait! Don't tell me. I don't want to know."

"I don't know what to do, Frank. I need your advice."

"Stacy, listen to me. You are in the midst of committing a very serious crime. And you're putting me in a very untenable position. If anyone were to find out we've spoken, I'd have to tell them everything you've told me. So don't even tell me where you are."

"What are you talking about, Frank? What do you mean you'd have to repeat what I'm telling you? I thought that stuff is privileged information. That fucking privilege is what started all of this in the first place."

"I told you there were exceptions to the privilege. And this is one of them. Communications with a lawyer in aid of the commission of a crime are not privileged. All I can do ethically is advise you to turn yourself in—*which I am doing right now*. If you were to tell me where you are right now with that girl, I would have to let the authorities know."

Stacy exploded. "I don't believe this fucking shit! Do you mean to tell me that that bastard who killed my son is protected by that goddamn privilege, but I'm not? What kind of police state are we living in?"

Frank answered her calmly. "They're different circumstances, Stacy. The driver of that car went to Scott Heller after he had committed a crime, in order to get legal advice as to what his rights were. The law protects those communications—the deed's already been done, the communications won't result in additional crimes being committed, and forcing their disclosure won't undo the crime that's already been committed. But you're calling me about a crime you're in the middle of committing. You're in the middle of a kidnapping, and you're holding someone for ransom. If I knew where you were, and the police asked me, I'd have to tell them. Shit, I'd probably have to pick up the phone and call them myself. So they'd be able to stop a crime in progress. It's that simple."

"That's fucked up," Stacy spat. "Really fucked up."

"There's one more thing you ought to consider, Stacy," Frank said. "If Heller's client is finally arrested because the police find out who he is through Heller's breach of confidence, you can probably expect a legal challenge by the client. I'm not saying it'll be successful, and in fact I don't think it would be upheld, but I'd expect his new lawyer to claim that his identification was illegally obtained and tainted. I'd say he'd try to get him off on a technicality like that."

"What are you telling me, Frank?" Stacy asked. "That that bastard is going to walk, and I'm going to be punished?"

"I'm telling you that extorting Heller into telling you privileged information is going to give the driver a technicality to seize upon. And I'm telling you *to turn yourself in*. If you want me to, I'll make some phone calls and arrange for your surrender."

"No thanks," she said, and she hung up.

■   ■   ■

She could not contain herself. She sent the place settings crashing to the floor with a sweep of her arm, and seeing a glass of orange juice still standing on the table, she picked it up and hurled it at the wall.

This fucking system. Why is this happening to me? She kicked angrily at one of the kitchen chairs, sending it toppling.

A shuffling sound caught her attention, and she turned to find Alex standing in the doorway.

"I'm hungry," she said softly.

Stacy's first inclination was to scream at the child. *God damn it, you little whining brat! I hate your father! Look at what he's done. Look at what he's made me do.*

The scene that greeted Alex, and the anger evident in Stacy's face, must have frightened her, and tears welled up in her eyes.

"What's the matter?" Alex asked quietly.

This simple question stopped Stacy in her tracks. What's the matter? She was forced to look at herself through Alex's eyes. To this innocent little girl, what *was* the matter? Her daddy knew who killed a little boy, and wouldn't tell the boy's mother who it was. The boy's mother was trying to make her father say who it was, but for some reason he wouldn't. Even though the lady could be kind of scary, she, Alex, agreed with her. Her father should say who killed the little boy.

Although she didn't really understand all of the grown-up stuff, the lady said she wasn't going to hurt her, and last night when they were talking about the boy, Ben, and looking at his picture, the lady seemed really nice. But this morning she was scaring her again. Throwing dishes around the kitchen, and kicking chairs across the room.

Pretty confusing for a nine-year-old.

"Did I do something wrong?"

For God's sake. In all her simplicity and innocence, little Alex was the only one who really did, really could, understand what was the matter. She knew what was wrong, she knew what was right, and she knew what ought to be done. She wasn't burdened by the artificial rules that most adults seemed to bind themselves to.

In all of this, she's the only friend I have.

"No, sweetheart, you didn't do anything wrong." Stacy said with a sigh. She righted the chair, and began picking up the dishes scattered across the floor. "Come here. If you help me clean up this mess, we can eat. I hope you like French toast and bacon!"

CHAPTER 43

Scott, Sharon, and Karen sat around the conference room table, each with a copy of the computer report that Scott had generated earlier that morning.

"All right," Sharon began. "Where are we?"

"I've come up dry so far," said Scott. "I've spoken with four of the six people on my list, and I've left voice mail messages for the other two. None of the four I've talked with have referred anyone to us."

"It's been slow going for me, too," Karen reported. "I've only managed to speak with two of my six. We only have home numbers for the others, and they must be at work. I was able to leave messages for all of them, but they probably won't get them until tonight. Hopefully they'll call back right away."

"And I've spoken with three of my five. They have nothing to report, and I've left messages for the others."

"Well, it's about ten thirty," said Scott. "My bet is that Stacy will wait till tonight to call again. I just hope I'll have something to tell her."

■ ■ ■

"Whaddya got?" asked Lieutenant Rob Weber.

Detective Roy Kluge sat across the desk from his lieutenant, ever-present notepad in his hand.

"It's the Altman hit-and-run, Loo. You know we've hit a brick wall there. We were able to make the car, but we haven't been able to do anything with it."

"Yeah, so whaddya have that's new?"

"A nasty turn of events. Not really our jurisdiction, but something we oughta keep our eye on."

"Go on."

"When I was at Heller's office in New York back in July, I made nice with the receptionist." He glanced at his notes. "Julie Fox. She seemed upset that her boss had gotten involved in the whole thing, and I just got the feeling that she might end up helpful in some way. So I gave her my card. Well, I just got a call from her. It seems that Heller's secretary..." He referred to his notes again. "Karen Allesio, let her in on a little secret this morning, and swore her to secrecy. The Altman woman went and snatched Heller's nine-year-old girl."

Weber whistled softly. "That's heavy shit."

"Yup," agreed Kluge. "She's called and demanded that Heller ID his client."

"Did he?"

"That's where it gets interesting. He can't."

"What? Whaddya mean 'he can't'?"

Kluge filled Weber in on what Julie had told him.

"Jesus Christ," swore the lieutenant. "Fucking lawyers. Of all the dumb-ass things!"

"My guess is that Heller hasn't gone to the local cops," ventured Kluge. "Otherwise, we'd've heard, being that Altman lives here."

"I think you're right," Weber agreed. "Maybe you oughta go talk to Heller, and see what you can find out."

"Right," said Kluge. "I'll head into the city now."

Scott was unable to get any work done, and he made no real pretense of trying. He called Win. Ordinarily, he would have confided in his friend about what had happened the previous afternoon and evening, but he just didn't have the energy to go into it. He simply asked whether Win had made any progress with the pager.

"My guy, the one who was going to run this down for you, is back in jail. Some Internet shopping scam. Usually, that doesn't slow him down, because he can accomplish a lot just from a pay phone, but he's been dealing with a lot of stuff since his arrest, so he hasn't gotten to it."

"It's important, Win. See what you can do, okay?"

"Sure thing. I gotta meet with him this afternoon. I'll mention it to him again."

He hung up, and wandered into Sharon's office to see if she had heard back from any of the clients she had left messages for. Nothing. He did the same with Karen. Nothing there either. He went back to his office and pushed papers around his desk.

At about noon, his intercom rang. Julie sounded nervous.

"Uh, Mr. Heller, Detective Kluge from the Perth Amboy police is here to see you."

Shit. What timing! What could he possibly want?

"Tell him I'm busy," he snapped. "Tell him to call Karen and make an appointment."

"He says it's extremely urgent, and that it can't wait."

Scott paused. The police must have known about Stacy's contempt and sentence. What if they've been keeping tabs on her? What if Kluge has news about Alex? He'd better see him.

"Okay, okay. Tell him I'll be right out."

Scott walked to the reception area, and found Kluge standing in front of the receptionist's counter. The detective extended his hand in greeting, and Scott shook it half-heartedly.

"Thanks for taking the time, Mr. Heller," Kluge began. "I know you have a lot on your mind today."

Scott shot a glance at the detective. *He knows*, Scott thought.

"I do. And I think you'd better come inside." He turned and

motioned for Kluge to follow him.

Scott escorted him into the conference room and closed the door.

"Mr. Heller, we know that your daughter is missing. We know that Stacy Altman has taken her."

Scott sat down in one of the chairs, and motioned for Kluge to do the same.

"How?" Scott asked. "How did you find out?"

"I'm sorry. I can't tell you that. But we want to help."

"With all due respect, Detective, we don't want it. And I mean that sincerely—the respect part. I appreciate your concern, and I appreciate your coming out here to see me. But I have the matter under control. She's contacted us, and made it clear that all she wants is the name and address of my client. We expect to hear from her again tonight, and I'm going to tell her what she wants to know, and Alex will be returned. If the police get involved, it'll just complicate things."

Scott saw no sense in letting Kluge know that he was frantically trying to find out just who his client was.

"It won't be that simple," Kluge said. "It's never that simple. You can't do this alone."

"Detective, I have to trust myself to do what's best to ensure the safety of my daughter. I don't want to escalate this any further. Besides, I have no idea where Stacy is, and you wouldn't know where to start looking. I have no choice but to depend on her to bring Alex back when I tell her what she wants to know. And quite frankly, I don't care what happens to her after she brings Alex back. She could vanish off the face of the earth, scot-free, for all I care. So I really don't see anything to be gained by involving the police."

Scott glanced at his watch.

"Now, like you said, I have a lot on my mind, so I'd like to be left alone."

Kluge stood.

"I think you're making a mistake, Mr. Heller. If you change your mind, you know how to contact me. You don't have to walk me out. I'll find my way."

■   ■   ■

It was almost one thirty, and Scott was restless. He assumed Stacy would be calling back, and although he had no idea what he was going to tell her—he was no closer to finding his client now than he'd been last night—he needed the contact. He needed to know that Alex was all right.

From his office, Scott could hear the telephone ring whenever a call came in to the firm. Each time it did, Scott jumped, thinking that it might be Stacy. The phone rang now, and Scott looked at his extension anxiously, waiting for the intercom to announce a caller.

"Mr. Heller," came Julie's voice. "Al Prescott is on line two for you."

Scott was surprised. Last night, Al had told him the e-mail was a dead end. Had he come up with something?

"Al," he said expectantly. "I didn't expect to hear from you. What's doing?"

"Well, buddy, you gave me a job to do, and do it I did."

"You traced the e-mail?"

"Indeed."

"But how? You said you couldn't."

"Yeah, but after I spoke with you last night, I got to thinking. And the solution was so simple. I don't know how I missed it the first time around."

"Tell me."

"My guy at the ISP told me that their log of dynamic address assignments goes back only fourteen days. For any day within the last two weeks, he could tell me what account holder was assigned what dynamic address. I was focusing on the fact that your guy sent his e-mail three months ago, and figured that it was untraceable because of that. But then I realized—when you log on to your Internet service and the service assigns a dynamic IP address, that address stays with you for your whole Internet session. Until you disconnect.

"I don't know about you, but at my office, I'm connected pretty much 24/7. I hardly *ever* shut down my computer, and I hardly *ever* disconnect from the Net. My connection is constant. I mean, there are times when I have to reboot—things go kerflooey with some program, the computer hangs, and the only way out is control-alt-delete. When I do that, and reconnect to the Net, I get a new dynamic address. But luckily that happens only once in a while."

"So you're saying that if the client's computer didn't disconnect from the Internet since he sent the e-mail, he would have the same IP address today as he did then?"

"Exactamundo. And guess what? We're in luck. My guy checked the log for the IP address that shows up in your e-mail… And according to the log, that address has been assigned to the same account holder for the last eighteen weeks! At first I thought it was something of a miracle that the guy wouldn't have had to reboot his computer in four months, but then I realized—and here it gets a little technical, so stick with me—the IP address probably isn't assigned to an individual computer. It's probably assigned to a router, a switch, or some other device through which a number of different computers share an Internet connection."

"Huh?"

"How many computers you got hooked up to the Net at your office?"

"Um, about ten or so, I guess."

"Okay. I'm guessing all of those computers are connected by cable to a piece of equipment in your telephone closet. That's gonna be either a router or a switch—probably a switch. A little box with a number of ports on it. The switch is what's connected directly to the Net, probably through a DSL or cable modem. All your computers connect to the one switch, the switch connects to the Internet, and your ISP assigns an IP address to the switch. On the local side of the network, the switch assigns a kind of internal IP address to the individual computers within the office, so it can direct the Internet traffic to the right computer. But as far as the outside world is concerned—anything on the other side of the switch—all the computers in the office have the same IP address."

Scott thought for a moment.

"So, as long as the switch is on, and connected to the Net, it keeps the same IP address? Even if I turn my computer on and off a couple of times?"

"That's it! And there's hardly *ever* a reason to turn off the switch. Now, I've given you a simplified version of what's going on, and there are any number of different configurations that might give similar results. But, I'm guessing that your guy has an office or home network, and accesses the Net through some kind of shared connection, and that the shared device that receives the dynamic IP address from the provider is constantly online. Hence, the same IP address for four months. There must've been some reason to restart the switch months ago, but who cares?

"My contact checked the IP address I gave him against the log, and that address has been with the same account holder for four months."

Finally. Something concrete to go by. *Maybe there's an end to this nightmare in sight.*

"Okay. Enough technical stuff. What's the name?"

The color drained from Scott's face when he heard what Al had to say.

CHAPTER 44

It had been about six weeks since Scott Heller's deposition. Vince Saldano hadn't had any contact with his attorney since the tense telephone call the day before the deposition, but he had seen the handful of news stories that had followed. To say that he'd been relieved when he'd read that Heller had followed through and asserted the attorney-client privilege, and that the court had upheld it, was to put it mildly.

In the intervening time, he'd seen no reason to reach out for his attorney again. To him, no news was good news.

Of course, he'd also followed the news stories about the Altman woman's activities outside the law. He wasn't happy with the fact that she didn't just accept the court's ruling and let the matter lie. That she'd defied a court order to stay away from Heller and gotten herself thrown in jail for contempt of court told him a lot about her mental state. Though he was still confident that there was no way Heller could betray him, it was discomfiting to know that there was an irrational woman out there hell-bent on finding him.

But when he considered the objective facts, he was beginning to think things might just work out. He just might come out of this okay.

■   ▦   ▦

Mike Harrison hung up the telephone and whistled softly. That Altman woman is something else, he thought. And as luck would have it, she'd chosen him to confide in.

It was just after noon, and it was rare that Harrison was at his desk at this time of day. Usually he was out in the field, but today he had a large volume of notes to sift through, so he had blocked out a time this afternoon to slog through them. He was glad he had. His telephone had rung, and he had been surprised to discover that it was Stacy Altman. He was even more surprised to hear the story she told.

When they had last spoken, she had told him of her inclination to defy the restraining order that had been issued against her and to confront the Hellers directly. He had watched the court docket, and had seen that she had actually followed through and had even earned herself some jail time. He had also learned of her little foray into the Hellers' house, and had done a short piece on the whole contempt incident.

She had just told him what she had been up to since she had gotten out.

The woman sounded unstable to him. *Unstable? Jesus! She had kidnapped a little girl to ransom her for information.* And the father couldn't tell her what she wanted to know? How bizarre.

What really appeared to tick her off was the advice her lawyer had given her yesterday. The attorney-client privilege protects the driver of the car that killed her son, but doesn't protect her. And her actions in forcing the information from his lawyer might actually furnish him with a technicality to get himself off on. *I don't blame her for being pissed off.*

"What are you going to do?" he had asked her.

"Well, I'm not putting my faith in the system anymore, that's for sure," she had answered cryptically.

Harrison decided then and there that if he could get an inside line with her, he would hold off writing anything about her contact until he saw what developed. He got her commitment to keep him advised of what was going on.

Yup. This one is worth watching.

■   ■   ■

I can figure this out, Stacy kept telling herself. I can make it so it all works out okay.

There was nobody for her to turn to for help, but when had there been since this whole ordeal had started? Her husband had been useless, wanting simply to put the matter behind him without caring a damn that his son's killer would go unpunished. Her mother had been there for emotional support, but she too had kept urging her to give up. She'd had hopes that Frank O'Connor would be her champion, that he would vindicate her rights—and Ben's—in the courts. That had turned out to be a sick joke.

No, she had only herself to rely on. She had taken control, and she was determined to learn what she had been seeking for months.

She had been skeptical at first of Heller's claim that he didn't know who or where his client was, but she just could not bring herself to believe that he would make such a thing up with Alex where she was. No, he had the incentive and he'd come across soon. *What was it they said? Necessity is the mother of invention? He'd figure out a way to find the information he needed.*

But after she found out who it was, what next? Turn him over to the police? According to O'Connor, the bastard would just hire another slick lawyer and twist the law some more. Cry that the police had found out who he was illegally. She took little comfort in O'Connor's advice that the challenge ought to be overruled. Heller's claim of privilege "ought" to have been overruled too. But the system was too preoccupied with making sure that criminals' rights were being protected to worry about actually doing some justice.

She'd be damned if she would stand by and watch her son's murderer walk away from this.

CHAPTER 45

Scott hung up from talking with Al Prescott and sat in stunned silence, trying to process the information that he'd just been given. A million questions flooded his brain, and he couldn't come up with a logical answer to any of them.

He had told Al that he must be mistaken. No way could the e-mail have come from that source. But Al had been adamant. "I have one hundred percent confidence in what my guy told me. That's your man."

Still disbelieving, Scott brought the client's e-mail up on his computer screen. The e-mail that Al had traced. With a few mouse clicks, he opened the header that showed the sender's IP address. Then he searched his mail folders for another message—one that he knew had come from the person Al had just identified. He brought up that header to reveal the IP address from which it had originated, and he compared it to the first.

They matched.

Scott stared at his screen vacantly, the words that Al Prescott had said to him moments ago reverberating in his head.

"Wait'll ya hear this guy's name," Al had said to him with a chuckle. "What a moniker."

"All right already," Scott had said. "What's the name?"

"It's a mouthful—Thurston Winslow Barton Honnicutt IV."

◼   ◼   ◼

"I have to see him *now*," Scott said to the receptionist in the small law office just off Foley Square in lower Manhattan. He hadn't bothered to telephone ahead. Instead, after he had spoken with Al Prescott, and then spent a few minutes confirming on his computer what he simply couldn't believe, he had rushed from his office to hail a cab, and was at the Law Offices of T. W. Honnicutt a half hour later.

"Tell him it's Scott Heller, and it's urgent."

But before the receptionist could do anything, Win appeared at the front desk.

"Heller!" he said, with a look of pleasant surprise on his face. "Slummin' it, I see. Come on in!"

"Cut the crap, Win. This has gotten way out of hand. That woman has Alex, and now I find out it's been you all along!"

Win's pleasure in seeing his friend turned to puzzlement.

"What are you talking about? Who has Alex?"

"Stacy Altman. How could you do this to me?"

Win glanced at the receptionist, and then turned back to Scott.

"I think you'd better come on into my office, and tell me what you're talking about." He led Scott down a short hallway, and stood aside to let his guest enter. In keeping with his characteristic eschewal of all things suggestive of affluence, the office was modestly furnished. He motioned to an austere upholstered chair at the far end of the room, and he took one identical to it on the other side of a low glass coffee table.

"Now, what's going on?"

"Damn it, Win! You tell me. All along, I'm trying to find out who this mystery client of mine is, and you even had the goddamn nerve to offer your help finding him. I don't know what's going on, but maybe you can explain to me why an e-mail that piece of shit sent me came from your computer!"

"Whoa, slow down there. What do you mean his e-mail came from my computer?"

"You're telling me you don't know what I'm talking about? *His* fucking e-mail was sent from *your* fucking computer. And now you'd better tell me who he is, and where I can find him, because Stacy Altman has Alex, and I have to deliver the guy who killed her son!"

Scott spent the next ten minutes describing the events of the last twenty-four hours, ending with Al Prescott's revelation of what the header on the client's e-mail told about the origin of the message.

"I couldn't believe it. But then I dug up one of the e-mails you sent me a few weeks ago. One of the jokes you forwarded on to me. Your IP address is there, plain as day. The same IP address as the client's."

Win had listened in silence. When Scott finished, he exhaled loudly.

"Scott, the most important thing is that we figure out how to get Alex back safely. But you have to know one thing—I have no idea how or why that e-mail led to my computer."

"So you're denying you have anything to do with this?"

"For God's sake, of course I am. Do you realize what you're accusing me of? You really think I'd do that? Use you like that?"

Win was looking directly at Scott, who averted his eyes.

"It looks like someone's setting me up for some reason," Win continued. "I didn't like it from the start, when you told me the guy used my name when he first called you. And now it seems he's closer to me than I'd like to think. Tell me how your techie traced this thing to my computer. You know how primitive I am when it comes to that stuff. But there's got to be an explanation."

Scott sat there, dazed. As much as he had hated thinking that his friend had deceived him, if Win *had* had something to do with this, he'd at least be one step closer to finding his client. And a step closer to getting Alex back.

If someone was playing Win, too, then unraveling this mess was going to take a much longer time.

■ ■ ■

"It gets a little complicated," Scott was explaining to Win. "The way Al explained it to me, depending on how your network is set up, a number of computers can be sharing the same Internet connection. That means e-mails sent from any of those computers would appear to come from the same place."

Win frowned in concentration.

"Think of it as a telephone with a bunch of extensions, I guess. As far as the phone company is concerned, calls from any of the extensions come from the same telephone number."

Win nodded.

"How many computers do you have here that are online?"

"Let's see," Win said, ticking them off on his fingers. "Mine and my secretary's, Jack Doherty's, the receptionist's, and the bookkeeper's. Five. And I think that switch thingy you're talking about is in the copy room."

"Remind me again. Who's Jack Doherty?"

"Guy who rents an office from me. I told you about him. Had a practice outside of Boston, and moved to New York the beginning of the year. He helps with my overflow when I need him, and I return the favor. You never met him?"

Scott shook his head.

"Nice guy. In fact, I want to bring him in here. He's the one who helped me set up this network stuff. Before he came, I was dialing in to the Internet on a modem. He got all my computers hooked up to each other, and to the Net. He should be able to help figure out what's going on here."

Win reached for the telephone extension on the coffee table and punched the intercom.

"Hey, Jack. Can you come here a minute? There's someone I want you to meet, and you might be able to help us with a computer question."

He hung up.

"He'll be right here."

A moment later, a man entered Win's office.

"You rang?"

"Jack…I'd like you to meet a good friend of mine. Scott Heller."

Scott's back was to the door, so he stood and turned to greet Jack Doherty. When he did, all hell broke loose.

First, a look of confusion on Doherty's face.

"Huh?"

Then, recognition and shock from Scott.

"What the—"

Scott lunged at the man and grabbed his shirt, and Doherty stumbled back against the door frame.

"For Chrissake, Scott!" shouted Win. He leaped from his chair and darted toward them.

"You son of a bitch! It's you! Who the fuck *are* you?"

Win had reached Scott, and he managed to pull his friend from Doherty. Scott twisted around to face Win.

"It's him, Win. *He's* my client! He's the guy who ran down Ben Altman."

Doherty shot a confused look at Win.

"Him?" This from Win.

"Yes, damn it. Him. He came to my office to meet with me when this whole thing started." He turned to Doherty, but continued addressing Win. "And now, I'm going to give his name to Stacy Altman so I can get my daughter back."

Doherty's eyes flitted between Win and Scott.

"Is that true?" Win asked Doherty.

Doherty recoiled at the question, and then stared straight at Win for a moment, silent. He seemed to be carefully measuring his response. Then, finally, he took a deep breath and exhaled.

"Yes, and no."

"Now what the fuck does that mean?" Scott snarled.

Doherty turned to Scott.

"Yes, I met with you, and yes, I spoke with you on the phone a few times," he said calmly. "But no, I am not the person who was driving the car that killed Ben Altman."

"Jesus Christ," muttered Scott.

"I think you'd better explain what you're talking about, Jack." Win physically directed Scott to the chair that he had been sitting in, and motioned Doherty to the other one. For himself, he dragged a third chair from in front of his desk over to the coffee table, and sat down. "What do you mean?"

Doherty seemed uneasy. He picked at the nap of the upholstered arm of the chair.

"He's a client. He wanted to make sure his name was kept completely out of it. I met with you, and told you I was the driver, but I'm really only a go-between."

"Jesus Christ," Scott repeated. "What about the privilege? I told him—you—that he was protected. And the court's upheld the privilege."

Doherty squirmed in his seat.

"He didn't trust it. He wanted to be sure, so he insisted on an extra layer. Your name is known in this office, so we—" He stole a glance at Win, who was watching him intently. "Uh, I brought you in. If the court rejected the privilege, you really had no way of finding him. And in the unlikely event you *were* able trace the contacts you had, they wouldn't lead to him. They'd lead to me."

"How *did* you find your way here, anyway? Or is it just coincidence that you came to see Win?"

"None of your fucking business."

"Enough," Win interjected.

"Well, I did find you," Scott said. "So now, tell me his name."

Doherty exhaled wearily, and looked from Scott to Win.

"I can't."

Scott gripped both arms of his chair, as if to rise, and Win put his hand up in a gesture of calm.

Doherty looked back at Scott.

"I can't tell you his name. It's privileged information."

CHAPTER 46

When they had finished breakfast that morning, Stacy had asked Alex if she wanted to see the rest of the farm, and the two of them had walked the grounds. Along the way, Alex had slipped her hand into Stacy's, and together they had explored. Stacy had tensed when they spotted one of the Bartletts' neighbors in the distance, an Amish man tending a nearby field, but Alex had just waved at him, and then barraged her with questions about the man's dress.

They'd returned to the house, and Stacy had suggested that Alex watch TV. "There's only garbage on TV," Alex had told her. "I hardly ever watch it, except for maybe some stuff on the Discovery Channel. Is it okay if I play out in the back?" Stacy had decided that the two of them had developed enough trust between them to allow this, and Alex had spent a few hours outside by herself.

It was now close to three o'clock, nearing a full twenty-four hours since Stacy had forced Alex into the car in front of 8 Apple Ridge Crescent. Her interaction with Alex during that time had been emotionally charged. She had begun by consciously forcing herself to view the girl dispassionately. Alex was a means to an end—someone for whom Stacy had no feelings, good or bad. Stacy quickly found, however, that Alex's presence magnified the loss that she had experienced. Things as simple as having the girl tell her she had to go to the bathroom, or wanted something to eat, evoked in Stacy feelings that had been absent since Ben's death—responsibility and the need to nurture.

Forced to remember what she no longer had with Ben, while being called upon to provide for Alex, she had begun to resent the girl. But Alex's innocent curiosity about Ben, and her simple declaration of what she thought her father ought to do, had kindled a connection, and their breakfast that morning had cemented a kind of mutual trust between them. She supposed she was experiencing some sort of reverse "Stockholm syndrome," in which she had formed an emotional bond with her hostage.

Throughout the day, she had fought the urge to call Alex's father to check the progress he had made in finding his client. If he was telling her the truth—and she had convinced herself that he was—he had a real bit of sleuthing to do, and she didn't want to distract him. Any more than he must be already, that is.

Stacy felt she was finally close to facing the coward who had run down her child. It was, in a sense, surreal. Until now, he had been a nameless, faceless person—more a concept than a being. Soon, she would be able to put a face to that concept.

His abstractness, however, had not prevented Stacy from cultivating a very real hatred toward him. For some time now, she had wondered what it would be like to vent her rage at its source—at him. She relished the thought of being so much closer to finding out.

But it all depended on Scott Heller. She had gotten his attention, that was for sure. And while his ignorance of his client's identity was a curve ball that she couldn't have foreseen, she felt he was now sufficiently motivated to ferret the monster out.

Earlier that day, she had told Mike Harrison that she was no longer putting her faith in the system. She had decided what she had to do for herself if—when—Scott Heller succeeded in finding his client.

She just hoped it would be soon.

CHAPTER 47

Scott Heller literally flew from his seat, rounded the coffee table, and grabbed Jack Doherty by the shirt.

"You piece of shit!" he screamed. His face was just inches from Doherty's. "Fuck you, 'it's privileged information.' She has my daughter! Now tell me his fucking name!"

For the second time in just a few minutes, Win wrested Scott from Doherty.

"Scott, for God's sake!"

"I've had enough of this shit, Win." Scott strained against Win's hold. "This isn't about the attorney-client privilege! My daughter's being held hostage by some crazy woman. I have to find this guy."

Doherty, who had been clearly shaken by Scott's explosion, regained his composure.

"Mr. Heller. Scott. You, of all people, should understand. The client's name is privileged information. I can't tell you."

Scott looked from Doherty to Win.

"I'm holding you responsible, Win. He's *your* partner. *Your* name is all over this thing. Get him to talk."

"Wait a minute, both of you. Please. Let's sit back down and talk this through."

Win eased his grip on Scott's arms, and when Scott did not move toward Doherty, he released Scott completely. He went back to his chair by the coffee table, and motioned for the other two to join him. Doherty did so, but Scott remained standing.

"First, Scott, for what it's worth, he's not my partner. He rents space from me. I can't tell him what to do."

Scott opened his mouth to speak, but Win held up his hand. He turned to Doherty.

"This is clearly a delicate situation, Jack. What can we do here?"

Doherty looked perplexed by the question. He sat there blinking at Win. After a moment, his shoulders slumped, and he sighed.

"There's nothing I can do. Ask him." He tilted his head in Scott's direction. "He knows there'd be serious consequences if I violated the client's trust."

"Consequences?" Scott took a step in Doherty's direction, but then stopped himself. "I'll tell you consequences. My daughter is being held hostage, and it's *your* fault. Every minute from here on in is *your* responsibility. And when this is over, I'll make sure you answer to me about that."

Win exhaled loudly, cheeks puffed and lips pursed.

"Hold on now. Let's see if we can figure this out…Scott, we'll get Alex back. Don't worry. Give me some time with Jack, and we'll figure something out. I promise."

"Win, we don't *have* time." He looked at his wristwatch. It was just after three. "She's going to be calling me soon. What am I going to say? 'You're not gonna believe this, but'? I have to know this guy's name. Now."

"I know, I know. Please trust me, Scott. Let me talk to Jack alone. Go home. I'm sure Jody needs you. When Mrs. Altman calls, tell her you're making progress—you are. I promise I'll call you later."

Scott reluctantly agreed to leave.

■ ▩ ▣

He couldn't go home. Not just yet. It was bound to be an emotional scene with Jody, and he had to sort out his thoughts before enduring that. He needed to talk it through with Sharon.

The hour being what it was, with rush hour traffic gearing up, a taxicab ride back to the office was impractical. He headed for the subway, and managed his way through the growing evening crowd onto a packed No. 4 Lexington Avenue Express. He had to stand for the two long stops to Grand Central Station, while the train lurched, squealed, and rocked along a tunnel that was periodically thrown into complete darkness. Luckily, there was a local waiting across the platform at Forty-second Street, and he hurried across for the final hop to Fifty-first Street.

Moments later, he sat in Sharon's office, waiting impatiently for her to finish a telephone call. When she had, Scott filled her in.

Sharon listened the whole time in silence, and when Scott had finished his narrative, she simply sighed.

"Shit, Scott. This is one major disaster."

"Sharon, there's got to be a way. There's got to."

"Let's think about this. We've got to go back to Judge Adams. We have to defeat the privilege. He may have just upheld it for us, but these are different facts. We have to find an exception that applies now that didn't apply then. We can start with Frank O'Connor's brief and see what there is in his argument that we can use. I'm sure he pulled out all the stops trying to overcome the privilege, so it's a good place to start. And Judge Adams's opinion from the bench. We'll go over his remarks and see if he gave any indication of what different circumstances might persuade him to go the other way."

"I don't like it," Scott said. He sounded defeated. "She warned about going to the police, and running into court isn't much different. As it is, Kluge already knows what she's done, and I persuaded him to back off. If we go into court, we'd obviously have to let Judge Adams know exactly what's happening. I'd hate to think what Stacy might do if word gets out that we've gone public."

"Maybe Adams'll seal the proceedings," Sharon suggested.

"Yeah, but think about it. What are we going to tell him? Make

Doherty divulge his client's identity so we can turn the guy over to the psychopath mother of the child he killed? I mean, it's one thing for the court to direct a disclosure like that in a wrongful death action, nice and orderly-like. But do you really expect the court to be a party to an extortion by a kidnapper? We have to figure something else out."

"Your friend, then."

"Win?"

"Yeah. Can he convince Doherty to talk?"

"I don't know. He promised me he'd try. He said he'd call."

"Then for the time being, that's what we have to hope for. That he can turn Doherty."

■   ▓   ■

Back in his office, Scott prepared to leave for the night. It was five o'clock, and there wasn't anything more he could do here.

He heard the telephone ring, and he jumped. Stacy? He didn't understand why she hadn't called yet.

"Mr. Honnicutt for you," Julie announced over the intercom.

Scott grabbed for the phone.

"Win, tell me you have the guy's name."

A pause. Scott didn't like that.

"Scott. I don't know what to tell you. He won't budge. As adamant as you were about the privilege, so is he. It's privileged information, he won't divulge it, and that's that."

"Shit, Win. What am I going to do? Now I've got to run home, because she'll be calling God knows when, and I first have to tell all of this to Jody." Panic was creeping into Scott's voice. "I'm going to give Stacy Doherty's name, then. I'll put her on to that bastard."

"I'd advise against that," Win said. "It won't accomplish anything. In fact, if you think about it, it'll complicate matters. If things heat up too much for Doherty, I think it'll spook him. If we try to keep things low-keyed with him, maybe we can make some progress.

"In the meantime, let me think on it overnight. But as far as Stacy's concerned, you may as well be honest with her. To a point. Just keep Doherty's name out of it for now. She couldn't possibly believe you'd make something like this up. Tell her you're working on it. But find out what she's after. I mean, suppose you get the name, then what? How and when does she let Alex go? Get her to focus on that. Talk like it's just a matter of time before you have the name, and she'll feel more hopeful. The more at ease she is, the more she thinks things'll work out, the better off Alex'll be."

"You think so?"

"Unfortunately, Scott, it's the best I can think of right now. You know, even though I didn't have anything to do with this, I *do* feel some responsibility. Jack may not be my partner, but I brought him into this office. And besides, you know I'll do anything I can to help you. Now go home. I thought you'd gone home from my office, and I called you there first. Jody needs you. Go home."

CHAPTER 48

Vince Saldano felt as if he'd been punched in the stomach. He fought to catch his breath, he felt nauseated, and he felt light-headed.

Only a few moments ago, Patty had stuck her head into the den, a concerned look on her face. "Honey, your lawyer friend is on the phone. He says it's important," she'd told him.

Important was an understatement. More like disastrous.

That Altman woman had gone and kidnapped Scott Heller's daughter. Scott Heller had tracked down Doherty. Altman was demanding his name in return for the girl's release.

It was all unraveling.

"You didn't give Heller my name, did you?" he had pressed.

"No. I told you. But he wasn't very happy when the privilege was turned against him."

"So now what?"

"We left it that I'd consider if there's a way to help him out of this."

"Like what?"

"Shit, I don't know. But he had to be told something. For Chrissake, she has his daughter."

"But what about me? Jesus, that sounds awful, doesn't it? 'What about me?' How old is his daughter? Nine, you said?"

"Yeah, nine."

"Shit."

Vince stayed quiet for a moment.

"So how is it you're gonna help him out of this?" he finally asked.

"I don't know yet...He's going to be talking to her again tonight. I've got to see what happens with that. I'll call you as soon as I hear. In the meantime, just hang in."

Just hang in. Easy for him to say. *I've killed one kid, and now I'm responsible for the kidnapping of another.*

Jesus Christ. What a clusterfuck.

■　　■　　■

He hung up the phone from the conversation with Vince Saldano, and sat in silence. He was, he thought, beginning to understand what Scott Heller had been going through. Sense of duty competing with gut instinct of what is right.

When this had all started, it was to have been a simple exercise. For all its intricate layers, it had been based on a simple legal concept. If it worked, great. If not, Vince would drop out of sight, and life would go on. The one thing he and Vince hadn't foreseen was Stacy Altman's determination. Her commitment to *her* sense of what was right.

He was faced with a choice now. He was not one to betray a friendship or a trust easily, for he liked to think of himself as a moral person. Truth be told, he'd been uneasy about the whole thing from the beginning because of the deception it entailed. But if it had gone as planned, there would have been no real harm done.

When he'd learned that Scott Heller's daughter had been kidnapped, he'd reacted instinctively. Now he had to decide the proper course.

He thought about it for a long while. He wasn't sure exactly how this would end, and a lot depended on what Stacy Altman said to Scott tonight. But he was starting to realize that the only choice was to betray someone who trusted him.

■   ■   ■

This was bad. Very bad.

How had this happened? Had she really thought that she could simply kidnap a child and get what she wanted? Had she been so desperate that she had been blinded to the realities of what she had undertaken?

Stacy sat on the floor of the Bartletts' kitchen, her cell phone in her lap. She had waited until seven o'clock, and then called the Hellers' home. Though she still refrained from using the Bartletts' telephone, and had placed the call on her cell, she no longer felt the need to be on the move in her car when she did so. She had decided that the Hellers were heeding her warning not to call the police. They wanted this to be over.

She was sure they wanted this to be over. But if Scott Heller was to be believed, they were trapped now, just like she was.

That damn privilege.

If the situation weren't so dire, she would probably be able to find some satisfaction, if not humor, in it. He had been so pompous, so arrogant, so removed, when she had pleaded with him to tell her who had murdered her child. He had hidden behind a legal concept—a technicality—that any rational person could see was just plain wrong.

And now that technicality stood between him and his own daughter.

Funny how things work out. A regular laugh riot.

"I have confidence in you, Mr. Heller," she had told him. She had tried her best not to let her fear and apprehension show. "With what's at stake, I know you'll convince him to talk."

For his part, he tried to be reassuring. He had pleaded with her. Please believe me. Please be patient. Please understand. Yes, it did give her some satisfaction to hear him humbled like this. But the bottom line was that he didn't have the information she wanted, and couldn't guarantee if, or when, he would be able to deliver it.

He had pressed her, though. When he found the client, what then? That, she had already decided. A meeting. He was to set up a meeting. Set up a meeting and you get your daughter back.

She realized that when she had begun, she hadn't really thought it through to the end. She'd known she had to do *something*, and she had done what her gut drove her to do. Now, as events unfolded around her, her course of action had become clear. There was only one possible outcome.

She sat there on the kitchen floor a while longer, contemplating that outcome. An eerie calm came over her.

CHAPTER 49

It was eleven in the morning, and Scott was back at his desk. He had managed to get home the previous night only minutes before Stacy called, so Jody heard of the day's developments at the same time he described them to their daughter's captor. He had tried his best to sound hopeful and optimistic, for Jody's sake and for Stacy's. For his own sake, too.

After the call, from Jody there had been tears, anger, outrage. And fear. Scott shared the same emotions, but he was too spent to show them. He went into the living room, sat down in an overstuffed chair, and promptly fell asleep. He made his way upstairs to bed somewhere around three o'clock.

He had gotten to the office early, started calling Win at eight, and finally got through just after nine. He told Win about his call from Stacy, and about her demand for a meeting with the client once he was located. Win hadn't anything new to tell him, but he tried to sound upbeat.

Now, nearly two hours later, Win called back.

"Win," Scott said breathlessly. "What do you have?"

"Good news! Great news, in fact."

"You found him? Doherty talked?"

"Scott, it wasn't easy. And we're going to have to do it his way. But the end result is the same. I think we can get this guy to a meeting."

"His way?" Scott asked. "What's that mean?"

"It means he still won't tell me the guy's name. But he's willing to give him up."

"Explain, Win."

"Let me tell you, Scott, I spent most of the night here in the office with him. I didn't let him out of here till after midnight. We talked about everything. The legal profession, legal ethics, morality, your family, your daughter. You name it. I pushed him hard.

"I'll bet you could recite to me chapter and verse what he said. About the privilege, I mean. You must have gone through it when Stacy first showed up in your office.

"First he talked about going to Judge Adams. Not for a directive that he *doesn't* have to talk, but for clarification that he *does*. So his ass is protected. I explained why that wouldn't work. Stacy's insistence that you not go to the authorities. That also took care of his idea about going to the police.

"Finally, when he promised to think about it, we called it quits for the night."

"And?"

"After you called this morning, I went in to him. Told him she wants to meet the guy. He said he'd thought about it overnight, and realizes he doesn't have a choice. He can't have Alex on his conscience. But like I said, we have to do it his way."

"All right already, Win. What does 'his way' mean? How is he giving the guy up without telling us his name?"

"He's arranging a meeting. He's naming the time and place, and he'll make sure the guy is there."

"Why that way? Why won't he just give us the name? I don't like it that I keep on going back to Stacy with stories."

Win paused.

"Well, he's not exactly being truthful with the client, Scott. The guy knows that you're the lawyer who's been dealing directly with the prosecutor. Jack's told him that they're getting close to finding him, and that now's the time to come in and make a deal. Before it's too late. Since you're supposedly the one who has the contacts at the prosecutor's office, he's convinced the guy to meet with you to discuss things. He hasn't said *anything* about Stacy being in the picture, and he's afraid if he gives you the guy's name, you or Stacy'll spook him, and he'll run...I've got to tell you, all things considered, I think it's your best bet."

Scott twiddled his earring and sighed.

"Yeah, Win. You're probably right. It shouldn't matter to Stacy, so long as the guy shows up."

"That's how I feel."

"Okay, then," Scott said. "Where and when?"

"You said you don't expect to hear from Stacy again till tonight, right?"

"Unfortunately. I have no way of contacting her. I have to wait for her call, and that didn't come yesterday until about seven."

"That's what I thought. So the soonest we'd be able to set something up with her is sometime tomorrow. Jack said the service area on the Garden State Parkway just south of Exit 123. Six p.m."

"Shit," Scott exclaimed. "I don't care where, but why wait until nighttime? Alex has been gone for more than twenty-four hours already. It has to be sooner."

"Can't, Scott. Jack says it has to be in the evening. I don't know why, but we'll have to rely on Jack to know what will work and what won't. It's the only way it'll happen."

Scott was silent.

"I'll be there too," he finally said. "That'll have to be when I get Alex back. How will I know him?"

"The guy will find you. Jack's given him a description."

Scott exhaled into the phone.

"I don't like it. I'd really like to know his name."

"Come on, Heller. It'll be over soon. Let's just get it done. Get Alex back safe and sound."

"Yeah, but—"

"But nothing. This is the only way. And it'll work. Just let me know as soon as you hear from Stacy."

Scott sighed.

"Okay, Win. Will do."

*   *   *

The first thing Scott did was to call Jody. The relief in her voice was palpable.

"Oh, thank God. Alex…"

"Yes. By tomorrow night, she'll be home."

After bringing Sharon up to speed, Scott spent the better part of the day considering what Win had told him, anticipating how his call with Stacy would go. He was uncomfortable about telling her that Doherty still refused to reveal the client's name. Admitting that would acknowledge to Stacy that he was not yet in control of the situation. He decided he couldn't have that any longer.

He'd leave Doherty out of it. As far as Stacy was concerned, he had convinced Doherty to name his client, and he had convinced the client to meet with him. He would tell Stacy when and where that meeting was to take place, and would demand that Alex be released there.

For once in this mess, he would be in control.

Scott went over in his mind what he would tell her that evening when she called.

*   *   *

"I hope you have something good to tell me," Stacy said without any preliminaries.

It was precisely seven o'clock, and Stacy was seated at the

Bartletts' kitchen table, cell phone to her ear.

"Yes. He's agreed to meet me. Tomorrow night."

"His name, Mr. Heller. Tell me his name."

"No."

"What?" she said incredulously. "I want his name."

"And I said no. I'm doing more than that. I'm delivering him to you. That's what you really want, isn't it?"

"I'm in no mood for games, Mr. Heller."

"I'm not playing games. You want the driver, and I want my daughter. If I give you his name, how do I know you'll return Alex safely?"

"For God's sake," Stacy said. "Do you really think I'm going to hurt her after all this?"

"Mrs. Altman. What I know is that you've kidnapped my daughter and are holding her hostage. Frankly, I don't know what you're capable of. But I also know I have something that you want, and I'm not about to give it to you until I know that Alex is safely back with her mother and me."

He was right. What did the name matter? She was getting him. The man who had killed Ben. Soon, he would be standing before her, and she would be able to look him in the eye.

"Okay," she finally agreed. "When and where?"

Scott told her.

"Good. I'll be there."

"What about Alex?" Scott asked.

"Don't worry. I told you. Her for him. She'll be with me."

She thought a bit.

"I'll be watching. You shake his hand when he introduces himself to you, so I'll know it's him. Then tell him you forgot something in your car. Tell him you didn't want to go back for it before he got there because you wanted to make sure you were where you were supposed to be when he got there. Excuse yourself and walk back toward your car. I'll send Alex off toward you. Then just leave us."

There was silence at the other end of the phone for a moment.

"This will end tomorrow, won't it, Mrs. Altman?" Scott asked.

"Yes, Mr. Heller. You have my word. This will end tomorrow."

After finishing her call with Scott, Stacy went upstairs to look in on Alex. Thank God the girl had settled in to a trusting frame of mind. Stacy hated to think of what an unmanageable nightmare this would have been if Alex had remained uncooperative. Earlier in the day, Stacy had found a copy of *Harry Potter and the Half-Blood Prince*, and Alex had jumped on it. A bit heavy fare for someone her age, but she seemed very bright. Stacy saw that she had fallen asleep reading about Muggles, wizards, spells, and incantations.

"Tomorrow, it will be over," she whispered to the sleeping girl.

CHAPTER 50

The newsroom buzzed with its usual morning activity. Mike Harrison was working on a story about an incident that had occurred the previous afternoon at the Interchange 11 toll plaza on the New Jersey Turnpike. A local gas station had been robbed, and the crew of a police cruiser in the area had spotted a vehicle meeting the description given by the station attendant. In the ensuing chase, which three other patrol cars had joined, the fleeing vehicle had found itself boxed in and forced onto the entrance ramp to the Turnpike. The toll plaza was jammed, and the robber had to abandon his car. He had started shooting, the police had returned fire, and the robber had been shot dead. So had an innocent driver in a nearby car. Last night, Harrison had interviewed a spokesman for the victim's family, and he was transcribing his notes when his phone rang.

"Harrison."

"Hello, Mr. Harrison. It's Stacy Altman."

Harrison flipped his pad to a clean page.

"I promised to let you know what was happening. I'm keeping my word."

"Well, Mrs. Altman. I appreciate that. Is Alex okay?"

"She's fine. She'll be reunited with her parents soon."

"Oh?" Harrison began jotting.

"Yes. Tonight." Stacy described the meeting that she and Scott had set up.

"And then what?" Harrison asked. "After Heller leaves with his daughter?"

"That's why I want you there," she told him. "I told you what my lawyer said. How this guy will just play the system and possibly get off. I can't let that happen and be buried with all the routine cases that nobody cares about. I want everybody to know what a travesty our system of justice is. You'll tell them."

"So, you want me to cover his arrest?"

Stacy paused.

"Yeah. Cover his arrest. But don't you call the police. Leave that to me. Just be there before six."

◼   ◼   ◼

"No Julie…I understand…You did the right thing calling… No, I won't let Mr. Heller know you called. Thanks."

Kluge hung up and walked directly to Lieutenant Weber's office. He knocked on the doorjamb and walked in. Taking a seat, he addressed the Lieutenant.

"Loo, you're not gonna believe this. I just got a call from the receptionist at Heller's law firm. Julie. She has some more information for us on Altman."

"Yeah?" Weber said. "I was wondering what was doing. Kid's been missing since Tuesday, and here it is Friday and there's been nothing in the media. What's up?"

"Seems that Heller is meeting up with Altman tonight to get the kid back. Appears he found the client, and he's delivering him to her. The receptionist's all sorts of nervous about having called, what with having told us about the girl's kidnapping in the first place, and now letting us in on this. But I think I convinced her that she's done the right thing, looking out for the kid's welfare."

"Where's the meet gonna be?"

Kluge told him.

"Hmmp. State Police jurisdiction. I guess we oughta let them know," Weber said. He thought for a minute. "Why don't you, uh, swing by there tonight, just to keep your eye on things? You got nothing else to do on a Friday night, do you?"

"Nah. I'll be there, Loo."

CHAPTER 51

Stacy had awakened that morning exhausted. She'd had the dream again. Once more, she'd had to endure the horrific sight of the speeding car bearing down on him. The unworldly sound of steel and chrome crushing flesh and bone. Once more, she'd been powerless to stop it, unable to reach him in time.

She'd awakened spent. She was never refreshed after a night that included the dream.

But it would stop coming after tonight. Maybe after tonight.

The recurrence of the dream put her in a reflective mood. Had it been only four short months ago that she had last shared her existence with her son? She thought of his last birthday party, his sixth. They had baked his birthday cake together. Ben's current hero had been Superman, and that had been the theme for his party. Stacy had found a character mold for the cake, and had supervised Ben as he measured and mixed the ingredients in a large bowl. He had insisted on icing the cake as well, and though the resulting cake may have been shaped like the comic book hero, it otherwise bore no resemblance to him. But Ben had been mighty proud of his creation. How reluctant he had been after he had blown out the candles to allow her to slice into it.

Stacy estimated that it was almost a four-hour drive to the service area on the Garden State Parkway. She wanted to get there by five thirty, at least a half hour before the scheduled meeting, so she planned to be on the road by one thirty.

There was one important thing that she needed to take care of before Alex woke up. Stacy quickly pulled on her jeans and a sweater, and walked around the bed to Greg's nightstand. She found what she was looking for in the top drawer, where she had come across it three nights ago when looking for a pen.

She took it, and hurried downstairs and outside. It would be best if she finished while Alex was still asleep.

■　■　■

Technically, Roy Kluge was off duty tonight. He and his wife made a practice of reserving Friday nights as "date nights," when they could get out and just enjoy each other—something that was impossible during the week—but like any other cop, he was never really "off." So while mildly upset, his wife wasn't terribly surprised when he told her he had some business to take care of that evening.

"I should be home by seven thirty. Eight o'clock tops," Kluge explained to her. "It's not even my jurisdiction. The lieutenant just wants me to watch the exchange go down. Keep my eye on things."

"Okay, then. I'll wait till you're home for dinner. Why don't you pick up a pizza on your way home, and we can see what's on HBO."

"You got it, honey."

■　■　■

Mike Harrison was supposed to be off as well. Though, he supposed, he was a reporter, and he ought to report news when it happened.

Even if it happened when he was off.

He had arranged to have a photographer come with him. There would be some good pictures. Kidnapper. Child hostage. And child-killer. The doorbell rang, and Harrison went to the door to let Kevin Loughran in.

"Hey, what's up, Mike?" the photographer greeted him. "We good to go?"

"Yeah," said the reporter, glancing at his watch. "It's about four now. Let's head down there and scope out the place. That'll leave us enough time to grab a bite to eat inside at Mickey D's before the show starts."

"Sounds good," said Loughran. He slung his camera over his shoulder and headed out to Harrison's car, Harrison following.

■　　■　　■

Scott passed through the high-speed E-ZPass lane at the Raritan toll plaza, just north of milepost 125 on the Garden State Parkway. A sign that stretched across the highway overhead announced that the Cheesequake Service Area was one mile ahead.

"Almost there," Scott said to Jody, who was sitting next to him.

Scott had not planned on having Jody accompany him, and had been against the idea when she had suggested it. "If he sees you, he'll know something's wrong. This is supposed to be a business meeting to discuss his surrender," he had said. But Jody had persisted. "You're meeting him right outside the door to the food court, and he probably expects that the two of you will go inside to talk. I'll stay in the car, and no one will even know I'm there. Alex'll be in shock over all of this. I have to come," she had argued. Scott had given in.

Scott looked at the clock on the dashboard, and saw that it was 5:40. They were nearing the exit, and just in case the client had arrived early, he wanted Jody out of sight when they pulled in to the rest stop.

"When we get to the exit ramp, get down, and stay down until I'm out of the car. Give me some time to get to the door."

A moment later, a sign advised Scott to move into the left lane for access to the service area, and Scott complied. As he approached the off ramp, he told Jody to get down.

"Give me at least a minute after I leave before you get up, so everyone'll be watching me instead of the car...Okay... We're driving past the gas pumps now. Up ahead on our left is the parking lot, and ahead of that is the building with the food court in it. I can see the door that I'm supposed to meet the guy at...There are people going in and out, but no one standing there...If I continue going straight all the way, this lane will take us back onto the highway. But before that, at the end of the building, I can loop around and come back on the other side..."

Scott reached the end of the building, turned left, and then left again to head back in the opposite direction on the other side of the building.

"I'm back in the parking lot on the north side of the building. I'm going to park the car now."

"Don't park too far from the door. We don't know where Alex will be, and I want to be sure she can see us so she doesn't have to be searching."

"All right," Scott agreed. "Here's a space about five spots in."

Scott eased the car into the vacant parking space. "I'll leave the key in the ignition, and the door unlocked," he said as he shut the car off.

Jody looked up at Scott, and reached for his hand.

"Be careful," she told him. "Bring Alex back."

Scott squeezed her hand and got out of the car.

◼   ◼   ◼

Mike Harrison and Kevin Loughran were inside the vestibule of the food court. A bank of three pay phones lined the wall, and

Harrison stood at one of them, receiver to his ear, pretending to be in conversation with someone. He had his back turned to the telephone so he could see out to the parking lot. Loughran stood next to him, ostensibly studying a road map, his camera casually slung over his shoulder. He glanced at his watch.

"Five forty-five."

■   ■   ■

Detective Roy Kluge sat in his Ford Taurus, a travel mug of coffee perched on his dashboard. He had arrived fifteen minutes ago, at five thirty, and had found a parking space along the edge of the lot at the northern end of the building. Julie had told him that Heller planned to meet the client outside, and Kluge had positioned himself so he had a clear view of both the parking lot and the door.

The lieutenant had notified the State Police of what was going to happen, and had emphasized to the officer he spoke to that Kluge would be there just to observe. Kluge looked around the parking lot, and wondered where the state cops were. He could usually spot an unmarked car, but did not see any likely candidates.

The detective had run a DMV search on Heller and found that the lawyer owned two cars, a Porsche Boxster and a Lexus LX 470. A few minutes ago, he'd seen a Lexus pull into the service area, matched the tag number with Heller's, and watched as the attorney pulled past the building. A minute later, he saw the SUV reappear on the other side and pull into a parking space.

The attorney got out of the car.

■   ■   ■

Stacy and Alex said little to each other during the long drive from the farm in Pennsylvania. Stacy was deep in thought about her upcoming encounter with the man responsible for turning her life upside down, and she suspected that Alex was anticipating her reunion with her parents.

Stacy's mood turned somber as she contemplated what was about to occur. That she was a criminal was no longer a foreign concept to her. She now accepted the title she had voluntarily assumed. But that she would shortly have to face the consequences for her crimes—those which she had already committed and that which she planned—was a sobering thought.

When it came time, would she have the nerve to up the stakes? Her eyes involuntarily glanced toward her handbag on the seat next to her.

Stacy slowed as she approached the toll plaza and guided the car toward an unmanned lane with an automatic ticket dispenser. She took the ticket spit out by the machine, and began the next leg of the drive, northbound on the New Jersey Turnpike.

Her thoughts turned to her husband. He had finally moved out of the house, two weeks earlier. They hadn't had anything to do with each other since the accident, and for a while he'd been staying in the spare bedroom, out of her way. Then, one morning, he told her he was moving out. He couldn't take it anymore, living in the same house without being a part of her life. He moved into a hotel in downtown New York, close to his office.

At first, he had telephoned every day. But then she began avoiding his calls and stopped returning his phone messages. She felt sad. She knew that in his own way he wanted what was best for her, but his way was to forget and move on. She wondered if a father could ever understand the depth of the biological bond between mother and child that made his solution impossible for her to accept.

What would it be like finally to dole out justice to the man who had caused her such immeasurable grief? Would she feel pleasure? She supposed she would derive some degree of satisfaction from inducing fear or inflicting pain on him. But not pleasure, she thought. She felt in her heart that she truly was seeking only justice. And closure.

Closure. She had always wondered about that word. She had often read news stories about people seeking closure on an issue. Convict the perpetrator. Bury the victim. Hold a memorial service for a missing loved one whose body could not be found. Do something so I can have closure. So I can put this behind me.

Tonight, I'll have closure.

Stacy continued her reverie until she found that she was nearing Interchange 11, where the Turnpike intersected with the Garden State Parkway. A moment later, she was through the tollbooth and on the approach to the Garden State Parkway south, just a few miles north of the Cheesequake toll plaza. The dashboard clock showed that it was about five thirty, so she would arrive at the service area only a few minutes behind schedule.

■   ■   ■

Stacy slowed as she drove past the gas pumps, and strained to see the entrance to the food court ahead of her to her left. She saw no one there obviously waiting. She surveyed the parking lot to her left, and drew in a breath when she saw Scott Heller three rows of cars away, walking slowly toward the building. He, too, scanned the parking lot as he walked.

Alex caught sight of her father as well. "Daddy!" she cried excitedly.

"Not yet," Stacy said to her gently. "I'll let you know when it's okay to get out of the car."

Stacy's adrenaline was pumping. This was it. The driver of that car was probably in the parking lot right now. She looked up and down the rows of cars as she drove slowly by. One of them might be the vehicle that had smashed into Ben. She shuddered.

Stacy pulled into the first slot two rows from the door. The car was facing the building, and she had a clear view of the entrance.

"Soon," she said to Alex. "I'll tell you when."

CHAPTER 52

Scott scanned the lot as he got out of his car, hoping to glimpse his daughter. Jody had told him that Stacy drove a Toyota Camry, and had even made note of the license plate number, but Scott could not see it. He assumed Stacy and Alex were here somewhere.

The client must be here by now, too. Scott looked around the lot once more, but realized he did not know what he was looking for. He didn't know what the guy looked like, or what kind of car he drove.

He thought about Jack Doherty, the lawyer who had dragged him into this whole mess. Though he'd been quick to blame Doherty, when he thought about it, the lawyer had done nothing but his job. And he'd done it brilliantly. He'd been hired to protect his client's identity, and he'd figured out how to do that. *Not much difference between him and me. That's what I had been doing. Or at least that's what I thought I'd been doing.* It wasn't Doherty's fault that things had gone the way they had. And when it came down to it, Doherty had finally done the right thing. He'd agreed to deliver his client.

Was Doherty a better man than he? He, Scott, had clung to the privilege, and had forced a grieving mother into a courtroom battle when all she wanted was peace for the memory of her son. His obstinacy had driven her over the edge. He'd known all along that what Stacy Altman had been asking was right. But he'd been worried about himself.

Doherty, though, had hesitated only briefly. He had seen that to do the right thing meant to place himself at risk, yet he had done so.

Scott's thoughts turned back to the client. The man at the heart of this all. He had no feelings for the man. He'd run over a child and had hidden, like a coward. Scott had never been totally comfortable when he'd thought he represented him. A man like that ought to answer for what he'd done. He never understood how Win could do it—represent murderers, rapists, muggers. Not for him.

Tonight, the man would be forced to face the consequences of his actions. He would face the woman whose life he had shattered, and then be turned over to the authorities. As he should be.

Scott strode toward the door of the food court.

■   ■   ■

Chi Chi Ramirez nudged Hector Vargas with his elbow.

"Heads up, bro. Dude's headin' for the door. Heller. Tall white guy, dark blue jacket."

"Shit, I know the man's white. Whatchu think, I'm stupid? Lawyer told us he's white." Vargas spit on the ground. "Anyway, how you know it's him? You ain't seen him before."

Chi Chi regarded his partner with a mixture of pity and contempt. Was it any wonder he'd needed a lawyer's services so often, carrying this imbecile with him all the time? A man with his skills, his vision, ought not to be tied down by a half-wit like Hector. But they were cousins, and Tio Luis would kick his butt if he didn't watch out for his *primo*.

Besides, look at the size of him. Hector was big as a bull, and he enjoyed throwing his weight around. There were lots of bar fights

Chi Chi would have backed down from if Hector hadn't been at his side. Chi Chi couldn't help it if he had a small frame. He was in good shape, and wasn't afraid of anything, but he was small. Wiry, that's what he was. But that had its advantages, too. He could move quickly, and could get in and out of tight places easily.

All in all, he guessed, he and Hector made an all right team. They complemented each other. But he really could be an *idiota*.

"No, I never seen him before. But if you was watching, you'd seen him get outta that Lexus. The one we was told he'd be drivin'. So that's him."

Hector was now alert.

"How 'bout the girl?" he asked.

"Not yet. Keep watchin'. The other guy can't be far neither."

Chi Chi shoved his hands in his pockets and bounced up and down on his toes. A nervous habit whenever something was about to come down. He had parked his Buick LeSabre close to the building so that standing outside they would have a clear view of the door and much of the parking lot. As Heller walked toward the door, Chi Chi looked around trying to spot either of the other two they were waiting for. So far, no sign of the girl or the man.

Their instructions were easy enough. Some crazy woman had snatched a little girl. Heller's girl. The other guy was here to get her released. He and Hector were to keep watch and make sure it went down like it was supposed to, and that no one got hurt.

"Hey, I think that's him," Hector said, pointing toward the door.

Chi Chi slapped Hector's outstretched arm.

"*Jesu Christo!* You wanna let that crazy bitch who took the kid know we're watchin'? Keep cool."

Chi Chi shook his head to himself, and took up watch again for the girl.

Kluge was ready now. He saw Heller approach the door, and watched closely for any sign of Stacy, Alex, or the client. The detective had been watching for a Montego blue Z4, but did not really expect that the client would still be driving that car.

Heller was outside the door now. Kluge saw someone approach, but he continued past the lawyer into the building. Then, from the other side of the lot came a lone man, walking purposefully toward Heller. The man stopped in front of the lawyer and addressed him.

■   ■   ■

Stacy kept the windows of the Jeep closed so Alex wouldn't shout out at an inopportune moment.

Scott Heller stood about fifteen yards away, in front of the door to the food court, still scanning the area. Stacy held her breath as each passerby neared him, to see which one would stop to greet him.

There. Someone appeared to be walking directly toward him. It was the driver. The killer. She was sure of it. She drew in a breath.

The man stopped in front of Scott and extended his hand, and Scott took it.

It *was* him.

Scott dropped his arm, looked around the parking lot, back at the man, and appeared to ask him something. He didn't seem to like the answer, and shot another look around the lot. Then he took a step toward the man, who backed away.

She could tell Scott was shouting now, though she was just far enough away that she couldn't make out what he was saying through the closed window. The man put his hand on Scott, apparently trying to calm him, and Scott shook him off.

The man continued to talk to him, and Scott started to respond, but stopped. His aggressive stance seemed to soften—his shoulders slumped a bit, and the balled fists at his side opened. He looked around the lot again, and then back at the man.

Scott—now calm—nodded to the man, and extended his hand as if in reconciliation. The man took it, and they shook.

Then Scott backed away in the direction of his car.

Stacy looked back at the man, who now stood alone.

So that's what a child-killer looks like.

Stacy felt for her handbag, and reached for the handle of the car door.

■   ■   ■

Kluge watched the interaction between Heller and the man, but wasn't sure what to make of it. Frankly, he was more interested in finding Alex. Another quick survey of the parking lot failed to reveal any sign of her or Stacy.

At that moment, Kluge heard the wail of sirens. He turned to his right and saw two State Police cruisers speeding into the service area from the highway, lights flashing blue and red.

Jesus H. Christ! What the hell do they think they're doing?

He turned back and saw Heller—who had been walking toward his car—stop in his tracks. The man he'd been talking to froze for an instant, shot a look at Heller, and started running for his car. And then Kluge saw her. Stacy Altman. Jumping from a Jeep Grand Cherokee not five cars away from him.

■   ■   ■

"Wha' the—?"

Chi Chi whirled around, trying to locate the source of the screaming sirens. The lights on the approaching police cars painted the scene in alternating colors.

"Shit, man," exclaimed Hector. "No one said nuthin' 'bout no cops!"

Hector already had the door on the passenger side of the LeSabre open.

"Let's get outta here!"

"Hey, bro, stay cool a minute. Lemme see what's goin' down."

All the same, he got behind the wheel and turned on the ignition.

"I'll tell you what's goin' down," Hector said. "The cops is what's goin' down. No one said nuthin' 'bout any cops. I'm outta here."

Chi Chi assessed the situation. They'd been hired to do a job, and he didn't like running. But if the cops were involved—like Hector said, no one said nuthin' 'bout that. So, really, this wasn't actually the job they'd been hired to do. Besides, with the cops there, both the girl and the guy ought to be all right.

"Okay," he said to Hector. "We're gone."

He eased out of the parking space, and headed for the Parkway North ramp.

■   ■   ■

Mike Harrison and Kevin Loughran had watched Scott Heller argue with the man, then curiously shake his hand and back away toward his own car.

Suddenly, sirens blared.

They bounded out of the door, and Loughran aimed his camera at the man that Heller had just left. The man, who had a panicked look on his face, ran for his car.

■   ■   ■

"Stay here!" Stacy yelled at Alex. "Don't move!"

Grasping her handbag, Stacy flung herself at the car door and sprang from the Jeep. She ran toward the fleeing man. The man who had killed Ben.

He had too big a head start on her, and he reached his car and leaped in.

No, God damn it. You're not getting away!

She fumbled in her handbag, as the man she was pursuing threw his car into gear.

◼   ◼   ◼

Alex! Where's Alex?

Scott had no idea what was going on, but this was not the way things were supposed to turn out. What the hell were those police cars doing here?

"Daddy!"

Scott's head whipped around.

"Daddy!"

There she was!

"Alex!"

She had darted from between two parked cars, and was running toward him.

A sound to his left caught his attention, and his eyes flicked over there.

"Alex!" he shouted. "Look out!"

The speeding car was barreling down on her. Alex heard it, turned, and froze.

"DADDY!"

Scott ran.

◼   ◼   ◼

Stacy pulled the handgun from her bag, and flung the bag aside. In college she had shot a gun, but that had been years ago. This morning, before Alex woke up, had been her only chance to practice with the pistol that she had found in Greg's nightstand. She would fire until it was empty, and hope that at least one shot would find its mark.

He was already in the car, and was speeding in her direction. Without thinking anymore, Stacy grasped the gun with two hands, and squeezed off shot after shot. The windshield shattered, and she kept shooting.

The car careened to her left, horn blaring. She heard a voice behind her shriek.

"DADDY!"

Omigod, Alex! I've shot him, and he's going to hit Alex.

She whipped around, and saw the girl frozen in fear.

■   ■   ■

It was her dream, all over again. Ben, paralyzed with fear as the speeding car bore down on him. Her, running as fast as she could, but being too far away to save him. His frightened scream—MOMMY! The sickening thud, and the squeal of tires as the car sped away.

"DADDY!"

She shook her head, violently, to shake off the image. It wasn't Ben. It was Alex.

It won't happen again. I'm going to stop it this time.

■   ■   ■

She ran. The car was almost upon the girl. It would be close.

Stacy threw herself with all of her strength. She collided with Alex, who was sent sprawling forward. Stacy was thrown high into the air.

CHAPTER 53

Marc Altman stood alone, the collar of his jacket turned up against the gentle wind that blew through the cemetery on Florida Grove Road. Just four months ago he and Stacy had stood here to watch as their son had been lowered into his grave. Two days ago, he had returned to bury his wife.

He was still trying to piece together what had happened, from what his friend Roy Kluge had told him, and from a series of newspaper accounts from a *Middlesex Herald* reporter who coincidentally had witnessed the entire thing.

One thing was known for sure. Stacy had sacrificed her life to save Alexandra Heller.

Ironically, though, she had shot dead the one man who could have told her what she had given her life to discover. She had shot Jack Doherty, the lawyer who represented the man who had run down their son.

According to the account given the newspaper by Scott Heller, Heller had been led to believe that he'd be able to identify the driver to Stacy in order to win Alex's release, but Doherty apparently had no intention of giving up his client. Doherty was to have arranged a meeting between Heller and the driver, but when Heller showed up, it was Doherty who met him instead.

Heller had confronted Doherty, who tried to calm him by explaining his plan. Doherty had told him that there were two men watching over things—"capable, street-smart guys"—who would see to it that everything went smoothly. The idea was to let Stacy think that he, Doherty, was the driver, so that she'd let Alex go. One of the watchers was to ensure that Heller got Alex safely to his car, and the other was to help Doherty "deal with" Stacy. Heller had given in and played along when he'd realized he didn't have a choice.

Then all hell had broken loose when the State Police showed up. Apparently, Doherty panicked and ran, and Stacy—thinking that the fleeing Doherty was the man who had run down Ben—pulled a gun and shot him.

And when she saw that Doherty's out-of-control car was about to hit Alex, she'd given her life to save the girl.

Truth be told, though Stacy had shot and killed the lawyer, Marc didn't have much sympathy for him. According to the Kluge, he'd not only shielded his client, he had also lured Heller into the scheme without his knowledge. Kluge had told Marc that the driver had hired Doherty to negotiate a plea on his behalf, and in order to protect the driver's name from disclosure, Doherty had posed as the client and had retained Heller to do the negotiating.

And Stacy, thinking that Heller was in contact with the driver, had become obsessed with making him reveal that information to her. Strange how the very privilege that Heller had invoked against Stacy had been turned against him when he'd discovered that Doherty had used him as a dupe.

The newspaper had reported, and Kluge confirmed, that the police were closing the investigation into Ben's death. After the debacle at the rest area, they had descended on Doherty's office, and interviewed everyone there. Doherty had been a sole practitioner, simply renting office space from some Win Honnicutt. He'd even done his own typing, and thus did not have even a secretary with whom he might have shared his secret. None of Honnicutt's personnel could shed any light on the matter either.

As to Doherty's files, the damn privilege still applied, and the police could not get access to them. In a compromise, Honnicutt had volunteered to look through Doherty's papers and effects, and to report whether there was any sign of the mystery client's identity. Though not technically kosher—Honnicutt had no professional affiliation with Doherty, and thus ought not be privy to his privileged information—under the circumstances, Honnicutt felt his intrusion was justifiable. In any case, he had come up dry.

The one or two other leads that the authorities had had led nowhere, so with Doherty's death, hope of finding the driver had all but vanished.

Marc tried to convince himself that none of this was his fault, but it was hard. Had he been more attentive to Ben, would his son be alive today? It was a freak thing, what had happened that afternoon. No father could be with his child one hundred percent of the time, and accidents happen. What had happened was an accident.

And his wife. If he had been more supportive of Stacy, would she have gone over the edge as she had? Must he shoulder the responsibility for her loss? No. He had done what he could. He had listened to her, talked with her about what had happened to their son. People make choices. She chose her path for herself. It had led her probably to the place she wanted to be.

He didn't know how long he stood there crying. Finally he turned to go home.

CHAPTER 54

Jack Doherty's funeral was a small, quiet affair. He had no surviving family. He had married, and divorced, and left no children. Both of his parents were dead. Since moving from Massachusetts earlier in the year, he had kept mostly to himself, and had not developed many friendships. Indeed, but for Win Honnicutt, and the staff of his office, few others attended.

One of the others in attendance was Win's lifelong friend from his prep school days at Choate. After the modest graveside service, Win and his friend went for a bite to eat.

"Sucks, doesn't it?" Win said, contemplating the Scotch and water that the waiter had just placed in front of him.

A sigh from across the table.

"I feel responsible," came the reply.

"Now don't go down that road," Win chided his friend. "I'm as much to blame as you are, but no one meant for any of this to happen. We all did what we thought was right. No one could have foreseen this."

No, no one could have foreseen it. But, thought Win, how had things gone so terribly wrong? He thought back to that Sunday morning in June, when his friend had called in a panic, begging him to meet with him that day. Win had rushed to his office.

■ ■ ■

"I don't know how it happened, Win," Vince Saldano said. "I just glanced away for a second, and there he was, out of nowhere. I know I should have stopped, but I panicked."

"Okay, Vince. Okay," Win said to him. "Let's talk it through and see where we are."

"Where are we?" Vince said. "Where am I? I killed a kid. That's where I am." His voice shook. "This'll kill Patty."

Win tried to calm him.

"I know how you must feel. I've defended drunks who don't give a shit, and they think they feel badly about it, when all they're really feeling bad about is that they might lose their license. I know you. I know it was an accident. You must feel like hell. But we'll get you through it."

Vince sat there, numb.

"What do they do to people like me?" he asked his friend. "Am I looking at jail?"

"Well, it depends on what you're charged with. The prosecutor has a lot of discretion in that area. It could be anything from careless driving all the way up to aggravated manslaughter."

"Assume the worst, Win. What's the worst?"

Win hesitated.

"Aggravated manslaughter. Possible thirty years. But that'll never happen. It might be what the statute says could happen, but in the real world it just never does."

"Shit, Win. What am I gonna do?"

"Don't worry, Vince. It's not going to come to that. First, I'll arrange for you to turn yourself in. Then, I'll talk to the prosecutor. There's no reason they should want to go for the max if you're cooperating. I'll be able to make a deal for you."

Vince sat there quietly for a minute or two.

"Turn myself in? I don't know, Win. If I knew I wouldn't have to go to jail, I could see that. But walk in to them without knowing? And maybe face up to thirty years?" He shuddered. "I can't do it."

"I think you'll be making it harder on yourself if you don't turn yourself in," Win told him. "It's bad enough that you left the scene. That's a whole separate offense."

"Can't you call them, uh, and don't tell them who I am? You know, just tell them you represent the person who did it? See what kind of deal they'd be willing to make?"

Now Win sat there thinking for a minute.

"Hmm…Not very orthodox," he mused. "Let's talk about that for a minute."

■ ■ ■

That's when Win had explained the attorney-client privilege to Vince. Anything Vince told him about what had happened was privileged information. Not even the court could force him to reveal it.

■ ■ ■

"I could withhold your name, and try to reach a plea agreement for you. If we make a deal, I tell them who you are. If we don't, your name stays a secret. Privileged information."

"Do you think it'll work? I mean, once you make the call, I'm kinda hangin' out there, aren't I? They'd have you, and you could lead them to me. How sure are you that they can't make you tell them my name?"

"I'm pretty certain of it. The attorney-client privilege itself is firmly established in our law. There are court cases that interpret the scope of the

privilege, and there have been some cases that dealt with the confidentiality of the client's name. They've gone both ways, but each one has depended on the particular circumstances. I think your circumstances fit the privilege. You'd be safe."

"Jeez, Win. I'm kinda lookin' for something more than 'pretty certain.'"

The lawyer contemplated the problem.

"What we need is additional protection," he finally said.

He sat in silence for a few minutes.

"I've got an idea."

And Win told his friend his plan.

"We need another lawyer to make the contact with the authorities— someone who doesn't know who you are, and who won't be told. That way, if the court rejects the privilege, he can't lead anyone to you."

Vince thought about it.

"Sounds like it would work."

"I have a guy in mind, too. Fellow I went to law school with. He's a corporate lawyer, but I make it a point to refer some criminal cases his way every now and then. Guy named Scott Heller."

"Yeah, but if the court makes him talk, won't the cops be on your doorstep the next day? Then, where are we?"

Win thought some more.

"Then we need a cut-out between Scott and me. Someone he doesn't know, and someone who'll be a dead end if Scott's forced to talk."

"Anyone in mind?"

Win spent the next few minutes in silence.

"Okay. Here's what we do. I think it covers all contingencies. In fact, I can't think of anything that can go wrong."

■　　　■　　　■

He had decided to bring Jack Doherty into the scheme and tell him that for his own protection, he could not know the name of the client. Doherty would retain Heller to contact the prosecutor.

Heller would be instructed to try to make a deal, but if he was asked to identify his client, he was to tell them it was privileged information. If the prosecutor went for it, and made a deal that was acceptable to Vince, Vince would come forward. If not, Vince would stay unknown.

As insurance, Doherty was to give Heller a false name. That way, if the court rejected Heller's claim that his client's name was privileged, and forced him to talk, all he would have was a name that led nowhere. Since he wouldn't be able to find Doherty, no one would ever find a trail to Win or to Vince.

■   ■   ■

"Okay. The only missing piece is how Doherty will come to call Heller. I'll have him tell Heller that I referred him. Giving him my name for that doesn't implicate me, but it gives him credibility with Heller...I refer stuff to him all the time, and he rarely calls me about it. And if he does this time, I'll just deny I ever referred the guy to him. I can't see any exposure there."

■   ■   ■

Doherty, himself, had added the twist of posing as the client. Win had liked that, since it made the story Doherty would tell Scott less contrived.

Then Stacy got on Scott's trail, and Scott had, of course, asked Win about the client he'd referred. He had denied doing so, as planned. When Scott became fixated on finding the client, Win had offered his help so he'd be kept abreast of Scott's progress. But he'd never believed that Scott would be successful.

When Scott had confronted him with the news that Stacy had kidnapped Alex, and that an e-mail from the "client" had been traced to his office, he had been consumed with guilt. He could never let his good friend know of his duplicity, but he had to do everything he could to make things right.

In what he now recognized was a selfish, last-ditch effort to save himself from exposure, he had called Doherty into his office, hoping that Doherty would quickly assess the situation and realize that he was the last line of defense between Scott and the truth. Doherty had realized what was at stake, stuck to the story, and refused to tell Scott anything, invoking the privilege.

After Win had convinced Scott to leave him—ostensibly to convince Doherty to talk—he had called Vince to let him know the unfortunate turn of events. He then contemplated the dilemma he was in, and the extent to which he had to betray his good friend Scott in order to preserve Vince's anonymity and avoid revealing to Scott how he had deceived him.

He and Doherty then hammered out a way to gain Alex's release. Since no one knew what the client looked like, Doherty would assume the role and appear at the meeting that Stacy had demanded. Win enlisted two of his regular clients, street thugs, to watch over things. Doherty would instruct Scott to identify him as the client, and Stacy would release Alex to Scott. Chi Chi would see to it that Alex was safely delivered, and Hector would ensure Doherty's quick departure from the scene.

And so, Jack Doherty had gone to the meeting.

■　　■　　■

Win downed his Scotch and water, and looked across the table at Vince.

"You know, I can never let Scott know my role in this. I put him through hell, and I sent Doherty to his death. Thank God Alex came through everything okay, but I can never let Scott know it was all because of me."

Vince nodded. "Some things are better left unsaid. There's

nothing to gain by telling him," he agreed.

They sat in silence for a few moments. Then Vince spoke again.

"Speaking of things best left unsaid, where does all of this leave me?"

"It leaves you, my friend, in the clear. According to the papers, the police have closed their investigation. And as far as everyone knows, the one person in the world who knew your name—Jack Doherty—is dead. It's over."

EPILOGUE

Vince Saldano felt like a child on Christmas morning as he flicked on the light in his four-car garage. He carefully removed the cover that had blanketed his BMW Z4 for almost a full year. An involuntary shudder came over him as he realized that eleven months had passed since his nightmare had begun. Eleven months since he had run down poor little Ben Altman.

He had put the car away immediately after the accident. Although no witnesses had ever come forward, he knew that he had lost one of the knockout plugs from his front bumper at the accident scene, and he had no idea if the police were capable of tracing that to his car. He had decided that, at most, they'd probably be able to figure out that it was a Bimmer, and there were thousands of them around. But there was nothing wrong with being careful.

In the weeks and months that followed the accident, no connection to him had been made, and even though Win had assured him right after Jack Doherty's funeral that the police had closed their investigation, he had been uneasy about returning the vehicle to the road. He wasn't sure which influenced him more—the guilt he felt when he saw the car, or the continuing fear that he could still somehow be tied to the tragedy by the instrument of death.

Patty had thought it strange that he garaged the car so soon after he bought it, and he had made hollow excuses which she didn't probe too deeply. He suspected she just chalked it up to a "men will be boys" thing—he'd bought a new toy, played with it a while, and tired of it. In the interim, he had leased a Lexus sedan—an LS 430. A lot of car, but without all the tempting sportiness.

The Lexus was boring.

Last week, more than half a year after Doherty had been killed, and the police had concluded that they'd hit a dead end, he had bought a replacement plug for the bumper. Even then, though, he'd driven to a BMW dealer in Rockland County to get it. Just a precaution, he figured.

Today was finally the day. He was ready to get behind the wheel of the Z4 again. Enough time had passed.

The cloth cover folded and stowed in its place, he opened the hood and disconnected the lead to the battery tender which, along with the fuel stabilizer he had added, hopefully had kept the engine ready to go. He dropped the hood back into place, hit the button on the garage door opener, and eased himself into the black leather seat. The sports car started up without too much trouble, bringing a smile to his face. He depressed the clutch and fingered the shift knob tentatively, and then decisively pushed it into first gear.

His face wore a huge grin as he peeled out of his driveway, on his way into New York to have lunch with Win.

■   ■   ■

Scott Heller strolled north on Centre Street, toward Worth. It was a warm day, for May, and he was in no hurry. The lunchtime crowd had begun to emerge from the state and federal courts bordering Foley Square, and the pushcart vendors hawking hotdogs, sausages, and mystery-meat-on-a-stick girded themselves for the noontime onslaught of business.

Scott's court appearance had taken less time than he'd anticipated, and his afternoon schedule was light. It had been a while since he'd seen Win, so he figured he'd pop in on him and see if he was free for lunch. He could have called ahead, but decided that since he was only a few blocks away, he might as well just wander over. Worst that could happen was that he wasn't in, or couldn't get away.

Ever since the whole Altman fiasco, Win had been rather distant. It appeared to Scott as if he blamed himself for what had happened. Despite Scott's assurances that he harbored no ill feelings—it had all been a scheme of Doherty's that had blown up—Win still seemed to bear a sense of responsibility that weighed him down.

Scott felt bad for his friend.

He turned west onto Worth Street, and made his way along the short block to cross over Lafayette, toward Win's office. Standing across the street from his destination, preparing to cross over, he caught sight of Win emerging from the building.

He was about to call out, when he saw a blue BMW convertible pull up to the curb. Win raised his hand to greet the driver, trotted over to the car, and got into the passenger seat. The top was down, and Scott could see the other occupant, but didn't recognize him. The Z4 pulled away.

No lunch with Win today, Scott thought, and he turned back the way he had come, to head for the subway.

Something about the car niggled at his subconscious.

Sitting on the No. 4 train, he remembered what it was. After the disaster at the Parkway rest area last year, Scott had read in the newspapers that the police had closed the investigation into Ben Altman's hit-and-run. Scott had called Detective Kluge to talk about it, and the policeman had explained that with Doherty's death, the trail had simply run cold. The only thing the police had been able to determine was the make and model of the car, from a knockout plug found at the scene. The car was a metallic blue BMW Z4.

Scott shook his head. Come on, he thought. How many Bimmers like that are there around?

But Win's strange behavior since it all happened. Whenever

they talked about it, he seemed uneasy, and was quick to change the subject. Scott had put it down to embarrassment over having been Doherty's unwitting dupe. No matter how many times Scott had reassured Win—they had both been victimized by Win's tenant— he never seemed to let it go.

Could there be more to it? Scott had always wondered what it was that was bothering Win so much, but he had never been able to figure it out. Now, for the first time, he wondered whether Win's awkwardness could be coming from a knowledge of what Doherty had been doing all along.

The blue BMW. If Win knew the driver—the *killer*—then Win not only knew what Doherty had been up to, he could even have been behind the whole thing.

Was his good friend capable of such deceit and treachery? Could he have known all along who the driver was, and stayed silent the whole time?

Scott considered confronting Win—asking him straight out. But if he was wrong—if he wrongfully accused him—he might do irreparable damage to a friendship he had valued for so long.

By the time he was back in his office, he had figured out how to handle it.

■   ■   ■

"That's right, Detective Kluge," he said into the phone. "And when you ask him who he had lunch with today, don't let him avoid the question. *That*, I can assure you, is not privileged information."